D1324249

ALSO BY PETER CLINES:

EX-PURGATORY

Peter Clines

DEL REY

1 3 5 7 9 10 8 6 4 2

First published in the US in 2014 by Broadway Paperbacks, an imprint of the
Crown Publishing Group, a division of Random House, Inc., New York.

Published in the UK in 2014 by Del Rey, an imprint of Ebury Publishing
A Random House Group Company

The Random House Group Limited Reg. No. 954009

Addresses for companies within the Random House Group can be found at:
www.randomhouse.co.uk

A CIP catalogue record for this book is
available from the British Library

The Random House Group Limited supports The Forest
Stewardship Council® (FSC®), the leading international forest-certification
organisation. Our books carrying the FSC label are printed on FSC® -certified
paper. FSC is the only forest-certification scheme supported by the leading
environmental organisations, including Greenpeace.
Our paper procurement policy can be found at:
www.randomhouse.co.uk/environment

Printed and bound by Clays Ltd, St Ives Plc

ISBN 9780091953652

PROLOGUE

SYLVESTER TAPPED HIS pencil on his knee. He did it like a drumroll, so the sound was sharp against his jeans. He always had a pencil, even though she couldn't remember him ever using a notepad. Three months now, a dozen sessions, and he'd never taken one note.

He was bald, but she was pretty sure he shaved his head. It made it tough to figure out how old he was. His tight goatee came to a perfect point under his chin. He had dark brown eyes, and his eyelids hung low. It gave him a relaxed, thoughtful appearance.

Sylvester stopped tapping the pencil, leaned back in his chair, and gave her a look. "How are you sleeping?"

She shrugged. "Same as always."

"Which means?"

Her fingers danced on the arm of her wheelchair. "I don't like the mask. If I try to do anything except sleep on my back it pulls at my head or leaves marks on my face. And it doesn't fit right. Air leaks out and blows over my eyes, so they're always dry when I wake up."

"Has it always been like that?"

She shook her head. "No. I mean, the whole thing only started a while ago. Near the end of senior year."

"Have you tried different masks?"

"Yeah. Dad tried altering them, too. It doesn't make any difference." Her lips twisted into a weak smile. "I think I've got a funny-shaped head."

"It looks fine to me," he assured her.

She blushed. Just a little. "Thanks."

"You understand why you have to wear it, right?"

She nodded. "Yeah."

"Do you resent it?"

"Didn't we go over all this ages ago?"

"We did," said Sylvester, "but I want to see if your answers have changed any."

She shrugged again. "It's keeping me alive. The doctors—the other doctors—they say I stop breathing as soon as I fall asleep. The first couple times it happened they were pretty sure I'd died in my sleep. Severe sleep apnea."

"One of the worst cases on record," he said.

"Yup. Mom gets worried whenever I stay up late because she's worried I'll nod off in class and asphyxiate."

"Big word."

"I've heard it a lot."

"So do you resent it? The mask?"

"It's keeping me alive."

"That's not really an answer."

She sighed. "I don't like it, but that's just the way it is, right? I wish I didn't need it, but I also wish I didn't need to use a wheelchair most of the time. And I wish I had red hair, too."

"Why red hair?"

"Because black hair and pale skin make everybody think you're some kind of Goth. Red hair and pale skin mean you're a sexy Irish girl."

"Are you Irish?"

"No, but nobody knows that."

He tapped the pencil three times on his knee, then a fourth. "Are you worried how the mask's going over at college?"

Sylvester had covered one side of his office with black-bordered motivational posters. She still wasn't sure if it was serious or a joke to make people lighten up. "A little bit," she admitted after a minute of poster-studying.

"Why?"

"Honestly?"

"That's the whole point of this." The pencil tapped twice for emphasis.

"I always wonder if everyone thinks I'm some kind of freak," she said. "Every study session, every party, every late night hanging out, I'm always the girl who has to get back to her room and strap this thing to her head before she falls asleep. And how's that—" She looked back at the wall of posters and stared at one marked *Desire*.

"And how's that . . . what?" he asked.

She glanced at the office door, toward her mother in the waiting room. "What if I meet a guy?" she asked. "What if I meet someone and things are going great? The chair's bad enough, how do I tell him, 'Oh, we've got to do it in my room because I've got to make sure I strap on my Darth Vader mask before I fall asleep or I'll probably die'? What guy wants to hear that?"

Sylvester smiled. "That's your big worry?"

Her mouth twitched into a smile for a moment. "It's one of them."

He took a long, deliberate look of his own at the door, at her mother in the waiting room. "I probably shouldn't tell you this," he said, turning his gaze back to her, "but I don't think you need to worry about guys in college *not* wanting to have sex. Even if you have to strap on an oxygen mask afterward."

She blushed again. "I just think it's going to be weird."

"Trust me. They won't care."

She turned back to the wall of posters.

He let the silence stretch out between them for a minute. Then he rapped the pencil on his knee once. "You're still having the dreams?"

She stared at the posters, then at her hands. He let her sit for a moment before he asked again. She nodded once. "Yeah. Every night."

"Exactly the same?"

She straightened up as best she could. "Not always. Sometimes I remember different parts of it. Different places, different people. But it's all the same. It's all . . ."

He tapped the pencil one-two-three-four times. "It's all what?"

"You know."

"It's important for you to say it," Sylvester said.

"Why?"

"Because how you remember things and how you describe them are little clues to what's going on in your head."

She sighed. "It's all real," she said. She waved her hand around the office. "The stuff in my dreams feels more real than all of this."

The pencil rapped three-four-five-six times against Sylvester's knee. "Your parents think it's because of this obsession you've developed with horror movies."

"I told you, the dreams came first."

"That's not what they say."

"They saw the movies first. I didn't tell them about the dreams until later."

The pencil spun twice between his fingers, then tapped against his knee. "And they're still suicidal dreams?"

"No," she said. "No, they've never been, I keep telling you that. They're just . . . I'm just dead in them, that's all."

"But not suicidal."

"No."

"If the dream is so realistic, how can you be dead? How are you experiencing it?"

"I'm supposed to be dead," she explained, "but I'm not. Not in the normal way."

"Buried alive?"

She shook her head. "No, not like that. I'm dead, like a vampire or something. But I'm different than the others."

"Others?"

"Well, most of the undead just want to eat you, right? I'm still me, I'm just . . . dead."

Sylvester's pencil paused in the air between taps. "Okay," he said. "Let me ask you this. In these dreams, can you still walk?"

She looked at her legs. "Yeah," she said. "Yeah, I can."

"So, you're having a dream that feels incredibly real where dead things walk around. And in this dream your legs—which have been 'dead' for ten years now—work again."

"Sort of. Is that a normal dream? It isn't, is it?"

"I have heard of it once before," he said. "Something a lot like it."

"You have?"

"It was in a movie. You've been watching a lot of horror movies, right?"

"Some of them, yeah."

"Did you ever see one called *Nightbreed*?"

She thought about it and shook her head. "I don't think so."

"It might be before your time. It's an older one by Clive Barker."

"The *Hellraiser* guy?"

"Yes."

"I met Pinhead at a convention in Seattle last year," she said. "The guy who played him, I mean. He was really nice, even though he seemed pretty bored."

"I think he's in this one, too." Sylvester drumrolled his pencil against his knee. "It's a film about a man who has dreams he's dead, and then he ends up becoming one of the undead. And parts of him that had stopped working start working again."

"Is that a sex thing?"

"Yes."

She shook her head. "It's not like that."

"That's good," he said, smiling. "The psychiatrist in that one turned out to be a homicidal maniac."

"No," she said. "You're not a maniac."

"I'm in the dream, too?"

She paused and weighed the question. "Lots of people I know are in it."

He tapped the pencil against his knee two-three-four times. "So, if I'm not a maniac in the dream, what am I then?"

She stared at her legs for another moment. "You're dead," she told him. "Everyone is. The world is dead."

"Was there a war?"

"It was a disease. A virus."

"Ahhh. A virus that made the dead walk?"

"Yeah." Madelyn bounced her fist on the arm of the wheelchair, breaking the beat of the pencil tap. "And I don't know why it's all different now."

THEN

I'M FALLING.

I'm not sure where I'm falling from. That's not part of the dream. I just find myself plummeting through the air toward the crowd below.

The crowd looks up at me. Men and women, young and old. It just seems to be random people. They're all talking. I can see their mouths moving but can't hear any words. The dream is silent.

My body tenses up as the ground flies up to meet me, but at the last minute I slow down. It's like coming to the end of a dive in a deep pool. My body just sheds momentum into the air. I step down onto the pavement as if I'm hopping off a bus.

The crowd surrounds me. They're all still talking. I still can't hear them.

No, not a crowd, a mob. A horde. They claw at me. Grab at me. Tug and pull and yank. One of them has my hair, because in the dream my hair is long and shaggy, like the hero on the cover of a romance novel. A pair of arms wraps around my neck like a bony scarf.

They want me.

The people are not well. They're lepers or burn victims. They have gray skin, like sand at the beach. Many of them are injured.

There's a woman with curly blond hair who looks like she's

been throwing up blood. One man has a long gash across his bald scalp and is missing an ear. A teenage boy holds up an arm that ends in a dark stump. An older, well-dressed woman is coated in blood, as if she works in a slaughterhouse.

And then, even though I've been looking at all of them since the dream began, I suddenly notice their eyes. All of them have the same dull, chalky eyes. Blind eyes. Their gazes don't settle on anything. I see one man whose eyes drift off in two different directions.

The people keep grabbing me and I realize—in that way you sometimes realize the painfully obvious in a dream—that this is a bad dream. A very bad one. I'm not surrounded by hurt people. These are *things*. There are monsters all around me. Sightless, sickly things.

A woman with a battered face opens her jaws wide and bites down on my arm. I can feel it and I wince, but her teeth can't make it through my leather jacket. Her mouth opens again and two of her teeth drop out.

I know I'm in a dream, but I also remember teeth falling out means this is a stress dream. Is that true for other people in your dream? Why is my mind so clear on some things and so fuzzy on others?

I throw a punch and one of the monster-people flies back into the crowd as if I've smacked it with a baseball bat. The physics of the dream seem a bit off. I grab another monster by the wrist and pull. It flies into the air and swings around me in circles. I'm making it fly, like a father spins a small child by the hands. I'm doing it with one hand.

If this is a flying dream, does it mean it's about sex?

The spinning monster strikes some of its companions and knocks them down. Then I let it fly free. It soars off into the crowd. Something moves near my feet and I stomp on it.

I hear a hiss of pistons and the whine of electronics. The dream isn't silent, I realize. There's been a sound here all along, a white noise I've grown used to and blocked out. And before I can think what the noise is, the ground shakes. Heavy thuds come from behind me.

I ignore the monsters and turn around.

A tan wall stretches out in either direction. Looming over me is a double archway and a pair of iron gates. It looks like a fortress. I've seen it before, but I can't remember where.

Stepping through the gate on the right is a giant robot. Blue and red armored plates accent its silver body. It must stand close to ten feet tall. It's shaped like a person. I'm sure it's female, in that odd way you just know things in dreams.

The robot looks at me with huge white eyes like tennis balls. Its metal skull nods once and then it holds up its hands. Electricity arcs between the thick fingers. It brushes its sparking hands against the monster-people and they collapse to the ground.

One of the creatures sinks its teeth into my shoulder like a vampire with bad aim. I shrug it off and knock it away with another physics-defying punch. The monster slams into another of its kind and they both tumble away.

The robot turns back to the gate and bellows, "Bring it out!" It has a woman's voice, like I suspected. It raises an arm and waves something forward.

A truck rolls through the gate. A big one, like the ones used by movers and film crews, but this one has been decorated with wide swipes of red spray paint. It crushes the monsters under its wheels. There are people in the back of the truck. They wave at me and poke at the creatures with long spears.

The monsters that look like people are all around me. For every one I push away, three more push forward. There is nothing to the world but pale, gaunt faces and grasping hands. They have my arms, my collar, my hair . . .

TWO

WITH REGRET, GEORGE admitted he was awake and squinted up at the ceiling.

It had been another rough night. It led to one of those mornings that felt like hell from the first moment of consciousness, and he tried to push coherent thought away one last time even as he buried himself back down into the pillow. The alarm had gone off early. He'd slapped the clock twice, and each time he hoped for another ten minutes of peaceful sleep. Just enough to make the day bearable.

The ceiling fan had other ideas.

The fan's beaded chain had come with the apartment. It wasn't the standard string of tiny silver balls. Someone, the rental company or a previous tenant or just a cheap repairman, had replaced it with a line of blue plastic crystals.

The crystals were just light enough to catch the subtle motion of the fan. The long strand built up momentum after a while and began to spin in an arc. The arc lifted the top two crystals high enough to scratch at the side of the fan. Again and again. The noise was loud in the quiet apartment. For a man trying to get back to sleep for a few precious minutes it was like Chinese water torture. He glared up and willed the beads to stop moving. They ignored him.

When George was happy with the fan, he liked to tell himself it was a line of Mardi Gras beads. At the moment, he thought about taking a kitchen knife to them and cutting the string in half. Stringisection. Stringicide. He was an easygoing guy, for the most part, but the string needed to be punished.

He turned his head and his hair rustled against the pillowcase. It was long enough that he could feel it bunch up around his ear. He needed to get a haircut.

George rolled over and stretched his legs out. At six feet he was just tall enough that his feet hung off the edge of the mattress. On the plus side, he was thin enough that the bed was spacious enough for two, even though he hadn't shared it with anyone in a while.

The alarm went off again. His ten minutes were up. Sunlight was creeping in through the blinds. If he delayed any more, he'd be late for work.

He sighed and rolled out of bed.

* * *

George made it to his car right on time—parked a block over from his apartment because of street sweeping—but somehow he'd caught the edge of rush hour. Traffic was piled up all along Beverly and he hit every light between his apartment and campus. The crosswalks were packed with people strolling along and taking their time. There was always someone in the road when the lights turned green and it always delayed him just enough that he missed the next light.

It's early morning, he thought to himself. Shouldn't anyone out at this hour have somewhere to be? Somewhere they need to get to?

He couldn't find any music or news on the radio. The only thing coming in was some self-help show. A man with a thick Spanish accent was talking nonstop about old relationships. George tried to tune it out for a while and then just shut it off.

Traffic got worse the closer he got to work. There were a lot of extra cars on the road, and while he sat at a red light he noticed a fair amount of them were packed full of boxes and gym bags. There were a fair number of pillows and stuffed animals, too.

All at once, his mistake hit him.

It was moving day.

He'd heard that different schools had different names for it, but the principle was the same. Three days after freshman orientation, all the returning students . . . returned. All at once, all on the same day. Thousands of them. With their families and cars and pickups and sometimes even moving trucks.

There wasn't going to be a scrap of parking anywhere on campus. Nowhere near where he needed to be, anyway. He'd have to find street parking and hope for the best.

How the hell had he forgotten it was moving day? That was why he'd set the alarm early, so he'd have time to take the subway.

He tried to turn and his car fought him for a moment. The transmission growled and the wheels felt like they were turning in mud. The last time he'd been at the garage the mechanic had mentioned tie rods, which had something to do with the wheels. George hoped that whatever they were, they could stay tied for a little while longer. His next paycheck had to go to rent, but the one after that could be car repair.

Three blocks from campus he found a space on a permitted street. He'd have to move it before four o'clock, which would mean ducking out early and asking someone to cover for him. The door stuck as he tried to get out. Extra repairs weren't in the budget, so he begged the latch to work and the door opened on the next try.

It took him another ten minutes to get to campus. He checked the time on his phone twice while waiting for the light to change at a crosswalk. The crowds of people pressed in around him. A man on his left grinned at him and showed off a mouthful of smoke-yellowed teeth.

The light changed and the crowd surged across the street. George pushed past most of them. According to his phone, he had five more minutes. He broke away from the crowds on the sidewalk and cut across the swath of grass.

A man headed across the lawn away from the physical plant

and toward George. The man had a severe limp, or maybe he was just stumbling-drunk. His headphones blared so loud George could hear the *tok-tok-tok* of the bass line ten yards away.

After another few steps, George realized the man's clothes were dotted with stains. The stranger's face was pale, as if he'd just thrown up. He was probably homeless, which meant George was supposed to call campus security.

He glanced around. Most of the students and parents were back toward the dorms. Maybe he could just give the man a warning and save him getting hassled by the rent-a-cops. "Hey, buddy," he said, "I think you need to get out of here."

The man staggered straight at George. He didn't say anything, but the dull click from his headphones got louder and louder. George still couldn't hear anything except the bass line.

"Seriously," George said, "if security finds you here they'll toss you off campus, and some of them are kind of jerks." He pointed over the man's shoulder. "Head back down into Westwood and they can't touch you."

The man kept limping toward George. The bad leg dragged behind him, like it was too heavy to move. A bruise on the side of his neck stood out against his pale skin. He was trying to talk, moving his jaw up and down, but he wasn't making a sound. Nothing George could hear over the bass line from the headset.

"Man, come on," he sighed, "don't make me . . ."

The headset cord swung away from the man's body with the next lurch. He didn't have an iPod. It wasn't plugged into anything. His eyes were chalk white. Three of his fingers ended in dark stumps. He bared yellow teeth at George and took another lumbering step forward.

George jumped back with wide eyes and raised a fist.

The man stumbled back, too, and held up his hands, fingers spread. Ten fingers. "Whoa," he said. "Calm down, dude."

George blinked. The man stared back at him. His eyes were pale blue, not white. His headset cord hung low and looped back up to the phone holster on his belt. The spots on his clothes were a subtle pattern in the fabric.

"Sorry," said George. "It looked like you were . . . Sorry."

The man shrugged his backpack higher onto his shoulder and shuffled past. One of his shoes had a double-thick heel, the kind to correct an uneven leg. It gave him a shambling gait.

George watched him go. The man looked back over his shoulder once and didn't look pleased to find George staring at him. He shuffled a little faster.

* * *

The physical plant still used an old-fashioned time clock. Someone in accounting typed up new cards for them every week and set them out Monday morning in alphabetical order. He ran his finger along the rack of cards. Tuesday morning and they were already a mess. It took him just under a minute to find his.

BAILEY George

His parents had been wonderful in so many ways. It never crossed their minds what he'd go through every December. Or every time he filled out paperwork. Or every time he introduced himself.

He got a moment of satisfaction from punching in five seconds before the clock ticked over to make him late. The card shuddered as the machine stamped down on it. He glanced at the red, sticky time code before he tossed the card back on the rack.

He slipped off his jacket and clipped on his ID. The jacket went into his locker and the tool belt came out. A few moments later he was getting his assignments from Jarvis. The shift boss had a dark beard shot through with white and silver.

The first two hours of George's day were spent replacing fluorescent lights in one of the labs. There'd been a power surge and three dozen tubes had blown out. Someone else had swept up all the broken glass, but he was stuck pulling out the jagged ends and installing new lights. It was slow work, but at least the halls were empty and he wasn't working around wandering students. Afterward he mopped the hallway to get any last fragments of glass or the chalky powder from inside the tubes. He didn't mind the mopping. He thought of it as a very Zen activity, although he was pretty sure he wasn't using Zen the right way when he thought that.

Just before lunch was a broken sprinkler head. Someone had kicked it or hit it or something a few days ago, and now it was shooting a jet of water right at one professor's window in the chemistry building. He'd complained two days ago and his complaint had filtered through the system and become an item George's boss assigned to him.

George poked and pulled at the sprinkler for about ten minutes before deciding to just replace it. A year or two back the sprinklers would've been groundskeeping's problem, but budget cuts had trimmed some departments and merged others. He still didn't know enough about the system to do fine repairs, so he had to go for big ones.

Lunch was a rectangular pizza slice with orange sauce and soft crust. He was pretty sure the pepperoni crumbles were just flavored soy meat. He'd read that once on the back of a frozen pizza box. The salad that came with the pizza wasn't much more than lettuce and dressing. He ate them both and read through the first few pages of a newspaper someone had left in the cafeteria. He had a glass of chocolate milk for dessert.

After lunch he went back to the sprinkler and installed the new one. There was a sheet of instructions in the box that helped. Nothing leaked or shook, so he called it done. He packed the soil back around the sprinkler and looked around while he wiped his hands on his Dickies.

He'd caught the lull when all the parents took their kids out for lunch one last time before heading home. The campus was dead. A few grad students stumbled between buildings and across the lawns, still hungover from welcome-back parties the night before. The lawn was overgrown, he noticed. More groundskeeping cuts. He'd mention it to Jarvis and volunteer to take care of it.

There was a poster on a nearby bus stop for a clothing store. George had never been into fashion, but something about the poster caught his eye. A blonde and a brunette flanked a stunning woman with dark skin and ebony hair. They all wore half-buttoned shirts and tight pants. The dark-skinned woman was barefoot. She looked familiar, and George was pretty sure she was the current "name" celebrity supermodel.

He just couldn't remember her name.

His Nextel walkie chirped. "George, you there?"

He pulled it free from his belt. "Yeah, what's up, Jarvis?"

"Bad news, m'friend. Somebody just broke a lobby window over at Birch Hall."

"How the hell'd they do that?"

"Backed an SUV into it trying to get close to the door," said Jarvis. "You drew the short straw."

"Dammit."

"Sorry. Mark's grabbing some plywood. He'll meet you over there and y'all can get it cleaned up."

George kept his finger off the button and sighed. Mark was a new hire this year. He'd been some level of film producer or development person—George wasn't sure which—who'd been let go after the economy started to dive and his last three movies in a row had tanked. After eighteen months of looking for work, the man had bitten the bullet and taken a job on the maintenance staff of his alma mater.

On one level, George admired the man for being able to swallow his pride. On another level, though, he couldn't stand listening to him complain about "how far he'd fallen" and the constant comments about "life at the bottom." In fact, George was pretty sure he was going to have firm words with Mark about it sometime soon.

After all, this was his life. He didn't need to listen to anyone badmouthing it.

THREE

GEORGE WIGGLED HIS fingers and settled his glove a little better on his hand. He reached up and grabbed the curved piece of glass. It was stuck in the frame of the big wall-to-ceiling window. The jagged point at the end made it look vaguely like an Arabian sword, one of the ones from the old Sinbad movies. A scythe? A scimitar. It was like a glass scimitar was buried in the frame.

Half the window had broken away. A collection of other glass swords and spikes hung in the window frame now, each a foot or two long. George had been doing this job long enough to know some kid—young adult—would end up stepping through the opening in the rush of moving day. And once one of them did, it would become a new doorway. At least, until someone got cut. Or worse. So his first priority was getting all the glass out of the frame.

He'd set up a few cones and signs from the dorm's supply closet and leaned a broom across them as a low barrier, but there were just too many people for it to do anything. A few hundred students were trying to move into the building, and most of them had at least one other person helping. There were close to a dozen bodies within five feet of his ladder at that moment.

The half-dozen shards on the ground had been easy. Now George was balanced on the ladder. He tried to lever the piece of glass away from the frame without breaking it or slashing up his gloves. Or his hands.

He pushed down on the shard's edge and felt the glass resist. The weight of his arms settled on it, then he added his shoulders. It was slow work, but rushing it would just break the glass and make a mess.

The sword-like shard tilted and slid free from the rubbery seal. George imagined it felt a lot like pulling someone out of quicksand—a slow, hesitant release. He got one hand under the two-foot piece of glass. His feet shifted on the ladder to keep his balance. The sword came away in his hands and he worked his way down the ladder.

George set the shard in the trash can at the base of his ladder. As he did, someone walked by and tossed a Taco Bell cup into the container. The paper cup popped open. Ice clattered and clicked down the glass.

He sighed and headed back up the ladder. The next piece was broad, stretching across the top of the frame. It probably weighed close to six or seven pounds. It also had a crack in it, which meant it would break apart when he tried to lever it out. The wide shard reminded him of a guillotine blade, waiting to drop. It would've been the first to go, but he'd needed to work out some of the big pieces around it.

He got one hand and part of his arm under the bulk of it and put pressure on the other side. That way, if it popped out or shattered, most of it should go away from the door, at least. The blade of glass resisted for a moment, then eased out of the frame.

"Hey, George," called Mark. "How they hanging, big man?" He dropped the sheet of plywood he'd been lugging and let it crash against the ladder. The fiberglass legs wobbled and tipped, just for a second. George shifted his weight. His arms tensed.

The shard snapped with a bang. George heard the zip of fabric coming apart and felt the cold glass slide along his forearm. The first thought in his head was all the morbid tips he'd heard about the "right" way to slit your wrists, going up and down instead of side to side. The huge blade whisked down across his thigh and cut off the thought.

Half of the guillotine shattered on the pavement, turning into crystal confetti that pitter-pattered across the ground. The second half hit a beat later, slowed by its passage through George's uniform, and added to the hail of glass. People shrieked. Mark grunted in surprise. George bit back a swear and grabbed at his arm.

"Job opening," cackled one student.

"Jesus, guy," shouted an older man. "There's kids all around here."

"Be careful, for Christ's sake!"

"Sorry," said George. "Everyone okay? Nobody hurt?"

A few more parents muttered at him. He shot Mark a look and hopped off the ladder. "What the hell?" he growled.

The other man looked at him, baffled. "What?"

George shook his head at the plywood. "What were you thinking?"

Mark had been an athlete in high school and college. He was one of those people who'd never quite outgrown the jock mindset of "the quarterback can do no wrong." He looked from the plywood to George, then to the ladder, and then to the glass-covered ground. "Are you saying this is my fault?"

"You threw a sheet of plywood against the ladder I was working on."

"It's not my fault you're a wuss who freaks out three feet up in the air," said Mark. He grabbed the broom. "At least man up and admit you made a mistake. You're just lucky nobody got hurt."

"Yeah, well—" The sensation of the glass blade sliding down his arm and across his thigh echoed in George's mind. He felt the cool draft inside his Dickies. His pulse quickened and he glanced down.

The pants were open across his thigh, just below where the pocket ended. He could see skin and leg hair. But no blood. He'd been lucky.

He held up his arm. The shirt sleeve was slashed open from his elbow all the way to his wrist. It was a smooth cut. Like his pants, the fabric of the shirt had parted between threads without a single hitch or pull. Even the cuff of his glove was cut. The blade of glass had gone right through the doubled-over canvas hem. He'd written his name on the cuffs ages ago, and the cut went right through the *A* in BAILEY.

His forearm wasn't even scratched. No blood at all. He flexed his fingers and they moved in the glove without any trouble.

George wiggled his fingers again. He'd had cuts that were so clean they were almost invisible. They'd stay shut for a few moments before opening up and gushing blood. He made a fist, squeezed it, and hoped his wrist wouldn't fall apart.

Nothing. And it had been three minutes since the glass had fallen. He poked at his forearm with his other hand and stretched the skin back and forth. Then he poked at his thigh.

"Damn lucky," he said aloud.

Mark glanced up from his half-assed sweeping. "Eh?"

George held his arm a little higher and flapped the edge of the cut.

Mark looked at the sleeve for a moment. Then his eyes bugged. "Fucking hell," he said. It got a couple of angry looks from parents. "You're damned lucky."

"I know."

"Another quarter inch and I'd be using a mop right now instead of a broom."

"I'd like to think you'd be using the truck to get me over to the Med Center."

"Yeah, well, okay. But then I'd be mopping you up."

George squeezed his hand into a fist again, but his forearm remained whole. The memory of the glass on his skin was so vivid, he was sure it had cut him. Maybe it had just been panic, like Mark said.

He shook his head and rolled the sleeve up. "Come on," he said. "Let's pull the last of this stuff and get the board up."

"Why don't you just knock it out with a hammer or something?"

George waved his hand at the crowd in the lobby and brought it back to the door. "Because I don't want to put a piece of glass in someone's eye on their first day back."

"Oh," said Mark. "Right."

* * *

They boarded up the window and Jarvis had new assignments for each of them. Mark had the truck, so he headed off to the far side of campus to deal with a blown fuse in another dorm. George had to go check on an abandoned couch in the middle of one of the parking lots. Day one and people were already abandoning furniture.

He found the couch right where it was supposed to be. He'd half hoped in the fifteen minutes it took him to get there some frustrated undergrad or parent would do the job for him. No such luck.

The threadbare piece of furniture had to be at least twenty years old. George understood why it had been abandoned. It was so ratty Goodwill wouldn't touch it. It sat kitty-corner along the dividing line of two spaces. One end was far enough out to make a third space awkward to use. As he walked up, one car proved that fact with an impressive seven-point turn.

"Who the hell brings a couch to college?" he muttered. He looked at the dumpster, sitting fifty yards away at the far end of the parking lot.

He gave the couch a tug and found out why no one had moved it. It had a foldaway bed, complete with steel frame, springs, and extra mattress. On a guess, it weighed three or four hundred pounds.

George had a few more thoughts about the couch's former owner as he yanked the cushions off and walked them to the dumpster. It was only a couple of pounds, but he figured every bit would help. He set them in the grass next to the steel bin on the off chance someone came running out to claim ownership before he threw the whole thing away.

The couch was still unclaimed when he got back to it. He sighed, bent his knees, and heaved one end up. It wasn't as heavy as he'd first thought. It went up on one end with no problem. He looked at the metal framework between the legs and wondered if maybe it was aluminum rather than steel.

A sedan beeped at him. The driver, an Asian man, gestured at the still-inaccessible space. "Can you get that out of the way," he called out to George, "so we can park?" The teenage passenger looked mortified. She winced and mouthed an apology through her window.

"Sorry," George said. "Just a second."

He decided to risk trying to lift the couch to his shoulder. It felt pretty light, and it was far enough away from the parked cars he was pretty sure he'd miss them if he had to drop it. He gave the upright couch a tug, knelt, and caught it on his shoulder. His arms wrapped around it and lifted.

The couch came off the ground. It wobbled on his shoulder for a moment and he steadied it with his hands. He took a few steps and it didn't tip. His back didn't twinge, either. He'd caught it at that perfect balance point where it seemed to weigh nothing. He turned until the dumpster came into his field of view, then started across the parking lot.

When he reached the dumpster he let the couch settle forward until one end sat on the rim. He worked his way backward, trying not to tear his shirt on the metal frame, until he had the other end in his hands. He heaved again. Gravity grabbed the couch and flipped it into the dumpster with a loud clang.

Slow applause broke out behind him. George turned and saw Nick leaning against his BMW. His friend was still wearing office clothes. The Beemer was parked in the center of the lot, blocking at least half a dozen cars.

"Very impressive," said Nick. He clapped a few more times, but his head was turned back to watch the young Asian woman unloading the backseat of the sedan.

"Don't ogle the students," said George.

"I'm not ogling," said Nick, "I'm appreciating. Look at those legs. I'm betting swimmer or gymnast."

Nick was two inches shorter than George, but made up for it with attitude. His dark hair was spiked out and his eyes were hidden behind a pair of sunglasses that probably cost more than George made in a week.

"So what brings you to campus?"

"I know I'm not supposed to be here," said Nick, "but I needed to talk to you. I need a favor."

"And you drove over here rather than called because . . . ?"

"It's a face-to-face, look-you-in-the-eyes kind of favor."

"Great," said George. "Take the glasses off."

"Hah. Hah," said Nick. A bad blood transfusion a few years back had left his eyes sensitive to light. He never took his sunglasses off outside, and rarely inside. "Coldplay at the Bowl next Thursday."

"It sold out, didn't it?"

"Yes it did. And my boss got a set of complimentary tickets this morning and doesn't want them, so—score. I'm taking Nita and you need to be my wingman because her college roommate's in town."

"Which one's Nita?"

"The publicist." Even as he said it, Nick glanced over his shoulder again. The young woman was walking across the lot with a swollen backpack over one shoulder and a suitcase in either hand. "Damn, she is really cute."

"Focus."

"Fine." The dark glasses turned back to George.

"So that's it? You need a wingman?"

"Yeah."

"What's the catch?"

"I'm asking you to spend the night with a woman you have absolutely no chance with so I can spend the night with a woman I have a pretty good chance with."

George frowned. "That far out of my league?"

"More like you're that far out of her circles of interest."

"So you're setting me up with a lesbian?"

Nick shook his head. "I'm not setting you up because we're all acknowledging there's no chance of anything happening. I'm just asking you to keep a third wheel occupied."

George smiled and shook his head. "Are you buying drinks?"

"I got the tickets."

"Someone *gave* you the tickets. And don't you want to impress

Nita the publicist with what a generous, high-powered agent you are?"

"That's not how I'm hoping to impress her," said Nick. "Fine, I've got you covered, don't worry about it. You in?"

George drummed his fingers on his thigh. "Yeah, sure."

Nick smiled and pulled out his phone. "Excellent. I'll lock things down with her right now."

"Hey," called a man. He stood by one of the cars Nick's Beemer was blocking. "D'you mind moving?"

Nick gave the man a quick wave and opened his door. "Talk more later," he said to George. "You want to meet up tomorrow night? Grab a drink or three?"

"Maybe." His Nextel chirped and he pulled it off his belt. He and Nick saluted each other with their phones.

The Nextel chirped again. "You there, George?"

George waved good-bye and the Beemer pulled out of the lot. "Yeah, what's up, Jarvis?"

"You need any help with that couch?"

"Nah, no problem."

"Get yourself back here, then. I need you to sign your time-card."

George checked the time on the phone. Half an hour until quitting time, and if Jarvis was calling him back to the office there wasn't anything left to do. Nothing that could be done in half an hour, anyway.

As he walked across campus he debated telling Jarvis about the falling glass. He didn't want to lose a day with an unnecessary doctor's visit. On the other hand, he knew a couple of people who'd held off mentioning injuries they thought were minor only to get a hassle from workers' comp later when they turned out to be serious.

Of course, as far as he could tell, the big blade of glass hadn't left any injuries, minor or otherwise.

George slipped past two families chattering away about classes and dorm life. Someone was already blasting music out of a window. A young man whipped past him on a bicycle.

He'd have to mention the shirtsleeve. It was too slashed up for a quick fix. He'd have to replace it. That would give him a chance to get the incident on record without actively claiming an injury.

A crowd of people approached. At least two or three families. They had the absent, flitting expressions of people trying to take in a lot of details while not really paying attention.

George stepped off the concrete path to go around them. If he picked up the pace he could be back in the office in under ten minutes. There was a slim chance Jarvis would even let him punch out early.

Then his stomach dropped. He'd forgotten to move his car. A day's pay just vanished to a parking ticket, assuming it hadn't been towed.

The crowd passed and revealed a woman in a wheelchair. She looked up at him and her face shifted. As George stepped back on the path he moved to the left and gave her a quick nod. He wanted to be sure she knew he saw her and wasn't going to collide.

She tugged on the wheels of her chair, rolling it back into his way. He caught himself before banging his shins on the wide wheel. His legs jammed up for a second and he came to a stop.

The young woman had large eyes and dark hair that passed her shoulders. Her skin was the pale hue of someone who never got outside. A look of relief broke across her face as she stared at him. "Oh, thank God," she said. "It's you."

George smiled. The price of wearing a uniform and an ID badge was everyone assumed you were there to help, but it didn't really bother him. "What can I do for you?"

"I wasn't a hundred percent sure you'd be here," she said. "I thought I remembered you saying once that you worked here before, so I figured it'd be the best place to start looking. Mom and Dad weren't happy with me switching schools at the last minute. I've been looking for you ever since we got here."

He blinked. "Sorry," he said. "Do we know each other?"

"George," the young woman said, "it's me. Madelyn."

He blinked and looked at her. There weren't many students he was on a first-name basis with, and he didn't remember any in a wheelchair. Then he had the awful thought that maybe the young woman hadn't been in a wheelchair the last time he saw her. He studied her face and tried to guess her height if she was standing.

She stared back at him and then her face fell. "Damn it," she said. "You don't remember anything, do you?"

FOUR

"YEAH, I'M SORRY," said George. "I think you might have me confused with someone else."

Madelyn shook her head. "Nope."

He tried to look apologetic. "I don't know you."

"I'm Madelyn Sorensen," she said. "The Corpse Girl."

"The what?"

"And you're George Bailey," she continued. "St. George? Formerly the Mighty Dragon?" She said the last two names—or maybe they were titles—in a hopeful way.

The use of his full name shook him until he realized that someone with good eyesight could read his name off his badge. And if she'd been in the wheelchair for a while, she was probably used to reading things from a distance. He glanced down at the gloves hanging off his belt, his name written on each one in big letters.

Madelyn watched his face. "Nothing?" she asked. "You don't remember me?"

He shook his head.

"You *have* to remember," she said. "What about Barry?"

"Who?"

"Stealth? You have to remember Stealth."

"Is that a person?"

She smacked the arm of her wheelchair. "What about dreams? Are you having dreams?"

George paused. He remembered waking up in the middle of the night, still exhausted in the morning. "What do you mean?"

"They probably seem more like nightmares if you don't remember anything," she said. "Are they—"

"Maddy," called a voice. "Everything okay, hon?"

She glanced back over her shoulder. "Yeah, Dad," she answered. "Just getting directions to the dining commons."

A man with a silvery-gray beard nodded to her and waved at George. George waved back automatically. The man looked like faculty. If not here, then somewhere.

Madelyn turned back to him. "Okay, listen," she said, "this is important."

George looked at her.

"This is all wrong," said Madelyn. "The world isn't supposed to be like this. None of these people should be here."

He looked at the crowds. "They won't be," he said. "It's just like this while everyone's moving in. In a day or two—"

"No," Madelyn said. "They shouldn't be here in the bigger sense."

"How so?"

"There was a plague," she said. "It broke out in the spring of 2009 and wiped out most of the world—"

"Spring of 2009?" interrupted George. "Four years ago?"

"Yes."

"Is this a game?" he asked her. "One of those LARP-things?"

"No." She shook her head.

"Is it the assassin one, where you're supposed to tag another student, because the university has some pretty solid rules about—"

"This is real," she said. "It happened. Everyone died. Even me."

"You're dead?"

"Yeah. For about four years now."

He looked at himself. "Am I supposed to be dead, too?"

She scowled. "Don't be stupid. If you were dead, how could I be talking to you?"

He smiled and tried to make it look sincere. "Right, of course."

"You have to believe me," she said. "Billions of people died. You gathered all the survivors into a film studio here in Los Angeles—"

"I did?"

"Yes."

"Me, personally?"

"Yeah. Well, I mean, I don't know how much you did by yourself, but you did a lot of it. Everyone trusted you to keep them safe."

George wondered if the young woman was a student. Maybe she was just a visiting relative, here to see her brother or sister or cousin off to school before going back to . . . therapy? Heavy medications? "Okay," he said. "And everybody trusted me because . . . ?"

"Because you're a superhero," she said.

"I'm sorry?"

"You're *the* superhero. The Mighty Dragon. I had a poster of you in my bedroom before everything fell apart."

Any student mentioning their bedroom set off warning bells in George's state-employed mind. He looked past her and tried to catch the eye of the bearded man. There was a quick contact and her father understood something was wrong.

Madelyn watched him for some kind of reaction. "None of this means anything to you?"

"Probably not the meaning you're hoping for."

"Everything okay here?" asked the bearded man, setting his hands on the wheelchair's handles. "It's taking a while just to get directions." He was a little older than George had first thought, and up close it was clear the beard needed a trim.

"I had a few other questions," said Madelyn with a bitter look at George.

"I hope I answered them," said George.

The bearded man held out his hand. "Emil Sorensen," he said. "It seems you've already met my daughter."

"Yeah," he said. "George Bailey." The bearded man's polite smile trembled and George tapped his ID badge. "Honest."

"And you're part of the welcome staff?"

"No, sir. Just with the maintenance department. They ask us all to help out where we can on the move-in days."

"Come on," Sorensen said to his daughter. "Your mother wants dinner and she'll be getting cranky soon if we don't get some food in her."

George took the moment to give a formal bow of his head to Madelyn and then to Sorensen. The bearded man acknowledged him and George slipped past them to continue down the path. The girl raised her voice to shout, "Wait!" and her father hushed her. George heard them argue for a moment, and then he was far enough away that their voices blended into the background noise of moving day.

He reached the next parking lot, squinted into the afternoon sun, and wished he'd remembered his sunglasses. Or his work cap. The light bounced off a hundred windshields and rear windows. At least there was shade on the far end of the parking lot.

A young woman on the other side of the lot, one of those people who felt the need to raise their voice two or three notches to talk on the phone, chattered on her cell. George could make out half her conversation from fifty feet away. She stumbled off an unseen curb, glanced back, and her laugh echoed between the buildings. She dug in her purse with her free hand, barely looking at the lot.

He hoped no one pulled out, because she'd never see it coming.

A few steps ahead of her, maybe as much as four or five yards, a man shuffled between the parked cars. He wore a suit coat over jeans and a T-shirt, and his hair was a ratty mess. He stumbled in the narrow space, and his head twisted up to look at the chattering girl. His mouth moved as if he was trying to say something, but George was too far to hear anything. Especially over the young woman.

The woman was still heading more or less in George's direction. There were a dozen yards between them. No more than ten parking spaces. She was two spaces from the man, ten feet at the most.

The three of them continued toward each other. George's

pace quickened. He couldn't put his finger on it, but the situation felt wrong.

The man's awkward movements weren't just because of the tight space between the cars. For a moment, George thought it was the same man he'd seen that morning, the one with the pale skin. But this man was taller, with darker hair and different clothes. He had the same half-drunken gait, though. He lurched toward the chattering woman with a certain focus that made George think of nature documentaries.

There were a few feet left between the man and woman. She pulled a set of keys free and gestured with them. A car behind George beeped twice. She looked up and saw George striding toward her.

Then the pale man wrapped his arms around her. He clawed at her chest and grabbed a mouthful of hair as she turned her head. He leaned into her and forced her away from the cars.

The young woman let out a brief shriek, as if she hadn't decided if the attack upset her or just surprised her. Her phone clattered to the ground. She slapped at the hands, swore, and tried to get a better look at the man. Her expression was a mixture of annoyance and curiosity. The pale man smacked his lips together. It made a wet popping sound with a hard tap beneath it, as if he was snapping his teeth down on her hair.

"Hey," called George. He broke into a run for the last few yards. "Let her go."

The man showed no sign of hearing George or of letting go of the woman. He pawed her some more and bent his head to the soft curve where her neck ran into her shoulder. She smacked him with her purse and her face tightened. The man was a stranger. She was getting attacked in broad daylight. He leaned on her even more, pushing her toward the ground.

George grabbed the pale man by the shoulders. The suit jacket was damp. The man was soft, with no muscle tone at all. George twisted and yanked him off the woman.

It was one of those perfect moments of balance and strength, the ones martial artists train for. The man was thrown through the air and crashed onto the trunk of an old sedan, raising a cloud of dust. George wasn't sure if it came from the car or the man.

"Fucking creeper," snapped the young woman.

George took a step to place himself between her and the man. "You okay?"

She tugged at her shirt. "Yeah," she said. She took a step, scooped up her phone, and scowled. "You're paying for this, asshole," she barked at the man, holding up the cracked screen.

The creeper waved his legs until he slid off the car's trunk. He ended up on his feet more from gravity and inertia than effort. He turned to George and the woman and smacked his lips together again.

The man was more of an oversized teen. His eyes were dusty gray, like old Plexiglas that had been scratched a thousand times. George wondered if he might be an albino, but didn't think the eyes were right for that, either. One side of the man's nose was a ragged flap, as if something had gone in his nostril and ripped out the side. His skin wasn't just pale, it was corpse white.

The creeper took a shaky step forward and his mouth opened and closed. There was something mindless about the movement, like a fish. George heard the man's teeth clicking against each other, as if they were chattering in the hot sun. It was a familiar sound, but he wasn't sure from where.

"Do you know karate or something?" asked the woman.

"No," said George. "I was just lucky."

"Well, feel free to kick his ass."

"Maybe you should call the police."

"Hello." She glared at him. "He broke my phone."

The pale man's arms came back up and he took two more steps. "Okay, you need to back off," George told him. "Just stop now before this gets any worse."

The man took another step and seemed to stumble. George reached out to catch him. The man bent down and bit George's arm.

"Oh, shit!" yelled the girl.

George shook his arm and slapped at the creeper's head. The man's teeth were caught in his sleeve, but he got it free. He took a few steps away from the man. The woman took a few steps back, too. She glanced at the arm. "Are you okay?"

"Yeah, it's fine. He didn't even break the skin."

"Lucky. You'd probably need half a dozen shots."

The creeper straightened up as if he wore a backpack full of weights. His head shifted side to side. His teeth gnashed together four times. One of them cracked and a gleaming piece of enamel spun to the ground.

George lunged forward, put his hands on the man's shoulders, and shoved. The pale man staggered back, hit the back bumper of the car, and tipped over backward. His skull bounced off the trunk with a loud clang, and his body flopped on the pavement between the sedan and a red minivan.

"Shit," said the woman. "I think you killed him with your karate."

"I didn't kill him."

"He's not moving."

The body on the ground moved. It groaned once. It rolled over. The oversized teen blinked twice, then twice again. "Whoooooo," he said. He burped and the smell of cheap beer wafted across George. "You have an awesome rack," the teen said to the side of the car.

"Asshole," said the woman. "You broke my phone."

George stared at the teen. Down between the cars, out of the direct sun, his skin didn't seem so pale, and his eyes were a faint blue, not the dull gray they'd looked like in the light. The side of his nose was covered with Magic Marker, and there were half-removed traces of it across his face. His hair had the stylishly rumpled look of someone who spent a lot of time making it look like they spent no time on their hair.

The creeper gave a drunken cackle. He rolled onto all fours and scampered between the cars. Once he was clear he staggered back to his feet and lurched away toward the crowds of students and parents.

"Asshole," she yelled after him.

"Do you want to call security?" asked George. "I saw it all."

The woman didn't even look at him. "Do you know who he is?"

"No."

"Well, that's not going to help, is it? Goddammit," she muttered, cradling the cracked phone, "I had plans for tonight."

George opened his mouth to say something else but she was already walking past him to her car. He looked after the creeper and caught a glimpse of the man stumbling through the crowd. He thought about calling security, but the girl was right. "Drunken frat boy" wasn't much of a description.

Plus, George admitted, he wasn't sure what the young man had looked like. He'd been so confident about the pale eyes and the torn nose, but it must've been his imagination. Probably from the girl, Madelyn, talking about dead people.

His Nextel chirped. "George," it twanged. "Where the hell are you, buddy? What's keeping you?"

He unholstered the phone. The whole half hour was gone. At this point he was running late. "Sorry, Jarvis," said George. "I got held up. A girl got jumped."

"Jesus. Y'all okay?"

"Yeah, she's fine. Just a frat boy copping feels. I got him off her."

"Security there?"

The woman's car started up and pulled out. She didn't even glance at George. "Nope," he said. "Once he was off her they both took off."

"Y'all want to make a report anyway? Just in case?"

"I'm pretty sure it was nothing."

"Well, then hurry it up," his boss told him. "I had Mark punch your card for you. You know they're getting all Nazi about overtime."

"Yeah," said George, "I know. I'm about five minutes away. See you soon."

He clipped the Nextel back onto his belt and took one last look over his shoulder. The shuffler had vanished into the human traffic between buildings. It struck George that he should go after the man, that the attack wasn't nothing, but he couldn't say why.

THEN

I FALL THROUGH the air.

There's a crowd of people below me, gathered in the street. It's dark out, but there are hundreds of people. Maybe thousands. I'm not sure what's brought so many people out at night.

Then, as one, they look up at me. Every head tips back at once, every set of eyes finds me at the same time. I see their eyes and remember I'm in the bad dream again. Dull irises stare at me. A constant stream of silent words pours from their jaws.

And there's something else in the crowd. Something huge. An even bigger monster than the ones around me, twice as tall with mottled, scaly skin. Its arms and legs are long and thin, and its tail lashes like an angry snake. It has curling horns and dozens of long teeth, but the same dull eyes.

I hit the ground behind the big monster, feet first. Some part of my mind knows falling from that height means I'm dead. The impact shakes me, but—as things happen in dreams—I don't break any bones. I don't even feel any pain.

One of the monster-people grabs at me and I kick it away. Another one reaches for me and I shove it back with my foot. I turn and one of them is right in front of me. It'd been a dark-haired man with a stubbly face. One of its eyes is gone. The empty socket looks sticky.

I throw a punch that catches the monster on the jaw. Like

falling from the sky, I barely feel it when I connect. It's as if the monster's head is just a paper sculpture. The skull bursts like a monster piñata. One side collapses under my punch and dark gore sprays out the other side. The monster crumbles to the ground. I've killed it.

No, I tell myself. I look at the dark stains on my knuckles. I haven't killed it. It's already dead. It's dead and walking around.

There's a name for a creature like this, but in the hazy world of the dream I can't remember it.

One of them paws at me from behind. I drive my elbow back and hear a crunch like a breaking bird's nest. My fist comes forward, takes the head right off another monster, and the ball of bone and flesh spins off into the horde. A second punch turns one of their faces into dark jelly. A sweeping backhand crushes two skulls.

And then the big creature's in front of me. It isn't just a monster, I realize. It's a demon. A real-life, actual demon.

Past the demon stands a spiked wall with people on it. Living people. They have guns. They're shooting the big thing and also the little ones. The instant I see them I feel like I know them, the way strange faces are familiar in dreams.

The demon holds on to the wall, on to the gate, with spider-like hands. The long fingers wrap around the spikes and pull. The gate shakes and squeals from its efforts.

I don't think. There's no time to think.

I grab the creature's tail. The beast is three times my size, probably four times my weight. I throw my shoulders back, pull, and the strange physics of this world take over. The creature flies into the air. It sails over my head and crashes to the ground behind me.

I jump, dragging the tail with me, and sail over the monster like the hero in a Hong Kong action film. I lash out at another—

Who do I watch action films with? Someone explained wire-work to me. Someone I watch a lot of movies with. It's a blank spot in my dream-memory.

I lash out at another one of the gray-skinned monsters as the wires lower me back to earth. I pull on the tail again, but this time I lean back, dig my heels in, and swing the demon to the side. The wires lift it up and spin it in a wide circle. Its scaly body smashes down dozens of the dead-people monsters.

I spin it once, twice, and let go. The beast soars through the crowd, crushing skulls as it goes. It crashes into the concrete pillar of a parking structure on the east side of Lemon Grove. The impact sounds like—

Lemon Grove. The street I'm standing on is called Lemon Grove. And so is—

The gate. The people on the gate are cheering. I glance over my shoulder as I backhand another dead man. A few of the people on the wall are calling my name. My real name. The one they gave me.

My name is Saint—

SIX

GEORGE SLUMPED BACK in the driver's seat. Another night without any quality sleep. Another red light on Wilshire Boulevard. Another crowd of pedestrians shuffling along without a care in the world, blocking the street long after the light turned green. He'd been late for work more in the past week than in most of his career.

The radio droned on. He'd ended up on some kind of retro station with lots of Matchbox Twenty and Green Day. At the moment, Bruce Springsteen was belting out the chorus to "Radio Nowhere."

He was going to have to start setting his alarm earlier. Not a pleasant thought considering how little sleep he was already getting. Unless he could figure out a better route to work, though, he wasn't going to have much choice. Traffic was stacked up on the road as far as he could see.

The light turned green just as he tapped another preset on the radio. An obese man with a thick beard waddled past George's car. He was too big to move any faster. His feet barely came off the ground as he walked. They scraped against the pavement with each step.

The car's engine revved. It growled like an angry animal. George felt it fight against the brake.

The man turned and glared at him. George tried to look apologetic and mouthed a "sorry." The heavy man stood there for a moment, wasting precious seconds of the green light.

"Just go," said the deejay on the new radio station. "Just run him down, man."

George's eyes flitted from the man in the road to the radio.

"Seriously, bro," said the radio. "Just let me run him down."

The brake pushed up against his foot. George gripped the wheel and pushed back. The deejay grunted and swore in Spanish.

The heavy man gave George a final, pointed look and then lumbered the rest of the way across the street.

The voice on the radio began talking about saints and the departed. The voice was very emphatic about it, but George was only half paying attention. He wondered how phrases like "run him down" had worked into the sermon.

Wilshire was clear for the rest of his drive. He stopped for one more light. The engine idled. He used the moment to switch from the religious channel to more music. The radio responded by singing about the virtues of Stacy's Mom.

And then, six blocks from work, his car died.

He was cutting over to Lindbrook when the engine coughed twice. The car lurched three times. The radio sputtered and went dead. George had just enough time to pull over before it stalled out. As it was, two of the cars behind him pounded their horns at him for slowing down.

He turned the key. The first time the engine made a wheezing noise. The second time the starter clicked twice. The third time the car did nothing.

George pulled out his phone and checked the time. Twenty-seven minutes until he was late. Again. He pounded the steering wheel. The car lurched and his heart leapt, but it was still dead.

He got out of the car and looked around. He could look for help and maybe get it in time to drive his car to campus, or he could start walking and hope the car wasn't ticketed or towed. There weren't any street signs in sight to give him a clue what would happen.

The car had stopped in front of a café that wasn't open yet.

The next building toward campus was a Denny's that looked pretty much empty through the big windows. One door back was an Army recruiting office with its lights on.

He decided to go Army.

* * *

Lieutenant John Carter Freedom stood by his desk and looked over his post. The recruiting office was a masterwork of marketing. Enough wood to feel homey but enough stark office furniture to seem formal. There were several posters but lots of open wall space. A portrait of the President hung in the back, flanked by an American flag on one side and the Army's on the other.

Freedom settled into his desk. It was a fair-sized desk but his legs barely fit beneath it. He was a very large man. Just shy of seven feet tall and 331 pounds as of his morning weigh-in. His office chair creaked and trembled whenever he moved, as if it was about to collapse.

He hated it.

Hate was a strong word, and he prided himself on not using it often. There were ideas he hated, like cowardice and betrayal, but he tried not to use the word in a more specific sense. When he'd been in Iraq and Afghanistan, he never hated the people there, even the people he fought against. While some officers prided themselves on whipping their soldiers into a frenzy of emotion and adrenaline, Freedom counseled them on duty and honor. Do what needed to be done but never blindly hate your enemy. That was their way, not the American way.

But, Lord, he hated the desk and the chair. Hated them with a passion.

He knew it was transference. That's what the Army counselors had called it. What he really hated was himself. He hated failing, and the desk was a constant reminder of how bad he'd failed and the fall he'd taken from it.

Twenty-three dead soldiers. Nineteen men, four women. Three staff sergeants, eight sergeants, seven specialists, a corporal, and four privates. Seventeen of them on their first tour, six on their second. Freedom had spent the past year learning every possible combination of those twenty-three men and women.

The court martial had been fairer than he'd expected. A general discharge had been discussed. In the end, he was taken off the front line, given a reduction in rank and a new career branch. And a desk facing out onto one of the most boring streets in North America.

Two other desks faced each other across the room. Each held a man in an Army Combat Uniform. Neither of them had chosen this assignment, either. One sorted and arranged paperwork, clicking his pen while he did. The other watched a television mounted in the corner.

Barely ten minutes into the day and Harrison was already lost in the recruitment video, tapping his fingers in time with the simple music score. It looked more like a sci-fi film, even when the Army banner flashed across the screen. The latest thing from DARPA—an armed and armored exoskeleton. On the screen the huge battlesuit stomped across an open field. Its armor plates were red and blue, and an American flag was stenciled across one shoulder. An M2 machine gun was mounted on each of the robot's arms. It turned to look into the camera with large white eyes.

It was impressive, but Freedom believed in men over machines.

Adams was a quiet man. Good soldier, very driven and single-minded. He wasn't supposed to be there in the office, either, but he accepted it and threw himself into the work. He went at the paperwork each morning like a machine. The only bad thing Freedom could say about Adams was the man kept clicking his pen. He'd write for a few minutes, then hammer on the button for a few seconds like he was back in weapons training doing trigger exercises.

Freedom knew the pen noise wasn't that bad. No one else reacted to it. Harrison never even noticed it, and the man hated random noises. He said they threw off his internal tempo.

No, it gnawed at Freedom because he was already on edge. He hadn't had a good night's sleep in ages. He kept having stress dreams. Nightmares, almost, where he was still a captain but he was surrounded by the bodies of the people he'd failed.

Dead bodies that walked. That fought. That tried to kill him.

Something moved on the edge of his vision and the electric eye chirped. He looked up. So did Harrison and Adams.

An older man stood at the door. Not old, by any means, but older than the usual people who came into the recruiting office. Freedom guessed he was in his mid thirties and in decent shape for a civilian. He had brown-blond hair that needed to be cut and an old bomber jacket covered with stitches, as if it had been patched and repaired dozens of times.

He shook his head. The man's jacket wasn't leather and it wasn't patched. It was just a trick of the light.

"Can we help you with something, sir?" Freedom asked.

"Hi," said the man. "Sorry to bother you, but my car just died out front. I don't suppose any of you have jumper cables or something like that?"

Freedom glanced at Adams, already back to his paperwork. The pen clicked three times to emphasize it. He looked over at Harrison, already watching the television again. "Harrison," he said. "Help the gentleman out."

Harrison glanced from the television to the man and back to Freedom. "Yes, sir, Lieutenant," he said. His eyes jumped back to the screen.

"Thanks," said the man.

Freedom gave a polite nod.

The man took a few steps and craned his head around to look at the television. "You see that?" said Harrison. "That, my friend, is the future of armed combat. Nine feet tall, fully armored, and it can throw cars like softballs. Its hands are Tasers. Those are fifty-caliber machine guns on the arms. This thing's a walking tank."

On-screen the patriotic-colored machine tore apart a concrete bunker, then the film cut to a shot of it throwing what looked like the wrecking ball from a crane. The footage played for another minute before the loop started over. "It's some kind of robot?" asked the man.

Harrison shook his head. "It's battle armor, man. Full-on Japanese sci-fi stuff." He gestured at the screen and grabbed a set of car keys from his desk. "That's just the engineering team testing it out. Another few years, you're going to see dozens of those on every battlefield. They want to start cranking 'em out by 2017."

On the screen, the battlesuit was blasting away targets at a firing range. Someone with a sense of humor had set up pictures of monsters instead of the usual black silhouettes. The shots punched softball-sized holes in each target.

"Wow," the man said. "That's pretty impressive."

"It's going to be out here next week if you want to see it in person," said Harrison.

"Yeah?"

The sergeant nodded. "Yeah. Kind of a pain in the ass, to be honest. The project head got some bug up her butt, insisted they had to bring it out here to Los Angeles for a demonstration. Put her foot down and wouldn't budge until they agre—"

"Sergeant," Freedom said without looking up. He put a certain emphasis behind the word and Harrison shut up. No need to discuss such things in front of civilians.

Across the room, Adams worked the button of his pen again and again and again while he went through his paperwork. Freedom closed his eyes for another moment. When he opened them, he saw the man giving the pen an annoyed look.

Thank the Lord, thought Freedom. It's not just me.

The man looked back at Harrison. "Does she ever miss?"

"Who?"

He tipped his head at the television. "The woman in the armor. It looks like she always hits."

"What?" Harrison looked at the screen again. "That's not a woman."

"It isn't?"

"Pretty sure," said Harrison. "Why would you think it's a woman?"

Freedom looked at the screen. The battlesuit was androgynous, but he couldn't shake the sense the civilian was right. He tried to put his finger on what it was about the hulking exoskeleton that made him so sure the person inside was female.

Then he shook it off. Like it or not, the suit would be here in a week. He could find out then. "Sergeant Harrison," he said, "would you please get a move on and help the gentleman with his car?"

"Yes, sir."

"Thanks again," said the man.

"Not a problem, sir," Freedom told him.

"If you get by your car, sir," said Harrison with a wave, "I'll drive around."

The man headed out and Freedom realized why he'd looked somewhat familiar. He looked like the man from his dreams. The man who helped him fight the walking dead.

* * *

Outside, George popped the hood and glanced at his phone. If they could get the car started in the next five minutes, he could still make it to work on time.

Two minutes later Harrison pulled around the corner in a hatchback. The car whipped past George, then backed up into the space before him. The sound equipment in the back bounced as the rear of the car bumped up onto the sidewalk. The hood popped open. Harrison climbed out and dragged a long set of jumper cables out from behind the driver's seat. "Sorry about the lieutenant," Harrison said as he connected the cables. "He's kind of had a stick up his ass since he got this job."

"He didn't seem that bad," said George.

Harrison shrugged and walked the other end of the cables over to the Hyundai. He stepped past George and clamped them onto the car's battery. "I get that he's pissed about being busted down and stuck here," the soldier continued. "I mean, I was supposed to be in the Army band and they gave me this. Adams isn't supposed to be here, either, but you don't hear him taking it out on everyone else. Ready to give this a try?" He gestured at George's car.

George slid into the driver's seat and Harrison dropped behind the wheel of his car. Their eyes met and the soldier gave him a thumbs-up. The hatchback's engine rumbled. George twisted the key. The starter clicked, the engine coughed once, and his car heaved itself back to life. The radio popped on and a string of Spanish came out of it. He was pretty sure the deejay was swearing. Then the voice faded away and a Beyoncé song rolled out of the speakers.

Harrison unhooked the jumper cables. "Good deal," he said. "You probably want to drive for at least fifteen or twenty minutes, let the battery build up some charge."

"I would," said George, "but I've got about six minutes left to get to work."

"Good luck, then," said Harrison with a grin. He gathered up the cables into a rough ball and shoved it back behind the driver's seat. "Might want to get your alternator looked at."

"Thanks again." George gave him a wave and pulled out. The car lurched once, reluctant to leave its resting spot, and then slid into the lane. The engine grumbled a few times, but he made it to work with seconds to spare.

SEVEN

GEORGE SIPPED SOME more milk and wrinkled his nose. The taste was off. The smell, too. He wondered if someone behind the scenes at the dining commons had let it sit out and get warm.

Lunch had been a dry cheeseburger. The salad bar had helped dress it up, but in the end it was still a sub-McDonald's burger. The tater tots were good, at least. The server had given him an extra ladleful of them.

He'd spent the morning hauling trash out of the dorms and down to the dumpsters. The first weekend was always one of the roughest. On the plus side, most of it was dry trash, though not as dry as his burger.

Someone had left a copy of *Maxim* on the dining hall table. It wasn't his usual kind of thing, but he knew if he didn't read something he'd just nod off. There was a short piece on the President's stylish tie collection and how his wife picked out most of them for him.

He made it halfway through an article about a "cleansing spa" before he decided it wasn't good lunchtime reading. He failed a fourteen-question quiz about whether his apartment would qualify as a "good loving lair."

One article made him fire off a quick text to Nick. It was just a sidebar piece about game shows, but it made something in his brain itch. He got an answer back a few minutes later.

Unless it jst happened in the past hr then no Trebek is not dead. Why?

He didn't bother to respond. He knew it was a stupid question when he asked it. But it still nagged at him. If not Alex Trebek, who was he thinking of?

Near the center of the magazine was a six-page pictorial with a short interview. It was the dark-skinned woman from the bus stop poster. Her name was Karen Quilt. She was thirty-three and had appeared in *Maxim* twice before, both times on the "Hot 100" list. She had doctorates in biology and biochemistry, plus a handful of master's degrees in other fields. Her mother had been part of the NSS, which sounded like the Somali version of the KGB the way the article spun it. Her European father had been some kind of mercenary or assassin. From the age of eight she'd been raised by an aunt and lived in New York City until she started traveling as a model.

Reading between the lines, George got the sense Karen Quilt didn't have a lot of patience for interviews or pictorials.

"Hi," said a voice.

He glanced up from the magazine and saw a dead girl in a wheelchair. Her eyes were dull and her skin was chalk-white. She wore a tattered collection of dusty clothes, and threads of black hair hung out beneath a Red Sox baseball cap.

He blinked and his eyes adjusted to the dining hall's fluorescent lights. They made the girl's skin look pale. The tubes reflected in her eyes at just the right angle to white out her irises. He shivered a bit at the afterimage in his mind.

He needed to get more sleep.

"We met a couple days ago," she said. "I'm Maddy. Madelyn Sorensen." She moved her wheelchair a few feet closer and held out her hand.

"I remember," said George.

"I've been looking for you," she said. "All over campus."

"I don't actually live here," he said.

"I know. I probably didn't make the best first impression."

He bit his tongue.

"I'm sorry about that," she said. "I was just . . . I kind of gushed, y'know?" Her hand was still out. She managed a weak smile.

George sighed. He reached out and took her hand. He hoped he wasn't going to regret it.

Madelyn's fingers were cold. He didn't think the air conditioning was up that high in the dining hall. He wondered if being in a wheelchair was bad for circulation. It couldn't be good, he figured.

She released his hand and gestured at the open space at the end of the table. "Can I join you?"

"I guess," said George. "Are you going to talk about people dying?"

"Yeah, sorry about that," she said. "I came across as a freak, didn't I?"

"Just a little." He brushed the magazine aside and gestured at the table.

The chair moved forward until it bumped the table edge. Madelyn reached over her shoulder and tugged the backpack off the handles. She pulled a bottle of eye drops from the front pouch and tossed the pack in the empty chair across from George.

"You're not eating?" he asked.

She tapped the arm of the wheelchair as she leaned her head back. "They bring my tray out for me. I could do it myself, but it'd take twice as long to reach a table using one hand." She blinked a few times to spread the drops around her eyes and tucked the bottle back in her pack.

One of the cafeteria workers—the same one who'd given George extra tater tots—appeared with a tray. She set it next to Madelyn and shot a quick smile at George. Madelyn peeled the bun and cheese off her first burger and attacked the patty with her fork.

"Low-carb diet?"

She shook her head. "Digestion issues."

"Ahhh." He watched her eat for a minute and wondered what she wanted from him. He picked up his last tater tot, rubbed it in the salt on the plate, and popped it in his mouth.

She finished the first burger and started stripping the second one. Her eyes drifted over to the magazine. She smirked and bit back a laugh. She turned the magazine around and looked at the pictorial, then turned it back to George.

"It's not mine," he said. "It was just here when I sat down. There wasn't anything else to read."

"She's pretty."

His mouth twitched into a smile. "That's an understatement."

"You know she's your girlfriend, right?"

He blinked. "Sorry?"

"She's one of us," said Madelyn. "A superhero."

He managed not to sigh out loud, but it showed on his face.

"I'm telling you the truth."

"I'm not a superhero. I'm not dating anyone right now." He tapped the magazine. "And I would definitely remember if I'd dated a woman like that at any point in my life." He pushed his chair away from the table and got up. "Anyway, I've got to get back to—"

She dropped her fork and grabbed his arm. "Wait," she pleaded. "I'm really sorry about the other day. I kind of lunged and hit you with everything at once, but it was such a huge relief to find you."

He didn't pull away. He also didn't sit back down. She sounded desperate again, and it kind of freaked him out.

"Ten minutes," she said. "Just let me talk for ten minutes and then I'm done. I'll even transfer back east if you want."

George sighed again and looked at the clock on the wall behind her. "My lunch break's almost over," he said. "I've got seven minutes."

He sat down.

"It'll be worth it," she told him. "I promise."

He crossed his arms and waited.

Madelyn took a long slow breath. "Okay," she said, "let me ask you something kind of weird."

"*Now* it's getting weird?" He couldn't hold back a smile.

She didn't return it. "Do you dream at night?"

"What?"

"Dreams. Are you one of those people who don't dream, or don't remember them?"

Images of falling and dead people and demons flitted through his mind. He shook his head. "No, I have dreams."

"Normal dreams?"

"What's that supposed to mean?"

She crossed her own arms. "I dream every night," she said. "Know what I dream about?"

"Look," he said, "this is going in kind of an uncomfortable direction. I'm not sure it's appropri—"

"Monsters."

He shut his mouth and stared at her.

Something sparked in her eyes. Her shoulders lifted. "And you do, too, don't you?"

He didn't say anything. He looked at the young woman and tried not to think of the image he'd seen out of the corner of his eye. The corpse in the wheelchair.

"There's thousands of them, right? Dead people walking around. They're kind of slow and clumsy, but there's just so many of them."

He set his hands on the table, then crossed them again. He studied her face. "How are you doing this? Is this some kind of magic trick?"

She shook her head. "What else do you remember?"

George thought about his dreams. "There's a wall," he said. "A big wall keeping them out. And a gate."

Madelyn nodded.

"And a robot," he said. "A battlesuit. But that's just dream stuff."

"No it isn't."

"It is. I saw it on a commercial for the Army this morning. It's some military project. The future of combat or something."

She smirked. "So you're telling me the battlesuit has to be part of your dream because it's real?"

"I'm saying I probably just saw pictures of it online. Maybe it was on the news while I was doing something else and it didn't register. And then, you know, the subconscious grabs it and puts it in a dream."

Madelyn reached down and tore a piece off the burger patty with her fingers. She popped it in her mouth. Her teeth were perfect. She swallowed. "The dream about monsters," she said.

"Yeah."

"That you have every night."

"I don't have it every night."

"Okay," she said. "When was the last time you didn't have it?"

George tried to remember his last good night of sleep. "I'm not sure," he admitted, "but I know I haven't always had it."

She tore another piece off the burger. "You haven't."

He drummed his fingers on the table. "So what makes you so sure your dreams are going to come true?"

"Already came true," she corrected him. "It's all real."

"But what makes you say that?"

"Because it is," said Madelyn.

"That's not really an answer."

She sighed and scrunched up her mouth. "Okay," she said, "do you have a television?"

He nodded. He figured he could humor her for a few more minutes.

"Prove it."

"What?"

"Prove you have a television. Right now."

He smiled. "I don't carry around photos of my TV."

"But you're sure you have one?"

"Yeah."

"You know it's in your apartment right now?"

"Unless someone broke in and stole it, yeah."

She smiled. "That's how I know your dreams are real."

George chuckled. "Okay, then," he said, "if this was true—"

"It is true."

"If this was true, why doesn't anyone else know about it?"

She poked at her tray. She'd eaten both burger patties and nothing else. All the meat was gone. "I used to have memory problems," she said.

The warning flares went off in George's brain again, but were swamped by a wave of pity. "Mental problems?"

"*Memory* problems," she repeated. "I had trouble forming long-term memories. Whenever I fell asleep I'd forget most of the previous day."

"And that doesn't happen anymore?"

She shook her head. "Not since I started having the dreams. I think . . ." She paused for a moment. "I think I forgot that I was supposed to forget everything. Whatever happened, I fell asleep and forgot that it happened, so it didn't affect me as much as all of you. So I'm here but I still remember there. Something like that."

He drummed his fingers on the table.

"Come on," she said, "this has to make sense on some level."

He glanced at the clock. He had just over two minutes before he'd have to call in to Jarvis. "Look," he said, "I don't mean to sound rude, but . . . well, what are you getting at?"

Her face dropped a little. "You still don't get it?"

He shook his head. "It's a fun story. A neat coincidence, I guess, that we're having similar dreams, but it's just a story. This is the real world, like it or not."

"George," she said, "this *isn't* the real world. That's my point."

He opened his mouth, then closed it again. Then he chuckled. "Okay," he said, "I was wrong. You came up with something less believable than the whole dating-a-supermodel thing."

Madelyn shook her head. "Something happened. I'm not sure what. And everything changed. We all changed. You. Me. Barry." She tapped the magazine. "Her. All of us."

"Who's Barry?"

"Barry Burke. He's your best friend. He's . . ." She closed her eyes and wrinkled her brow, the look of every student trying to remember something. "He's in a wheelchair, too, and he's . . . he's bright."

"Smart?"

"I think so. He told me he used to work out at a lab in New Mexico." She snapped her fingers. "Sandia Labs. The people with the Z Machine."

"The what?"

"It's a big machine in New Mexico. It has something to do with physics. They make particles there."

"That's not really helpful."

She waved her arm around her. "Give me a break. I'm just a sophomore."

"I thought you knew all this," he said. He tried to give her a good-natured smile. "You said you remembered everything."

"I remember most of it," she said. "I remember enough to know we're not supposed to be here."

One minute left on the clock. Somewhere in the dining hall a knife was tapping on a glass. He wasn't sure if it was to get attention or be annoying. Or both.

George thought for a minute about how to word what was in his head. "Okay, let's say you're right," he said. Her smile lifted and he held up his hand. "Just hypothetically. Let's say there was some kind of epidemic and half the world died and turned into monsters. And you and I know each other there and we're leaders or heroes or something."

She nodded.

"So why would we want to go back to that? Why would anyone want to 'fix' things so billions of people are dead? What would it accomplish?"

"Because the people there are depending on us," she said. "They're depending on you."

George leaned back in his chair and tried to ignore the shadows her words had cast. He tried to think of something gentler to follow up with when his Nextel chirped. "George," called Jarvis's voice, "you there?"

Habit made him unholster the phone. "Yeah, I'm here."

"You done with lunch?"

He looked at Madelyn and mouthed a quick apology. "Yeah, I think I'm all done here."

Her face fell.

"Can you head over to Ackerman? Bathroom's flooding on the second floor."

He looked out the window toward the student union building. "Seriously? Don't you have plumbers over there right now? Real ones?"

"Sorry, buddy. I'd give it to Mark, but . . . well, trust me. You got the better job."

"Great. I'll be there in ten."

"You the man, George."

He pushed his chair away from the table and stood up. Madelyn said nothing. "Sorry," he said. "I've got to go." He piled his napkins and glasses on the tray.

She slid the magazine across the table to him. "Keep it," she said. "Maybe she'll help you remember."

He shook his head but she pushed it at him. He sighed, folded the magazine, and shoved it in his back pocket. He could toss it once he was outside. "It was . . . fun," he said. "You should write all this stuff down. I'm sure someone in Hollywood would buy it."

She sighed. "One last question."

"If you're quick."

"Are you strong in your dreams? Really, really strong?"

He thought of the impossible physics when he fought the monsters. How their bones crumbled beneath his fists. How he'd yanked the demon into the air. "Yeah," he said. "How'd you know?"

"Because that's who you are."

EIGHT

THE TRASH BARREL had two plastic wheels on the bottom. Over the years one of the wheels had been worn away by too many trips down the stairwell and over curbs. It was closer to an oval now. Almost a rectangle.

George dragged the trash barrel across the parking lot and some more of the oval wheel crumbled away. The plumbers had dumped all the old tiles and soggy plaster in the trash room rather than carrying the material down to the dumpster like they were supposed to. If he had to guess, the barrel weighed over three hundred pounds. Maybe over four.

He paused to let a group of students go past. They were chattering away and barely acknowledged him as they rushed between classes. He started to pull again and one last kid walked by, cracking his gum.

George heaved. The trash barrel scraped across the pavement. By the time he got it to the dumpster he was pretty sure he'd worn the other wheel flat, too. He tossed both lids open and stopped for a breather while he figured out what to do next.

He knew he should just call Jarvis and tell him to send Mark over for an assist. He should've called ten minutes ago, but the thought of listening to Mark ramble on about the life he was supposed to have seemed especially grating at the moment.

If he could get the barrel off the ground, even just a little,

George was pretty sure he could work the top of it up onto the edge of the dumpster. Then he could just push it forward and tilt it until the whole thing tipped. It was the same move he'd used with the couch last week.

The couch that had been so much lighter than he'd expected.

Madelyn's lunchtime stories flashed through his mind. That he was strong. It was nonsense, but right now he wouldn't mind if it were true. Unfortunately, he knew the barrel weighed a lot more than the couch.

He gave the top edge of the trash bin a nudge. It bent away from his finger. The weight had settled to the bottom of the container, but the top was still just plastic. He could feel the barrel resist as his hand slid down and pushed.

He shook the thoughts from his head and tightened his lifting belt. The Velcro flaps rustled into place over his abs. He got behind the barrel, bent his knees, and pushed at the top with his left hand. It tipped forward just enough for him to slip his fingers underneath it. He tightened his fingers, braced his arms, and heaved up with his knees.

The trash barrel jumped two feet into the air.

George fell back for a moment, convinced his grip had slipped, then lunged back in to grab the barrel. It crashed down on the ground. It was so bottom heavy there was no chance of it tipping.

A last few passing students glanced over at the noise of the impact. It had been loud. Over five hundred pounds loud, easy.

George straightened up. The *click-clack-click* of newly broken tile echoed inside the bin. A faint haze of dust circled the top. He gave it another prod with his hand.

Are you strong in your dreams? Really, really strong?

Most of the students were gone now. Class schedules weren't exact, but there were periods of high and low foot traffic on campus. At the moment, there was no one nearby to watch him try something dumb.

He bent down again. With one move, without thinking about it, he scooped up the bin. It came away from the ground and fell into his arms. It weighed nothing.

He held it by the mouth and the bottom. He tipped the whole thing forward and shook it out. A wave of trash poured out into the dumpster. Soggy papers, wet plaster, ceramic tiles. It all crashed down inside the metal container.

George dropped the plastic bin and looked at his hands. His gaze traveled up his arms. There weren't any bulging muscles or swollen veins. His shirt didn't feel tight. His limbs didn't look any bulkier or more powerful than they ever did in the bathroom mirror.

He looked at the old tiles and plaster chunks piled up in the dumpster. There was also a bunch of old pizza boxes, a dozen or so plastic trash bags, and what looked like some shelving with twisted brackets. The dumpster wasn't full, but it'd need to be emptied in a day or two at the most.

Still no one nearby. He stepped to the side of the dumpster and put his hands on the big sleeve the trash trucks slid their forklifts into. They used them to flip the dumpsters up and over the cab. He slid his fingers under the sleeve and lifted.

The end of the dumpster rose into the air with a squeal of stressed metal. The wheels went one-two-three feet in the air. Half a ton of steel and trash, easy. Hell, the dumpster alone weighed over five hundred pounds. Even considering two of the wheels still sat on the ground, he had to be lifting five or six times his own weight.

And it barely took any effort at all. He was aware of the weight, but it felt like nothing. He could've been lifting a bag of groceries.

George set the dumpster down. He didn't want to make any noise. Any more noise, at least.

The life he was supposed to have.

He reached down and grabbed the underside of the steel bin with one hand. The rusty bottom flaked away beneath his fingertips. He felt something small and slick skitter away from the tip of his pinky. His other hand grabbed the edge of the dumpster's wide mouth. The pose put his head almost against the forklift sleeve.

"Just like picking up the trash bin," he whispered. He took in a deep breath. His fingers tensed.

A car horn blared out three quick beeps. He fell against the dumpster. Its side echoed with the *clang*.

One of the department trucks sat in the walkway a few yards behind him. It was covered with dust. The front tires were flat, and it made the whole vehicle lean forward. Behind the wheel was the body of a man. Its skin was gray with a few freckles of black. Its eyes were dull pearls. The body was dusty, too. A cobweb stretched from the brim of its department cap to its nose, then down to its collar.

The dead man's head rolled to the side to look at him. Withered fingers reached up to paw at the steering wheel and the half-open side window. One arm pushed through the opening and it stretched out, trying to reach George. Its teeth snapped together, as if the dead thing thought it could bite him from twenty feet away.

George spun away and stumbled back against the dumpster. It made another loud *clang*. He looked back at the dead thing.

Mark popped open the door of the truck. "Hey," he called out. "What the heck are you doing?"

George looked at the dumpster and at the empty trash bin, then back at his coworker. He straightened up and looked in the dumpster. The garbage was all still more or less centered. None of it looked tilted or piled up as if someone had just lifted one end of the dumpster three feet in the air.

He felt very stupid and sleep deprived. Mostly stupid. The girl's stories had gotten into his head.

"Think I strained something," he said. "Trying to stretch my shoulder."

"Want me to pop your back?"

"No, that's okay."

"I'm really good at it. Seriously."

George shook his head. He shot another look at the truck. It was clean and shining. Both front tires were fine.

Mark walked over to him. He made fists and put his knuckles under his chin. "Put your arms like this," he said.

George held up a hand. "I'm okay. Thanks."

"Just trying to help, man." He gestured at the plastic trash bin. "Didya hurt yourself trying to flip it?"

"Yeah. It was full of tiles and crap the plumbers had dumped in it."

"Lazy bastards. Why didn't you just call for some help?"

"Ahhh, you know. I didn't want you calling me a lazy bastard."

Mark snorted out a laugh. "C'mon, get that thing put away. We've got to get one of the courts pretty in the gym for tonight." He gestured across the street.

George grabbed the trash bin. Both its wheels were worn flat now. It lurched along as he dragged it. "What's tonight?"

"I don't know." Mark shrugged. "Something that isn't football. Get a move on."

NINE

THE CLUB WAS somewhere in Hollywood, east of Highland but north of Sunset. They'd parked Nick's car in a lot and gone on foot for two blocks. The line stretched halfway down the sidewalk, but Nick guided them past it. The doorman smiled at him and shook his hand. George was pretty sure money was exchanged in a subtle, professional way. The velvet rope lifted away and George followed Nick into the club, along with three women he was pretty sure were just old enough to be inside. Years on campus had given him a good eye for ages.

The club was loud and dim with flashes of colored light. There was more open space than he'd expected, but it was still far from empty. Nick guided them through the crowd to the bar and exchanged a few quick gestures with the bartender. A moment later she handed them two drinks and they were seated at a side booth that fell beneath the blast of the speakers.

"Why don't you ever just want to go out to a bar?" George half shouted to his friend.

Nick gestured behind them. The spinning lights flashed off his sunglasses. "They've got a bar." He pulled the tiny straw from his Seven & Seven, tossed it on the table, and took a deep drink.

"They've got a cover charge."

"Which you didn't pay."

"Yeah, because you bribed the doorman."

Nick waved him off with a smile. "There's better girls here," he said. He tilted his head at two women dancing with each other. "You wouldn't see that at a bar."

George shook his head. The crowd on the dance floor parted and across the room George caught a glimpse of white eyes and messy hair. He straightened up, but the dancers swayed and shifted and hid the sight from him.

"Truth is, I shouldn't be here," said Nick. "I've got to do a phone meeting in the morning. And I think the owner here doesn't like me. I helped set up a party here for one of our dumb-fuck clients and it didn't end well." He had another mouthful of whiskey and soda. "So what's gnawing at you?"

"What do you mean?"

"You suck at hiding your feelings, George. You always have. Something's been bugging you all night. Ever since I picked you up."

He shrugged and sipped his own drink. "Weird stuff."

"Weird kinky or weird strange?"

"Not weird kinky," George said. "I've just felt really . . . off, lately."

"Sick?"

"No."

"Good. Get me sick and I'll beat the crap out of you. So what is it?"

George shifted on his side of the table. A new song started and a few people in the crowd cheered. He raised his voice. "Have you ever had one of those dreams that were just . . . real? One of those ones that's so real, when you woke up it took you a while to figure out if it had happened or not?"

"This is about a dream?"

"Answer the question."

Nick settled one arm on the table. He was good at leaning in and not making it look awkward. "Once or twice, I guess. I remember once when I was a kid I dreamed my dog was dead and I freaked out in the morning when I couldn't find him."

"Where was he?"

"My brother took him for a walk."

"What about one of the ones that are fresh and solid in your mind when you wake up, but then a couple minutes later they're gone. Wiped clean. There's just a . . . a dream-shaped hole in your memories."

"Yeah, okay, sure."

George took a sip of his drink. "I've been feeling like that for a few days. Maybe a few weeks. I'm not sure."

"Feeling like what?"

He tapped the side of his glass. "Like I've forgotten something. I pretty much always feel like there's something I should remember and I can't. Something right there that I just can't see, y'know?"

"You're acting weird because you forgot a couple of dreams?"

"No." George shook his head. "It's not dreams, it's life. I feel like this when I'm awake. I've got this constant, nagging feeling I've just forgotten something."

"Like a dream?"

Over Nick's shoulder, a gap opened at the bar. There was a woman there with stringy blond hair. It looked like she hadn't washed it in months. In fact, it looked like there were things tangled in it. One of the thin straps of her top had slid off her shoulder, and that side sagged dangerously low. She didn't seem to notice or care. Her skin looked pale against the dark top.

Her head swung in a slow arc that made him think she'd been drugged. Her eyes were blank, pink circles in the club's red lights. Her mouth opened and closed like a fish gasping for air. George was sure if the music hadn't been so loud he would've heard her teeth hitting each other from here.

Then the bartender stepped forward to set some drinks on the bar and blocked the woman from view. When the gap opened again, the woman had turned around. Then a couple of guys filled the gap and she vanished.

Nick held out his hand and snapped his fingers. "Hey." He glanced over his shoulder, scanned the bar, and looked back at George. "Someone over there I should know about?"

"I don't think so," he said. "I just . . . I thought I saw someone I recognized."

"A girl?"

"Yeah?"

"From campus."

"No." He wasn't sure where he knew the woman from, but he was pretty sure it wasn't work. He shook it off.

"So you're just in some kind of . . . what, existential funk?"

"Maybe? I don't know."

"We so need to get you laid." Nick gestured at the two women dancing with each other. "Two of them, two of us, what do you say?"

"What about the publicist? Nina?"

"Nita. I was thinking of blowing her off and inviting that gymnast we saw in the parking lot the other day."

"I don't know if you're pathetic or . . . something else."

"I'm good with something else." He settled back into his side of the booth. His sunglasses reflected the dance floor, and for a moment the spinning lights gave the lenses a mechanical look, like a camera iris.

"You want to hear something even weirder?"

"Something weirder than you ignoring two hot, scantily clad women putting on a show for us?" Nick sat up. "Please, tell me. I'm dying to know."

George gave the women an obligatory glance and then took a sip of his drink. He was already a bit hoarse from raising his voice to be heard. "Okay, you know how when you have the realistic dreams, your mind fills in all the missing parts? If you're a pirate you know all the crew names and how you all met, that kind of thing?"

"You're dreaming you're a pirate?"

He shook his head. "No."

"Freak," said Nick. "Is this about a parrot fetish or something?"

"Anyway," George shouted over the music, "I think there are holes in my dreams, too. I'll be dreaming, but there are still things I can't remember. It's like I know I've forgotten things in the dream." He sipped his drink. "Have you ever heard of anything like that before?"

Nick laughed. "With the roster at my agency? I hear crap like this all the time. If it wasn't you, I'd say you need to stop taking pills from strangers at clubs."

George sighed and looked out at the dancers. On the edge of the crowd a tall woman in a tight blue tank top swung her hips. She'd painted her spiky hair fluorescent red, and it almost glowed in the club's lights. Two men were near her, waiting to be acknowledged, but she didn't seem to notice them.

He'd known a woman with wild hair once. A past girlfriend who had . . . spots? Stripes? He was pretty sure it was someone he'd slept with and felt ashamed that he couldn't remember a name or even a face.

"You could score with her," said Nick.

"What?"

He pointed at the fluorescent-haired woman. "Her. She's looked at you half a dozen times now at least. You've gotta pay attention to this stuff."

George took another look at the woman. She had muscular arms, but lots of curves. She smiled at him. Then her gaze slid off him and over to the bar. It slid in a way that clearly meant he was invited to come ask what she was looking at.

He followed her gaze, just for a moment, and then froze.

The stringy-haired blonde was on the dance floor. Another woman was with her. This one wore a T-shirt with a dark stain across the collar and chest. The second woman turned to George and he saw she had blank eyes, too, and her mouth was ringed with messy lipstick. Maybe some kind of sauce from food she'd crammed into her mouth.

Maybe something else.

The second woman grinned at George, a wide grin that showed a lot of teeth. He realized after a moment her lips and part of her cheeks were gone, showing off her bare jaw. Her teeth clicked together, keeping time with the pounding bass line from the speakers.

They weren't women. They weren't even alive. They were monsters.

"Jesus," muttered George.

Nick followed his gaze. "What?"

They flanked a man. He didn't see what they were. He swung his hips and pumped the air even as they fell on him. The blonde sank its teeth into his bicep. The other one bit into his shoulder. Their jaws worked back and forth as they tore loose mouthfuls of meat.

George leaped up. His thigh hit the edge of the table hard enough to tilt it and knock over both drinks. The table wobbled and fell over onto Nick.

"Fuck!" he barked.

George glanced down and saw himself reflected in his friend's glasses. Then he looked back to the dance floor, stepping forward as he did. It took him a moment to find the two . . .

Women. Just two women with hair that had been arranged and styled to look unkempt. They wore a lot of dark makeup around their eyes. They were grinding against the guy. He looked like he was having a lot more fun than George.

All three of them glanced his way. They looked at him and then at the fallen table. They never stopped dancing.

He looked around for a moment, confused. His eyes landed on the fluorescent redhead and she winked at him. It was a very promising wink.

George looked back at Nick. He pushed against the table edge until it tipped back the other way. "Cheap-ass hardware," muttered Nick. He looked at the base of the table. "The bolts snapped right off."

"You okay?" asked George.

"Are *you* okay? You jumped up like something bit you."

"What? Yeah, sorry, I just thought I saw—"

"Damn it," said Nick. His sunglasses were focused at the far end of the bar. "We should go."

"Why?"

"Remember I said I thought the owner didn't like me?"

"Yeah."

Nick angled his sunglasses toward the bar. "Well, it looks like we just broke a table in his club."

Across the room a buzz-cut man in a glossy suit glowered at

them. Two oversized men in black polo shirts lumbered toward them.

"We didn't do anything," said George.

"Great," said Nick. "We can feel really superior when they drag us out by our necks. Come on." He gestured toward the dance floor.

"Why?"

"Because there are a lot of people here and my boss'll be pissed if he hears I got thrown out of a club. We're going to dodge them and leave on our own." Nick started walking.

George took a few steps and someone grabbed his arm. He looked over at the fluorescent-haired woman. She was almost as tall as him. "About time," she said with a grin. "I was going to come over there and climb into your lap."

He tried to think of a good answer and his shirt got tight. It twisted into a knot between his shoulder blades. Right above the spot where he . . .

What was important about his shoulder blades? He tried to focus on the thought. It slipped away.

The knot in his shirt pushed him past the red-haired woman. Her hand slipped away from his arm. Another hand—a larger, heavier one—grabbed his wrist and pulled it back.

George slapped his foot down and looked over his shoulder. The man behind him was bald and his black polo shirt said SECURITY over his heart. His face was set in a flat expression that leaned close to a scowl. He was one of those guys treading a line between beefy and fat. Over the man's shoulder, the fluorescent-haired woman stared at George with a confused look.

The big man shoved again and George resisted, more out of instinct than any planned action. He pushed down on the floor and levered himself against the man's arms.

Just for a moment the heavy man's scowl cracked. His brow furrowed as George refused to move. The man pushed again, but it felt like he wasn't putting any real force into it. It was more of a nudge, a gentle guide in the direction he wanted George to go.

Then the moment passed. The next shove sent George sprawling, and only the fist twisted into his shirt stopped him from falling face-first on the dance floor. The club rushed past him, a side door loomed in front of him, and he was out on the sidewalk next to Nick.

Nick muttered something and pushed his sunglasses tight over his eyes. He dusted himself off and brushed the lapels of his coat back. For some reason it made George think of the sheriff in an old Western.

"Okay," said Nick, "want to hit somewhere else?"

THEN

I'M FALLING AGAIN.

This time, I'm falling sideways. The ground rushes by below me. I've been thrown or launched. I'm not sure which. That isn't part of the dream.

The ground rushes by. I see pavement, a quick glimpse of people, a white truck, a wall topped with spikes. And then I see them.

The crowd of monsters tilts their papery faces up at me. They all look thin and gaunt, and they stare at me with undeniable hunger. Some bend their heads so far back I see them fall over. As always, their jaws move but don't make any sound.

I lose momentum and crash down through the crowd. I get my arms up as I plow into some of the monsters. They fall under me as I drop to the street. The impact doesn't hurt. Dream physics saves me again. Or maybe the dead people broke my fall.

They swarm over me. They grab at my clothes and tangle their fingers in my hair and wrap themselves around my arms and legs. A woman with ivory skin falls on top of me and bares her gory teeth.

A prickling sensation sweeps over me. It reminds me of pins and needles, a sleepy leg or arm waking up, but it's localized in patches across my body. I tug away from the hair-pullers and look down at myself.

They're biting me. All of them are. The dead creatures are gnawing on me with yellowed teeth. They chew on my arms and fingers and calves and ...

They're trying to eat me!

I panic even as I realize they're harmless. They've been dead so long their teeth fall out when they try to bite me. Some just crumble. How long does someone have to be dead for their teeth to crumble against skin?

I push myself up and I'm back on my feet. Most of the creatures fall off me. A few have wrapped themselves on tight enough that I drag them to their feet as well. They must be very light. They're still biting me, even the ones with no teeth left in their mouths.

Parrots, I think. *These are parrots.* While dream-me understands the term, on a deeper level—the level where I know I'm in a dream—I know it's a nonsense phrase. More garbled memories.

Something pulls at my back. It's itchy. Whatever it is, it lifts me up and out of the horde of monsters. I soar into the air and a few of the creatures come with me. They're tangled in my limbs or snagged on my leather jacket. One's hooked its arm over my boot. The wirework spins me in a circle and the dead things tumble away. They fall on top of others in the mob and knock them to the ground.

Someone punches me. Hard. Twice. I twist in the air and look around.

A soldier's shooting at me. The man—the *huge* man—stands on top of the white truck I glimpsed earlier. It's tipped over, so he's standing on its side. The soldier has a video game pistol, something too big and bulky to be real.

As I look at the pistol, the soldier fires another burst at me. I flinch away, but all the gunshots just feel like punches. They knock me around and hurt a bit, but I can tell they aren't doing any real damage.

"Please stand down, sir," calls the huge soldier. The words echo out across the silent dreamscape. He has a good, deep voice. "I don't enjoy doing this."

It's stupid. I know this. The soldier and I are on the same side. We're supposed to be fighting the monsters. It's all a misunderstanding.

The wires I'm hanging from sag as the dream bullets hit me. I dangle down enough for the monsters below to reach me. One of the taller ones wraps its dead fingers around the toes of my boot. Another one brushes my heel.

The light grows brighter. Part of me wonders if it's one of those moments in a dream when night suddenly becomes day or you go from inside to outside. But I'm already outside in the early morning, so I'm not sure what's changed.

Then I see the other man. The other man hanging in the sky. The soldier turns to face him, too, and fires more dream bullets that do nothing.

At first I think the new man is wrapped in tinfoil. He's nothing but reflections of the sun. Every now and then the brightness shifts and ripples, as if threads of even brighter light are racing across his odd outfit.

He's very bright.

Then the gleaming figure speaks. Its voice sounds like static. Or a distorted hum. It takes an effort to understand the words, but I do understand them, because that's how things work in a dream.

Well, says the glowing man. He holds up his hand and it gets even more brilliant. It's like the tinfoil man is holding the sun in his hand. Even the air ripples and twists from the heat around his fingers. *That was all pretty impressive up until the part where you got here.*

ELEVEN

GEORGE WOKE UP with a headache.

The fan chain *tick-tick-tick-tick*ed against the side of the fan. The beads wobbled back and forth and tapped the motor housing again and again. He couldn't block out the sound.

He focused on the chain of beads. There was something wrong with it. And then his eyes focused past the chain and he saw the dark mildew stains stretching across the stippled ceiling. He blinked and sat up in bed.

While he slept, someone had destroyed his apartment.

His television was gone, along with his DVD player and his pathetically small collection of movies. The squat bookshelf the television lived on had been smashed and collapsed into moldy sections of particle board. The closet hung open and empty. Shoes, shirts, all of it gone. Even his—

What did he keep hidden in the back of the closet? Something important. Something he was proud of, but didn't want anyone to see.

The futon he was lying on was damp. He could see white threads of mold stretching across one corner like cobwebs. The opposite corner looked like it had been ripped open. Maybe chewed open. His blankets and sheets and pillow were gone. They'd been taken off him during the night.

They'd been taken *out from under him* during the night.

The room was covered with dust. The window was smashed. Even part of the frame was gone. There was a puddle on the floor beneath it, and a damp wind blew in from outside. The paint peeled off the walls in thick strips. Where they weren't peeling, the walls had the glossy sheen of condensation spotted with mildew.

He heard a scuffling noise from behind him. He flipped around on the bed and got a glimpse of his intruder. He saw outstretched arms, pearl-colored eyes, bared teeth, and then the dead woman lunged at—

* * *

George woke up with a headache.

He stretched his arms out from under the blanket and covered his eyes. Another night of too many vivid dreams and not enough restful sleep. The chain of beads *tick-tick-tick-tick*ed against the side of the fan. The beads wobbled back and forth and tapped the motor housing again and again. The noise accented the awareness that he wouldn't be getting back to sleep, even though the clock said he was awake more than an hour early.

His arm was sore. It tingled and felt a little raw. He wondered if something had bitten him during the night. A few people in his building had complained about bedbugs and demanded the managers spray or fumigate or something. Up until now, George figured he'd dodged that particular bullet.

He stepped off the bed and yawned. For now he had an extra hour to kill before heading in to work.

Like most people in such a position, he turned to the Internet.

George checked his e-mail and Facebook and skimmed a few articles on Yahoo! News. The President was coming into town for an appearance on one of the late-night shows. Things were still at a constant near boil in the Middle East. The big weekend movie was being savaged by critics and bloggers.

Halfway down the entertainment section was a picture of Karen Quilt wearing a long black dress and making it look casual. She was taking part in some charity gala in Los Angeles tomorrow night. She was also using the time to tour the Jet Propulsion Lab out in Pasadena. Aerospace engineering was one of her hobbies. The article phrased her interest in a condescending way, like a parent explaining that their child wants to be an astronaut when they grow up.

He wondered what Miss Quilt thought about that particular reporter.

The folded-up copy of *Maxim* was on his desk. He'd tossed it there when he came home the other day and hadn't touched it since. He flattened it out and opened it up to one of the first pictures. Karen Quilt sat at a desk in an English study with lots of books and a wooden globe. She was wearing a black suit and owlish glasses. It was a naughty librarian–type pose.

Someone had scribbled in the margin at the bottom of the page, alongside the introductory paragraph that talked about Karen Quilt's parents and early life. George tilted his head, then turned the magazine.

Try to remember—Madelyn

She'd included her phone number and dorm room, too. He tried to think when she would've had time to write without him noticing. Maybe when he'd answered his Nextel? Had he looked away from the table?

Madelyn's story drifted through his head. A girlfriend he didn't remember and a best friend he'd never heard of. George looked at the naughty-librarian picture again and shook his head. Guys like him didn't get women like that. Not in the real world.

What was the guy's name? His supposed best friend. He remembered the first and last name had the same sound. There was a term for that, when two words started with the same sound. A lot of old superhero names were like that, their secret identity names. Peter Parker. Clark Kent. Bruce Banner. Wally West.

He chuckled at the mental list of superhero names. He hadn't read a comic book in years, not even any of the popular graphic novels. But Madelyn had given him heroes on the brain.

She'd mentioned where the best friend worked. Something in New Mexico. A power station of some kind. Or was it a lab?

He tapped a few keys on his computer. It took him five minutes to find Sandia National Labs in Albuquerque, New Mexico, and their Pulsed Power Project. One part of it was a huge array called the Z Machine.

The Z Machine. Z. Z. Z. It sounded appropriate somehow.

George didn't understand half the factoids Wikipedia listed about the Z Machine, but apparently it was used to create phenomenal amounts of energy. There was a photo in the article showing a crackling web of electricity stretched over banks of equipment. He was pretty sure it was just a split-second photograph, not an ongoing effect, but it was still impressive.

The main website for the project didn't have a crew roster he could find, but there were a few pictures. George lingered on one showing a half-dozen people gathered around a table. Seated off on the left was a skinny black man with stubble-short hair.

The website had contact information. A set of e-mail addresses and a pair of phone numbers. The lab was open—or answered the phones, at least—during regular business hours. He unplugged his cell phone from the charger and tapped in the number. New Mexico was an hour ahead, which meant it was . . .

Seven-thirty in the morning there. They probably had a George of their own who was just showing up to empty the trash. No one else would be there for hours. If they were, they'd ignore the phone.

He felt silly.

Madelyn's story had struck a nerve. Some idealistic dream from childhood about helping people, great power and great responsibility, or some such thing. Part of him almost wished her story was real. Minus the killing-millions-of-people part. He put his phone back on the desk and closed the magazine.

George threw his arms over his head, locked his fingers, and stretched. A good night's sleep would get everything right in his head. That's all he needed.

The alarm went off behind him. He banged his knee on the desk when he jumped. It was time to get ready for work.

* * *

Once again, pedestrians made the drive in a headache. Every intersection was packed with people, all of them taking their time. George sat through the whole green light at Fairfax as men and women shuffled across the street. On the plus side, everyone could see the crowd, so nobody started honking their horns. The only thing more frustrating than traffic delays was a jerk behind you who didn't acknowledge them.

It also didn't help that the brake on his car seemed to be slipping. He'd get to an intersection and the Hyundai would try to lunge forward at the figures in the crosswalk. He could feel it fighting his foot as he pushed down. With the constant cries on the radio extolling different religious figures for aid, it gave the drive in a surreal tone he didn't enjoy.

There seemed to be a lot of homeless people out that morning. At least half the people crossing each intersection wore stained, ragged clothes. George knew Los Angeles had a huge homeless population, but they weren't always so visible. Or maybe he'd just become more aware of them somehow.

He made it most of the way to campus before the car sputtered and died again. George swore and guided the vehicle to the edge of the road before it lost all momentum. He turned the key again and again. The dash lights didn't come on. Not even one click from the starter. The radio was silent. He glanced at the street to get a sense of how far he was from campus.

His car had come to rest in front of the recruitment office again.

Something moved in his peripheral vision and a huge figure lumbered out of the early morning haze. It was the bald officer he'd seen last week, the man with arms the size of George's waist. He was wearing a tan T-shirt and breathing deep, the kind of measured breathing people did after exercise. He pulled some keys from his pocket and headed to the office door.

In the back of George's mind, he realized the car must have died just as it passed the big man, half a block or so back.

He stepped out of his car. "Excuse me," he called to the man.

The giant turned. Confusion flashed across his face, but he clamped down on it. "Yes, sir," he said. "How can I help you?" Only some of the confusion slipped into his voice.

George gestured at his Hyundai. "Sorry to bother you," he said. "I stopped here last week. I've been having car trouble. It just died again."

"I remember. Do you need another jump?"

"I'm not sure. I can't figure out what's going on with it, to be honest."

A sound echoed down the street. A foot slapping against the pavement. There was a faint scraping sound, then another slap a few seconds later. George looked down the street. A handful of homeless people were shambling up Wilshire toward them.

Something about them gave him a chill.

"We should go inside," said the soldier with a nod at the approaching group. "I've been generous in the past and now they can get a bit demanding. I've found it best to avoid them." He unlocked the door and waved George inside.

The giant flipped the dead bolt and tapped out a quick code on a keypad near the door. His fingers were very nimble for their size. He flipped on the lights and walked across to his desk.

"Thanks," said George.

"Not a problem," said the soldier.

"I'm George."

"Lieutenant Freedom," said the giant. He held out a broad hand.

George's fingers barely reached across the palm. He smiled as they shook. "Freedom? Is that some recruitment tool or something?"

The officer's face tightened. "It's a family name, sir." He turned away and headed toward a door in the back corner. "Sergeant Harrison's not in for another half hour or so, but we might have some jumper cables in the back. There's a junk closet with a lot of odd supplies in it."

A thump came from the front of the office. One of the homeless people was pressed against the window. His teeth were a rotted mess and his eyes were filled with cataracts. He was muttering, but George couldn't hear him through the glass.

His eyes swept back around and Freedom had a pistol out and pointed at him. The muzzle was enormous. George stumbled back with his hands up, tripped, and fell on his ass.

Freedom blinked. "Are you all right, sir?" He held out an empty hand. Both his hands were empty.

George looked at the huge man, then back over his shoulder. The homeless people were shuffling away. The one with bad teeth had left a smudge on the glass. "You had a gun," he said.

"Sir?" Freedom looked at his bare hip. "I'm not armed."

George climbed back to his feet as the pieces fell together. "You shot me," he said. He gestured back at the window. "Those things were all around and you shot me with some big-ass pistol."

The soldier's gaze didn't waver, but his face shifted.

George stared back. He sounded crazy. He knew that. He tried to ignore the endless pen-clicking and focus his thoughts. "I think I know you," he told the other man. "I think we've known each other for a while."

Freedom straightened up. He was almost a foot taller than George. "I'm pretty sure we just met for the first time last week."

The sound of his voice freed up something else in George's mind. It came rushing out so hard and fast it made his head ache. "You were a captain," he said. "Harrison said you'd been demoted and I didn't make the connection. You're Captain Freedom. John Carter Freedom." The words spewed out, as much of a surprise to him as they were to the lieutenant.

The officer pressed his lips together. George wasn't sure what kind of expression the man was biting back. He also wasn't sure where he'd pulled the name from. He glanced over his shoulder at the empty office and then back to the giant.

"Sir," said Freedom, "I think you should leave now." He crossed his arms across his chest. He wasn't making a request or suggestion.

* * *

George wandered outside. A few of the homeless people saw him and switched direction, but he was back in his car before they came anywhere close. He checked his pockets and the dish under the emergency brake, but he didn't have any change to offer them.

He flopped back in the driver's seat and pressed his hands over his eyes. He couldn't believe he'd babbled on like that. He'd accused an Army officer of trying to kill him! His lack of sleep was now officially making him act like a maniac. He wondered if he should take a sick day or two and just try to get caught up on rest.

A thump made him look up. A filth-covered woman pressed herself against his window. She had pale blue eyes, almost gray. She would've been pretty if not for her stained shirt and all the dirt on her face.

George glanced at the time. He was going to be late for work. He started his car and pulled back out into traffic. If the lights were in his favor, he could still make it on time.

He was parking on campus when he realized his dead car had started back up with no problem.

TWELVE

GEORGE SPENT THE morning cleaning windows. It was a mindless job, and on a normal day he'd have been glad for it and let himself sink into the Zen of window washing. Today, though, he didn't want any extra time to think.

His eyes kept drifting over to one of the other buildings. It bothered him for some reason. He had a nagging sensation he'd forgotten something about it. There were lecture halls in there, a bunch of biochem labs, and two or three of the larger storerooms. He couldn't shake the feeling there'd been a fire there at some point, or maybe some kind of explosion.

Something in the back of his mind insisted he'd been *in* a fire in one of the buildings.

It was almost noon when he heard two kids chattering away as they passed his ladder. What they were saying didn't make sense to him, so he pulled out his phone and shot a quick text to Nick. The answer came back a minute later.

> **Hugh Laurie is not dead, either. Y U on such a morbid streak?**

George sighed. Nick was right. He was getting morbid. Madelyn's talk of doom and destruction mixed well with the weight of sleeplessness.

He flipped the phone in his hand and his fingers brushed the screen. It jumped to the default phone keypad and he paused. A string of numbers stretched across the screen. He didn't recognize them, not even the area code. It took a moment for him to remember tapping them into the phone that morning. It felt like ages ago.

He knew he should just erase the number to Sandia. It was tempting fate. He didn't want to call and ask a bunch of stupid questions that would make him sound like an idiot. An idiot if he was lucky. It was a national lab. He wasn't sure what that meant, but he felt pretty sure if they told the FBI about weird phone calls, their complaint would end up a little higher on the list than most.

And calling would just feed this whole delusion the girl had shared with him. Her fictional dreamworld where everyone was dead and he was some kind of superhero. He didn't need to get mixed up in that sort of thing, especially with a student.

Then again, if he was a superhero, shouldn't he be brave enough to make the call?

His thumb hovered over the keypad for a moment. Then, without any real thought from him, the thumb dropped down. The little handset icon flashed once and the screen changed under his fingertip.

Dialing.

There was still time to hang up, he told himself. Even when the call connected and he heard the first ring, he knew he could hit the red **End** button. It wasn't like they'd call back on a hang-up.

The phone picked up just after the second ring. "Sandia National Labs," recited a male voice. "How can I direct your call?"

"Ummmm . . ." said George. "Hi. I'm looking for, that is, I'm trying to reach . . ."

"Sorry?"

The name leaped to his tongue. "Barry. I think his name's Barry . . . Burke."

"Oh," said the voice. "Sure thing. One second."

The phone clicked and a Muzak version of Bruce Springsteen's "Radio Nowhere" echoed over the lines. His heart raced. He hadn't felt this way about a phone call since he was fourteen.

A minute passed before the phone clicked again. "This is Barry," said a new voice.

"Hi," he said. "Barry Burke?"

"The one and only. I'll be appearing in Las Vegas next month from the fifteenth 'til the sixteenth. And this is . . . ?"

"I'm . . ."

Stupid. George suddenly felt very stupid. The girl, Madelyn, had played him. She'd looked up the Pulsed Power machine, found some names online, and convinced him to make the call. Reverse psychology or something like that. It was some sorority prank or something.

"I'm sorry," he said. "I think I've got the wrong number."

The man on the other end laughed. He sounded like a guy who laughed a lot. "I'm the only Barry here," he said. "If there's another Z Machine somewhere with another Barry Burke, he'd better have a goatee and a sash."

George chuckled. "No, it's just . . . I'm sorry. I think this is just a big mistake. Sorry for wasting your time."

"Ummm . . . okay. You sure?"

George looked over at the lab building. He thought about his dreams and the strange homeless people he'd been seeing. He remembered Madelyn's story about a best friend he couldn't remember.

"Look," he said, "this is going to sound really stupid, I know, but can I ask you something?"

Another laugh echoed from New Mexico. "You're keeping me from a boring staff meeting, stranger on the phone. Ask me anything."

"Are you in a wheelchair?"

The voice on the other end went silent. George realized what a jackass he sounded like. The silence stretched out for ten seconds, and he wondered if the other man had hung up on him.

"Who is this?" Barry Burke asked.

"I'm sorry," he said to the phone. "That was really insensitive of me. I didn't mean to be so—"

"Is this George?"

The phone jumped away from his head. Or maybe his hand spasmed. He stared at it for a moment, then pulled it back to his ear.

"Are you still there?" asked the man in Albuquerque.

"Yeah," he said. "I'm still here. I just . . . you know me?"

"Your voice is familiar," said Barry. "I couldn't place it and then I realized you sound like the guy in my dreams. Which sounds very different than I intended out loud."

George felt light-headed. He slumped against the wall next to his bucket of soapy water. "You have dreams about me?"

"I guess. You're six feet tall, blond-brown hair . . . Ummm, I don't suppose you're super-strong, by chance?"

He thought of the dumpster. "Maybe?"

Barry whistled. "Who's the redhead?"

"Sorry?"

"There's a redhead in my dreams, too. Kind of cute. I think she wears . . ." His voice trailed off. "I think she might be a knight. Like a King Arthur–Excalibur–type knight. Or maybe a Gundam pilot."

"I'm sorry," he said. "I don't know. I haven't . . . I don't think I've actually dreamed about you."

He sensed the shift, even over the phone. "You haven't?"

"I don't think so."

"So how'd you know to call me?"

"There's a girl out here," explained George. "A young woman. She knows . . . she claims to know a lot of stuff. She says I've forgotten things. That everyone has."

"Is she dead?"

"What? No. She's just—"

A set of sounds and images flashed across George's mind. Meeting Madelyn for the first time on moving day. Meeting her again in the cafeteria.

"I'm Madelyn Sorensen," she said. "The Corpse Girl."

He glanced up from the magazine and saw a dead girl in a wheelchair.

His voice trailed off.

Barry cleared his throat. "Still there?"

"Yeah, sorry. This is all . . . this is all a little weird. And overwhelming."

"Tell me about it. I've been thinking I was going nuts or something."

George thought of the other thing Madelyn had mentioned. "Is there anyone else in your dreams? Any other people?"

"A bunch," said Barry. "There's you, the redhead, this huge Army officer—"

"I've met him," George said. "He's here in LA. Lieutenant Freedom."

"Lieutenant? That doesn't sound right."

Something pulsed behind George's left eye, the faintest hint of an oncoming headache. "I didn't think so, either, but it seemed to make him upset to talk about it."

"But he's real? You've actually seen him."

"I shook his hand this morning."

"Frak me," said the other man. "Anyway, there's all of them, a ninja, the dead girl, and a ghost."

Now the pulse was behind both of his eyes. It had grown from a firm hint to a scheduled meeting in no time at all. "Did you say a ghost?"

"Yeah. I think that may just be a dream thing. I don't think it means anything." He paused for a moment. "Can I tell you something else? Or ask you something else, I guess?"

"Sure."

"This one's going to sound really weird."

"Weirder than the whole 'random strangers hundreds of miles apart sharing dreams' thing?"

"Yeah," said Barry, "I think so. This is like first-season-*LOST*-level weirdness."

"Okay."

"Have you ever heard of George Romero?"

He wrinkled his brow. It took a minute to get his mental footing again. "The film director?"

"Yes!" The voice on the phone sounded relieved. "Okay, part two. Do you know what kind of movies he makes?"

"Errrr . . . horror movies?"

"Yeah, but what kind of horror movies? Can you be more specific?"

George rubbed his temple. The headache was swelling inside his skull. "Ummm . . . monster movies, aren't they? Gory ones."

"But what kind?" insisted Barry. "Vampires? Werewolves? What's the monster?"

"I don't know," George said. "I'm not really into the whole horror thing."

"Well, I am," said Barry. "I'm a big ol' geeky fanboy. One of the biggest. And you know what?"

"What?" George's headache arrived and settled in. The sun hurt his eyes. The sounds coming from his phone were sharp and grating, like needles in his ear.

"I don't know what kind of monsters they are, either," said the man in Albuquerque. "I've checked Google, Netflix, Amazon, a couple fansites. I've been trying to figure it out for days and I don't know."

THIRTEEN

GEORGE'S PHONE SLIPPED from his fingers. His head was pounding. His pulse was pounding in his ears like a car blasting its subwoofer. He'd never had a migraine before, but this had to be worse. Some part of him wondered if a blood vessel or something might've burst in his head. Maybe an aneurysm. It wasn't hard to believe these could be the last seconds of his life.

He heard a rasping noise in front of him. He lifted his head and forced his eyes open. It took a moment for his vision to focus.

A group of people stood in front of him. Students and faculty, on a guess. There were three women and two men. In the corner of his eye he could see another man walked toward him. A couple watched from a few yards away.

They were all dead.

The corpse closest to George had a red fire axe buried in the top of its shoulder. The axe wobbled and sent the dead thing close to tipping over every time it moved. A woman's shirt had three bullet holes ringed with dark stains. An overweight young man held out arms that were gnawed down to the bone. At least half his fingers were missing. A dead girl with one eye had a monkey backpack looped over her shoulders.

Their jaws moved up and down, and their teeth cracked together again and again. Some of them had chipped or broken their enamel. The axe man had nothing but jagged stumps. The sound of their teeth was like hail or bubble wrap, a constant *click-click-click*.

George twisted away from them and took a few steps along the side of the building. The long grass brushed his knees. He glanced up at the gray building. Thick grime coated the windows he'd been cleaning. Years of dust and condensation, streaked and spotted from rainfall.

The dead people staggered after him. The corpse with the gnawed arms stumbled and fell face-first into the side of the building. Its face crunched against the brick. The others made slow adjustments and shifted their paths to follow.

His head was still pounding and nausea tickled the back of his tongue. He thought about calling campus security, but his phone was somewhere back in the tall grass. Even if he could get past the creatures, he wasn't sure how long it would take him to find it. He ran in a wide circle around the dead things and headed out along the long walkway of the Court of Sciences.

At least two dozen more monsters staggered in the courtyard. Maybe more. A few wore gore-splattered suits and ties. Some others had backpacks or messenger bags. One dead woman wore a UCLA sweatshirt. Something with one leg and long hair was dragging itself across the pavement. It had worn its face and chest down so far George couldn't tell if it had been a man or a woman. The sound of clicking teeth echoed between the buildings.

A dead thing over by the Geology building was wearing a campus security uniform. It was missing an arm. It raised the arm it did have at George, as if it could grab him from across the plaza.

The court looked old. Weeds pushed up between the bricks. The small trees were withered and brown. Dark stains dotted the whole area, along with a few pieces of sun-dried garbage that looked like dead animals, but not enough to hide what they'd really been. The few windows around the court that weren't shattered had more streaks of grime.

Part of him, some animal, instinctive part, told him to run. Just run. That part shrieked in time with his pulsing headache. The corpses were still spread out wide enough to dodge. But he wasn't sure where to go. Back to the maintenance office? Back to his car?

And another part of him wanted to fight. Something told him these things weren't a threat. Not to *him*, anyway. Buried right down next to the instinct to run was a certainty the dead things couldn't hurt him.

Running still won out.

George ran a dozen feet and the throbbing pain in his skull made his eyes water. He made it a few more steps and fell to his knees. His stomach was churning and his throat trembled with the promise of impending vomit. Something burned at the back of his mouth.

The dead people closed in around him. They dragged their feet. Fingertips brushed his shoulders. They gnashed their teeth and the *click-clack-click-clack* of ivory hit a rhythm with the pounding in his skull.

He tried to get up but the nausea had crippled him. He bent over, his throat convulsed, and something hot forced its way into his mouth. It felt like wet smoke and acid streaming out between his teeth.

"Jesus," said someone. "You okay, guy?"

George managed a deep breath and opened his eyes. He'd retched nothing onto the pavement. His nausea and headache had vanished like a light being turned off.

He looked up. A man in a suit and a campus security guard stood over him. "You looked pretty bad there for a moment," said the suit. He was bald and wore square eyeglasses.

A ring of people surrounded George. Most were a polite yard or two away. Several watched from nearby tables.

George stood up. "Sorry," he said. "Didn't mean to freak anyone out. Just a . . . a bad migraine."

Half the crowd sighed and strolled off, their hopes for a serious incident dashed. A few lingered to be sure they weren't going to miss anything. "You okay now?" the suit asked.

"I've got some Advil," said a woman in the dwindling crowd. She slung her backpack off her shoulder and rooted through a side pouch. "I get killer ones now and then."

George waved her off. "I'm good, thanks."

The suit—probably a doctor of some kind—helped George onto a bench and checked his eyes and pulse. Whatever he found seemed to satisfy him. The suit squeezed George's shoulder, told him to get some rest, and headed off across the plaza. Most of the bystanders vanished with him.

The security officer waited until the suit was gone. "You been drinking?" he murmured. The name on his silver tag was Crosby.

"What?" George shook his head. "No."

Crosby's eyes dropped to George's ID badge. "If you've been drinking I need to report it," he said. "You know that."

"I haven't been drinking. Honest."

The security officer nodded. "Okay, then. Take care of yourself. Don't let it happen again." He walked off with an air of confident superiority and left George on the science court. A few last people glanced at him, and then they wandered away, too.

He waited two minutes to see if the headache returned. When it didn't, he retraced his steps. Aside from a random coffee cup and an overflowing trash can, the court was pristine. No weeds. No cracks. The dozens of windows around the plaza were all whole and clean.

He found his phone sitting in the short-cut grass next to the window-cleaning supplies. He'd almost dropped it in his squeegee bucket. According to the log, twenty minutes had passed since his call with Barry Burke ended. He didn't remember hanging up. He wondered if the other man had stayed on the line. Had he heard anything?

George was staring at the phone when it chirped. "George," it said, "y'out there or what?"

"Yeah, I'm here, Jarvis."

"I been trying to get you for five minutes now."

"Dropped my phone in the grass. Sorry."

"Those windows done?"

He looked up at the building and sighed. "Got to be honest," he said, "I'm about half an hour or so behind."

Jarvis was silent for a moment. George could picture the salt-

and-pepper man cursing back at the office. "What's the problem?" he asked.

George looked back at the Court of Sciences. "I think I'm coming down with something. I don't feel too hot."

"Don't mess with me, George."

"I'm serious," he said. "I've been having killer headaches. I almost threw up a few minutes ago."

Another silence from the phone. "If it was anyone else," said Jarvis's twang, "I'd tell 'em to suck it up."

"Sorry."

"You need to go get checked out?"

He considered that option for a few moments. "No. I think I just need to get some rest."

"Yeah," agreed Jarvis. "You've been looking a little ragged. I'll punch you out. Go home and sleep. Don't be sick tomorrow or I'll fire your ass."

* * *

George couldn't remember Madelyn's phone number or dorm, but he remembered where he'd flipped the couch into the dumpster. The unusually light couch. He found a good central position between a few of the buildings and waited.

His stomach grumbled. It was lunchtime. He considered hitting one of the vending machines, but he didn't want to miss the girl. It crossed his mind she might be down at the dining commons looking for him, but he didn't want to lose time second-guessing himself.

Two guys crossed the courtyard reciting British comedy to each other. "I discovered," said one, "the only reason that it had been sitting on its perch in the first place was that it had been *nailed* there."

"Well, of course it was nailed there," said the other. "If I hadn't nailed that bird down, it would have nuzzled up to those bars, bent 'em apart with its little pecker, and . . . voom!" They walked off, amusing themselves with their performances.

He was there for an hour when he saw Madelyn coming up the path. Her palms ran along the hand rims and moved the wheelchair at a decent pace. She didn't have any trouble keeping up with some of the other walkers.

She was a dozen yards away when she saw him. A flutter of emotions crossed her face. She slowed down. It took her two minutes to cross the last thirty feet.

"I wasn't sure I'd see you again," she said.

"I've been thinking about some of the stuff you told me."

"Yeah?"

"I called the guy in New Mexico. Barry Burke."

Her face lit up. "Zap!" she said. She buzzed the Z against the roof of her mouth so it stretched out, like she was saying it in French or something.

"I still don't remember him," said George. "He seemed to know me, but . . ."

"But?"

"But that's it."

She crossed her arms and stared up at him. "That's it?"

"He asked if you were dead. He said in the dreams he's having there's a dead girl, but the way he says it is like . . . like she's not really dead."

Madelyn smiled. "That's me."

He paced in front of her for a minute. Then he realized he was pacing and stopped. "This can't be real," he said.

"It is."

"It's silly."

"Is that why you're here?" she asked. "You just wanted to be a jerk and come tell me this is all silly?"

"The monsters."

She looked back at him. "What about them?"

The back of his skull pulsed. Just once. The sensation traveled forward through the bone to echo in his eye sockets. A reminder not to push it too far. "I think I'm . . ."

Having some kind of nervous breakdown crossed his mind.

"I think I'm seeing the things from my dreams," he said. "While I'm awake."

Madelyn looked around. "Seeing them *here*?" she asked.

He nodded.

"Do you see them now?"

He shook his head. "It comes and goes."

Madelyn looked over at a nearby trash can. "Is there a newspaper in there?"

"What?"

"In the trash. Is there a newspaper or magazine or anything?"

He glanced in the bin and shook his head.

She rocked the wheelchair back and forth for a moment. "Can you come up to my room? You need to see something."

The standard reaction flashed across his mind. This was serious getting-fired territory. It was also, he had to admit, crossing another line. In a way, that one scared him even more.

"Yeah," he said. "Sure."

George followed her into one of the dorms. They waited on an elevator, and when it came she slid inside and spun her wheelchair around so she could tap the controls. It wasn't a large elevator. He felt crowded.

The doors opened on the third floor and Madelyn led him down the hall. She dragged her backpack around, pulled out a keychain on a black scrunchie-cord, and unlocked the door.

"Sorry," called a voice from inside. "I didn't expect you back."

Madelyn pushed her way into the dorm room and tossed her backpack on the bed. Her side of the room looked empty to George, but he couldn't figure out why. Then she spun her wheelchair around to the desk. The standard chair was missing.

Two oxygen tanks stood next to the bed. They looked like a scuba diver's rig mounted on a small dolly. A clear tube ran off the left tank, coiled around, and hooked into a clear mask shaped to fit over the nose and mouth.

Madelyn saw him studying the tank. "I need it to sleep," she explained. "I don't breathe when I'm unconscious."

The other side of the room looked like an art project. Posters and magazine pages showed Olympic gymnasts, dancers, and martial artists. It was a look George was familiar with. A month or so into the semester, as the new students finally accepted they were unsupervised, there was always an explosion of creative decorations, clothing, and relationships. Some of it stuck around. A lot of it didn't.

The young Asian woman sitting cross-legged on the bed wore a baggy white sweatshirt with bold rainbow stripes on it. A textbook sprawled in her lap, and her long braid brushed the pages. She glanced up from her textbook as Madelyn settled in. She struck George as familiar.

"Hi," she said. "I'm Kathy."

"George."

She studied him for a moment. "Hey," she said. "I know you. You're the couch guy."

He smiled and remembered her slouching deep into the passenger seat of the car. "Yeah."

"I'm sorry about how my dad talked to you. He and Mom are having major separation anxiety."

"Don't worry about it."

"That was kind of awesome. You picked it up like it didn't weigh anything."

"It's . . ." George glanced at Madelyn. Her fingers were brushing back and forth across her laptop's touchpad. "It's a balance trick," he said. "It looks impressive, but there's nothing to it."

Kathy smiled and let her eyes drop back to her book. "Your friend's kind of cute, too."

"Sorry?"

She blushed. "With the glasses? How old is he?"

"Hey," interrupted Madelyn, "pay attention."

"Sorry," said George. He glanced at Kathy, but she waved off his eyeballed apology and went back to her book.

Madelyn's desk held nothing but her laptop. The shelf above it was packed with two dozen black composition books. Each one had a piece of paper with a set of dates taped to the spine. At the far end were a trio of what looked like pocket diaries. She glanced at him, then followed his gaze up to the notebooks. "Journals," she said. "Well, it started out as diary, but I think I should call it a journal now."

"You planning on writing a memoir or something?"

"Remember how I said I had memory problems for a while?"

"Yeah."

"Writing a journal helps me remember stuff." Her fingers slid back and forth on the computer's track pad. "I had a lot to remember."

There was a calendar on the wall and next to it was a list of words. They'd been printed out in large font.

Corpse Girl (ME)
St. George / Mighty Dragon
Captain Freedom
Stealth
Zzzap
Cerberus
Driver

She followed his gaze over to the list and pointed at the top. "That's you," she said. "You're the Mighty Dragon. You used to be, anyway."

He bit his lip. "Okay."

Madelyn tapped a few keys on her laptop and brought up a web page. A news headline from that morning showed the President and First Lady at some event. George remembered seeing a notice about them being in town.

"This is what you wanted to show me?" he asked.

"When I first realized who he was," she said, "I just thought it was part of this weird history-rewrite thing. He used to work for my dad. I think I even talked to him on the phone a couple times when I was in high school." She pointed at the picture. "Do you know who he is?"

His headache was coming back, and his nose was starting to run, too. He sniffed and pressed on the bridge of his nose. "The President?"

She sighed. "Yeah, but past that."

"What do you mean, past that?"

"Okay, how about this." She grabbed a box of tissues from the corner of her desk and tossed it to him. "Do you recognize his wife?"

George pulled out two and wiped his nostrils. He looked at the picture of the First Lady and nodded. She was six years older than her husband, but it looked like more because he was so well preserved. He'd laughed off accusations of plastic surgery more than once. "She used to be a councilwoman here in LA, back before they got married."

"Christian Nguyen."

"Yeah."

"Yeah." Madelyn tapped the picture of the President again. "I'm pretty sure he's behind all of this."

"All of what?"

"Us being here instead of in our world. You and everyone else not remembering you're superheroes. All of it."

George stared at her for a moment. "Okay," he said. He balled up the tissues in his hand. "Now the President is part of this?"

"I think so, yeah."

He dabbed at his nose again and tried to keep from sounding too harsh. "The most successful President in history? A guy who's so universally loved there's a bipartisan movement in Congress right now to repeal the Twenty-second Amendment so he can run for a third term?"

"Yeah. He must still have his powers for some reason. Probably because he's the one who did all of this."

George drummed his fingers on his leg. He'd almost bought it. He'd wanted to believe her. "So I'm a superhero," he said, "but I don't remember it."

"Right."

"And I'm supposed to be dating an Abercrombie and Fitch model who's also a superhero. I'm guessing she doesn't remember it, either. And you're one, too, except you're supposed to be dead."

"Not like that," she said. "That's my superpower."

"Being dead doesn't count as a superpower."

"It does in my case."

"Right. But on top of all this, you want me to believe that

President John Smith—who I voted for—is some kind of super-villain?"

"Yeah," she said. "Something like that." Her eyes dropped to the Kleenex in his hand.

He looked down. The tissues were spotted with thick blobs of red.

FOURTEEN

FOURTEEN

GEORGE WIPED HIS fingers under his nose. They came back streaked with blood. Across the room, Kathy's eyes went wide.

"Oh, jeez," he said. He grabbed a few more tissues from the box.

Madelyn leaned forward in her wheelchair. "I think your nose is bleeding because you're fighting him," she said. "John—Captain Freedom—said he does things like this to people."

"He did?"

"Yeah."

"So he remembers, too?"

She made a point of not looking at George. "Well . . . he told me before all this changed. Back in our world." She tapped the image of the President and the First Lady. "It's what Smith does," she said. "He makes people believe things. It's how he killed my mom and me."

"Your mom's dead?" asked Kathy.

"She isn't dead and neither are you," George said. "I saw her on moving day."

"We're supposed to be," said Madelyn, "in our world. But he sent us here somehow and he made you forget you have superpowers. He tried to make all of us forget."

He dabbed fresh tissues against his nostrils. "I don't have superpowers. I think I might have a brain tumor or something."

"You're just remembering. Don't you get it, George?" She waved her hands up and down, taking in all of him. "You're so much more than this. Everyone looks up to you. Everyone trusts you."

"Because I'm a superhero," he said. He looked over at the list on her wall. "Because I'm 'The Mighty Dragon.'"

She shook her head. "Because you're St. George."

The name echoed in his ears. It was the name from his dreams. The name he'd never quite been able to remember.

"If you don't believe me," said Madelyn, "believe her."

She clicked her mouse and another window rose up on her screen. A photo of the supermodel, Karen Quilt, in the black dress. It was the same article George had been looking at that morning. The one about her being in Los Angeles.

Morning seemed like a long time ago.

"After my dad," said Madelyn, "she's one of the smartest people I've ever met. She'll know what's going on. She'll get it."

George stared at the picture. The woman looked so damned familiar. More than that. She just looked . . . right. He looked at her and felt content.

Then the pain in his head faded away, and the contentment faded with it. He was just a guy trying to buy into some fantasy of a better life. More to the point, he was a guy ogling online supermodels in a teenage girl's dorm room.

"Look," said George, "I know you want to believe this stuff. I'd like to believe it, too. But there aren't superheroes or supervillains. There aren't monsters. And women like that," he said, pointing at the computer screen, "do not end up with janitors. Things just don't work like that in the real world."

"I keep telling you," Madelyn said, "this isn't the real world. Not our world, anyway."

He thought about saying something, but closed his mouth. He walked the few steps to the door and opened it. "I wish I could believe you," he said. "I really do. But I need something more than just you saying it's true."

"Then, please," said Madelyn, "go talk to her. She's here in LA this week. Find her and talk to her."

He took a last look at her. The screen reflected on her eyes and made them look white. She stared at him like a hopeful puppy.

"We'll see," he said.

Her face dropped. "When my dad says that, it means no," she said.

George smiled. He stepped into the hallway and closed the door behind him. Just before the door latched he heard Kathy call out, "It was nice meeting you."

* * *

George walked across campus, sure he was dragging a balloon that marked him as an idiot. His sleepless nights were getting to him. Madelyn's stories were getting to him. He'd put his job at risk going up to her room. He'd done it because of a phone call that was probably a practical joke, plus a hallucination brought on by lack of sleep.

The girl was just plain nuts. She had to be. Superheroes. Epidemics. Monsters. Presidential conspiracies. Just thinking about it made his head spin like a drunken blitz.

And yet . . .

Underneath it all, what she was saying made sense. He'd just been talking with Nick about how he always felt like he'd forgotten something. About the dream-shaped holes in his memory.

But superheroes?

He shook his head as he marched over to staff parking. A man in a sweater vest fumbled with a briefcase next to a car. George pegged him as either an older grad student or a younger professor. It was just a sense that developed over time. The vest had a set of large diamond shapes on it, like oversized argyle socks.

George couldn't see his car. He took a moment and tried to slow down his whirling thoughts. It wasn't good to drive so worked up and distracted, anyways. A few deep breaths and he spotted his rear bumper poking out a dozen spaces over.

Two young brunettes were heading across the parking lot

toward him. They were dressed in loose, tie-dyed shirts and pants. More freshman freedom. A brawny, crew-cut guy in a football jersey was heading to intercept them.

As the distance shrunk between them, George realized the two women weren't that young. Their thin frames had made them seem close to their teen years, but as they got closer he could see their angular faces. Then he noticed the irregular pattern to their tie-dye. It wasn't bands or radiant patterns. It was splatters and sprays, all in browns or reds.

He took a breath. The guy in the jersey was headed his way, too. And there was a shuffling sound behind him. The guy in the sweater vest.

In the corner of his eye, off in the distance, he could see dozens of figures scattered across campus and down toward Westwood. They moved in slow motion. Each one tilted and staggered as it walked.

George stood still and tried to stay calm. The hallucination would vanish in a few moments, just like the others.

The women were close enough for him to see their wounds. The one with almost-black hair had a gash that opened its mouth back along its cheek, showing off all the teeth on one side. The other one, the one with golden-brown hair, wasn't wearing much of a shirt. Rags of clothing hung from its neck and shoulders, and its torso was a shredded mess of gore and pale flesh. It had been hit by a shotgun blast. Maybe two or three. Or a grenade.

They were twenty feet away now.

Behind him, the scraping sound was very close. George wasn't going to indulge the waking dream by looking, but he guessed the vest guy was ten feet away at the most.

Jersey guy lurched toward him. A dozen yards left between them, tops. The walking corpse didn't have a crew cut. Its hair and scalp had been torn away from its skull. The ragged tufts of gristle and blood had dried into little points across the bone.

George closed his eyes. When he opened them, there would just be normal students around him. Maybe a faculty member behind him. Nothing else.

With his eyes closed, he was more aware of the smells of dust and mildew. They were so thick he could feel the scents in his nose. And the wafting odor of meat was getting stronger. Closer.

He could hear their teeth clicking together. *Click-clack-click-clack-click.* It was the sound of a speed typist with a wooden typewriter.

Something leathery wrapped around his wrist. A wave of nausea boiled up in his throat. His eyes flicked open.

The women were just a few feet away. Jersey guy was a yard behind them. Another dead man, this one in a long coat, stumbled out from behind a car on the far side of the lot. George looked over his shoulder and found himself face-to-face with the sweater-vest man. His skin was the color of cobwebs. One of his eyes was gone. The other looked like frozen milk.

His teeth snapped at George's nose and missed by an inch.

George yanked his arm away from the grasping hand and stumbled back into the women's embrace. They wrapped their arms around him from behind. Their hands pawed at his chest. One nibbled on his ear, then sank its teeth in and tried to rip the ear off. The other chewed on his shoulder. He could feel it gnawing through the fabric of his shirt.

The sweater-vest monster staggered forward with its arms wide. George brought up his foot and lashed out. His work boot slammed into the center diamond of the vest and the dead man flew back. It hit a car ten feet back, spun over the hood, and smashed into the windshield of the next car over with an explosion of glass and dust.

He turned and the two dead women spun with him like they weighed nothing. Something pitter-pattered on the ground. The dead woman chewing on his ear was losing her teeth.

Jersey guy loomed in front of him. George drove his fist into the dead man's gut. The force of it folded the corpse over. It landed a few yards away in a heap that showed off its gory scalp, but its limbs had barely settled when it struggled back to its feet.

He reached across his chest and grabbed a handful of golden-brown hair. It was dry and brittle in his fingers. He yanked and the dead woman flipped over his shoulder like a bag of leaves. The body hit the ground near jersey guy.

George took a deep breath. Acid burned in the back of his throat. He felt a deep need to throw up but bit it back and swallowed hard. He couldn't risk being helpless while he got sick.

He rolled his shoulders and knocked the ear-biter away. The dark-haired monster staggered for a moment before it fell against a car and found its balance. Its jaws hinged up and down. The slash in its cheek flapped open and shut. The dead woman staggered forward and he threw a punch. The jaw crumbled like old plaster. The bottom half of its face sagged. Teeth scattered on the pavement.

It didn't seem to notice. The left side of its face twitched as dead muscles tugged at the shards that had been its jawbone. The motion shook another tooth free from the ragged hole of its mouth.

George pulled his arm back and punched again. He didn't hold back. The dead woman's head shattered like a piñata. A double handful of wet tissue splattered across the hood of a parked car. The body tumbled to the pavement.

Jersey guy's arms wrapped around George. They were thick and meaty, the arms of an athlete. Even in death, they were pretty strong.

George threw himself against the dead man. They hurled back, and jersey guy's teeth scratched between George's shoulder blades. He had a moment of intense déjà vu and realized he was living his dream—tumbling through the air and fighting monsters.

They crashed into something solid. An SUV. Jersey guy took most of the impact. George heard glass crackle and metal squeal. The arms holding him twitched and sagged.

He stepped away from the big truck and looked at the monster. The impact had caved in its rib cage. It slid down the side of the SUV and tried to raise its arms. Without anything to push off of, its shoulder blades flopped under the football jersey.

George reached down and grabbed it by the jaw and the back

of the skull. It tried to bite his fingers, but it didn't seem to have any strength. Like a puppy trying to be savage, it couldn't even break the skin.

He twisted the thing's skull, just like assassins and other bad-asses did in the movies. There was a double-snap, like popping bubble wrap, and the body went limp. Its jaw kept gnawing at his fingers. He let go and the monster slumped next to the SUV.

He turned around. They'd staggered back much farther than he thought. His kick had propelled him and the monster over fifteen feet.

The corpse in the long coat had crossed the parking lot. It reached for him and he grabbed its wrists. He twisted around and sent it sailing into the trunk of a primer-colored muscle car. It hit the trunk skull-first and collapsed.

The dead woman with the golden-brown hair flailed on the pavement. On a guess, he'd broken its back when he flipped it over his shoulder. He reached down and twisted the woman's head around. It felt right, somehow. Merciful. They were already dead, but this way they were more at rest. They weren't walking.

George looked at the parking lot and the bodies and the dust-covered cars with smashed windows and the distant figures shambling across campus.

He waited for the hallucination to end.

His nose was bleeding again.

FIFTEEN

TWENTY MINUTES LATER George blinked and the world changed. The bodies vanished. The cars were clean and whole. The people in the distance picked up their pace and moved with smooth, even gaits.

He stood in the parking lot a few yards from his car. According to his phone, ten minutes had passed since he walked out of Madelyn's dorm room, not the thirty-odd ones he remembered. There was no sign of the grad student with the argyle sweater vest.

There was blood on his knuckles. It was thick and grimy, more of a sludge than a liquid. His fingertips had oily grime on them. Residue from the dead woman's crushed skull. It was under his nails. It smelled a bit like rust without the sharp tang.

He walked to the closest dorm and found a bathroom. There was no soap because it wasn't intended to be public. He considered finding one of the supply closets and grabbing some soap and paper towels, but he didn't want to wait to clean himself.

He cranked the hot water and washed his hands twice. The water felt hot, but not hot enough to scald him. He scrubbed his face, too, and snorted some water into his nose. It rinsed out red, then pink, and then clear.

His fingers were free of all residue. The nails were clean. The knuckles didn't have any cuts or scrapes.

None at all.

He turned his head and pulled at his ear. The dark-haired dead woman had chewed on it for almost a minute. He twisted the lobe back and forth, but couldn't see a scratch. He unbuttoned his shirt and pulled his collar down. His shoulder wasn't even bruised where the other monster had gnawed on him.

A young man walked in wrapped in a towel. He was carrying a bucket of shower supplies. He glanced at George, smirked, and headed into one of the shower stalls. A moment later the sound of running water echoed in the bathroom.

George buttoned up and headed back out to his car. He stood by it for a moment and looked around. A trio of students walked across the parking lot. He closed his eyes, counted to five, and looked at them again.

Still just students.

He dropped into the driver's seat and pushed the key into the ignition. It took him a minute to gather his thoughts. Then he pulled out his phone. He tapped a few keys and closed his eyes again while it rang.

The ringing stopped. Nick's voice echoed over the phone. "Hey," he said. "What's up?"

"I need a favor."

"Yeah, sure, what?"

George paused for a moment. "It's a face-to-face favor," he said, "but I can't get over there, and I don't think I can wait until next time we go out."

"Okay."

"I need a work favor."

"What?"

"I need you to find out something for me."

He could hear Nick's brow furrowing. "Okay."

"You said your agency represents pretty much every big name, right? Actors, directors, models."

"Yeah, right. If you know their name, odds are pretty good they're with us."

"What about Karen Quilt?"

Nick made a sound like a grunt. "Pretty sure she is, yeah."

The *click-click-click* of a keyboard echoed over the phone's speaker. "Yeah, we rep her. And I can tell you right now, she's not dead."

"It isn't that."

"You want an autograph or something?"

"I need to know what hotel she's staying at."

Silence stretched out between them. When Nick spoke again, his voice was lower and more muffled. "George," he said, "I can't give that sort of thing out."

"I just—"

"I can get *fired* for giving out that kind of information," stressed Nick.

"It's important," George said. "I swear. It's nothing creepy or stalker-y, it's just . . ."

"Just what?"

"Do you trust me?"

"What?"

"Yes or no. Do you trust me?"

"Yeah, of course," said Nick. "I'd trust you with my sister. Or money, even."

"Then just believe me," George said. "It's important, okay?"

Another silence lived out its brief life. "No," said Nick. "Sorry, this is one of those lines I can't cross, y'know?"

"Nick, please—"

"No," he interrupted. "The conversation's over, okay? Done. Finished." There was more tapping of keys. "I've got to get back to work. I'll talk to you later."

Nick hung up.

George slumped in the driver's seat. It had been a stupid request. Nick had told him horror stories of people doing similar things. He'd just become one of *those* people.

Except those people couldn't pick up dumpsters. They didn't get attacked by walking corpses. And if they were, he was pretty sure the monsters' teeth didn't break on their skin.

He had to find Karen Quilt.

He reached for the ignition. His fingers were three inches from the key when the car started. The engine purred. The dash lit up. The radio flared to life. It was between songs. "That," said the deejay, "was totally awesome. Good to see you in action again, man."

He froze. Had he turned the key? It was a muscle-memory thing he did a lot of the time without thinking. There were so many things going on in his mind he might've started the car and then just blanked it out until he went to turn it again. Maybe a wiring issue? He could've turned the ignition earlier and it didn't engage until he moved and made something in the car shift. It was a lame explanation, but of all the things going on, his car starting without a hitch didn't rate that high. Heck, a wiring problem might even explain why it kept stalling in the mornings.

The deejay launched into a diatribe about divorcées and saints. George shut the radio off. How did it keep getting back to religious stations, anyway? More bad wiring?

He brushed it from his mind. He needed to head home and scour some articles online. Maybe he could find a hint about where Karen Quilt was staying. He'd been assuming it was a hotel, but maybe she had a condo somewhere in Hollywood or Santa Monica or somewhere. Common sense told him there were enough celebrity-stalking websites out there that someone had to have a general sense of where she was.

His phone beeped. Nick had sent him a text.

Four Seasons on Doheny—for fuck's sake, don't make me regret this

George smiled and backed his car out.

* * *

The Four Seasons in Beverly Hills stood tall, flanked by a handful of massive palm trees. It bristled with balconies but still had the color and faint lines of Spanish architecture. The entrance was discreetly blocked off from the rest of the world with a series of hedges and smaller trees.

George drove past the entrance. Through the gap in the high

shrubs he saw several valets and very few parking spaces. He went a little farther down and turned onto a side street. It took him another few minutes to find parking, and two more to find a sign that told him how long his car would be safe there.

He walked back to the hotel. He paused to tuck his shirt in and brush himself off before he stepped through the pillars of greenery and onto the grounds. There were a few life-sized iron statues of people scattered around the entrance. He kept glimpsing them in his peripheral vision as he crossed the driveway. Their stillness was a bit unnerving. They flickered in his eyes and for a moment he saw them covered with years of green tarnish.

The men at the valet station didn't give him a second glance. George was sure he wasn't the first person to dodge valet parking. He returned the doorman's tight smile and stepped inside. The lobby looked expensive in an elegant way. It was the kind of expense that didn't feel the need to flaunt it by being oversized.

He saw the counter off to the side and tried to decide if he needed to speak with the regular clerk or the concierge. His experience in fancy hotels was limited to a pair of parties with Nick, neither of them at this hotel. He chose the main desk on the hope lower-ranking staff members would be more helpful than higher ones. A slim man and woman in matching shirts and blazers stood behind the high counter.

"Good afternoon, sir," said the man as he approached. "Welcome to the Four Seasons. How can I help you?"

"Hi," George said. "I'm trying to get in touch with one of your guests."

The man's hands slid to a keyboard. "Of course. What room number?"

"I'm afraid I don't have it."

"Name?"

He drummed his fingers on his thigh. "Karen. Karen Quilt."

The man looked up from his computer screen. He locked eyes with George for a moment, then his gaze slipped to something just over George's shoulder. There was a large mirror behind the desk, and in it George saw a man by the elevators straighten up.

He was a large man, as tall as George but wider in the chest. He wore a black tee with his dark suit.

"Is Miss Quilt expecting you, sir?" asked the clerk.

"I'm not sure," he said. It felt like an honest answer. He looked at the phone by the man's hand. "Could you tell her . . . George is here."

"George . . . ?"

"George Bailey."

The man's face twitched. Not in a good way. His eyes flitted back to the large man wearing the T-shirt with his suit.

George was ready for it. He'd been dealing with it his whole life. "No," he said, "really. That's my name." He slid his driver's license from his wallet and held it out to the clerk.

The man looked at the license, then to George, and then back at the license. He tilted it between his fingers under the light, then handed it back. "You have very cruel parents," he said with a polite smile.

"They were pretty cool past the whole name thing," said George.

"However, Miss Quilt was very clear she did not want to be disturbed this afternoon."

"I know," ad-libbed George, "but this is kind of important, and she's not answering her cell phone." He decided to risk winging it. "Neither is her assistant."

The clerk sighed. "I will check, sir, but I'm quite sure what the answer will be."

George put up his hands. "If she doesn't want to talk, I'll move along quietly."

"Yes," said the clerk, "you will."

His fingers danced on the keyboard's number pad and he picked up the phone. He turned halfway from George so the handset muffled his voice. He spoke for a few moments, listened, spoke again, and then listened again. His eyes flitted from George down to his computer screen.

George turned away and tried to look casual. He gazed around the lobby. His eyes met the large man's for a moment, and George gave the man a polite nod that wasn't returned.

"Sir," said the clerk. "She's waiting for you. Sixteenth floor, the Royal suite." He gestured at the elevators.

George stood for a moment, just as stunned by the news as the clerk was. He was pretty sure the clerk was hiding it better, though. He managed a "thank you" before he walked away.

The elevators were all mirrors and brass. Like the lobby, they felt expensive. George looked at his reflection in the doors and brushed a few more wrinkles out of his jacket. He saw his boots and wished he'd switched into sneakers or something more casual. He was pretty sure there was a pair of sneakers in his car. He wondered how long it would delay him to run and get them.

The elevator doors opened to reveal a smaller lobby, just as elegant. He checked the signs and headed down the left-hand hallway. It was dotted with small tables and flower arrangements.

A man was waiting for him at the door. He was maybe an inch taller than George, but slim. His dark clothes accented that slimness. The man's steel-colored hair was bristle-short, and a pair of round spectacles balanced across his nose. George couldn't decide if the John Lennon glasses made the man look more like a hipster assistant or some sort of undercover Nazi officer.

"Mr. Bailey?" His voice was dry, but not in a weak way. It was the kind of dryness found inside pyramids. A powerful rasp with tons of weight and history behind it.

"Yeah." George nodded and held out his hand.

The man made no move to take it. He didn't even seem to notice it. He gestured George through the open door and closed it behind them.

George followed the man into the hotel suite. It was cream colored and gigantic. He was pretty sure his entire apartment would fit inside the main room. One wall was all windows and French doors leading out to two different balconies. He walked past a sprawling, L-shaped couch and a glass-topped table to stare at a flat screen the size of his bed. George was pretty sure any one of them cost more than his monthly rent.

"You have ten minutes," said the man. He pointed at a chair with two fingers. The chair looked expensive, too.

"Thank you, Father," someone said.

George turned and saw the woman on the couch. She was slouched just low enough that he hadn't seen her there. She set her book aside and straightened up without using her hands. Her body flexed and pulled her up to a sitting position. She also gestured at the chair.

Living in Los Angeles, George had seen more than a few celebrities. He'd run into Lindsay Lohan once hiking up in Runyon Canyon, and seen Scott Bakula at a pizza place in Larchmont. One time, around Christmas, he'd stood in line at Target with Biff from *Back to the Future*, and one summer he'd sat across from the redhead from *Six Feet Under* at a coffee shop for half an hour. It made him aware of how human celebrities were. Without special lighting or an hour of makeup, when you just saw them from any old angle, most of them lost a degree of beauty and appeal. They were still all a lot more attractive than him, but it was clear they were just people like everyone else.

Karen Quilt looked better in person than she did in photographs and on television. She wore a black tank top and form-hugging sweatpants. If she had any makeup on he couldn't tell. Her dark hair draped across her bare shoulders. Her arms were muscular.

Her gaze flitted down to his shoes and back up to his face. She had gorgeous eyes. Sky blue. They had an edge to them that was hard but didn't look cruel. He kept watching them, hoping to see a spark of recognition.

If there was one, she hid it well.

"George Bailey," she said. "The main character in the 1946 motion picture *It's a Wonderful Life*. I would recall meeting someone with such a distinctive name."

Something sank inside him. "You don't remember me?"

Her dark brows shifted. "Remember you from what?"

"From . . . I don't know, remembering me."

She smiled. The smile was even more formal and polite than the desk clerk's downstairs. "I generally do not associate with janitors."

His heart lurched back up in his chest. "You know I was a janitor," he said.

Karen pointed at his hand. "There are seven round spots on your right sleeve," she said, "each discolored to a different degree. They are from drops which splashed up when you were soaking a mop, and do not appear on your left arm because it would be held higher from the bucket. The discoloration was caused by a diluted industrial cleaner, meaning you were most likely not mopping at home. The varying degrees of discoloration mean it happened multiple times with different ratios of water to cleaner. Mopping is a regular action you perform when not at home, thus, a janitor."

He smiled. "You're like Sherlock Holmes," he said.

"Except I am not fictional," she said with a slight bow of her head. The motion made a few strands of hair slide across her forehead and cheek. "What do you do now?"

"Sorry?"

"You said you *were* a janitor. What do you do now?"

He rewound his words in his head. "I . . . I don't know why I said that," he admitted. "Nervous, I guess."

"Why?"

"Why what?"

"Why are you nervous?"

He juggled a few possible answers. "Because it's important you know me."

"Why?"

He shrugged. "I don't know," he said.

"You are lying," she said, "and you are not good at it."

His mind raced and he realized just how unprepared for this conversation he was.

Karen slid a bottle of water from an ice bucket on the table. She made no move to open it. There were three left in the bucket, and he thought about taking one to give himself a few moments. He wasn't sure how stepping toward her would go over, though, and it seemed rude to take one if she didn't offer it.

His eyes drifted across the table to her face and stopped at the elaborate hotel phone. The call with Barry flitted across his mind. "Can I ask you a question?"

She ran one finger around the bottle cap and wiped off the excess water. "Very well."

"Do you know who George Romero is?"

"He is an American film director who began his career making commercials and short films in the Pittsburgh area, most notably doing a feature for the children's show *Mister Rogers' Neighborhood*. He is best known as the creator of the *Night of the Living Dead* horror series."

"Yes!" said George. "What are those about?"

She raised an eyebrow.

"Please," he said, "it's important."

She stared at him for a moment. "An unknown force causes the dead to become animate and attack the living. In most of the films in the series, the plot revolves around a small and isolated group of characters dealing with the dead."

"But what are they called?"

"The characters?"

"The dead."

"Romero has said in several interviews that he and his fellow filmmakers did not give the creatures a name, although he was inspired by the legend of the ghoul."

George shook his head. "No, not ghouls. They're called something else."

The dark-skinned woman opened her mouth to reply and her expression shifted. Her eyes softened. Then she straightened up. Her shoulders squared off. "Despite my status as a celebrity," she said, "I am not a student of popular culture. It is not uncommon for me to miss references to motion pictures."

"This isn't a reference," he said. "It's just a name. A word." He met her gaze and her eyes softened again, just for a moment. "And you don't know what it is, do you?"

It was the wrong thing to say. Her eyes hardened. The corners of her mouth twitched. George had the distinct impression he'd just insulted her somehow.

"Is there a point to this meeting, Mr. Bailey?" she asked.

"Look," he said, "I know this is going to sound insane, and I bet you hear crazy stuff like this all the time, but I think you and I . . . I think we're supposed to be somewhere else."

"Where?"

"Somewhere . . . else."

"That is not very informative," she said.

"It's hard to explain."

Her mouth twitched again. Her eyes hardened a bit more.

"You have dreams about monsters," said George. "Dead people who walk, like in the Romero movies. And I'm in the dreams, too, aren't I?"

"No," she said, "you are not."

His heart dropped again. "I'm not?"

"I do not dream," she said. She stared at his eyes. "Not since I was a child. I practice a form of polyphasic sleep."

Another moment stretched out between them and became a full minute. She still held the water bottle, but didn't drink from it. George felt pretty sure at this point she wasn't going to offer him one.

He was pretty sure she didn't blink, either.

"So," he said, "none of this means anything to you."

She shook her head once. Left. Right. Her eyes never left his.

"You don't know me at all."

Again, one time side to side.

"Then why did you invite me up?"

"She didn't," said the thin man from behind George. "I did."

George looked at him. So did Karen. "Father?"

"Your name is George," said the older man. "Like the saint?"

The comparison made his head throb. The air rushed out of his lungs. "Yes," he coughed. "Yes it is."

Karen's father looked at her. "You call his name in your sleep."

Any last hints of softness left her face. Her expression would've fit well on a grim teacher or soldier. "Nonsense."

His chin went up and down once. It was an economical, efficient motion, like Karen's. "For three weeks now," he said. "When the clerk said there was a man with this name asking to meet with you, I said to send him up."

She glared at him. "You gave access to a complete stranger? What if he was dangerous?"

The thin man glanced at George. He made a dry sound that might've been a chuckle. "What if he was?"

Something clicked in George's mind. He remembered who—*what*—Karen Quilt's father was. He remembered the links he'd found while browsing the Internet and the articles those links had brought up. Some of the pictures in those articles were worse than the things he dreamed about.

The man in the John Lennon glasses, he realized, was far closer to Nazi officer than hipster assistant.

The thin man met his daughter's gaze. "If there is nothing else," he said, "I believe Mr. Bailey's ten minutes are up."

Karen stood up. It was a smooth, graceful motion, just what one would expect from a professional model. She held out her hand and he took it in his. Their fingers fit perfectly against one another. She had a very strong grip. "This has been interesting," she said. "It has been a pleasure speaking with you, St. George."

Another needle of pain stabbed George in the back of the eye and he winced. Her father raised an eyebrow. George let go of her hand.

"Forgive me," said Karen. "It was a slip of the tongue after my father's earlier reference. It was not intended as an insult."

"It's okay," he said. "It's safe to say I deserved it if it was an insult. You've been very generous with your time."

Her father put a hand on George's arm and guided him back to the door. The suite flew by in a blur and George was in the hallway again. He met the thin man's gaze again and then the door closed. There was a double click as the dead bolt locked and the safety bar hinged shut.

While he waited for the elevator he considered going back and knocking on the door. Then he thought about banging on the door and demanding another few minutes, but by that point he was already stepping into the elevator. He considered going back up and trying to force his way past the thin man, but some part of him understood this was the absolute worst possible plan to act on. And by then he was already walking out the front door.

The doorman watched him exit with chalky eyes above a mouthful of ruined teeth. George made a point of not looking at the man, but he heard the teeth gnash together like glass splinters. He got a few feet away when the dead man called out, "Have a good afternoon, sir."

He walked back to his car and tried to figure out his next move. Something in the back of his mind was telling him to give up on the whole stupid idea, but he forced past it. He'd have to talk to Madelyn. Maybe he could call Barry Burke again, too. He should've called him already.

And then he got mugged.

The young man in the black hoodie appeared from nowhere in front of him. The way the oversized sweatshirt flapped around him, George guessed the teenager had leaped down from somewhere, although he didn't think there was anything around to leap down from. He raised his fists and the mugger slapped them away before he even got them all the way up. And then he saw the cleavage and the satin skin and the blue eyes and he realized the slim figure wasn't a young man.

"I would like to offer you another ten minutes to explain yourself," Karen said.

SIXTEEN

GEORGE LOOKED OVER his shoulder, then back at the woman in front of him. She was still wearing the sweats and tank top, but had pulled on the hoodie and a pair of what looked like combat boots. "How the hell did you get ahead of me?"

"You are wasting your ten minutes," Karen said.

"Seriously," said George. "I walked straight out here and you didn't pass me. How'd you get down here so fast?"

"I went down the side of the building. It was the most direct route."

He looked up at the pastel building and considered the columns of balconies. There were over a dozen of them, one on top of another. "No, really."

The corners of her mouth went up. Just a bit. "Perhaps I chased you in the next available elevator, then." She stepped to the side so they could walk next to each other. "You now have nine minutes, fifteen seconds."

He fell in next to her and they walked down the street. "Why am I getting another ten minutes?"

An older couple approached them from the far end of the block. Karen tugged her hood down another inch. The shadows against her dark skin hid her face. George found himself thinking it was kind of a creepy look, but she pulled it off.

After the couple had passed, she raised her head. "Forgive

me," she said. "It is sometimes difficult for me to have a private conversation. I would prefer if this one remained so."

He looked around. "Paparazzi or something?"

She gave the front of the hood another tug. "There were two outside the hotel, and a third on the street. They did not see me leave, but I could still be recognized by regular citizens."

"So," he said, "why are you here?"

"The matter of George Romero's monsters intrigues me," she said. "As I told you, I am not well versed in matters of popular culture. However, I have studied several mythologies and folk-lores from across the world and have near-perfect recall. It is un-likely I could not come up with at least a comparative name for these cinematic creatures, yet I can think of no name for them."

"If it makes you feel better," George said. "you're not the only one."

"The dreams you spoke of with these monsters? You are having them?"

"Yeah. Me and a few other people."

"Interesting," she said. "Are you a fan of Romero's work?"

He shook his head. "I'm more of an action-movie guy. Some comedies."

"So you have not seen these films, or others like them?"

George thought about it. "I'm pretty sure I haven't, but I seem to know a lot of them. Maybe I was at a party or something and they were on in the background." He gave her a look.

"What?"

"I just think it's kind of interesting that I blabbed on for ten minutes and the thing that got your attention was realizing you didn't know something."

"It was not the only thing," she said.

"What else?"

She didn't answer him. They walked on for a few more yards. Eight concrete slabs passed by under George's feet.

"Is this counting toward my ten minutes?" he asked.

"In the past eight years," she said, "I have received over one hundred marriage proposals of a semi-serious nature. I would estimate close to seventeen thousand men and women have professed their love for me in e-mails or on various web pages. There have been substantially more declarations of a strictly sexual nature."

"That sounds like more of a reason to avoid me than follow me," George said.

"You did not make any such statement," said Karen. "You stated that we were supposed to be somewhere else. Our togetherness was a secondary factor." She took in a slight breath to continue speaking, then walked past three more sections of sidewalk.

"And?"

"When we said good-bye . . . your hand felt right."

Something fluttered in George's chest. He felt like a teenager asking the head cheerleader to the prom. "Sorry?"

"It felt right to hold your hand," said Karen. "It bothered me when you let go."

They walked for another half-dozen slabs. Part of him hoped she'd reach out and take his hand again, but her fingers stayed tucked away inside the pockets of her sweatshirt. They walked past his Hyundai and continued down the street.

"Why do you believe we know each other?" she asked.

"I'm not sure," he said. "I noticed posters of you before I knew your name, but probably anyone could say that. To be honest, this girl I met told me you and I are in love and . . . well, she's been right about a lot of stuff."

"I see."

"Does that sound like me professing my love for you?"

She looked at him. "Are you, George?"

He counted another three slabs of concrete in the sidewalk. "Your hand felt right, too," he said.

They reached the end of the block before she spoke again. "This young woman is having similar dreams?"

He glanced both ways and they crossed the street. "Yeah, but she seems to remember a lot more than me. At least, she remembers it a lot clearer than I do."

"Does she know the answer to your George Romero question?"

"I haven't asked her. Her name's Madelyn Sorensen."

Karen blinked as they stepped up over the curb. "Dr. Emil Sorensen's daughter?"

"Maybe," said George. "I met her dad on moving day. He came across like a professor. Do you know him?"

"I know of him," she said. "He is a renowned biochemist and neurologist. He was expected to be awarded the Nobel Prize in 2007, and some felt he was more deserving than the team that received the honor. Why are you so averse to being called a saint?"

A muscle behind his eye twinged. "What do you mean?"

"When my father compared you to St. George, you closed your eyes and lowered your head. When I referred to you the same way, you reacted as if the words caused physical pain. And just now the muscles around your eye contracted."

"I don't know," he said. "Madelyn called me that, too. It just feels strange, people calling me a saint. And she keeps telling me I'm supposed to be a superhero."

Karen's eyebrows went up. "I beg your pardon?"

He looked ahead. "Yeah. According to her we all have superpowers. That's how we fight the monsters. I'm supposed to be super-strong."

It occurred to him he was spewing out a new level of madness, so her response caught him off guard.

"Are you?"

"Sorry?"

She looked at his arms. "Do you have superhuman strength? You said she has been correct about many things."

Something twinged again. "Maybe? Why, do you?"

Karen Quilt straightened her back and looked at the sidewalk ahead of them. "From a very young age, my father trained me to be capable and independent. Circumstances required that he was absent from my life for many years, but I continued training on my own."

"What's that supposed to mean?"

She turned to him. "I saw the look on your face back at the hotel, George. You know who my father is."

His lips twisted before he could stop them. He pushed them flat again. "Yeah."

"With that in mind, what do you think he would consider 'capable'?"

"Jesus," he said, "you really are a superhero."

"If I decided to follow such a path, I could be, yes."

George decided not to dwell on what other paths her father might have been training her for. He took in a deep breath. "I think I lifted a dumpster the other day," he said. The words made his head flare with pain, but it felt good to say them.

Karen looked at him. He couldn't read her expression. "You think you lifted it?"

"I was having a migraine," he said, "and I think I may have been seeing things."

"Things such as dead people who continue to walk?"

"Yeah."

"How high did you lift the dumpster?"

"I . . . I couldn't get under it," he said. "Somebody saw me. I got it to here." He held his hands out a few feet above the sidewalk and mimed lifting something.

"Was it difficult?"

He shook his head and cleared away some of the pain. "Not really. I lifted a couch the other day, too. One with a hideaway bed built into it."

"Impressive."

"Did you really come down the side of the building to catch me?"

"I did. It is a Parkour technique."

He glanced over his shoulder at the tall hotel and the columns of balconies. "Wow."

Karen tilted her head, then reached up and touched her nose. Her fingers came back spotted with red. "Pardon me," she said. "I seem to be having a mild headache of my own which is causing a nosebleed."

Across the street, just behind Karen, a trio of men headed for them. One wore a suit, the other two had dull jackets. The paparazzi had spotted them. Their conversation was over.

Then George saw the pale skin and chalky eyes. One of the men raised an arm that ended just past the elbow. Another wobbled on a leg that had two round, ragged holes near the knee. They stumbled off the far sidewalk and into the street.

In the blink of an eye, the world changed. Dust covered the cars on the street, and spiderwebs of cracks blossomed across several of their windshields. Leaves spread across the pavement in drifts. Weeds had forced their way up between the sidewalk slabs.

He glanced over his shoulder. Four more monsters staggered on the sidewalk behind them. The two in the rear of the quartet looked a lot like the older couple he and Karen had passed a few minutes earlier.

"We should speak more with Madelyn Sorensen," said Karen. She dabbed at her nose again, then wiped her fingers twice against the cuff of her sweatshirt. "If she does remember more of this alternate world, she may have information she does not realize is relevant."

George glanced at her. "So you believe me?"

"It would seem I have little choice."

"How so?"

She pointed down the street ahead of them. "There are three people walking toward us who all appear to be dead."

The blonde in the lead had frizzy hair. A large clump of it had been torn out to show a patch of bald bone on the dead woman's forehead. Glasses hung from one ear of the next corpse. The last one's face had been burned or scraped down until there was nothing left but teeth and eye sockets. George wasn't sure if it had been a man or a woman.

"Ahhh," he said. "So you can see them, too?"

"Yes. Three in front, three to the side, four behind us."

"Good," he said. "I was thinking there was still a chance I might be crazy."

Karen's feet shifted on the pavement. "Do they have any notable strengths or weaknesses?"

"They're kind of slow," he said. "They like to bite. Head and neck injuries seem to put them down pretty fast. Don't worry, this has happened to me a few times now and I can . . ."

His voice trailed off as she grabbed his arm. For a brief moment he pictured Karen half swooning against him like the love interest in some old movie poster. It made him feel a bit heroic.

Then her other hand grabbed the top of his shoulder and pushed down hard.

She swung up and over him like a gymnast vaulting off a horse. Her boot lashed out at the trio in front of them and caught the blonde in the jaw with a solid crack of bone. Karen twisted her body, brought her other foot around, and slammed the heel into the dead man's head. The glasses shattered. She landed in a crouch, spun, and swept the legs out from under all three monsters.

George turned to the side and found the dead thing with the severed arm was a yard away. He stepped forward and slammed his palm into the corpse's chest to shove it away. He barely felt the impact, but the creature flew back as if gravity had shifted and dropped it down the street. One of its flailing arms struck another shambler and spun it around. George threw a punch and another dead thing's chest collapsed.

Karen grabbed George's shoulder again with both hands and vaulted up, over, and behind him. She drove her heels into the two creatures there and rode their skulls down to the ground. Her open hands batted away the withered fingers that grabbed for her, then knifed out efficient strikes to the jaw, throat, and spine. Two more dead things collapsed and gave her room to snap another neck with a spin kick.

In the moment he spent watching her, one of the last monsters, an emaciated woman, sank its teeth into his hand. He felt it clamp down with its jaw, heard the teeth grind against the bones of his palm. He yanked his hand away and drove his fist into the dead woman's face. The head snapped free and bounced down the street.

"Are you injured?" asked Karen. Her hood had fallen back to expose her face. She looked at his hand with wide eyes. Not scared, but very focused.

George held up his palm. "Not even scratched."

"You are fortunate."

"Or maybe invulnerable," he said.

"Perhaps," she said. "Increased strength would be of little use without an epidermis and skeletal structure which could support additional mass."

"I was joking," he said.

"I was not."

He looked at the circle of bodies around them. A few of them still wiggled their jaws. The fight hadn't even lasted a minute. Karen had put down three of the creatures for every one he'd stopped.

"I'm guessing most supermodels can't do that?"

"No others I am aware of. The city has changed as well."

She pointed down the street. There were a few crashed cars in the middle of the road that looked like they'd been there for a while. A few bodies sprawled on the pavement, too. One building was a burned-out husk. Another looked like it had been barricaded at one point, and the barriers torn down.

"Yeah," said George. "At first I just saw the monsters, but now it's spreading to everything."

"You did not mention that earlier."

"I was trying not to sound too crazy."

She raised an eyebrow. Then she gestured down the street. In the distance, a half-dozen figures were staggering toward them. "How long do these altered states last?"

"This is my third one today," he said. "The last one was half an hour."

"We should retreat to the hotel. The lobby is not safe, but the higher floors should be defendable."

"If you say so."

They stepped over the dead monsters. A few of them snapped at their feet. George stomped on one and crushed the skull to paste. They walked back up the sidewalk with quick strides.

Karen glanced at him. "Are you a violent person?"

"What?"

"Are you prone to acts of violence?"

"No, not at all. Why?"

She looked back over her shoulder. "You did not hesitate to destroy these creatures, even though they had once been human. Most people would have a natural reluctance to overcome."

He shrugged. "It just seems clear they're not people anymore."

"If Madelyn is correct," she said, "you may have more experience dealing with them than you remember."

"Maybe," George said. "So this hasn't happened to you before? The dead things and everything changing?"

Her head went side to side once. "It has not."

"You're sure?"

She gave him a look. "I am quite certain."

"Does it strike you as odd that you're diving into this full force?"

"How do you mean?"

"I've been having little glimpses and flashes of the monsters for a week or two now," he told her. "They kept building and growing. It's only been the past two days that the world started to change. But you're starting right where I am."

"Perhaps because I am with you," suggested Karen.

They turned the corner and saw the entrance to the Four Seasons. The burned hulk of a limousine sat in the driveway. It stretched back far enough to block one lane of traffic. Two dead things shuffled around it.

Karen looked in his eyes. The muscles of her neck tensed. He clenched his fists and felt strong.

And then the world flickered. The streets cleaned out and the wrecks vanished or were made whole again. The restored limo lurched into motion and pulled into the hotel. A man standing near it snapped a few quick pictures with a small camera.

"It appears to be over," Karen said.

George glanced behind them. The bodies were gone. The weeds had vanished. "Yeah, I think so."

The man with the camera stared down the street at the two of them. Karen flipped her hood up and turned her back to the man. "I have been recognized," she said. "Give me your phone."

"What?"

The man took a few steps toward them, gaining speed with each step. His camera rose. "We will have to continue our discussion later," she said. "I will give you my personal number. Call later this evening. We shall make plans to meet tomorrow."

The idea that a supermodel was forcing her phone number on him crossed George's mind. He bit back a chuckle as he pulled out his phone. She took it and her fingers danced over the keypad. She went to hand it back to him and paused.

"Your phone is a Katana LX, manufactured by Sanyo."

"Yeah. I've been meaning to get a new one, but I'm kind of stuck in my contract and—"

"It is five and a half years old," she said. "This model should no longer be supported."

"It is, though."

She handed him his phone and pulled her own from the sweatshirt pocket. It spun in her hands to reveal a sunken keyboard. "The T-Mobile G1," she said, "with the new Android operating system. It was given to me as part of a promotional deal for a series of print advertisements."

"You're right," he said. "That blows my phone away."

Karen shook her head. "It does not. This phone was an early release in autumn of 2008. It is also five years old." She looked at him. "Why would I still own a first-generation phone which is half a decade old?"

The photographer snapped off half a dozen pictures of them examining the phones. In a wide shot, it might've looked like they were holding hands. George imagined pictures of him and Karen Quilt with provocative captions showing up in magazines between shots of pop stars and hot actors.

Then he realized he couldn't picture a single actor or actress who was considered the new big thing. He couldn't name a new song or the person who sang it.

There was a plague. It broke out in the spring of 2009 and wiped out most of the world.

"What's the last new song you heard?"

The phone spun and collapsed in her hand like a quick-draw artist with a pistol. "I thought I had made it clear I follow very few popular—"

"Anything," he interrupted. "Anything at all. Can you name one song that's come out in the past couple of years?"

She shook her head.

"Movies? Books?"

Her head moved side to side again. "I cannot."

"No new phones," he said. "No music, no books. Do you see any new cars?"

Karen scanned the street. "All the models I can identify are 2009 or earlier. With the economic downturn, this is not an impossible occurrence."

"In this part of town? At this hotel?"

The photographer was close, barely fifteen feet away. Another one ran down the street to join him, and a third not far behind. "We shall talk later," she said.

She turned and spun the sweatshirt off her shoulders and into her arm with the practiced grace of a runway model. The cameras focused on her as she strode away from George and back to the hotel. George was pretty sure the first guy had already taken at least a dozen photos of them together, but he still used the chance to slip back around the corner and head for his car.

His 2002 Hyundai. Over ten years old.

THEN

I'M FALLING THROUGH the air.

There are over a hundred people marching in the street below. Their boots kick up dust on the dirt road. They're all wearing military uniforms, but they don't move like the military. They're wobbly and erratic, only loosely in sync. It's as if the whole crowd is drunk. The crackling popping sound of teeth echoes up to me.

I realize I'm not falling toward the crowd, but toward a building on the side of the street. And I'm not falling alone. The man in the tinfoil suit, the brilliant man, is falling alongside me. The gleaming suit buzzes as we fall, and the buzzing makes words. *If you don't mind this part of the base being annihilated in the process, sure.*

I'm not sure what the bright man is talking about. The dream has dumped me in the middle of a conversation. I can't remember how it started, so I'm not sure how to respond.

The flat roof rushes up at us and only slows just before my boots hit. They never touch, or if they do it's so gentle I can't feel it. My arms shift and a third person enters the dream. I'm carrying an older man, with messy hair and an overgrown beard. He doesn't seem to weigh anything. He looks like a professor who hasn't slept in days. He's familiar, both to dream me and to real me, watching the dream from some other vantage point.

I set the man down on the roof and a voice speaks. My voice. It takes me a moment to recognize it, and by the time I do the few words have passed and been lost. The old professor looks at me and nods. "I understand. I'll be fine."

And then I'm falling again. Some of the parrots—the monsters—see me coming and raise their arms. Up close I can see their uniforms are incomplete. Some have digital-patterned jackets, others T-shirts, and a few just wear sand-colored tanks. A few have belts. One or two have caps. I drop into the center of the crowd and they turn on me.

I grab a monster by its outstretched arm and swing it like a medieval flail. The corpse batters down a dozen of the dead soldiers. I swing my improvised weapon back the other way and clear a path to a large, hangar-like building. It's a tomb. I know this in the way people know things in dreams.

My weapon twists at the end of the swing and the dead body comes apart at the shoulder with a wet sound. I'm holding an arm and most of the shoulder. A yellowed knob of bone glistens at the end of the limb.

Another monster lumbers out through the entrance into the building. I put my hand on its chest and push it back inside. It stumbles away from my hand and knocks other corpses down behind it.

I grab the huge door—it's half the front of the building—with one hand and pull. It squeals on metal wheels and shrinks the opening. Dead things gnaw and claw at my hands, but I know they can't hurt me.

Something hisses behind me and the shadows jump and vanish. The tinfoil man hangs in the air with his arms stretched out to push at something. Clouds of black ash in front of him hold the shape of soldiers for a moment, then drift apart. Near the edge of the clouds are three or four other charred monsters that break apart as I watch.

The man isn't tinfoil. He's hot. White-hot.

My knuckles punch through a dead soldier's skull. The punch becomes a backhand that crushes another head. I grab a body with each hand and throw them like dolls.

I speak to the white-hot man and he talks back. I say something else, but the words are lost in the muddle of the dream. We have a whole conversation that I can't hear.

No. That I can't remember. That's important, part of me knows. I'm not not-hearing this. I'm not-remembering it.

The monsters are all dead. I've thrown them all into a pile and the white-hot man has incinerated them all. It makes him get pale.

I look up at the old professor on the roof and jump up to him. Like my other dreams, I'm carried up by invisible wires that make my back itch. I hold on to the older man and we fall down to street level together.

Not fall. This is something else important. These aren't falling dreams. They're—

The ground shakes and disrupts my thoughts. It's a heavy, steady thumping—the sound of construction sites and dinosaurs. Reflections tremble in the windows of nearby buildings.

A few buildings down, something smashes through the doors of another hangar. The long slats fold like cardboard. Rivets pop and scatter like bullets. Without thinking, I pull the old man back and step in front of him. Shards of metal patter against my body. I feel them, but they don't hurt.

For just an instant, the huge robot stands in front of the hole it's made. Then it turns and runs down the street away from us. The trembling ground goes with it and—

EIGHTEEN

GEORGE WOKE UP to the *click-click-click* of the chain against the side of the fan. He couldn't stop it. The sound had even made its way into his dreams.

Then he remembered he was awake.

He lunged up and the parrot chewing on his arm staggered back. It had been a woman once. Very petite. Strawberry-blond hair cut short. Small teeth that had probably made her look even younger. Back when she was alive.

The dead thing's camisole was thin, almost sheer. If it hadn't been caked with blood it would've been see-through. The corpse wore tiny shorts and had bare feet. The woman had died in her sleep. Or been killed in her sleep.

The dead thing stumbled forward again. He grabbed it by the shoulders and kept it at arm's length. The skin felt like cold meat. It bent its head and snapped its teeth at his wrists. He slipped his hands down onto its arms and kept them pinned at its sides. Its hands pawed the air between them at elbow height.

His apartment was destroyed again. Not destroyed, he realized, as much as neglected for years. The broken windows. The peeling paint. Mildew everywhere near the windows, dust everywhere away from them. It was derelict. Abandoned.

And he was wrestling with a dead woman. In her pajamas. While he was in his pajamas.

George walked the parrot—why was it a parrot? That was from the dreams—back through the apartment and toward the door. The corpse weighed as much as he thought, but it had no balance or coordination. Each push or tug made it stumble.

Past the dead woman's bobbing head he could see the apartment door hanging open. The lock had been smashed. The wood was cracked and splintered around the dead bolt. The hallway beyond looked as neglected as his apartment. A dark stain decorated one wall. It wasn't mildew.

He twisted the monster's arms and levered it back a few more steps. It tripped on its own foot and thumped off a wall. He almost shifted his grip to catch it, but then the gnashing teeth and chalk eyes reminded him it wasn't a woman.

Another few steps and the dead thing was in the hall. It kept biting the air between them. He bent his arms a little bit and one of its fingers brushed his stomach. The painted nails almost got snagged in his T-shirt.

He shoved hard and the corpse staggered across the hall to crash into the opposite door. Its skull cracked just below the faux-iron numbers, right on the peephole lens. The dead thing slumped for a moment, then pushed itself back up against the door. Its camisole dragged down to expose more gray skin and a purple nipple.

George stepped back and slammed his apartment's door. The broken wood around the lock jammed it before it could close all the way. He gave two more hard shoves and wedged it into the frame. He reached for the dead bolt out of instinct, then fumbled with the chain instead.

The door shook as the petite woman hit it from the other side. It shook again. And a third time. Then he heard lacquered nails clawing at the wood.

It would be as hard to force the door open again as it had been to close it. He could use the remains of the couch to block it even more and give himself a few minutes to think. And find some clothes.

He double-checked the chain and turned to look at his apartment.

The carpet was clean. The blinds were half-down over the windows. Sunlight streamed in through the glass. He turned back at the door, nestled in its solid frame.

"Son of a bitch," muttered George.

* * *

He stepped closer to the door but heard nothing. He lowered his eye to the peephole. The fish-eye view of the hallway didn't show him anything. It was empty.

He slid the chain loose and flipped the dead bolt. The door glided open on the hinges. He stepped into the hall and looked both ways. The dead woman was gone. There was no stain on the far wall.

George went back into his apartment and closed the door behind him.

He didn't remember turning the ceiling fan on last night. The nights were getting cool, even in Los Angeles. But the blades were swinging in lazy arcs. The beads wobbled back and forth and tapped the motor housing again and again.

He'd come home and eaten some leftovers. He remembered wondering when he should call Karen, and not being sure what was the best time of night to reach a supermodel. Then he'd just called and they'd talked for ten minutes. He'd made a joke about all of their ten-minute conversations. She hadn't laughed, but he'd sensed she didn't look down on him for it.

He was supposed to be meeting her at a coffee shop near her hotel at ten o'clock. He looked at the clock. He'd overslept. It was almost seven. Rush hour was in full swing, which meant it'd take him close to an hour to get over to the—

It meant he was going to be late for work!

Panic made his heart pound. He could skip his shower, put on some extra deodorant, or maybe a spot of the cologne he wore once a month or so. He'd get crap from the other workers but it meant he could be on the road as soon as he was dressed.

And then he took another breath. He'd made this decision

last night. Whatever was happening to him was more important than work. He'd call Jarvis halfway through the day and tell him the illness had gotten worse.

Seeing Karen again was more important than work.

He shook the nerves out of his arms and gave his apartment another look. Not a single sign of the devastation he'd woken up with. Woken up with twice now.

George double-checked the locks on his door and headed for the shower.

* * *

He'd parked his car around the corner. This morning was a scheduled street-sweeping day, which meant last night the whole neighborhood's parking habits had shifted. As an early riser, these days usually meant easy parking the night before—George would be long gone before the parking fines kicked into effect. But last night he'd decided to park somewhere safer, just in case, and that had meant parking a block and a half away from his apartment.

He waited to cross the street as a black sedan with tinted windows rolled past him. There were a few gangs active in the area, and his first thought was somebody was cruising very early in the morning. The car was too basic for that, though. It wasn't a flashy vehicle, it was a workhorse. A Crown Victoria or something like that.

So his second thought, right on the tail of the first one, was that it was a cop. Which was also kind of reassuring after the first thought. But even through the tinted windows he was pretty sure the man and woman in the car weren't cops. They wore dark suits. The woman stared back at him through the glass as they drove past.

He stepped out behind the sedan and headed across to the corner. He saw his car and grumbled. A black van was double-parked in the street, blocking him in his space. The other driver didn't even have his hazards on. George steeled himself for a possible confrontation. He knew most folks would move without question and look apologetic when they did, but there was always that small percentage who got angry at the suggestion that every road in LA wasn't built to be their private parking spot. As he got close, though, the van pulled away fast and headed up the street.

George pulled out his keys and heard a squeal of rubber. The van had made a wide turn and cut off two other cars. Not just a turn—a U-turn. The van roared back toward him, cutting across the yellow line. It twisted in at the last moment and almost kissed the front corner of his Hyundai just before it came to a stop.

The two men in the front of the van were both staring at him. The side door slid open and George saw two more men in the back. All of them wore dark suits.

Another squeal of brakes made him spin. The black sedan had doubled back, too. It stopped in the road right behind him. Its nose was inches from the Hyundai's rear bumper. The two black vehicles and his own car had him surrounded on three sides. Even as he thought it a second car pulled up in the far lane. They formed a tight box around him.

The passenger door opened while the sedan settled and a short blonde stepped out. The woman he'd glimpsed as they drove by outside his apartment. Her hair was cut short. She had a face that might've been cute when she was younger, but had gotten lean and harsh as she matured. She wore the same dark suit as the men in the van, and her driver.

The blonde held up something dark in her hand. A twitch of her fingers opened it to show a gold shield, a photograph, and some tiny words on a white background. George registered a capital S, but the wallet closed before he could read anything.

"George Bailey," the woman said. It wasn't a question. It was a statement. She was just letting him know everything was intentional and deliberate.

George realized an instant too late he should've spent that thinking time trying to run.

A man grabbed either arm. A third one dropped the bag over

his head. It was made of heavy black material, like denim. He heard a zipping sound as it cinched around his neck.

He fought back. The man holding his right arm let go. George swung his arm around and heard a grunt of pain from someone. The man holding the other arm let go, but then someone slammed into him. The world spun inside the black bag, something hit him in the side of the head, and everything stopped.

NINETEEN

IT WAS VERY stuffy.

George realized the darkness wasn't unconsciousness but something draped over his head. He reached up to pull it away and something cold clicked and cut into his wrists. Then he remembered the van and the men and—

"He's awake."

The bag whipped off his head. The blonde was standing in front of him. She was going through his wallet. She had his driver's license out and was holding it up to the light. She tilted it back and forth, checking the holograms.

They were in a square room. One of the dark-suited men stood in each corner. One had a bruise on the side of his head that hadn't been there when they grabbed him. Another one had splints on two fingers and his thumb. The only furniture was the chair George was handcuffed to and a table off to the side.

There wasn't a mirror. He thought there was always a one-way mirror in these rooms so people on the other side could watch what went on. He craned his head around. No mirror, and also no cameras.

He wasn't sure if that was good or bad.

The blond woman tossed his license on the table. His credit cards were already there, along with what little cash he had and a few receipts. "George H. Bailey. *H* stands for Harrison." She shook her head. "Seriously, with a name like that you'd think Homeland would've picked you up years ago."

"It's my real name," he said.

"I know," she said. She pulled a few grocery store cards from his wallet, glanced at each of them, and tossed them on the table. "Your parents were Beatles fans?"

She stared at him for a moment and George realized she was waiting on an answer. He swallowed and tried to stay calm. "*Star Wars*," he said. "Dad said I was almost George Han Bailey, but Mom won out."

The man in the corner to George's left, the one with the bruise, bit back a snort.

The blonde's gaze didn't waver. "Are you a sci-fi geek?"

"When I was a kid."

"Not anymore?"

"No more than anyone else, I guess."

Another long pause stretched out. Her eyes were bright green. The longer he looked, the more he was sure she wasn't a nice person.

He looked away from her eyes. "Ummmm . . . What's this all about?"

The blonde tossed his wallet on the table. "You do any sports?"

"What?"

"Football? Weightlifting? Maybe a little soccer on your lunch break?"

"I . . . no."

"Nothing?"

"I ride my bike to work sometimes in the summer. That's it."

"Ever take anything for that?"

"What?"

The blonde nodded at the man with the splints. "You put up a real fight when we grabbed you."

"I was scared."

"A lot more of a fight than a guy your size and build should be able to. Especially against guys like these." She paused again. "My friend here thinks you're on steroids."

He shook his head. "No. Absolutely not."

"That's what I told him."

"Good," said George. "You're right."

"You're way too skinny to be on steroids. My bet was meth."

He blinked. "I'm not on anything."

"You sure about that?"

"I have to do a drug test every six months. I don't even smoke."

She held out her hand. One of the men placed a cell phone in it. George realized it was his. She made a few quick swipes at the phone's screen and then held up the call log for him to see. "Yesterday morning," she said, "you placed a call to Sandia Labs in New Mexico. The Pulsed Power Project. The call lasted just under nine minutes."

This pause was twice as long. George wasn't sure if she wanted an answer and he didn't want to risk interrupting her if she started talking again. Once he was sure she was waiting on him, he gave a quick nod. "Yeah," he said. "I did."

"Why?"

"Why what?"

"Why did you call the lab?"

"I was looking for someone."

"Barry Burke?"

"Yes."

"And you found him." Another statement, not a question.

"Yeah."

"How do you know Mr. Burke?"

"I . . ."

The blonde set his phone on the table and crossed her arms. "It's not really a tough question," she said. "How do you know him?"

"I'm not sure I do," admitted George.

"So why were you calling him?"

George started to talk, then closed his mouth.

"Well?"

"I think . . . I think I'd like to talk to a lawyer," George said. "Counsel. Whatever you call it."

The blonde's mouth twitched into a new shape. If it was a

smile, it was a cruel one. "A lawyer?" she echoed. "What year do you think this is, George? I don't have to give you a bathroom if I don't want to. Answer the question. Why were you calling Barry Burke?"

Something burned at the back of his throat and he swallowed it down. "To see if I recognized him. Recognized his voice."

"But you don't know him?"

"I don't think so."

"You don't think so? Have you ever met?"

George shook his head. "No."

"Ever talked on the phone before?"

"No."

"Exchanged e-mails? Online chat? Message boards? Anything?"

"No."

"So how would you recognize him?"

George closed his mouth again.

"According to the receptionist you were on hold for a minute and a half while Mr. Burke got to the phone. You talked for a little over seven minutes. What did you talk about?"

"Nothing."

"You didn't say anything? You just stood there with the phone in your hand?"

"No, of course—"

"So what did you talk about?"

"I asked who he was. He made a joke."

"What kind of joke?"

George tried to roll his shoulders. The cuffs bit into his wrists. "I said I thought I had the wrong person. He said if there was another Barry Burke, he probably had a goatee and a sash."

The blonde furrowed her brow. "What the hell does that mean?"

"*Star Trek*," said one of the agents behind George. "In the mirror universe all of the *Enterprise* crew wore sashes to show their rank, and the evil Spock had a goatee."

"Shut up, Winston," she snapped.

"Sorry, ma'am."

"I just told you to shut up." Her gaze settled on George again. "So," she said, "did you recognize Burke?"

He thought about it for a long moment. "No."

"You sure?"

"Yes."

"Did he recognize you?"

George paused with his lips half-open. "I don't know."

The blond woman stared at him. "In the past week you've stopped twice at the Army recruiting office on Lindbrook. Why?"

"Look, I think I at least get to know what this is all about. I'm pretty sure that's in the Bill of Rights."

"We're getting to it," she said. "Why were you at the recruiting office?"

"My car broke down. I was looking for help. Somebody with jumper cables."

"And the second time?"

"Same thing."

Her eyebrows went up. "Your car broke down twice in one week, both times in front of the same office?"

"No," said George. "The first time was half a block away. The second time was a little before it, but then I knew they had the cables."

"Who did you talk to there?"

"A sergeant, I think. I don't know military ranks that well. And a lieutenant."

"Names?"

He shook his head. "I don't know." The huge officer's name floated up in his memory. "The big guy, the lieutenant, was named Freedom."

The blonde traded looks with one of the men behind George. Not the *Star Trek* fan. He glanced over his shoulder and saw the man thumb-typing into a BlackBerry.

"Yesterday afternoon," the blonde said, "you visited a woman named Karen Quilt at the Four Seasons Hotel."

"Yes," said George.

"Do you know Miss Quilt?"

"No. I mean, just from her pictures and stuff."

"Never met her? Never sent her any e-mails or anything?"

"No."

"You have any feelings for her?"

He blinked. "What?"

"Do you have dreams about her? Fantasies?"

George paused, then shook his head. "No."

The blond woman noticed the pause. "Are you stalking her?"

"No!"

She picked his phone and her thumb swung back and forth. She held it out so he could see the message on the screen. "Nikolai Bartamian texted her address to you. The hotel she's staying at."

Something twisted in his gut. "Yes."

"I'm guessing for someone in his line of work, that's very frowned on. You know there's a good chance he'll get fired for that, right?"

"Yeah," said George. "He said he might."

She gave him another long stare. "So you're not stalking her, but you're willing to risk your friend's job to get the address of a woman you've never met. Am I getting this right?"

"No."

"So clear it up for me."

"I just . . ." He hung his head.

"You wanted to see if she recognized you?"

"Yeah."

"Why did you think she would know you?"

"I don't know," he said. "I can't explain it, I'm sorry."

"Did she recognize you?"

He sighed. "No."

"According to her security force in the lobby, you were in the penthouse with her for almost twenty minutes."

"It was only ten," he said. "A lot of that was elevators and finding the room."

"If she didn't recognize you, what were the two of you talking about for ten minutes?"

"Old movies," he said. "And Sherlock Holmes."

"Don't fuck with me, Bailey."

He pressed his lips together in a line.

The blonde held out her hand again. The man with the splints took George's phone away and handed her a brown folder. She tapped it against her hand twice before opening it. Her gaze left George and dropped to the pages inside the folder.

"Are you aware," she said without looking up, "Miss Quilt is connected to a suspected terrorist? A man wanted by the CIA and Homeland Security, not to mention MI5 and pretty much every other intelligence organization on Earth?"

"I thought everybody knew that," he said. "Hasn't it been in *People* magazine and *TMZ* and all that?"

"You watch *TMZ*?"

"No."

"Read *People*?"

"No. I think it was an issue of *Maxim* I found in the cafeteria."

"And you looked it up online, didn't you?"

The back of his throat sizzled. He swallowed again and nodded.

"It's funny," she said. "We've been going over your browser history, and it seems like you double-checked a lot of this information last night after you met with her."

She held up a photograph. There was a string of numbers and letters down the side of the image. The photo was fuzzy, and the subject's head was shaved almost bald, but there was no mistaking his harsh features and small glasses. They were sunglasses in the picture, and George found himself wondering if Karen's father wore polarizing lenses.

The blonde pushed the photo closer to George. "Have you seen this man?"

He looked at the photo for a long moment. "I'm not sure."

"Think carefully, George," she said. "Your answer could influence the next thirty-five to forty years of your life."

And then, just when George was ready to give up, the door opened and the President and First Lady walked into the room.

The President looked at George in the chair. Christian, the

First Lady, put her hand up to her mouth, aghast. She turned back to another suit in the doorway and murmured something.

"What's all this?" President Smith asked. "I just asked you to get him for a talk."

The blond woman looked confused, but hid it quickly. "The assignment was snatch and grab for interrogation, Mr. President."

"What?" The commander in chief shook his head. "No, just a talk. Literally, just a . . . oh, for God's sake, uncuff him."

The blonde shot a look at one of the agents behind George. A lot of her confidence had vanished. It made her face softer, but she still didn't look nice.

The *Star Trek* fan released the cuffs and George brought his arms around. He expected horrible welts from the tight restraints, but his wrists weren't even bruised.

As soon as George's arms were free the President waved the others away. "Out," he said. "Give us a minute."

The agents looked at the blonde. She gave a quick nod and they filed out of the room. President Smith looked at her, but she squared her shoulders and let her hands hang loose at her sides. He sighed and turned to his wife.

"Just a minute, hon," he said.

She smiled. "I'll be right outside if you need me."

Christian Smith stepped into the hall and the door closed. The President gave the blonde another look and she took a half step back. Then he focused his attention on George.

"I'm sorry," he said. "I didn't intend for this to be so crude. I didn't want them yanking you out of your life. You probably didn't want to be yanked out of it, either, did you?"

"No," said George. "Not really."

The President had the face of a young man. The shape of it, the tone of his skin. The past few years had aged him, as it always aged the men who'd held office before him, but he'd managed to hold off the worst of it. Some of his very few detractors accused him of dyeing his hair, which the First Lady always laughed about.

Just above the collar of his shirt, George could see the scar. The war injury the President couldn't hide. An insurgent had stabbed him in the throat and a Naval corpsman had kept him alive long enough for a field hospital to save his life. It made his voice sound older.

"Mr. Bailey," said the President. He wrung his hands. "May I call you George?"

George nodded. He wasn't sure what else to do. After half an hour of near panic, his mind was blank.

"George, I have a problem," said the President. "This may be hard for you to believe, but we have reliable intelligence there's a terrorist cell operating here in the southwest United States. We believe several members of it are here in Los Angeles. And we think you've had contact with them."

George shook his head, but the President held up his hand.

"Don't worry," he said. "We know you're not involved with them. Not deliberately. But we need your help if we're going to beat them, George. Can I count on you to help us? To do your duty as a citizen of this great country?"

"Of course."

President Smith beamed. "I just need you to answer one question for me, okay? It's very important, George. Your answer is going to tell us how much they know, and how we need to adjust our plans."

The commander in chief dropped to one knee. It made him shorter than George, so he straightened his back until they were eye level with each other. The two men looked at each other for a moment before he spoke.

"Do you know who I am?"

George blinked in confusion. "Of course I do," he said. "Sir. Mr. President."

The President shook his head. "No," he said. "I mean, past that." He leaned in and looked George in the eyes. "Do you know who I am?"

A splitting headache sprang up in the back of George's head, the worst one yet. It felt like someone had driven a nail halfway into his skull, and now that someone was just tapping the nail hard enough to make it shiver in the bone.

"I ... sorry," said George. He blinked a few more times. "You're ... You're John Smith. You're the President of the United States."

Smith smiled. It was the smile from dozens of photo ops and press conferences. It was a wide, well-practiced smile. "And you're sure of that?"

The hammer tapped the nail a few more times and George's skull trembled. His eyes got wet. "Yes," he said. "Of course I'm sure. I voted for you."

"No doubts at all?"

Something splashed in George's lap. A drop of red. His nose was bleeding. "Sir," he said, "Mr. President ... I'm not sure what you—"

"I asked if you had any doubts. Do you have any doubts, George? Have we ever met before? In any other capacity?"

The idea of having met the President and forgotten it would've been funny most of the time. Right now, with the nail ringing in the back of his skull, the idea almost made him scream. His nose-bleed had become a thin stream across his lips. Any more and it would be gushing.

"No," he whispered. The sound of his own voice made him wince.

The President's smile grew at the edges. "Of course we haven't," he said. He patted George on the cheek. "Let's try to remember that."

TWENTY

THE ALARM WENT off and George woke up.

He felt well rested. His head didn't ache. The bed was firm but comfortable.

His fan was silent.

He'd met the President yesterday. The President of the United States. He and the First Lady had been very apologetic about the misunderstanding, and grateful for his help. George didn't think he'd told them anything important, but they seemed to think he was some kind of great American hero.

It gave life a degree of clarity.

The ride to work was as slow as usual, but he didn't mind. It was just part of life. Same with the pedestrians and the swarms of homeless people. To think just a few days ago he'd been seeing conspiracies and monsters. His radio was on the religious channel again. He didn't even waste time looking for another station. He just shut it off. The radio blurted out, "C'mon, man, gimme something," before he twisted the knob.

George reached the time clock five minutes early and couldn't find his card. He searched behind a couple of the others, looking for his last name in bold print. It wasn't there. He grumbled and started a new timecard, knowing it would get him a lecture from accounting.

The clock snapped down on it like a set of hungry jaws.

Jarvis's eyes bugged a little when George stepped into the office. "Hey," said the supervisor. A long moment stretched out before he added, "I didn't expect to see you."

"Why not?"

The salt-and-pepper man's gaze darted left and right, as if he thought someone was hiding in the closet and behind his messy bookshelf. "The feds were here yesterday looking for you."

George sighed and nodded. "Yeah, I know. It's okay, they found me."

"The NSA," said Jarvis.

"It's okay," he repeated. "They found me. We talked. Everything's okay, it was just a misunderstanding."

Jarvis showed no sign of hearing him. "They took everything. All your assignments, my log book, your employment history. They even went up to accounting and got all your old timecards." He shook his head. "They interviewed pretty much anyone who'd ever talked to you. All of us, some professors, even a couple of students."

George pictured the blond agent's determined glare and didn't have trouble picturing what his coworkers had gone through. "I know this sounds crazy," he said, "but the President wanted to talk to me."

His boss stared at him.

"I'm serious. It was a mix-up."

Jarvis closed his eyes. "You're not one of those kooks, are you?"

"What do you mean?"

He waved his hand at the computer. "You don't act all sane at work and then go home and spend all night ranting in the Yahoo! comments about impeaching the President or conspiracy theories or something stupid like that?"

"What? No, of course not."

"You on some sort of watch list?"

"No. Well, not anymore, I think."

"You think?"

George raised his palms. "If they thought I'd done anything wrong, would they have let me go?"

Jarvis flopped back in his chair. "People were freaking out," he said after a minute. "They're going to freak out more now that you're back."

"How so?"

"How d'you think? These days what's everyone think when the government comes looking for your neighbor? Nobody's getting the Nobel Peace Prize, that's for sure. Half the people who talked to me yesterday thought you'd been arrested and shipped off to Guantanamo or something. If they see you . . ."

"What are you getting at, Jarvis?"

The supervisor scratched his salt-and-pepper beard. "Look," he said, "just keep a low profile for a while, okay? Try not to . . . I don't know, draw attention to yourself. Don't do anything weird. Maybe this'll cool down in a couple of days."

George's phone buzzed. It was a text message from **Karen Q**. He deleted it without looking. "Yeah," he said. "I'll do that."

"I'm doing you a favor," said Jarvis, "'cause you've been here forever and you're a great worker. Please don't light yourself on fire or anything."

"I'll do my best."

Another text came through. He deleted it.

* * *

His first job was changing a flickering bulb in one of the lecture halls. Not a big deal, but it needed the big fifteen-foot A-frame ladder. When that was done, Jarvis sent him to deal with a backed-up toilet in one of the dorms, and then he emptied trash in some of the other science buildings. It was more mindless work. The most challenging part was mopping up after one trash can that had received a mostly full cup of coffee.

George dumped the last bin in the dumpster. Loose papers, Doritos bags, and paper cups rained down onto the other trash. There were old clothes in the dumpster, plus a few swollen bags and some parts that looked like they might've been the guts of a television, or maybe an old computer monitor.

He let the bin drop and rested his hand on the edge of the

dumpster. He closed his eyes, rolled his neck, and pushed down. There was a knot in his shoulder he wanted to pop. He turned a bit more and levered his shoulder against the dumpster.

When he opened his eyes, Karen Quilt was staring at him.

She was dressed in black slacks and a blazer. She wore a tie but no shirt, and held the jacket more or less shut with one hand. The poster was less than ten feet away. Someone had put it up between his trips to the dumpster. He didn't recognize the name along the bottom, and wasn't sure if it was a brand or a store. Maybe both.

She looked disappointed in him.

This girl, Madelyn, she keeps telling me I'm supposed to be a superhero.

He looked away from the poster and his eyes fell on the dumpster. It was almost full of trash. Most of it was paper, but the whole thing probably weighed close to three or four tons. His hand tightened on the edge and he gave it a shake.

The steel container trembled.

According to her we all have superpowers. That's how we fight the monsters.

He stepped to the side. It had the same sleeves as the one he'd lifted—that he imagined lifting—the other day, but they were lower on this model. It'd be even easier to put a hand on it and get the other one underneath. And this one was far behind the building. No one would see him.

I'm supposed to be super-strong.

He set one hand on the sleeve and his head flared. His fingers leaped back to his temple and felt the vein pulsing there. His nose started to run, and when he wiped it with the back of his glove it left a red streak.

Another one. He couldn't believe he'd had a nosebleed while talking to the President. Six-year-olds get random nosebleeds. It was tough to think of something more embarrassing, short of wetting his pants. At least the President and the First Lady had been gracious about it. Christian had given him some of the tissues one of her assistants carried for her, and even offered to have their medic look at him.

George shook off his glove, tilted his head back, and pinched his nose. He walked away from the dumpster, dragging the plastic trash bin behind him. He passed the poster of Karen Quilt without looking at it.

* * *

According to the menu, the cafeteria was serving chicken parmesan. George was pretty sure it was just a fried chicken patty with tomato sauce and mozzarella cheese, but he also wasn't sure what actual chicken parmesan was supposed to be. With the spaghetti, a pair of rolls, and a trip to the salad bar it made for a solid lunch.

He found a table with an abandoned newspaper and paged through the news. More on the President's visit to Los Angeles. A sidebar about the First Lady talking to police and schoolchildren. As he finished his chicken patty, he found a short article in the entertainment section. Karen Quilt had been spotted with a mystery man outside her hotel. It was two paragraphs long, one of which was her bio. There weren't any pictures. George wondered if the President had suppressed them somehow.

Either the lettuce or tomatoes had gone bad. He wasn't sure which. He pushed the salad to one side and split a roll with his fingers.

Someone cleared their throat. He looked up and saw a young woman sitting across from him. Her dark hair was braided into a tight ponytail.

She wasn't sitting at the table. She was in a wheelchair. It was the crazy girl.

"Hey," Madelyn said. "I didn't hear from you yesterday."

He ignored her and let his eyes drift back to the newspaper.

She peered at it upside down. Her finger darted out to tap the Karen Quilt article. "I saw that online," she said. "Was that you? Did you go talk to her?"

Her hand was pale under the cafeteria's harsh fluorescent light. He could see dark veins under the flesh and faint bruises under her fingernails. Part of him tried to insist a living girl's hand couldn't look like that.

"Please leave me alone," said George.

Her eyes went wide. "What?"

"Go away."

Madelyn looked down at the article again. "Didn't she know you? She had to know you."

He drummed his fingers on the table. Then he killed another few seconds by having a sip of milk. It was on the edge of spoiling, and the tang of it made his nose wrinkle. Something was wrong with one of the cafeteria coolers.

"George," she said. "What's wrong?"

"I am not part of this," he said. "Whatever fantasy world you're making up, leave me out of it."

He might as well have slapped her. "What did you say?"

He flipped the newspaper shut. It wasn't as dramatic as slamming a book. "You," he said, "are crazy. You need to talk to a therapist or a psychiatrist or someone. And I'd appreciate it if you would just leave me alone in the meantime."

"What happened to you?"

"Nothing happened," he said. "I'm just not going to play this game with you anymore."

"Game?"

"All this superhero nonsense."

"You *are* a hero," she said.

He shook his head. "I'm just a guy," he said. "Just a regular guy trying to do his duty as a citizen of this great country."

She blinked. "What?"

"Please," he said, "just leave me alone." He lowered his eyes to the newspaper and set his hands flat on the table. He could feel his veins pulsing in his temple. She was giving him a headache.

He could see her in his peripheral vision. Her head was bowed, and he thought she might be trembling. He wasn't sure what kind of outburst could result from that. He could guess a few possible ones.

Instead, her pale hand reached out again. It came to rest on the front-page headline. The one about the President.

"Did he talk to you?"

He shoveled another mouthful of salad into his mouth. It tasted foul. The lettuce was slimy and the tomato was acidic. He forced himself to chew it.

She tapped the picture of President Smith. "George, did he talk to you? Did he ask you anything? It's important."

"George!" called someone else. Kathy, the crazy girl's roommate. "Hey, how are you?"

He pushed his fork through another lettuce leaf, but he couldn't eat it. His stomach was churning after the last mouthful. On the plus side, his nausea was overwhelming his headache.

Kathy stopped a few feet from the table. "Are you guys fighting about something?"

George shook his head.

Madelyn ignored her. "Smith gets into your head," she told George. "I told you, it's what he does. If he talked to you, we're back to square one here."

"I didn't mean to interrupt," said Kathy. "Sorry." She gave a meek wave and walked away.

Madelyn opened her mouth and the Nextel cut her off with a chirp. "George," called Jarvis. He sounded tired.

He wrested the phone off his belt without looking at Madelyn. "Yeah, boss."

"Where are you right now?"

He shot a glance at her. "Lunch."

"Finish up and come on back to the office."

"Did you want me to deal with that broken mirror?"

"I put Mark on it. Come back to the office."

George loaded his tray. He thought about taking the newspaper, too, but Madelyn still had her hand on it. He stood up. "You need to get some help," he said.

"What do you think I've been trying to do?"

He felt her eyes on him as he dropped off his tray and left. He tried not to think about her. His nausea was gone, but his head was pounding again.

* * *

"I think I need to give you a couple of days off," said Jarvis. "Just 'til this all calms down."

It was a kick in the gut, even though he'd felt it coming. "No," he said. "Come on, Jarvis, you can't."

He shook his head. "I don't have a choice."

"I did what you said," George told him. He wondered if someone had seen him talking to Madelyn. "What happened?"

"That bitch from HR came looking for you. The lawyers wrote up some sort of disclaimer for you to sign, something to show parents. I said you were over working in the chemistry labs and her head almost exploded."

It took a moment to sink in. "You've got to be kidding me."

Jarvis shook his head. "They're suspending you while they 'investigate.'"

"I didn't do anything!"

"Yeah, but you can't prove it," his boss said. "Did the feds give you a letter or a number to call or anything?"

"Well . . . no."

Jarvis threw up his hands. "They're paranoid, George. You and I both know there's a few thousand parents who'll be calling in if they find out there's a suspected terrorist working here."

"I'm not a—" George bit his lip. He clenched his fists. "This is bullshit."

"I know, buddy. I know. But my hands are tied." He paused. "I need your ID. And your keys, including the keycards."

George stood in front of the desk for a few more moments. Jarvis studied something on his computer screen. Then he grabbed a pen and tapped it on the desk. It *click-click-click*ed for almost thirty seconds before the fight went out of George and he pulled the lanyard off his neck.

"You're still going to get paid," said Jarvis. "Won't be any overtime or anything, but it's something."

"Thanks."

* * *

It was clear there had been people in George's apartment while he was at work. Books were shifted on the shelves. Some of his

DVDs were out and opened. Half his clothes were on the floor and the closet door—

What did he keep hidden in the closet?

—the closet door was wide open. The cabinets were ajar and a few drawers left open an inch or two. He wondered if the government hired two types of agents—the ones you sent in when you didn't want any sign they'd been there, and the ones you sent in when you wanted someone to know they'd been there. Maybe they were trained for both options.

He tossed his phone and wallet on the kitchen table, kicked off his shoes, and started to clean up. He did easy stuff first. Pushed in drawers. Shuffled books and DVDs back into place.

He shoved all the clothes in the hamper. They looked okay, but he didn't like the idea of wearing clothes a lot of other people had been handling. Plus he'd seen enough *CSI* shows to know they could have been sprayed with different chemicals to show blood or gunpowder or chemical residue. Lots of stuff he could've told them they wouldn't find.

His laptop was open and on. The password probably hadn't slowed them at all. For that matter, he realized, what about all his other online passwords? Bank of America? His e-mail? Facebook? Amazon? He'd need to reset them all.

Although, would it make a difference? The President had seemed straightforward, but George still didn't feel like trusting the blonde who'd snatched him off the street. He was probably being monitored somehow. Despite what he'd told Jarvis, it was a good bet his name was already on tons of Homeland Security lists. There might be cameras or microphones in his apartment, too.

He was annoyed to find the browser history had been wiped clean on his computer. Half his bookmarks, too. It wasn't a real surprise, it just felt kind of petty for them to erase stuff like that. Even if he had no plans to look up any of those sites again.

After two hours George decided his apartment wasn't any messier than it had been when he went to work. His stomach grumbled. There wasn't much in the way of food in his apartment, but he knew he couldn't blame that on the CIA or the

Secret Service or whomever the blonde had worked for. He ate out once a week, just at the Mexican place up the street or the Thai restaurant a block over, but after missing a day and a half of work he wasn't sure he should be spending any money he didn't need to.

There was a knock at the door.

He felt more cautious than usual and checked through the peephole. He didn't see anyone for a moment, then saw the little girl's head in the bottom of the fish-eye view. He unlocked the door and swung it open.

Not a little girl. A girl in a chair.

"What are you doing here?" George asked.

"Looking for you." Madelyn rolled the wheelchair forward a few inches, but he didn't open the door any wider or step out of the way.

"How'd you find out where I live?"

"You pointed the building out to me once," she said. "While we were out scavenging."

"No more games," he said. "I'm done. How did you get my address?"

She sighed. "I had wild wheelchair sex with a guy in the university's payroll department. Is that what you want to hear? Let me in."

He shook his head. "You need to go home. Or back to the dorms. Just go away."

"I'm trying," she said. "Don't you get it? This isn't our life. We're supposed to be somewhere else."

Her words made his head ache again. "Please," he said, "just stop."

"You're super-strong, George," she insisted. "You're invulnerable. You can breathe fire. You . . ." She took a breath and stared him in the eyes. "You can fly."

He closed his eyes and counted to five. The pounding in his head faded. When he opened his eyes again, she was still staring at him.

"You need to go," he said again.

She sighed. "Okay, then."

He waited for her to turn and head back down the hall.

She didn't move. "I'm sorry," she said, "but we need to get past this, and I can't think of a better way to convince you once and for all."

Madelyn pulled something out from between her hip and the arm of the wheelchair. It seemed to swell in her hand as George realized what it was. She pointed it at him.

"Whoa!" he said. He put his hands up. "Hang on. You don't want to—"

The gunshot rattled the window at the end of the narrow hallway.

TWENTY-ONE

AMID ALL THE jostling and the shock, it crossed George's mind he'd never been in an ambulance before.

The oxygen mask and the gurney straps limited his movement, so he couldn't get a good look at his chest. The woman with him—he wasn't sure if she was a paramedic or an EMT or something else—kept asking him questions. His name. What year it was. Who was President. He was pretty sure they were supposed to distract him.

The woman had strapped an oxygen mask over his face and stabbed at his arm with three different needles. She cut open his shirt and probed at his chest with her fingers. She pushed a wad of gauze against him and held it with one hand. The driver said something and she turned her head to talk over the sirens.

She looked worried.

He'd been shot. Madelyn had shot him at point-blank range. He'd seen enough cop shows to know what that meant. He was maybe an hour from death, crippled if he was lucky. He tried to wiggle his toes, and it felt like they moved, but he couldn't see them. He knew amputees felt phantom pain and itches in limbs they hadn't had for years.

He also remembered reading somewhere people never felt extreme pain. The human body had some kind of built-in system for deadening nerves. People never felt the full pain of broken bones or other severe injuries.

George felt a dull throb in his chest. Nothing else. Combined with the woman's worried expression, it had him on the edge of panic. He tried to talk but she pressed the oxygen mask against his face.

They pulled the gurney out of the ambulance and rolled him down a hallway. There were white panels and fluorescent tubes, just like the endless ones he changed at work. A new woman and two men leaned over him. He glimpsed a police uniform on one.

The gurney slipped through another door and came to rest inside a circle of curtains. The police officer had vanished. The new woman moved her hands around his chest. She was younger with dark hair tied back in a short ponytail. She pushed and prodded and asked if he could feel any pain. Then she vanished, too.

Had they given up on him? There was a word for it, when they stopped wasting resources on hopeless cases. His heartbeat felt strong. He wasn't having any trouble breathing. He couldn't feel anything in his chest. Even the dull ache had passed. He guessed it was all the shots they'd given him in the ambulance, even though his mind still felt very clear.

The dark-haired woman reappeared. "George," she said, "I'm Dr. Velez. We need to take some X-rays. It's just going to be a few minutes. Don't worry."

She was gone before he could ask anything. The gurney moved again, through the curtains and back into a hallway. It was chilly without a shirt on. A few minutes later a new face loomed over him. "George," the man said, "we're going to shift you." They didn't wait for him to respond, but lifted him onto a separate bed. It was cold, and a machine like a cannon loomed over him. The cannon made a loud click, he heard things clack beneath him, then another clack as the man switched something out.

Then he was back on the gurney and moving through more halls. He settled back inside the curtain just in time to hear people arguing. Velez reappeared. "We've got to do this again," she said. "Sorry." The ceiling shifted and he went back down a familiar hallway. They slid him under the X-ray machine again, the plates *click-clack*ed below him, and then he was headed back to the curtain room.

His hand felt its way across his torso. He couldn't feel any stitches or bandages. He wondered if he was numb.

He was there for twenty minutes before he heard a voice. "You," said Dr. Velez, "are a very lucky man." She patted him on the arm and unfastened the strap across his hips.

George looked at her, then craned his head to look at his bare chest. "What do you mean? Am I going to be okay?"

The doctor smiled. "You're going to be fine," she said.

He tried to think what "fine" could mean. "It missed organs," he said. "I've seen that on television, when the bullet goes through you but misses everything. Is that what happened?"

"Not exactly." She pulled an X-ray from an oversized folder and pushed it up into the light box. The black and gray image flared to life. In real life, an X-ray was a lot darker than they looked on television. She looked back at him and her stubby ponytail swished on her collar. "You the morbid type?"

"What?"

"Do you read about attempted suicides? Darwin Awards? That kind of stuff?"

"Now and then," he said. "No more than anyone else, I guess."

"Ever hear any of those stories where somebody gets shot in the head in just the right place, at just the right angle, and it bounces off?"

He looked at the X-ray, then back at the doctor. "What?"

"It's rare," she said, "but it does happen. Bones are strong. A lot stronger than people give them credit for. Think about the punishment you can put a body through, and figure the skeleton's taking most of it."

"I . . . I'm not sure what you mean."

She pointed at the gray skeleton on the light box and traced a line down the center of the rib cage. "You were shot, but the bullet hit you right on the sternum, between the fifth and sixth ribs."

His fingers pressed against the thick bone in his chest. It felt tender, but he couldn't find the wound. "What do you mean?"

"It bounced," she said. "Hit dead center against the bone and flicked off. No breaks, no fractures. Didn't even break the skin. You've got a bruise where it hit, but that's it." She tapped the X-ray with her pen. "Just the right place at just the right angle."

The temperature in the room seemed to rise three or four degrees. A wave of relief washed over him. "I'm not hurt?"

Velez shook her head. "A bit of shock, understandably, but I can't see anything. No fractures, lungs are clear, your heart's in sinus rhythm. We could do a CT scan, but if you're not in serious pain I think it'd just be a waste of time."

He tried to sit up, but she'd left the one strap across his chest. He bent his arms back to fumble with it. She walked back over and released the clasp. George sat up and looked down at his body. A faint purple-blue spot sat at the center of his chest. It was a little smaller than a quarter. It ached as he moved, just enough to remind him it was there.

He waved a hand at the dull X-ray. "You're sure there's nothing?"

"Positive."

"It's really dark."

"Yeah, we did two sets. The first films were dark and we thought it was bad stock. Turns out our machine needs maintenance, the levels are really down. Or maybe X-rays can't get through your skin, either." She smiled and winked. "Seriously, though, don't start thinking you're bulletproof or you'll end up right back here. Just be happy you can tell the coolest bar story ever. I can give you a prescription for some ibuprofen. Or just go home and have a good stiff drink. In a day or two you won't even feel it."

Dr. Velez pulled the curtain aside. Doctors flitted around the rest of the emergency room. George glimpsed what looked like a dog attack victim before another curtain was yanked shut. He heard the click of instruments on trays from the other side of the green cloth. "I don't mean to sound harsh," said Velez, "but if you feel well enough to walk, we could really use this bed for someone who needs it."

"Yeah, I see that," said George. He looked down at his stocking feet. "Do I have shoes somewhere?"

The doctor shook her head. "I think that's how you came in. Sorry."

He slid off the bed. The cold floor reached up through his socks and prickled his feet. He patted his backside. No wallet, either. It was still sitting back on his kitchen table with his phone.

He followed a line that led him to a set of wide double doors. No shoes, no shirt, no wallet, and he needed to get home from whatever hospital they'd brought him to. After he'd been shot. This was not going to be one of the better nights of his life.

He pushed through the doors into the waiting room. It was a large, antiseptic chamber with rows of blue plastic chairs and a television showing an episode of *Seinfeld*. The far wall was all windows and a sliding door to a glassed-in foyer that led out of the hospital.

The woman by the door was Karen Quilt. She stared at him from across the room. Her arms were crossed over a dark trench coat that looked made for substance more than style.

They looked at each other for a moment before she crossed the waiting room in eight long, precise strides. She settled less than a foot from him. "You were supposed to meet me for coffee."

"Yeah," said George. "I ended up meeting the President instead." A vein pulsed behind his eyes as the words left his mouth.

Her lips flattened out. "It is a very rare thing for a man to miss an appointment with me."

"I wasn't really given a choice."

"You also did not return my calls."

"Yeah," said George. "I was busy being shot."

"You did not return my calls before you were shot."

"Sorry. What are you doing here? It must be close to midnight."

She crossed her arms again. "I have been waiting for you. I heard the shooting reported on my father's police scanner. I went to your apartment to investigate, then came to make sure you were uninjured."

He patted the bruise on his sternum. "Pretty much, yeah," he said.

"There is no entry wound?"

"They think the bullet bounced off my rib cage."

She mulled over the idea.

"Did you say you investigated at my apartment?"

"It was important to examine the scene before the police contaminated it," Karen said. "While their methods are fine for standard crimes, I thought your shooting might require a more open interpretation of the facts."

"What's that supposed to mean?"

"Where are the rest of your clothes?"

He shrugged. "This is all I've got. I wasn't wearing shoes when they picked me up, and they cut my shirt up in the ambulance."

Her eyes ran down his body and back. "Wait here," she said.

"What? Why?"

She turned on her heel and stalked out the door.

George settled into a plastic chair and crossed his arms over his chest. It was odd, sitting around with no shirt on, but with the random homeless people scattered through the waiting room he didn't stand out too much. One bulky man was barefoot. Another one looked like he hadn't bathed in months. They both drew more stares than him.

He turned around and looked into the face of a little girl with pale eyes. She was standing on the chair behind him. Her teeth banged against each other as she chomped on her gum.

He was pretty sure she had gum.

She leaned toward him. George got up and the little girl tumbled over the seats to land where he'd been sitting. She didn't cry. She kept gnashing her teeth as she slid off the chair and onto the floor. He took a few more steps away, around one of the homeless people—a tangle-headed woman—and settled himself against one of the windows.

Shouldn't there be police waiting to do an interview? George thought. Take a statement or something like that? He looked around, but didn't see any uniforms or anyone who looked like they might be a detective.

It didn't feel chilly, but he could hear lots of teeth chattering in the waiting room. The little girl's father turned around to stare at George. The man's neck popped twice as he moved. The homeless woman had twin cataracts that made her eyes white. The nurse behind the counter let her jaw hang open as she stared. Her dark red lipstick contrasted with her ivory teeth.

He blinked and they looked away. The little girl whined. On the television, George Costanza tried to explain the difference between coffee and *coffee*.

The automatic door whisked open behind him. Karen reappeared with a large bag and handed it to him. "Everything should fit," she said.

He checked the inhabitants of the waiting room one more time, then looked in the bag. It held a new dress shirt, some generic-looking sneakers, and a pullover fleece with the hospital logo on it. He unwrapped the shirt and pulled out the first few pins. "Where did you get all this?"

"The hospital gift shop."

He saw the tag on the shirt wrapper and tried not to flinch at the gift shop prices. "How much do I owe you?"

She shook her head and brushed the question away with a wave of her hand.

He pulled the cardboard out from under the collar and unbuttoned the shirt. It was stiff and had sharp creases in the fabric, but it fit fine. He rolled his shoulders. "How'd you know my size?"

"I have been a runway model for twelve years," she said. "I can size someone on sight." She glanced at him as he buttoned up the shirt. "It is even simpler when they are not wearing clothes."

"I've got pants on," he said. He leaned against the door frame and pulled one of the shoes on. The sneaker had thick Velcro straps instead of laces. It was a perfect fit. He tugged the other one on.

"We should go," said Karen. "Now."

He looked up. The waiting room inhabitants were all staring again. A half dozen of them had climbed to their feet. The sound of chattering teeth echoed in the large room. They staggered toward George and Karen. The little girl was at the front of the small crowd.

Karen led him out the door and across the parking lot. He paused to stuff the bag and packing material in a trash can and then took a few quick steps to catch up with her. "It would be best if we did not separate," she said. She held up her keys and a sports car a few yards away chirped. "Whatever these hallucinations are, it is clear they are more difficult for you to process alone."

"Why do you say that?"

She looked at him. "Did you not say you had a meeting with the President?"

He tugged the fleece over his head. "Yeah, but that really happened." A spike pushed its way into his head as he spoke.

Her mouth flattened again. It wasn't much more than a line at this point.

"It did," he insisted. The spike in his head grew long barbs that pushed in every direction. He could feel them against the back of his eyes, his sinuses, scratching the inside of his skull. He ignored them.

Then he paused. "How did my car get here?"

Karen stood by a Tesla Roadster. It was a convertible, low to the ground and glossy black. It looked fast. "I beg your pardon?"

George pointed at the Hyundai. It was a few spaces down from the Tesla. "That's my car," he said. "Did you get someone to bring it here or something?"

She shook her head.

He walked over to it. He glanced at the back and recognized his license plate and the parking sticker from work. His battered Payless sneakers sat in the space behind the passenger seat.

The door was unlocked. He lowered himself into the seat. The ignition was empty. He glanced at the dish under the gear shift and saw the small collection of coins. He looked in the glove compartment and checked the CD holder strapped onto the sunscreen. "What do you think the chances are someone stole my car, didn't take anything, and ended up at the same hospital?"

"Unlikely." Karen studied the Hyundai. She placed a hand on the hood. "Is it possible you drove yourself here?"

He shook his head. "Up until about twenty minutes ago I thought I'd been shot and was going to die. I'm pretty sure I was deep in shock."

"People have driven vehicles under similar situations."

He got out and walked around to look at her over the hood. "So where are my car keys?"

She looked back at the hospital. "If you were in shock, it is not hard to believe you could have dropped your keys somewhere between your car and the entrance."

He shook his head. "I was brought in by an ambulance crew." He got out of the car. "I'll have to come back and get it later."

The engine started. It revved twice, hard enough to make the chassis tremble. The headlights lit up a nearby shrub and a section of cinder-block wall as they flickered on and off.

George and Karen exchanged a glance. "Are we seeing things?" he asked.

"Perhaps. I believe your car is attempting to communicate in Morse code."

"What?"

She gestured at the shrub. The headlights blinked in a series of long and short flashes. George watched for a moment before he saw the pattern.

"Is that an SOS?"

"The pattern it is repeating is OSO," said Karen, "which is why I said 'attempting.' It is a common mistake for those who do not know Morse code."

The engine growled and the pattern of flashes changed. The radio switched on and shouted some talk radio at them. Outside the car, with the engine running, it was just distorted squawks.

"Do you think it's going to turn into a giant robot?"

"Doubtful," Karen said, "but I am becoming more open to what I would normally consider foolish ideas. I believe we should contact Madelyn Sorensen. I would like to hear more of her insights into this other world we are glimpsing."

"That could be a little difficult," said George. "She's probably in a jail cell right now."

"Why?"

"She's the one who shot me."

Karen shook her head. "As of one hour ago no arrests had been made and no suspects named. Your next-door neighbor across the hall heard gunfire and called the police. She claimed she did not see the shooter."

"So she's still out there somewhere?"

"I believe she did not intend to hurt you, George. She believed you would not be harmed and was attempting to prove it."

"She could've just pricked me with a thumbtack or something. Next time I may not be so lucky."

Karen gave him an odd look.

He gestured at his chest. "Like I told you, it was a million-to-one shot. The next bullet could've—"

"The next bullet did nothing," said Karen.

"What?"

She stared at him over the car's hood. "I told you I examined the scene of the shooting," she said. "I discovered eleven bullets and shell casings. All were on the floor in the doorway of your apartment, all flattened from impact. Based on estimated range and damage to the surrounding walls, it was clear all of them struck some impenetrable object which had been removed since the shooting occurred."

George looked down at his chest.

"At this point," Karen said, "I believe it was taken away in an ambulance."

His hand slipped up onto his ribs. Even through the fleece and the crisp new shirt, he could feel the sore spot fading. "You're lying."

"All the evidence suggests Madelyn Sorensen fired eleven rounds into your chest. Six while you stood, five more once you were on the ground."

He rubbed his chest. His head was throbbing again. "The police would have said—"

"The police report said multiple shots fired. Their training tells them the bullets could not have hit you because that number of gunshot wounds would be fatal."

George shook his head. He could feel moisture swelling in his nostril. Another nosebleed getting ready to go.

"Were they all lucky shots?" Karen asked. "Did each and every one of them hit a bone and bounce off?"

"There was only one bruise," he said. It felt like a stupid excuse.

"I believe your doctor has succumbed to the same line of thinking as the police," said Karen, "rationalizing something she cannot explain with traditional knowledge. She claims one bullet hit your sternum and was deflected. I believe only one bullet struck a bone. The rest hit soft tissue in your shoulders, abdomen, or throat which absorbed the impact."

George remembered the huge pistol in Madelyn's hands. The sound of it going off in the narrow hallway. The punch in his chest. Had it been dead center? He'd been looking right down the barrel, so shouldn't the bullet have hit him . . .

Had she shot him in the head?

The pain behind his eyes faded a bit. He sniffed once, hard. The blood flow dried before it got severe enough to leak.

"Get in the car," he told her.

She looked at the Hyundai and raised an eyebrow. "My vehicle is better suited for any—"

"Just get in," said George. He got back into the car. The radio started to babble and he slapped it off. "I need to think, and it's not going to happen here."

TWENTY-TWO

UNDER OTHER CIRCUMSTANCES, George would've been having fun. Traffic had been heavy on the 101 and at a near standstill on the 405, but his Hyundai wove in and out of the lanes, slipping between other cars without a moment of hesitation. He considered turning on the radio for some driving music, but didn't want to risk more religious-show shouting in front of his passenger.

"You are an excellent driver," said Karen.

"Thank you, Rain Man," he said with a faint smirk.

The corner of her mouth trembled. It was the closest he'd seen her get to a smile. "Have you taken defensive driving courses?"

"Not that I remember."

The ever-so-faint smile vanished and he realized what he'd said.

In truth, the Hyundai was responding like a high-end sports car, as if it knew just what he wanted to do and predicted his moves. The steering wheel almost moved by itself. The car didn't slow down once until they pulled off the freeway in Santa Monica and waited on a red light.

A group of pedestrians made their way across the crosswalk. It was a large group for such a late hour, even in this part of town. They walked as if they'd all had a few too many drinks. Most of their clothes were ragged and soiled. A few of them stared at the Hyundai's windshield with chalky eyes.

The engine growled at them.

Karen turned her head to him. "Are you attempting to kidnap me?"

"What?"

"You are driving in an evasive pattern, to throw off followers. You have not told me our destination. I would be worth a considerable ransom if this was your plan."

He met her gaze and tried to figure out if she was joking. Then he shook his head. "The car's stopped," he said. "Your door's unlocked."

"I am aware of that."

"I think if you thought I was kidnapping you, I'd be unconscious in the backseat or something like that, right?"

She turned her eyes back to the road. "Something like that," she told him. "The light is green."

The gas pedal dropped away from George's heel and the steering wheel turned left in his hands. They wove around another car and headed west.

"Okay," he said. "There's a guy out in New Mexico. Barry Burke. He's been having the same dreams as us."

"Who is he?"

"I don't know. Madelyn told me about him. I know he's in a wheelchair, and I think he's a scientist."

"Have you contacted him?"

George nodded. "I talked to him on the phone for a few minutes. He works at a lab out there. Sands? Sandy?"

"Sandia Laboratories," she said. "Located in Albuquerque, New Mexico."

"Yeah. That's where I got hold of him."

The clock on the dashboard said it was one in the morning. Karen pulled her own cell from her pocket. "Do you have a home or cell phone number for him?"

George shook his head. "I was having . . . head issues."

She tapped three buttons and put the phone to her ear. "Albu-

querque, New Mexico," she said. "The number for Barry Burke."
There was a pause, and a distant, tinny voice. "May I have the
street names for all five?" Another pause. "That one, please."

"You found him?"

"I have. They are connecting me."

"Are you sure it's the right one?"

"There are three B. Burkes and two Barry Burkes listed in Albuquerque. The second Barry is on Wolf Creek Road, which is
just over half a mile from the Sandia Labs complex. A man for
whom traveling is complicated, such as a man in a wheelchair,
would most likely choose to live as close to work as possible."

"They told you where the road was?"

"I have memorized street maps of all fifty state capitals, along
with several other major cities such as Los Angeles, San Diego,
Dallas— Good evening," she told the phone. "I am trying to reach
Barry Burke."

* * *

Barry knew his dreams were of the geek persuasion.

In his dreams he always wore X-ray specs, just like on the
back cover of old comic books, except these worked. People were
walking skeletons surrounded by sparkling muscles and infra-
red auras, all wrapped in a glowing nimbus of electromagnetism.
He could pick out individual wavelengths and energetic particles
like a kid sifting through a bin of Legos. He could see fillings and
surgical pins and pacemakers by the way they twisted and bent
the magnetic waves.

And he could fly.

Which was good, because the other part of his dreams was
sci-fi/horror geek stuff. Dead people filled every street and
crowded around buildings. Hungry dead people. Their teeth
clacked together again and again. The noise was like a hundred
kids shaking a thousand dice in their hands at once. It was the
sound of the saving throw you could never hope to pass.

They were the undead. They were ghouls. They were . . .

Frak, he thought, what the hell were they?

His voice was always distorted in his dreams. He'd never questioned it. It was probably related to the way people couldn't recognize recordings of their own voice. Something about cranial resonance and sound waves. In his dreams, he sounded like a bad '50s robot. Or a kazoo.

On a normal dream-night he fought the waves of the undead with blasts of pure energy—blasts of *him*—that turned them to ash. It was like aiming a BFG, and the blasts did tons of collateral damage if he wasn't careful. Even if the dead things got close enough to touch him, his skin burned them away.

His skin was white in his dreams. Milk white. High-watt fluorescent light white. And kind of blurry. He was sure some psychologists would have a field day with that. It didn't bother him.

He also fought side by side with a giant robot, which was cool. And the robot was also strangely attractive. Sometimes, despite the flying and the undead and the X-ray vision, it felt like things were tipping into a very different kind of dream. Although flying was supposed to indicate a different type of dream anyway.

This dream had the flying and the undead and the giant robot. But then he heard a low sound, like a brass horn section warming up. The noise rose over the chattering teeth in slow pulses and grew louder by the moment. The robot didn't seem to hear it. Barry looked around and tried to figure out where it was coming from.

And then Barry recognized the sound. It was the sound of a blue police box, a kind that hadn't been used in over fifty years, materializing out of the time vortex. His heart raced for a moment, and then he realized his phone was ringing.

Then he realized he was awake.

"Damn it," he grumbled.

He rolled himself over. The phone's brightness made him wince. He closed his eyes and felt around on the nightstand until the phone was in his hand. He glanced at the screen and saw **Blocked** as he answered. The voice on the other end was naming cities. "You better be very pretty or offering me a lot of money," he said.

"Good evening," said the woman. "I am trying to reach Barry Burke."

"This is he," said Barry with a yawn. "So is it pretty or money?"

"I am calling about your dreams."

He was much more awake, just like that. "Who is this?"

"I believe we have a mutual friend. I am with George Bailey."

He chuckled. "George Bailey, the loveable martyr of Bedford Falls? The guy who runs the Building and Lo—wait! George?" He sat up in bed. "You're with George?"

"I am."

"Hey," called another voice beyond the phone. Barry remembered it from a few days ago, and from countless nights. He'd been kicking himself for not getting the other man's number before they lost their connection.

"You have been having dreams of another life," said the woman.

"Yes," said Barry.

"A life where the world is overrun with animated corpses and you possess some form of superhuman abilities or powers."

"Yes," he said. "Yes I have. Are you one of the final five Cylons, too?"

"I believe the answer to that would be yes."

"Wow." Barry shifted himself back so he could lean against the bed's headboard. "Okay, question for you. Do you know who George Romero is?"

"Our mutual friend has already shared this question with me. I also do not know the proper name of Romero's creations."

"Damn it."

"A few moments ago you made a popular culture reference to the television series *Battlestar Galactica*, correct?"

"Yeah," he said. "You sound very pretty, so please don't tell me you're one of those freaks who think the original series was better."

"You are a follower of such genre material."

"A follower?" he echoed with a chuckle. "Yeah, I am. Do you know me?"

"Please name another science-fiction series which is currently being aired."

"What?"

"*Battlestar Galactica* aired almost five years ago. Can you name a network series since then? One on the air or even one which was canceled?"

Barry racked his brain. He'd been watching reruns of the second season of *Chuck* with a bit of *Deep Space Nine*, the later stuff where the Dominion War really took off. He tried to think of anything new that stood out. He'd been meaning to check out the new season of *Doctor Who*, but realized he wasn't sure which season that was. Had the BBC taken another weird on-again, off-again hiatus, like they did with Tennant's last year in the lead role? For that matter, what season was *Chuck* in? And how had *LOST* ended? He was pretty sure it wasn't on the air anymore, but couldn't remember a final episode.

"Mr. Burke?"

"Give me a minute."

He couldn't even think of any new cartoons. Every morning with breakfast he'd been watching an episode of *Battle of the Planets*. He knew it was soft-core by some standards, but he'd grown up on this version before he'd ever heard of the original *Gatchaman*. And off that thought another memory shoved its way forward.

"Oh my God," he said. "You're the ninja."

"I beg your pardon."

"In my dreams," said Barry. "I recognize your voice. You're the ninja. You've got guns. And a cape."

There was a pause. "Shall I take this to mean you cannot name a current television show?"

"I just told you you're a ninja with guns and you still want to talk about television?"

"It is more important," said the woman on the phone. "Have any elements of your dreams appeared in the real world?"

"Sorry, what?"

"Have you seen any elements from your dreams while you were awake?"

"Like a guy in a red and green sweater with a glove made of knife blades?"

"The walking dead."

"Ahhh. No, not that I can . . ."

There'd been a staff meeting a few days ago, right after George's call, when his coworkers had gotten quiet and looked very pale under the office lights. They'd all stared at him without blinking for a moment, then the meeting continued as if nothing had happened. And there was a smell in his office he couldn't track down, a sort of under-scent of mildew and rot. It clung to everything. Sometimes he even brought it home with him.

"Maybe," he said. "I think maybe I have, yeah."

There was a pause on the other end. Then the woman spoke again. "I believe it is in our best interests to be together," she told him. "Can you travel to Los Angeles?"

A handful of thoughts flashed through Barry's head. The casual meeting he was supposed to have with Mike from maintenance about the smell. Jerry and Vanessa talking about component testing schedules. Keith asking for reports. His weekly Warhammer game with the guys down at the store.

He thought about his dreams and how right they felt. Not just in a geek-fulfillment sense. In a simple, basic sense. Speaking to the woman on the phone, speaking to George, he knew his dreams were true.

"Yes," said Barry. "Yes I can. I can be on the first flight out of the Sunport and be in LA before ten o'clock."

"I will arrange for a car to pick you up at LAX."

"Cool," he said. "I'll see you then."

She hung up and he set the phone down. He thought about what he'd just agreed to, and was pretty sure it was going to mean the end of his career at Sandia. They were always on a tight budget, and he wasn't high enough up the chain to have any sort of protection. He was throwing it all away over a dream.

A dream where he could fly.

Barry reached up and grabbed the handle over his bed. Most folks called it a trapeze, but he always felt if you were going to tell people you had a trapeze over your bed it needed to live up to certain expectations. He pulled up on the handle and swung his body across the bed and out over his wheelchair. His legs dragged behind him.

It was a little after two in the morning. He could be packed and ready to go by three-thirty and at the airport by five. Then he just needed an accommodating flight.

* * *

"He will be here in the morning," Karen told George. "I will have my father pick him up at the airport."

He glanced at her from the driver's seat. "Is that wise?"

"How so?"

"I mean . . . well . . ." He tried to think of a polite way to phrase his worry and gave up. "Is it safe for your dad to go to an airport?"

Her eyebrow went up.

"Isn't he kind of . . . wanted?"

The corners of her mouth trembled again. The almost-smile. "My father long ago perfected the art of hiding in plain sight. If he does not want to be noticed, he will not be. How else could he be staying in a hotel surrounded by paparazzi?"

George decided to call the matter closed. "Okay, then," he said.

They were still on surface streets. Somewhere deep in Santa Monica. He didn't know exactly where, but according to the street numbers he'd hit the beach in another dozen blocks if he kept heading down the road they were on. After that . . .

"Let's stop and get a beer," he said.

Her eyebrow went back up.

"We're driving around with no plan and the car's got a quarter tank of gas. Let's stop and make some kind of plan."

She glanced at her phone. "Last call will be in the next fifteen minutes at most establishments."

They passed two clubs before settling on a bar. George parked across the street, went to shut off the engine, and realized he still didn't have a key. The engine revved. It sounded like a grumble.

"We'll be right back," he said to the dashboard. "Half an hour at the most."

The car revved again and then turned itself off.

"You are talking to your car," said Karen.

"I don't know if you noticed," he said, "but the car's talking back."

She opened her mouth to respond, but decided against it.

They walked across the wide road. An oversized man sat on a tall chair near the bar's door. A tall table with a desk light and a beach umbrella created a small check-in station. The doorman looked up from his book when he saw them approaching and straightened up. George went to reach for his wallet and realized it was back at his apartment, but the man waved them through with a broad smile at Karen. He took a quick step to make it clear they were together. It felt awkward, and under the stark lights the folds in his shirt stood out. They scraped on his arm and he had to make an effort not to scratch and draw more attention to them. The itch moved up to his bicep and he raked his fingers across it.

The bouncer shook his head and smirked. George scratched at the itch again and the man's smirk broke into a wide smile. He had bad teeth. One of his incisors was missing.

The bar could hold a hundred people, but it was almost empty. Two men sat in the booth farthest from the door, and a man and two women sat in the one closest. A woman in a dark T-shirt cleared a table that looked like it had held a fair-sized party in the recent past. A half-dozen young student types—film students, said something in George's university-experienced mind—chattered away at the other end of the bar. George heard enough names and terms to grasp they were having a serious talk about comedy. One of them started reciting lines about Winchesters and pints with a bad British accent.

A thick-built man with thinning hair was wiping down the bar as they walked in. He glanced over his shoulder at the clock as they reached him. "Only got time for one," he said. "What can I get you?"

George pointed at one of the taps. Karen examined the row of bottles behind the bar and ordered a vodka martini. A few moments later the bartender presented their drinks and vanished to get final orders from the film types.

Karen held the stem of her glass and lifted it to her lips. The liquid shifted, touched her tongue, and she set the glass down on the bar napkin. The base of the martini glass was centered on the square of paper. "And now?" she asked him.

George sipped his beer. "I'm not sure," he admitted.

They sat in silence for a moment. Neither of them touched their drinks.

"I got shot a few hours ago," he said.

She waited for him to continue.

"I was shot, and the day before that I was snatched by the feds and my apartment was trashed. And I think I met—"

A spike of pain shoved into the back of his skull. The room spun for a moment. He winced. The tip of his nose felt wet.

"I think I met the President and the First Lady."

She let the martini brush against her tongue again. "Why do you think you met the President?"

"Because I remember it."

"No," said Karen. "Why did the incident occur?"

"They thought I might be—" The spikes pushed at his eyes again. He ignored them and forced his memories forward. "He wanted to know if I knew him."

"The President?"

"Yeah," said George. "Madelyn said—" The spikes shot forward another quarter inch. They grew thorns. He could picture them making deep dimples across the back of his eyeball. "Madelyn said he can make people believe things. He's from somewhere else, like us."

She slid the bar napkin out from under her drink and held it out to him. "Your nose is bleeding again."

"I know," he said. "I think . . . I think it bleeds when I get too close to the truth. And the truth is, a crazy girl told me I had superpowers, and then she shot me a dozen times in the chest and it didn't do anything." He tugged at the shirt and looked down past his chin. "I think the bruise is already fading."

She reached across the bar and pulled two more napkins from a small tray. The bartender glanced over and saw George with the wad of red paper. "You okay, buddy?" he called over.

"Fine," said George. He wrapped his fingers around the napkin to hide most of the blood. "Don't worry about it."

"For the sake of argument," said Karen, "let us assume everything Madelyn has told you is true. We are superheroes trapped in some alternate universe or time stream."

"It sounds a lot more believable when you say it," George said.

"If this is all true," she continued, "why would we go back? This world offers us everything we would have tried to achieve. It is free of the dead creatures which overwhelmed that reality."

"But it's not where we're supposed to be," he said. "If she's right, it means there's another world out there that was depending on us. A world we've abandoned, even if we didn't know we were doing it." He dabbed at his nose again with a fresh napkin.

Karen stared at him for a moment. "The perfect prison," she said.

"Sorry?"

"Prisons are built around certain inherent ideas, chief among them being the prisoners do not wish to be there and the threat of death or injury overrides the desire to escape. For people such as you and I, that threat is greatly reduced, if not nullified. So how does someone imprison us?"

George folded the napkin in half.

"They create a prison we have no reason or desire to escape from."

At the end of the bar the students had shifted topics. Two of them were acting out a scene from something. It took George a moment to recognize the skit.

She followed his gaze. "Is there a problem?"

"No," he said. "I don't think so. It's just . . . This may sound stupid, but I've been hearing a lot of Monty Python lately."

Karen looked at him for a moment. "This is important how?"

"I don't know," he admitted. "It's just kind of weird. All these years on campus, I must've heard people doing Monty Python skits a few thousand times. But I can't remember anyone ever doing Steven Wright, Seinfeld, Eddie Izzard . . . anyone else. It's always old Python stuff."

"I am not familiar with their individual skits," she admitted.

A slim man with glasses raised his voice to a near-manic tone. "It's a stiff!" he shrieked. "Bereft of life. It rests in peace! If you hadn't nailed him to the perch he would be pushing up the daisies!"

George waved down the bartender. "Sorry," he told the beefy man. He nodded at the group at the far end of the bar. "Are they in here often?"

The other man shot a quick glance at the film types. "We get a lot of those folks in here. There's a couple of little production companies in the buildings across the street. They too loud?"

George shook his head. "No, I just . . . What's that skit they're acting out? It's on the tip of my brain and I can't think of it."

The bartender smirked. "It's Monty Python."

"Yeah, but what's the actual piece they're doing?"

The beefy man shrugged and turned his head. "Hey, Shaun?"

The skinny man paused in his recitation and returned the gaze. He had blue eyes behind wire-rimmed glasses.

"What's that sketch you're doing?"

"It's classic Python," said Shaun. "The parrot sketch."

Parrots.

Shaun and his partner, a man with horn-rims and shockingly blond hair, picked up the sketch, turning themselves to face their new audience. Their voices rose to match, reaching a manic pitch in the reenactment.

"If you hadn't nailed him to the perch," repeated the thin man, getting back into the part, "he'd be pushing up the daisies! His metabolic processes are now history! He's off the twig! He's kicked the bucket, he's shuffled off his mortal coil. It's run down the curtain and joined the choir invisible! This," Shaun declared emphatically, "is an *ex*—"

A railroad spike slammed into George's skull. Just before the pain forced his eyes closed he saw Karen's hands fly to her own head. He heard her shift in her chair, and a faint grunt of pain.

His skull cracked and let in a brilliant light. It was so bright closing his eyes did nothing. Covering them with his hands made no difference. No matter what he did, he could still see it.

He forced his eyes open against the searing pain and looked at Karen. She was already staring at him. Her eyes were wide. He slid his hand across the bar and she seized it with a grip like a vise. George felt blood run across his lips, enough that he heard it splash on the bar.

"Hey," said the bartender, "you two okay?"

Memories poured into George's head like molten steel, burning everything else away even as they cooled and hardened. He saw himself. He saw his world. He saw *them*.

The undead.

The zombies.

The ex-humans.

A ripple washed over him and made the hair on his arms stiffen. A smell that had lurked in the background rose to the fore. It was the twin scents of must and mildew, and the tangy odor of rot lurked behind them like an aftertaste. He looked at the small puddle of blood on the dusty bar. His beer bottle crumbled away into a few shards of broken glass. The napkin under it collapsed and left a square of fragments and dust.

In his peripheral vision, a handful of people in the bar vanished.

The rest of them died.

The dead ones turned to stare. Their eyes were balls of chalk. Their skin was brittle pages from old books.

Their jagged teeth tapped together. It was a sharp, hard noise. The sound of crackling glass and clicking pens and beads hitting the side of a fan again and again. The sound echoed in the bar.

He pushed himself off the bar stool.

And St. George, the Mighty Dragon, stood to face the exes.

TWENTY-THREE

THE PLACE HAD been well looted. The shelves behind the bar were empty, and had been for years if the dust meant anything. What couldn't be carted away had been smashed. Broken glass was everywhere. The padded cushions of the booth had been torn out.

St. George counted fifteen exes in the bar. The dead couple in the closest booth were trapped by the table, unable to rise and not smart enough to move to the side. One of the exes from the far booth had already fallen onto the floor. It crawled across the bar toward them.

Most of the film types were still there. Shaun was a desiccated husk. Its glasses hung loose off one ear. The half dozen or so exes around it banged their teeth together and shuffled around to face the heroes. Their arms reached for them. The ex with the blond hair raised hands that had three fingers between them. It looked like they'd been torn off in the same incident that had claimed the dead man's chin and nose.

"You see them," asked Karen. It was a confirmation more than a question.

No, not Karen, he corrected himself.

She was Stealth.

"Yeah," he said. He pointed around the room. "Two there, another four, I think seven over there. The doorman by the entrance. I don't see the server anywhere." He glanced over his shoulder. "And the bartender."

The bartender snapped its jaws behind them. Its cheek hung open on a flap of pale flesh and showed off a row of yellowed teeth. One of them stood out, bright white against the others. St. George figured it was an implant. The dead man's fingers reached across the bar and brushed St. George's arm.

Stealth rolled her shoulders inside her trench coat. She'd loosened the belt to give herself a better range of motion, but he could see it still pulled in the shoulders. Her fingers flexed in the thin leather gloves and batted away the bartender's grasping fingers.

"I'll take care of the big group," he said. "Can you get the others?"

"Of course."

"Do you have any weapons?"

Stealth raised an eyebrow at him. "George," she said, "have you ever known me to need a weapon?"

She turned and snapped out a punch like a snake striking. It caught the dead bartender on the bridge of the nose. There was a sharp crack as the bone pushed back into the skull and its face flattened out. The ex collapsed behind the bar.

He smiled. "Good to have you back."

"And you."

St. George stepped forward and caught the dead thing that had been Shaun by the neck. He lifted the ex off its feet and snapped its neck with a quick shift of his thumb and forefinger. The dead man's jaws kept snapping at him even as its arms and legs sagged. He hurled the body back into the crowd and knocked down two of the others.

Not as strong as he should be, he noticed. That throw should've taken out the whole crowd. He wondered if it was some sort of residual block in his mind.

Behind him, Stealth brought her boot down on the crawling ex. It slammed face-first into the floor and left a dark stain on the carpet. A second kick to the back of the head made the dead man slump. A puddle of dark liquid spread out from under its head.

St. George grabbed another ex and twisted its head around. A third one, the blond man, latched onto his arm and bit down on his elbow. The ex's teeth left a sticky circle on his sleeve and then splintered apart. He brushed the teeth fragments out of the fleece and then drove his fist through the blond man's face.

The front of the zombie's head collapsed beneath his punch and his knuckles broke out the back. For a moment the dead man's skull hung on his wrist like an oversized bracelet, the limp body dangling beneath it. St. George shook his arm until the rest of the head cracked apart and the corpse fell free. It hit the ground with a thump. He kicked it away and it crashed into the booth where the two exes struggled with the table.

Another step and he grabbed two more exes, a dead man in a suit and a slim woman with bristle-short hair. Their teeth beat out a constant *click-click-click*. He swung them and their skulls cracked together like billiard balls. Another swing and both of them slumped to the floor.

The last of the film types stumbled toward him and he grabbed its outstretched hands. A twist of his wrist spun the dead woman around and dislocated one of its arms. He put his hand on its back and pushed. The ex flew across the bar and crashed over a table.

Something slammed into his back. The oversized doorman. Its jaws swung open, and St. George realized it was missing most of its teeth. A collection of splinters stuck up from its lower gums. Shards of bone and enamel were white against its dark tongue.

It bit down hard on his shoulder and what was left of its teeth turned to dust. He reached up, put his hand on its forehead, and shoved it away. The needles left in its jaw tore furrows in his shirt as it staggered back. Its gnashing jaws made a sound St. George could only describe as pulpy.

He took a step after the dead man and brought his hand around. The edge of his palm tore through soft flesh and brittle bones. The zombie's head rolled to one side even as the momentum of the blow carried it to the other. It spun off the ex's shoulders and fell to the floor. The body crashed on top of it a moment later.

St. George flicked some of the gore off his fingers. He turned and Stealth looked at him. A trio of exes slumped on the floor at her feet. "Most impressive," she said. "You seem confident in your abilities."

He looked at the bodies scattered around the bar. "To be honest, I'm just acting on instinct," he said. "There's still a lot of stuff going on in my head."

"I understand. I am having similar issues trying to distinguish my own history from this alternate one." She dropped to her knee and drove a punch into the back of an ex's neck as it tried to rise. There was a loud pop and it collapsed.

He glanced at the door, and then up. "Do you think these shifts affect all of us at the same time?"

"I do not have enough data to predict such a thing." She walked over and took his hand. Her fingers felt good threaded between his. "You are worried about Barry?"

St. George nodded. "It would suck to be him if he was in mid-air on a plane and shifted back to our world."

Her eyebrow twitched. "If such a thing happened, his own abilities would most likely activate on instinct to save his life."

"We don't know that, though," said St. George. "I'm still feeling kind of weak, and most of my other powers haven't kicked in." To emphasize the point, he glanced down at his feet. He tried to make them rise, but they stayed on the floor of the bar. There was a trick to getting off the ground, but he couldn't remember it. He flexed his toes, tried to imagine rockets thrusting out of his feet, pictured huge wings lifting him into the air.

He stayed on the ground.

"From what I understand," said Stealth, "you have not needed your abilities past strength and invulnerability. I am sure I could throw you from the top of any structure of significant height and your ability to fly would reassert itself."

"Thanks," he said. "I love you, too."

"I am still unsure what has caused this—"

"Smith," said St. George. "He's back."

Her mouth snapped shut. "Are you certain?"

"Who's the President right now?"

Her lips pressed even tighter together. She remembered Agent Smith, formerly of the Department of Homeland Security.

"Madelyn knew," St. George said. "She's never even met him, but she knew all along. She tried to tell me, but the way he'd rewired my brain made me reject the idea. I told her she was crazy."

"It would seem you owe her an apology," said Stealth.

"Yeah. I'm guessing he found something out at Groom Lake that let him send us into another reality or something. Then he rewired our brains so we'd never know."

She looked at him and raised an eyebrow. "This is not another reality, George."

"Sorry?"

"This is our world. I suspected as much for some time, but knowing Smith is involved confirms it. He altered our perceptions so we did not see reality. This is why the exes were erased from our minds, so we would not realize what was around us."

He shook his head. "That's not possible."

She pointed past him to the decapitated ex on the floor. "Its teeth were broken."

"Yeah, so?"

"They were recently broken," she said. "There was little discoloration on the inside edges and there were still shards in its mouth."

"Okay, and . . . ?"

She gave him the look that told him he'd missed something obvious. "There is only one thing in the bar it could've broken its teeth on, George."

It took him another moment. "Me?"

"When we entered the bar you scratched your left arm. The arm closest to the doorman."

"The shirt's kind of itchy. It's still got those right-out-of-the-package folds that are pretty much starched into it."

"The doorman was an ex. It was biting you."

"No it wasn't."

"It was."

St. George shook his head. "He sat on his stool the whole time. I would've noticed if he was chewing on me."

Her eyebrow went up again and she looked at her arm. "Much in the same way Captain Freedom thought he would have noticed if ninety-three percent of the people at Project Krypton had died?"

When they'd first met the captain, his entire base had been under Smith's influence. They believed they were a thriving military base with over fifteen hundred soldiers and support staff. Then the heroes had arrived and revealed that barely a hundred people were there.

St. George shook his head. "This isn't convincing us things are a bit better than we thought they were, though. This is him telling us things are completely different. It just seems way beyond what we saw him do before." He tugged at the sleeve of his fleece. "And if we aren't hopping between worlds, where did this come from? It's not mine."

Stealth didn't respond. She was studying her arms. She pushed the sleeve up on one and ran a finger across the skin.

"Wait," he said, "are you okay? Did you get bitten?"

"I did not," she told him. "I have no injuries at all."

He sighed in relief.

"I am, however, also wondering where these clothes came from."

He looked at her outfit. "They're not yours?"

She shook her head. "I have only three civilian outfits at the Mount. All of them were chosen to be inconspicuous. Each of these items has been tailored to me."

"Are you sure?"

She raised an eyebrow at him.

"So if we're not jumping between worlds, where did you get a tailored outfit?"

"I am not sure. It is possible Smith had them constructed to add to the illusion of another world." She pushed the sleeve back down. "Our first priority is to locate the others. You know where Madelyn is?"

"Yeah. And Freedom, Gorgon, and . . ."

He stopped. He closed his eyes for a moment. He took a breath and opened them again.

She was looking at him. Her eyes had the faint wrinkle at the corner that let him know she was concerned. "Gorgon?"

"Yeah," he said. "I forgot. I forgot he was dead. I've been dreaming about a lot of dead people."

She reached out and squeezed his hand. "Madelyn and Freedom, then."

He nodded. "They're over in Westwood, but they're both alone. We get them, we figure out where the hell Barry and Danielle are, and then we get back to the Mount."

Her eyebrow twitched again and an expression that looked like confusion flitted across her face. Then she bowed her head. "I concur."

He walked to the door. It was a solid piece of wood at least an inch thick with no windows or peepholes. He rapped his knuckles against it four times and waited.

The other side of the door was silent.

They exchanged looks. He pushed the door open and slipped outside. Stealth was a beat behind him.

The street was deserted. Nothing moved. Nothing made a sound. They moved past the sidewalk and into the street, keeping their backs to each other.

"East is clear as far as I can see," said St. George.

"As is west." She held up her hand when he went to speak again. She turned her head to the north, then to the south. "I hear nothing," she said.

"Neither do I."

"I hear *nothing*," she repeated. "There is no sound of teeth."

St. George closed his eyes and listened. He turned and looked around. "What are the odds there isn't a single ex within four or five blocks?"

"Low," said Stealth. "The street is clean. No leaves, no trash, no debris of any kind. However, all nine streetlights I can see from this position are unlit."

"My car's gone," said St. George. He looked up and down the street. "Actually, weren't there at least four or five parked on the street when we went in?"

"There were six on this block," said Stealth, "not counting your own Hyundai. Two Fords, two Hondas, a Chrysler, and a Volkswagen."

A low growl made them turn. St. George balled his fists. Stealth raised an eyebrow. She didn't look worried.

The car roared around the corner and lit them up with its headlights. The vehicle shot toward them without slowing. It tore down the road with its driver's-side tires riding on the line of yellow dashes. Stealth took two quick steps back to the sidewalk. St. George stood his ground and stared into the headlights. The car missed him by inches. It was an old Mustang, a classic muscle car. Half of its body panels were still bare primer, the other half were glossy black.

It slowed at the corner stop sign, long enough for the driver to give St. George the finger and call out a few muffled insults. Then the Mustang rumbled back up to full speed and vanished down the street. The sound of its engine echoed in the air for a few moments and then faded away.

"Son of a bitch," said St. George. He blinked away a few spots the headlights had left in his eyes. The street stayed bright even after the spots vanished.

They looked around at the street. Now there were five cars scattered along the curb on either side of the road, gleaming in the streetlights. One of the Hondas was gone, replaced with a small drift of leaves. George's Hyundai was still nowhere to be seen.

In the distance, he heard the faint rumble of more cars. The bars were closing down and people were either heading home or out to after-parties. Most of them were heading east or south toward the freeways.

"Your hands are clean."

He looked down. The smears of blood and dark tissue across his knuckles had vanished. The stains on the fleece jacket were gone, too. He looked over his shoulder at the bar. "Okay," he said, "as far as everyone in there knows, did we just run out without paying for our drinks?"

"Focus, George," she said.

"We don't want them calling the cops on us."

"There are no police to call. This is all just an illusion."

"Right." He looked west. "How long do you think it'll take us to reach Westwood on foot?"

Stealth flexed her fingers. "It depends on what we find on the way."

TWENTY-FOUR

FREEDOM RAN PAST the packs of homeless people gathered around a few grates. People assumed Los Angeles was always sunny and wonderful, but the past few years had taught him otherwise. There wasn't any snow, but it got cold enough at night to endanger anyone's health. Even now, half an hour before sunrise, he caught wisps of his breath.

His morning run was almost done. It was a winding route from his Hancock Park apartment, through Beverly Hills, and then down to the recruiting office. He'd measured it out to an even eight miles. He ran it every day, rain or shine, in under forty-five minutes, depending on traffic lights. At the end of the day he ran it home.

The Army may have been done with him, but he was determined to stay worthy of his uniform.

There were more street people all along his route. They held out desperate hands as he strode past them. There seemed to be hundreds of them these days. He knew the economic crash had left many people in a bad place, but it seemed like the number of homeless had doubled or tripled in the past few months. A few of them tried to follow him every morning and night. They'd stagger toward him with their hands out, mouthing silent pleas. At his pace, they fell behind before most of them even reacted to his passing. He tried not to think about them while he ran.

Sometimes, though, in the deserted city of predawn, there was something unnerving about them. In the shadows their poses and sluggish movements struck him as aggressive, even a bit dangerous. He wasn't sure why. Their hands seemed less pleading and more ... hungry.

There was one stretch of Wilshire Boulevard that cut through the Los Angeles Country Club, right between Beverly Hills and Westwood. Tall hedges bordered the road on either side. If he encountered other pedestrians or bicyclists here, it meant stepping off the curb and running in the road. There was nowhere else to go for two-thirds of a mile. On those dark mornings, when the homeless were gathered there, he often thought of it as Donner Pass. He wasn't sure what made him pull that particular name from history. The street wasn't high in the mountains or buried in snow. Which left one option. The hungry option.

At West Point he'd had a recurring dream after writing a paper on the Donner Party and how their situation could've been resolved aside from resorting to cannibalism. The dream had come back, as of late, and he'd had it two or three times in the past month. Maybe more.

In his dream, however, eating other men hadn't been a last resort. The settlers had changed into soldiers under his command. He was a captain again, in charge of leading them to safety, but he kept getting conflicting orders from the President for them to stay put. Then the whole group, dozens of men and women with skin gray from frostbite, came at him like some ancient horde. Their teeth snapped at his fingers, their hungry hands grabbed at his arms and neck.

Wilshire sloped down a steep incline toward the Federal Building and 405 (he still hadn't picked up the Californian habit of addressing all freeways as "the"). Freedom pumped his arms and thrust his legs at the ground. Banks, stores, and apartment buildings flew past him. There was no traffic on the road to judge his speed by, but he was sure he was breaking the posted speed limit.

He cut down Manning Avenue and slowed to a walk when he hit Lindbrook, still three blocks from the office. There was something on the sidewalk up ahead. For a moment he thought a car might've gone up over the curb. Whatever it was had more than enough mass.

Then the shapes firmed up in the morning haze. A dozen crates and shipping containers, the super-sturdy ones edged with steel, sat in front of the recruiting office. They reminded him of the cases he'd seen at traveling USO shows, the ones designed to hold equipment.

A woman half leaned in the door frame behind one of the larger cases. Her head was turned away from Freedom, and her red hair was twisted into a messy braid. She wore jeans, but her top was an Army Combat Uniform jacket with fuzzy patches instead of insignia. Her arms were crossed in a way that seemed more defensive than casual.

He let his boots hit the ground a little harder as he covered the last few yards between them. The slap echoed along the sidewalk and she turned. Her face was dotted with freckles. Just enough to keep her looking young, although the scowl lines around her mouth helped cancel it out. "Good morning, ma'am," he called out to her.

"Morning," she said. "You Freedom?"

He held out his hand across the crate. "Lieutenant Freedom. What can I do for you?"

She pried one of her arms away from her chest, took his hand, and shook it once. "Dr. Danielle Morris," she said. "I'm supposed to do a recruitment demonstration for your office?"

"I wasn't expecting you so early."

He released her hand and the arm folded back to her chest. "They wanted to drop everything off before breakfast. I'm guessing rush hour is pretty nasty around here?"

Freedom gestured at the eight-lane street with his chin. "This is going to be pretty close to a parking lot in another hour. Didn't mean you had to come, though, ma'am. The demonstration's not until noon."

Dr. Morris patted the crate in front of her. "Cerberus is still my baby," she said. "I go where it goes."

Freedom kept his face straight and managed not to grind

his teeth. Another civilian who didn't understand schedules. He glanced at the crates. "So this is it?"

"Yep. The Cerberus Battle Armor System."

Freedom looked up and down the street. "Weren't you a little worried leaving all this on the sidewalk, ma'am?"

"I didn't leave it," she said. "I've been with it the whole time."

"I meant, weren't you worried someone might take it?"

"Again," she said, "sitting here the whole time. Plus, these are all a little too heavy for a snatch and grab." She gestured at one of the cases, a two-foot cube, with her chin. Her arms seemed glued to her chest. "That's the lightest one and it's close to a hundred pounds."

He studied her for a moment. "Are you all right, ma'am?"

"I'm fine."

"Because you seem a bit tense."

"I'm fine, I just ..." Dr. Morris took a deep, calming breath and forced her arms down to her sides. "Can we get inside? I don't ... I'd rather talk inside."

The crates were about five feet from the recruiting office doorway. He glanced between the entrance and the pile a few times. "Is it just you?"

"The rest of my team should be showing up around ten. They're still back at the hotel." She followed his gaze. "I was told there'd be a hand truck," she said.

"There may be," he said. "Do you mind waiting a few more minutes while I check the back room?"

She closed her eyes for a moment. "Sure. No problem."

After unlocking the door and deactivating the alarm, Freedom learned there was, indeed, a hand truck. He pushed two cases of flyers off it with his foot and wrestled it out through the office. She looked relieved to see him again, and even more relieved once she stepped inside.

It took just under half an hour for him to work the crates through the door and stack them in front of Taylor's desk. Dr. Morris watched from just inside the door and gave instructions as he loaded and tilted the cases. He could tell she was trying not to snap at him when one of them bumped the door frame.

When he was done he let the door swing closed. Her shoulders relaxed a little when the latch clicked. "Better, ma'am?" he asked.

"Yeah," she said. "I'm sorry for acting strange."

"Quite all right."

"I have agoraphobia," she said. "It's usually pretty mild, I just felt . . . I don't know, really exposed out there. And I'm sorry if I messed up anything you had planned."

"Beg your pardon, ma'am?"

She waved a hand at the cases stacked in the center of the office. "I pissed off a lot of people insisting on this trip, didn't I?"

"I couldn't say."

She smirked. "Couldn't or won't?"

"I couldn't say."

"Yeah, that's what I thought. I'm sorry if I messed anything up. I know the Army loves schedules."

Freedom almost laughed. Almost. "If you don't mind my asking, ma'am," he said, "why were you so insistent on coming out here?"

The smirk faded and Dr. Morris stared down at the crate. "I was pretty sure . . . I thought you'd need Cerberus here."

"I'm sorry, ma'am?"

She squared her shoulders and stared at him. "I remember what LA is like. I knew you'd need me here. Me and Cerberus."

"Los Angeles isn't as bad as some folks think," he said. "It's not a paradise, but it's nowhere near as bad as it was back in the seventies and eighties. Or so I'm told." Freedom furrowed his brow and tried to remember all the information they'd sent him about Morris. "You've been out here to Los Angeles before?"

"August of 2009," she said. "I flew in with the suit for . . ." Her voice trailed off. "My mind just went blank, sorry."

"Not a problem."

"I came here in 2009, on a military transport," she said. It wasn't so much directed at him as thinking aloud. "My team was on another plane, I was with Cerberus, and we were out here for . . ." Her face twisted in frustration.

They stood there for a moment in silence.

"If you're settled for the moment, ma'am," he interrupted, "I need to wash up before opening the office." He gestured at his running clothes.

She gave him an absent nod.

Freedom stepped into the back, stripped off his T-shirt, and left it hanging in his locker. He spent ten minutes washing up in the small bathroom behind the office. One advantage of his shaved head was easy cleaning. When his run had been scrubbed off, he toweled off his face and chest and swiped some deodorant under his arms.

He set his towel aside, tugged a fresh tee over his head, and pulled on his coat. He checked his nametag and patches in the mirror and bit back the usual pang of regret at the sight of the single bar on his chest. A glance at the clock told him he had another twenty minutes before the office needed to open. Plenty of time to get Dr. Morris squared away and maybe still get caught up on—

Someone rapped on the front door.

He paused. It was early for someone looking to enlist, and all of the staff members had keys. Sometimes the homeless banged on the windows. Every now and then a car would kick up some gravel. But the noise had sounded much more deliberate.

"Ummm . . . Lieutenant," called Dr. Morris. Another set of quick raps echoed on the glass of the front door.

He brushed himself down and stepped out into the office.

Across the room, the front door framed two figures. One was the man who had appeared at the office earlier in the week. The one who'd brought up Freedom's demotion. The other figure was a beautiful dark-skinned woman in a black trench coat who looked familiar. It crossed his mind she might be an actress, although he couldn't think of what he might've seen her in. Or why the crazy man would be with her.

"I think they want to get in," said Dr. Morris.

"They're not part of your team, are they, ma'am?"

She shook her head. "Nope. I think . . . they look kind of familiar, though."

As Freedom crossed the room, other people appeared out on the sidewalk. At least a dozen figures were closing in on the couple at the front door. More homeless folks in ragged clothes. Their pleading hands were held out and their mouths moved in a constant stream of words that came through the glass as pops and clicks.

For a brief moment, he considered ignoring the couple. The homeless people could be annoying, but he'd never heard of them hurting anyone. Not in this part of town, anyway. Then the thought of Donner Pass danced across his mind. And the hungry hands.

He sighed and unlocked the twin dead bolts on the door.

The couple slipped through the door as soon as they could fit. The woman pushed it closed again and snapped the locks shut, one with each hand. Up close, Freedom was even more certain he'd seen her in a commercial or magazine.

But there was something else about her, too. Her stance. The way she held herself. Something about the woman made him think of career soldiers, although he couldn't remember ever serving with a woman even remotely as gorgeous as this one.

"Thanks," said the crazy man.

"Of course," said Freedom. He glanced at the figures out on the sidewalk. "Is there something I can help you with?"

The woman glanced at his insignia. "Lieutenant John Carter Freedom?" She glanced back at the man. "He is not a captain?"

"No."

Freedom bit back a growl.

The man looked at Dr. Morris across the room. A smile broke out on his face. She stared back at him. "Wait a minute," she said. "Is your name George?"

"Yeah," said the man. "Do you remember me?"

That was right, Freedom remembered. He'd said his name was George.

"I think so," Dr. Morris said, "but I'm not sure from where. Are you with DARPA? Or a college?"

"Not quite."

The other woman, the supermodel type, studied the cases. "This is the Cerberus suit?"

"Yeah," said Dr. Morris. "How'd you know?"

Freedom wondered as well. The Cerberus Battle Armor System wasn't a secret. The recruiting office had been showing footage of it for a few months now, and there were YouTube clips of it online. It wasn't getting major news coverage, though, and yet here were two people who happened by his office on the day it arrived. Both of whom seemed very familiar with the battlesuit and its creator.

Maybe too familiar.

He straightened up. "Ma'am," he said, "sir, what can I do for you this morning?"

"We're here for you," said George. "Both of you."

Dr. Morris raised an eyebrow. "Sorry?"

George glanced at the supermodel, who gave a slight nod. "This is going to sound a little strange," he said, "but you've both been having a lot of dreams, haven't you? Things that should be nightmares, but aren't?"

"Yeah," said Dr. Morris. Her arms pulled back up and crossed over her chest. "How did you know?"

George gestured at the crates. "Do you dream about being in the battlesuit? About fighting monsters?"

Her eyes went wide. "Yes," she said. "They're always all around me. They're like a swarm. A horde."

Freedom stiffened at the word. He wasn't sure why at first. Then he remembered the Donner Pass.

The supermodel noticed his reaction. She was sharp. "You are having similar dreams," she said. It was more of a statement than a question.

"No," he told her, even as an image of gray-skinned settlers flashed in his mind. It occurred to him he still didn't know who the woman was. "No, I am not."

"It's okay," said George. "Someone did something to our minds. It's not your fault you can't remember."

"My fault?" said Freedom. He felt his hands clench into fists and forced them straight. "What are you implying, sir?"

"Someone did what to our minds?" asked Dr. Morris.

"We are wasting time," said the supermodel. "Convince them the direct way, as Madelyn convinced you."

"She didn't really convince me, remember?"

"George," she said, "we do not have time."

He sighed and looked at the crates. He pointed at one the size of a desk and glanced at Dr. Morris. "That's the back section, right? Armor plates, spinal computer, all that stuff? It's, what, three hundred and fifty pounds, not counting the case?"

"Yeah," she said. "How'd you know?"

"I've helped you get in or out of the armor a couple hundred times. That's the only case big enough for it."

Her face twisted up. "Who are you people?" she asked.

George grabbed the sturdy handle. The road case leaped into the air and he caught it with his free hand. Dr. Morris gasped. Freedom tensed. George balanced it for a moment, then pushed it up to the roof with one hand.

They stared for a moment, and then Freedom set his jaw. "Sir, that's government property," he said. "Set it down."

"Gently!" snapped Dr. Morris. "Do you have any idea what that costs?"

George let the case drop back down so he could balance it in both hands. "You're always so worried about it," he said, "even though it's built like a tank."

Freedom took a step and placed himself between George and the rest of the boxes. "I think you and your friend need to leave, sir."

George looked at him for a moment. "Catch," he said as he tossed the case at Freedom.

Dr. Morris snarled. Freedom lunged forward. He grabbed the large case in his arms like a man catching a baby. He held on to it for a moment, not wanting to shift his balance until he was sure he had it.

"It would seem," said the dark woman, "George is not the only strong one."

Freedom set the case down. It thudded against the thin carpet. He stared at it for a moment.

Dr. Morris looked at the case, then her eyes darted between the two men. "How did you do that?" she asked George.

"How did I pick it up? With my arms."

"No, seriously. How did you lift it?"

The thin man took a slow breath. "Well," he said to Freedom, "I can tell you how you did it."

"Adrenaline," said Freedom. "I've seen men do amazing things in combat." It was true. He'd seen soldiers kick down doors with no effort and hurl opponents across rooms. One man had bent the door of a burning Hummer when he pulled it open to rescue a squadmate. The human body was an amazing machine, powerful and durable all on its own without any help from . . .

Where had he heard that phrase? He'd heard it from an Army physician. A doctor.

"You were part of a special project," said George. "They were trying to create super-soldiers. Well, not just trying. They *made* super-soldiers."

Freedom felt his eyes start to roll and managed to keep his gaze locked on the smaller man. Dr. Morris made no such attempt. "Seriously?" she muttered. "That's the best you've got?"

"You were stationed at the Yuma Proving Ground," said the supermodel, "on a subbase designated Project Krypton. The man in charge of the program was Dr. Emil Sorensen, considered one of the world's experts in neurology and biochemistry, among other fields."

Krypton. Sorensen. The names sparked a headache right behind Freedom's eyes, like nails going through his temples. He turned his head away to focus and found himself staring at the portrait of the President. John Smith stared down at Freedom and smiled. It looked like a fake smile.

"This is nonsense," he said.

"It's not," said George. "It's real."

The pain in his head got worse. It was like someone tapping on his skull. The old Chinese water torture, obsolete now that more ruthless ways had been found to torture people with water.

"I'd like you to leave, sir," he said. "And you, too, ma'am."

"Sorry, Captain," said George. "Not without you."

He turned around. "I'm not a captain anymore."

"You are," George said, "someone just told you to forget."

He looked over at Dr. Morris. She was wiping her hand across her nose. There was blood on her lip and on her fingers. "You want to hear something funny?" she asked the room. "I kind of dated the President for a while. Back before he got married."

"We know," said the dark woman.

"I hadn't thought about that in . . . in ages, I guess."

Freedom took a step toward George. "Get out now," he said. The clicking pen was playing hell with his headache. He set a hand down that covered the smaller man's shoulder. "Please don't make me use force."

George shot a glance at the dark woman. She bowed her head once and he looked back up at Freedom. "If it helps," he said, "just remember this is the rematch you always wanted."

"Sorry, sir?"

George pushed out his hand to shove Freedom in the chest. It wasn't a particularly fast or skilled move. It made Freedom think of Combatives training. His own arm dropped down for an easy block, and he started thinking of ways to politely throw the couple back out on the street.

George's hand pushed past the block. It was like trying to stop a moving truck. Or a tank. Freedom had just enough time to remember how the man had held the steel-lined case up over his head and then George's palm connected with his sternum.

The front door flew away, the office blurred, and something slammed into Freedom's back just before he heard wood crack and splinter behind him. He found his footing and glanced over his shoulder. His desk had been crushed between his back and the far wall of the office.

George stood a dozen feet away with his hand out. Dr. Morris's mouth hung open. The supermodel had the faintest hint of a smile on her face.

Freedom stood up and brushed himself off. Then he took three running steps forward and slammed his fist straight into George's stomach. It was like hitting a tree trunk, but he'd already committed to his follow-through punch. His knuckles cracked against George's jaw, but the smaller man's head barely moved.

He hadn't even raised his hands to defend himself.

Dr. Morris swore. Then swore again.

Freedom stepped away from George and glanced over. Dr. Morris was standing in the center of the room. She looked angry and confused. Her arms were pulling in toward her body, being forced back out, and pulling in again. "Where is it?" she snapped. "Where'd it go?"

It took him a moment to figure out what she was talking about. Nothing looked out of place. He was too used to seeing the middle of the office empty.

The cases for the Cerberus Battle Armor System had all vanished.

Freedom felt a surge of suspicion again, but he knew it was foolish. It would be impossible to move all the crates in the few seconds he'd been fighting with George, let alone to do it without anyone noticing.

"What did you do with it?" Dr. Morris glared at the supermodel.

The woman and George ignored her. They were both looking around the recruiting office. "Our perceptions have switched back again," said the supermodel.

"Yeah."

Then Freedom noticed the office itself. The floor wasn't carpet, it was a dark, industrial-looking tile. It was covered with faded takeout menus and drifts of broken glass.

One of the picture windows had a pile of tables in front of it, a makeshift barricade. The other one was cracked. A huge spiderweb spread across the glass. The threads at the center were blurred with dark brown smears he recognized as dried blood. The wooden walls were just a cheap laminate. It was peeling off in places. The recruitment posters were gone. A bland painting of yellow and blue flowers sat on the floor. Its frame was cracked.

His desk had vanished. In its place were a counter and the remains of a large glass case. A cash register sat on its side on the floor. The presidential portrait was now a large chalkboard. Half of it was a colorful menu of pastries and coffee drinks. The other half had been blurred into pale streaks and replaced with messy letters made of thick pink strokes of chalk.

END OF WORLD
SPECIAL
$6.66

Something dripped on his lips. He reached up and his hand came away red. His nose was bleeding, just like Dr. Morris's was. He didn't remember George punching or head-butting him. His mind flitted down a list of airborne toxins and the location of the pro-masks in the back room even as he registered that George and the women were fine.

Adams's pen clicked away. And then Freedom realized Adams hadn't come in yet. In fact, it was his day off.

He turned toward the sound.

Adams's desk was gone. A table large enough to sit five or six people was there. It had been pushed back against the wall, pinning the one occupant in its seat.

It had been a man. It was wearing a threadbare, old-pattern camo jacket from the eighties that had faded well past cook whites. It had the same color hair as Adams, but much longer. A larger nose and wider jaw, too. Its eyes were dead white and its skin was gray. Settler gray, just like Freedom's dreams.

The dead man reached for them across the tabletop, its dry fingertips drawing lines in the dust. Its mouth snapped open and closed again and again. The clicking teeth echoed in the room.

Dr. Morris made a low noise, something between a growl and a squeal. Her arms had wrapped tight around herself again. "What's going on?" she hissed. "What the *fuck* is going on?"

Another half-dozen dead people crowded the door, and Freedom could see more in the street wandering toward the office. Or coffee shop. Whatever the place was. Some of the dead people were missing eyes or teeth. One looked like it had been scalped. A woman near the front of the group wore a shirt that said NAVY in large letters. It was splattered with blood. So was her mouth.

"Where in God's name are we?" asked Freedom.

"We've switched back," said George. "We're seeing the real world now."

"What's that supposed to mean?" said Dr. Morris.

"Look, you just have to trust us," said George. "Someone's been messing with our minds, making us see the world the way he wants to get us out of the way." He walked over to the dead thing at the table and placed his hand on top of its head. Its neck flexed for a moment as it tried to stretch its mouth up to his fingers. Then George turned his palm and twisted the corpse's head around like a man opening a bottle. The dead thing's spine popped twice, like a log in a fire, and it slumped on the tabletop. Its jaws still hinged back and forth.

It struck Freedom he'd made no move to stop George, and had no reaction to the snapped neck. He knew on some level it hadn't been a murder. It had been weeding.

"You both need to come with us," said George. "We're heading onto campus to pick up someone else, and then over into Hollywood."

"Do you have a car or a truck or something?" asked Dr. Morris.

"We do not," said the supermodel. "We are on foot."

The redhead blinked. "On foot? With those things out there?"

The dead men and women pawed at the glass and banged their teeth against each other.

"We'll be okay," said George. "We can hold them off until we get to the Mount."

The name resonated in Freedom's head. "The Mount?"

"Our base of operations," said the dark-skinned woman. "Your memories have been clouded so you do not remember. An epidemic has decimated the world. The survivors here in Los Angeles have formed a safe compound in Hollywood."

"We need to find the armor," said Danielle, wiping her nose again. Her hand was covered with blood. "I can't go out there without the armor."

"It's probably at the Mount," said George. "Waiting in your workshop."

Danielle shook her head. "It better be," she muttered. "If I find out Cesar went joyriding, I'll . . . Who the hell is Cesar?"

"Good," said George. "It's starting to come back to you."

Freedom closed his eyes and tried to will away the pain in his skull. "I need more than this, sir," he said.

George glanced at the door and the figures pressed against the glass. "More than that?"

"You're asking me to abandon everything I believe in," said Freedom.

The dark woman's gaze dropped to his chest, and her brow furrowed. "It would appear" she said, "that we are not."

Freedom looked down. His ACU was old and worn. He could see two seams where it had been repaired, and recognized the careful stitchwork his mother had taught him as a boy. On his chest was a Velcro patch with two black bars on it, faded to charcoal.

His captain's rank.

TWENTY-FIVE

ST. GEORGE STARED at the exes outside the door. Another seven or eight of them had wandered over to the little coffee shop while he and Stealth convinced Danielle and Freedom. He counted fifteen out on the sidewalk now. Another twenty or so out in the street hadn't figured out there was food in the café, but they would soon enough.

He looked back at the others. Stealth had found a broomstick somewhere in the back. It was one of the longer ones from the oversized, industrial push brooms, and there were a few swaths of duct tape on it. He wasn't sure if she was planning on using it as a spear or some kind of fighting staff.

Danielle still had her arms wrapped around herself, but she didn't seem quite as panicked as she had a while ago. She kept looking around the room. He was pretty sure she was hoping the armor cases would reappear.

Freedom walked up to him. The huge officer had pulled a thick pair of gloves from one of the pockets of his uniform and was working them tight around his fingers. "What's the plan, sir?"

"Well," said St. George, "I'm thinking we open the doors, I'll push these first few back, and then we'll loop around and head down Glendon Avenue back to campus."

"Where Madelyn is," said Freedom.

"Right." He saw the officer's expression. "She should be safe until we get there," he added. "The exes probably don't even know she's there."

"It would be safer to travel on rooftops," said Stealth.

"It would." St. George nodded. "But I think you're the only one who could get up there. Danielle's human, Freedom's still a bit unsure of his abilities—no offense, Captain."

"None taken, sir," said Freedom.

"—and I still can't fly for some reason."

"I'm sorry," said Danielle. "Did you just say 'fly'? Like in, fly through the air?"

"Yeah," said St. George. "Just like Superman. Sort of."

"Yeah, right."

"Says the woman with the computerized battle armor."

She snorted and looked around the café again. "Not at the moment."

"So we're stuck on the ground," said St. George.

"It is almost nine," said Stealth. "I estimate it will take us at least seventy minutes to retrieve Corpse Girl. If our goal is to cross the city and reach the Mount before sundown, we should proceed."

"Agreed," said Freedom. "From what you're saying, the last thing we want is to be out after dark."

"Okay, then," said St. George. "I'll take the lead. Stealth, you follow. Freedom, watch our back. Danielle, stay between us and keep safe. We'll have you back inside Cerberus before you know it."

She grunted and forced her arms down to her sides.

"Everyone ready?"

They all nodded.

St. George shoved the door open.

*   *   *

The first ones were the easiest. He spread his arms wide as he marched out of the door and gathered them up. A few lunging steps carried the exes to the curb. It was a six-inch drop, but it was too much for the mindless dead. They stumbled and tripped and fell over. Two of them hit the pavement hard, skull first. Their teeth stopped chattering.

Out in the road, the other exes saw the movement. Chalk eyes turned to him. The dead all shifted their gait and staggered toward him.

He thought about setting fire to the pile of exes. In the back of his throat he could feel the light touch of smoke. He knew there was a trick to it, a way to make the smoke turn into flames, but he couldn't remember it. Like getting off the ground, it was something Smith's blocks were still keeping hidden from him.

He glanced over his shoulder. "Come on."

The four of them worked their way down the sidewalk. St. George grabbed exes by their jackets and shirts and blouses and hurled them out into the street. Behind him he heard Stealth's makeshift staff slice through the air twice, each time followed by the sound of breaking bone. Freedom let out two quick breaths—boxer's breaths—and St. George heard two more bodies fall.

They made it to the corner and he looked down Glendon. There were fewer exes, but the street seemed a bit narrower. He risked a quick glance back. "How's it looking behind us?"

"If we can keep up this pace, sir, we should be fine," said Freedom. "We're moving faster than they can catch us."

St. George gazed at the zombies on Glendon. They were already shuffling in their direction. "It might be getting rough, then," he said.

He looked around and spotted a 2 HOUR PARKING sign. He batted an ex away and heaved on the sign until something underground snapped and it came loose in his hands. He spun the square pipe once to get a feel for it. Then he brought it around like a club and crushed four skulls with one swing.

They moved down the center of the street. St. George took a few steps, shifted the pipe in his hands, and the steel sign changed from blunt instrument to edge-on blade. One swipe and it cut open three exes. A man and two women. Their clothes parted, their flesh gaped open, and their guts spilled out in front of them. Thin and thick intestines uncoiled onto the pavement. Stomachs, hearts, and other gray pieces of meat he couldn't identify tore loose and splatted against the ground. The exes swayed for a moment, their center of balance gone, and then tripped over their own insides.

Another swing of his signpost-axe, a little higher this time, and two skulls spun into the air. They cracked against the pavement as their bodies slumped and fell. St. George swung again, aimed it better, and took off four more heads. One of the dead things, a man with an Arab scarf draped around his shoulders, was a little shorter. The metal sign smashed through its skull at eye level. Its teeth snapped three more times before it collapsed.

They passed a jeweler and a Christian Science reading room. A car had plowed into an overgrown tree. There was a skeletal body under the flattened front tire. On the opposite side of the street was a quartet of ragged pop-up tents and some cases with National Guard markings.

"Looks like a checkpoint," said Freedom. "We should look for supplies."

"Maybe on the way back," said St. George said. "I don't think we want to stop moving right now."

"But, sir, there could be—"

"There will be nothing," said Stealth. "The Westwood National Guard outpost was lost on July 27, 2009. Best estimates had it looted by August fourth. That was before the South Seventeens consolidated their territory to the east in Century City and looted the surrounding area."

Freedom grabbed an ex by the arm, twisted it around, and slammed it back into two others. The trio of zombies stumbled and fell. "Very well," he said. "Let's move on, then."

Half a block from the outpost, a pile of withered corpses dominated an intersection. St. George guessed there had to be at least two hundred of them. They all had head wounds. Mostly bullet holes, but a few caved-in skulls as well. The pile was marked off with bright orange cones and a handful of yellow sawhorses.

He glanced back and saw Danielle shudder. She was fighting not to curl up in a ball. He could see it on her face.

They passed a three-car collision and a row of stores with all the picture windows smashed. St. George put down another dozen exes with his signpost, and he was pretty sure Stealth and Freedom stopped as many between them. At Le Conte Avenue he glanced back at the group. "We're about a third of the way to her dorm room," he told them.

Danielle frowned. "How do you know she'll be there?"

"I don't," he admitted. "I just don't know where else to look."

Freedom threw a kick that crushed an ex's rib cage. "More important, sir," he said, "how do you know where her dorm room is?"

"Relax," said St. George. "She spent two weeks trying to get me to remember all this."

Stealth lunged forward and thrust with her staff. The tip smashed through a dead woman's teeth and up through the roof of her mouth. The ex closed its jaws on the broomstick once, twitched, and fell over.

As the body slumped, a breeze blew down the street. St. George heard a growl that grew into a roar. It took him a moment to recognize it. He looked up and saw Stealth focusing, trying to locate the sound.

Danielle took another step forward.

"Hang on," he told her.

A bus plowed through the intersection. Its brakes hissed once and then it moved on. A poster for KTLA Channel Five stretched across the side of the bus.

A horn blasted behind them. A green Jetta was a foot from Freedom's shins. The driver banged on the horn again and gestured them out of the street. It wasn't a polite gesture. A few cars backed up behind him honked as well. The tail end of rush-hour traffic flowed around them while they stood in the street.

They glanced at each other and St. George took a step toward the sidewalk. Stealth gazed at him. "What are you doing?"

"Getting out of the street."

"It is not a real car."

"I know," St. George said, "but it's going to be easier to think without all the imaginary horns going off."

They stepped out of the lane into a parking space. The Jetta driver blared her horn again as she drove by. The rest were more concerned with making the next light.

Freedom went to step up onto the sidewalk and Stealth grabbed his arm. A trio of men in suits walked toward them along the sidewalk. One was on a cell phone, the other two were talking.

"They're just people," said Freedom.

"No," said Stealth. "They are exes we are being made to perceive as people."

"Are you sure?"

The men got closer and St. George raised his signpost. They walked past without slowing. One of them glanced at St. George, then his gaze swept over to Stealth and her broomstick. They didn't look back. The one on the phone swore as a teenager flew by on a skateboard. The teen didn't even glance at the four heroes in the parking space.

"If all the people are . . ." Danielle closed her eyes and snapped her fingers three times. "If they're all exes, why aren't they attacking us?"

Another bus slowed and spat out a handful of people. They scattered in different directions. None of them glanced over at the heroes. A young woman in a UCLA shirt jogged past them, her headphones blaring. She glanced up at Freedom and smiled.

"That," said St. George, "is a good question." He lowered the sign.

"A better one," said Stealth, "is why were we not attacked before?"

Freedom glanced over his shoulder, back toward Wilshire. "Before what?"

"Before regaining our awareness of the world," she said. "If we have been wandering through Los Angeles for weeks under Smith's influence, how are we still alive? St. George may have survived with his increased damage resistance, but the three of us have no such abilities. We should be dead."

"Cheery thought," Danielle muttered.

"She's right, though," said St. George. "Just because we don't see them as zombies doesn't mean they'd stop acting like them."

"Maybe we just got lucky."

Stealth shook her head.

"There were about forty of those things around this intersection," said Freedom. "I'd guess there's close to twice as many people now, not counting the ones in cars."

"And there's five times as many cars," added Danielle. "Are they all just hallucinations or whatever?"

"Let's keep moving," said St. George. He lowered the sign a little more, letting it hang level with his hip. "Same formation. Don't let anyone get too close."

A crowd of students slid past them, heading onto campus. Most of them ignored the heroes. One looked at the signpost in St. George's hands and grinned. He gave the hero a cheerful "Dude," before continuing on his way.

"Keep a safe distance from them," said Stealth. "They may appear benign, but they could be attacking us." She shifted the staff in her own hands. It stayed out away from her body and extended back to help shield Danielle.

St. George led them past the medical plaza, then headed west. He glanced over at the facilities management building and wondered if Jarvis was there. At this time of day he'd just be finishing with all the new requests.

Then he remembered that Jarvis had never worked on campus. It had been so many years, and the false memories were still crisp and clear. He remembered Jarvis—the *real* Jarvis—had joked about the Zombocalypse taking care of his unemployment problem.

"George," murmured Stealth.

He glanced up and realized he'd let a trio of young women get close to them. Two women and a very effeminate young man, he realized a moment later. They glanced at St. George and the others, but kept walking. A female voice slipped back to them a beat later. "Did you see? That guy was carrying a street sign."

A man and woman in ROTC uniforms paused and snapped quick salutes to Freedom. He returned them automatically. They waited for him to go by and then continued on their way.

As they passed the tennis courts, two young men in sweatshirts stared at Stealth and whispered to each other. One pulled out his phone and snapped a photograph. "What's going on?" asked Freedom.

"They recognize her," St. George said.

"How?"

"Before the uprising," said Stealth, "I was considered a minor celebrity."

"And still are in this world, it would seem," Freedom said.

"This world that we're imagining," added Danielle.

"Yes," Stealth said. The edges of her lips twitched down and her brows furrowed.

They went another ten feet and the world shifted.

St. George blinked and the grass grew a foot. A construction site became a mass of rusted girders. Two nearby cars lost their windshields and faded from years in the sun. Another became the victim of a long-ago sideswipe. The sounds of the city vanished and were replaced by the white noise of clicking teeth.

A handful of exes staggered in the street. Three dead men, two women, and two that weren't recognizable as either. One was too thin and wore shapeless, genderless clothes. The other looked like it had been scalped, and most of its face had been torn off in the process.

One of the dead women was closest. St. George shifted his grip and brought up the signpost. The first swing would crush the ex's skull and put him in position to take out the next two. Out of the corner of his eye, St. George saw Freedom move to get between Danielle and the faceless thing.

Then a jet flew by overhead and reality came crashing down on them again. The closest ex became a living woman with an oversized backpack. The parked cars were whole again. One tried to pull out and got honked at by a truck on the road.

No, George corrected himself. Not reality. The illusion.

"Goddammit," muttered Danielle.

The woman with the backpack gave St. George a frosty look. He realized he still had the signpost up and ready to swing. He lowered it as she marched past him. The sign scraped on the pavement.

"Just so we're all on the same page," said Danielle, "everyone's seeing a non-zombie world now, right?"

"Correct," said Stealth.

"Yes, ma'am," said Freedom.

"Yeah." St. George looked over his shoulder. "Everyone good? We can keep moving?" Freedom and Danielle nodded.

Stealth stared across the road at a man who looked like a young professor or teaching assistant. "Something wrong?" St. George asked her.

"I am not sure," she said. "I am forming a hypothesis, but I do not feel I have enough data to make a firm statement."

"Well, what are you thinking?"

Stealth stared at the man for another moment.

Then her phone rang.

She pulled the cell from her pocket and looked at the screen. Then her thumb slid across the screen and she held the phone up. "You are on speakerphone," she said.

"Hey," said Barry.

Danielle's eyes went wide. She mouthed something to St. George, the back half of which looked like *know that voice*.

"How did you get this number?" asked Stealth.

"You called me the other day, remember? I work with high-energy subatomic particles for a living and you think I can't star-sixty-nine someone?"

"This number is unlisted."

"Nothing's really unlisted," Barry said. "You've just got to know where the lists are. Speaking of which, even though we weren't, are you going to tell me your name at some point?"

"You do not know?"

"I do, I'm just checking to see if you know."

"Is that an attempt at a joke?"

"I guess it was, yeah."

Stealth looked at the cell for a moment. "My name is Karen Quilt," she said. "You may remember me by the name Stealth."

The voice on the phone chuckled.

"Something amuses you?"

"Yeah," he said. "Did you know you've got the same name as a former *Jeopardy!* champion? I bet you hear that a lot."

"Not often," she said. "Four minutes ago did you experience a reality shift?"

"Sorry?"

"Four minutes ago, did your view of the world change for twenty-six seconds and then revert back to normal? Did you see the undead we spoke of last night?"

"No," said Barry. "Maybe? Everybody always seems a little like the undead in baggage claim. Especially the TSA people."

"You're at the airport?" asked St. George.

"Yup. Which is why I called. Didn't you say you were going to have a ride here for me, Miss Karen Quilt or maybe Stealth?"

"I did."

"Did your guy take off without me or something, then? Took these idiots over half an hour to get me off the plane. You'd think they'd never dealt with a guy in a wheelchair before."

"You are looking for a thin man with glasses. He should have a white sign with your surname on it."

"Nope," said Barry. "I've been looking for twenty minutes now. Wasn't outside security or at baggage claim."

"You are certain?"

"I'm in a wheelchair, not blind. Besides, I've always wanted to say, 'Yes, I'm Mr. Burke,' and get whisked away in a limo. He's not here."

Stealth pressed her mouth into a line. "Hire a cab," she told him. "Go to the Four Seasons in Beverly Hills. Depending on traffic you should be there within the hour. I will cover the expense when you arrive."

"Okay," he said. "Does that mean I don't have time to do the Universal Studios tour?"

Danielle bit back a snort, and St. George felt his lips twitch into a smile for a moment. Stealth said nothing.

"Okay," Barry said after a moment. "No jokes. Got it. I guess I'll see you in an hour."

"You shall," she said, and hung up the phone. She looked at George. "He does not seem to be taking the situation seriously."

"I think that's kind of normal for him, isn't it?"

"He didn't experience the shift," said Freedom. "And he didn't know you."

"No," she said. "He did not."

"Maybe he's just not up to speed," said Danielle. "I mean, I think I'm eighty percent there, but I'm pretty sure there's still some holes in my memory."

St. George looked at Stealth's face. "Is it something else?"

She looked at the phone, then at the street around them. Her brows furrowed again. "We agree that we are still in the real world," she said. "Agent Smith has used his powers to affect our perceptions."

"Yeah," said St. George. Danielle and Freedom nodded in agreement.

"If that is so," she said, "and this is all an illusion, how is Barry calling my cell phone?"

TWENTY-SIX

"BUT WE'VE ALL been using our cell phones," said St. George. "I called Barry. I called you. I called . . ."

"Maybe he's using his powers," said Danielle. "He's got . . ." She closed her eyes for a moment and snapped her fingers again. "He's got some sort of energy powers, right? He talks straight to walkie-talkies all the time, doesn't he?"

"Correct," said Stealth. She held up the phone. "However, to transmit to a cell phone he would still require an active network to tap into. There has been no such thing for fifty-one months now."

"I remember that," Danielle muttered. "The annoying habit of knowing everything."

"Also," Stealth continued, ignoring them, "Barry cannot partially manifest his powers. If he is not Zzzap, he has no such abilities."

"And if he's turned back into Zzzap," said St. George, "why does he think he's still in a wheelchair?"

"Is it a cell phone when we switch over?" asked Danielle. She patted herself down. "Maybe you're talking to him on a walkie. I mean, maybe we've all been using walkies."

Stealth shook her head. "If his mind is still confused it is possible . . ."

"Ma'am, sir," said Freedom, "perhaps this is a conversation we can continue in a more secure location? We don't want to be trapped out in the open if there's a longer shift." As he spoke he stepped to stay between Danielle and an exhausted jogger plodding along the sidewalk.

"Agreed," Stealth said. The phone vanished back into her pocket. She nodded to St. George. "Continue."

"We're almost there." He pointed ahead to a tall brick building. "That's her dorm."

* * *

Madelyn's roommate, Kathy, opened the door. She was dressed in baggy sweatpants and a loose tank top, but didn't look like she'd been woken up. Her eyes widened when she saw George. Then her jaw dropped when she saw Stealth.

"Oh my God," she said. Her jaw pulled itself up and became a wide grin. "Oh my God."

St. George felt a kick in his own stomach. He hadn't recognized her before. The last time he'd seen Banzai alive and without her mask had been almost five years ago, the morning of the day she'd died. They'd all met up to discuss strategy against the exes. She'd been dressed in her rainbow-colored karate uniform with her mask slung over her shoulder, standing next to Gorgon as they'd all studied a map of Los Angeles.

"Hey," he said, forcing the memories away. "Is Madelyn here?"

"Oh my God," said Kathy. Her eyes were still locked on Stealth.

"How do you do," said Stealth. She held out her hand. St. George could tell she was shaken, too, although she did a much better job of hiding it. "It is a pleasure to meet you. Is your roommate here?"

"Oh my . . . yes. Yeah, she is." She stared at the hand like she was both thrilled and terrified by it. Then she stepped back and pulled the door open. "Maddy, it's for you."

"Who is it?"

Kathy looked out again and noticed the wall of digital camo behind Stealth. Her gaze went up until she saw Freedom's face. "It's your friend," said Kathy. "And Karen Quilt. And a giant."

She stepped out of the way and waved them in. St. George glanced back at Freedom, then drew a line between Kathy and Danielle with his eyes. Freedom nodded his understanding.

They filed into the dorm room. Madelyn was stretched out on her own bed in sweats and a T-shirt, holding a textbook open above her head. She glanced over and sat up when her eyes settled on Stealth. "It's you," she said. "You're here."

"I am. You know me?"

"Sort of. I know your voi—John!" Madelyn used her hands to bounce to the end of the bed and lunge at the captain.

Freedom caught her in one arm and hugged her. St. George saw the huge man's face shift. It was still formal and serious, but a layer of tension washed away as he held the girl.

Danielle pushed the door closed behind them. Kathy retreated onto her own bed and pulled her MacBook into her lap. A moment later the sound of YouTube comedy clips buzzed over the speakers. She stared in awe at Stealth over the top of the screen.

George realized, without much surprise, that Kathy was watching old Monty Python clips.

The captain set Madelyn down in her chair. "It's good to see you, too," he said.

"At least you remembered not to call me 'ma'am.'" She smiled.

"So," said St. George, "first off, I don't think you should shoot anyone else to help them remember."

Her face dropped. "I'm sorry," she said. "I didn't know what else to do. Smith had got to you again and you just kept denying stuff."

"Where is the weapon?" asked Stealth. "It is best if I take possession of it."

Madelyn twisted around and grabbed the backpack hanging on her wheelchair. She pulled it into her lap, fished through it, and pulled out a pistol.

Kathy gasped. "You've got a gun?!"

Stealth held out her hand and Madelyn handed her the pistol butt-first. The supermodel checked the safety, ejected the magazine, and yanked the slide back. "Sig Sauer Pro 2009," she said. "Four rounds remaining in a magazine which holds fifteen. You are too young to purchase a handgun in California. How did you acquire this?"

"I know a guy."

Stealth reloaded the pistol and tucked it into the waistband of her slacks so it would be hidden beneath her trench coat. "Who?"

"His name's Hector. He's a member of the South Seventeens. He got it for me."

"Hector de la Vega?"

Madelyn nodded. "If it makes you feel better, it freaked him out, too."

"If you were shooting at him to convince him," said St. George, "that might be why he freaked out."

"I said I'm sorry."

"How much have you seen?" asked Stealth.

"Huh?"

"Twenty-two minutes ago all of us experienced a shift in perceptions which allowed us to see the world as it is instead of the reality Smith has implanted in our minds. Has this happened to you?"

Madelyn shook her head.

"Have you seen any of the walking dead?"

"The walking dead?" echoed Kathy from her bed. St. George took a half step and placed himself between the girl and Stealth.

Madelyn shook her head. "I haven't seen them. I remember them from our world."

Stealth shook her own head. "There is no other world."

"No, there is," she insisted. "We're not supposed to be here. In our world, there was a virus that—"

Stealth held up a hand. "I am aware of the timeline," she said. "However, there is no other world. We are in our world now, but your perceptions and memories have been altered so you do not register it."

"What? No, my memories are fine. I mean, they're fine for me."

Stealth looked at Madelyn. "You are familiar with the writer-director named George Romero?"

She smirked. "Yeah, of course."

"What were the monsters called in his movies?"

"What?"

"It's important," St. George said. "It's a test, sort of."

"I . . . I don't know. They're just dead things, right?"

Stealth shook her head. "There is another name for them."

Madelyn shrugged. "No idea."

Kathy peeked out from behind her laptop. "They were zombies, right?"

St. George and Stealth both looked at her. "That is correct," said Stealth.

Kathy smiled.

"Ex-humans," said Danielle. She dragged the word off her tongue.

Madelyn scowled.

"Do you trust us?" St. George asked her.

She looked at him, then at Freedom. "Yeah, of course I do."

"Then that's all that matters for now. Pack anything you might need and let's get going."

Madelyn spun her chair around, pulled opened a drawer, and grabbed a pair of jeans. "Ummmm . . ." She looked up at Freedom and St. George. "Would you guys mind waiting in the hall for a few minutes?"

St. George glanced at Kathy, then at Stealth and Danielle. "Will you be okay in here?"

Stealth nodded.

"If it's all the same," said Danielle, "I'll wait outside with you guys."

They shuffled outside. The dorm hallway was empty, although the echoes of voices and footsteps came from either end. St. George could hear a shower running somewhere, too.

Freedom stood with his back to the door. Danielle pressed herself against the wall near a fire extinguisher. "A wheelchair's going to cause problems," she said. "If we have another shift we could be trapped somewhere."

"Technically we're already trapped somewhere," Freedom said. "The shift should make it easier because we'll actually be able to see where we are and what's around us."

"And if we have another shift," added St. George, "she shouldn't need it anymore, anyway."

Danielle shrugged and looked down the hallway. A young man in a towel strolled out of a bathroom and across the hall to a room. The clunk of his door echoed in the hallway.

"Worst-case scenario, I can carry her," said Freedom. "Or she could just ride piggyback."

"This *is* the worst-case scenario," Danielle muttered. "We're running for our lives and we're almost helpless."

* * *

Madelyn hauled herself back onto the bed and pushed the sweat-pants down her legs. She tried not to think about getting naked in front of a woman who was a thousand times more attractive than her, but it was kind of tough when she was forced to wrestle with her jeans. It reminded her that her thighs were kind of fat for her height and Karen Quilt's were perfect.

"If you want it," she said, "there's a black hoodie in the closet. It's a little too big for me. You can have it."

Karen—no, Madelyn thought, Stealth. We always call her Stealth—arched an eyebrow. "I am warm enough, thank you."

"No, I didn't think you were cold. I just meant, if you wanted it because—"

"I am aware of what you meant. Thank you, but no. Do you require assistance?"

"It's okay. I've gotten pretty good at it." Her fingers hooked into the belt loops and pulled the jeans up. She dropped onto her back and the jeans slid over her hips. "Everyone tells me I got really sick when I was nine, that's why I'm in the chair, but I don't remember it. You think I'll be able to walk again once we're out of here?"

"It would seem once we each consciously realized Smith was

affecting our perceptions, we began to find ways around the blocks he has created. As our minds create these new pathways and associations, our memories and abilities have begun to return."

"But I've had my memories all along," she said. "So why do I need the chair?"

Stealth looked at the other side of the room. "I am not sure," she admitted. "It is reasonable to assume the unique nature of your mind has allowed you to remember certain elements of the actual world. It is unclear, then, why certain aspects of the illusionary world appear to be locked in your conscious mind."

Madelyn twisted her lips. "So this might be permanent?" She shifted her legs over the edge of the bed and slid back down into the wheelchair. She landed hard and winced.

"Again," said Stealth, "I am not sure. There are too many inconsistent facts." She looked at the far side of the room again.

"What do you mean?"

Stealth said nothing. She just stared at Kathy. The other girl traded looks with Madelyn and shrunk down a little more behind her laptop.

* * *

Freedom pushed Madelyn's wheelchair down the hall. Danielle hovered behind him. St. George and Stealth brought up the rear.

"Returning to the hotel should be our new priority," she said.

He glanced at her. "Why?"

"Barry will be arriving there within the hour and will be unprotected. Also, my father always insists on traveling with certain items. There are weapons there which we can use."

"Are there?" asked St. George. "I mean, it's just going to be an empty hotel room, right? Most of the hotels and motels in the city were pretty well looted in that first year. Hell, we looted half of them."

She took in a small breath through her nose.

He looked at her. "What?"

"There may be more to these perceptual illusions than we first believed."

"What do you mean?"

"My initial hypothesis of our situation, based on our knowledge of Agent Smith's abilities, may be flawed."

"What makes you think so?"

"You did not tell me Banzai was Madelyn's roommate."

"Well, I didn't know it was her until fifteen minutes ago," he said. "And, I mean, it's not really her, right? The real Kathy's still wandering somewhere around in . . . what, West Hollywood last time we saw her?"

"It is," said Stealth. "Madelyn never met Banzai while she was alive, and has never encountered her as an ex-human. Neither has Captain Freedom. Banzai died nineteen days before Cerberus was deployed to Los Angeles, so Danielle has only known her as an ex."

"So?"

The corner of Stealth's eye tightened. She was frustrated with him. He was missing something.

"George," she said, "how could they be seeing and hearing an actual person they have never met? The illusion cannot be based on memories they do not have."

He glanced back up the stairwell, toward the dorm room. "Maybe Smith planted the memories the same way he plants suggestions."

"Smith has also never met Banzai. How would he know so many precise details of her appearance, voice, and personality?"

"Maybe it's a perception thing," he said. "Maybe what we're seeing isn't what the others are seeing."

Stealth shook her head. "There are too many common references for us to not all be seeing the same things."

They stepped out into the sunlight. The sounds of the campus washed over them. There was a faint breeze from the west. St. George's street sign lay in the freshly mown grass by the door with Stealth's broomstick crossed over it.

"So, you mean . . . this really is another world?"

Stealth's eyes tightened again, harder this time. "I do not

know," she said. "Either conclusion is inconsistent with the evidence."

"Which means what?"

"Which means there is a third conclusion which is consistent with all the evidence. Unfortunately, at the moment I do not know what it is. Even our clothing is inconsistent. Ours and Danielle's remain the same in both worlds, yet Freedom's uniform changes."

"Yeah, I noticed that." He picked up the improvised weapons and handed the wooden stick to Stealth. "Are you okay?"

"Of course."

"I just ask because I know illogical things drive you nuts."

She took in a short breath. "It is . . . frustrating," she admitted. "I appreciate your understanding."

"Hey," shouted Madelyn. Freedom had already pushed her a dozen yards down the sidewalk. "Come on! We've got to go be superheroes."

TWENTY-SEVEN

THIS WOULD BE a lot easier if we had a car," said Danielle. "Or got a cab. Or just took the bus."

"Until we switched over," said Freedom, "and realize we've been standing in a derelict bus with twenty or thirty exes."

They'd made their way back to the recruitment office and were headed up the steep climb into Beverly Hills. St. George had the lead, while Stealth had fallen back to bring up the rear. Freedom had Madelyn's wheelchair.

They'd been walking for twenty minutes when squealing brakes echoed across Wilshire. Half a block ahead of them, a car whipped across from the eastbound lane, cutting off half a dozen vehicles in the process. It pulled up alongside them, double-parked, and revved its engine. Then it honked its horn twice. St. George glanced over. It was a Hyundai, just like his. The driver was...

There was no driver.

The horn went off again. The passenger's-side door popped open.

"That is your car," Stealth said to St. George.

Two cars slowed down to veer around the Hyundai. The third didn't slow at all, but its horn blared as it went past them. The next lane wasn't slowing, and more cars started to honk. A few brakes screeched. The Hyundai's hazard lights popped on.

"No," said Danielle. Her eyes widened. "It's Cesar."

The horn let out three long angry blasts.

She smirked. "I am not calling you 'the Driver.'"

St. George looked at Stealth. "What do you think?"

"I do not know," she said. "I am unsure why Cesar retains his powers while the rest of us are still limited."

"I meant, do we risk getting in?"

"I am aware of your question, George. I do not know."

"I do," said Danielle. "I'm tired and my feet hurt." She glanced over at Freedom. "I'm guessing you're going to want shotgun?"

He smiled. "I'd prefer to drive, but it's not my car."

Danielle flipped the seat forward and crawled into the back. Freedom and Madelyn looked at St. George, then at Stealth. "Are we doing this?" Madelyn asked.

"There is no room for our weapons," Stealth said.

St. George tossed the signpost on the sidewalk. "At the worst," he said, "twenty minutes from now we're sitting right here in an abandoned car. At the best, we're at the hotel."

"At the worst," corrected Stealth, "we abandon our weapons, switch, and find four exes in the car with us."

Another car honked at them as it drove by.

"There's no exes," shouted the voice on the radio. "I'm clean, ma'am."

"As far as you know," said Stealth. She tossed her broomstick away.

The captain helped Madelyn out of her wheelchair, then crouched to set her into the back of the Hyundai. Danielle helped her in. Stealth slipped in next to them while St. George folded the wheelchair and stashed it in the trunk. The suspension squealed as Freedom squeezed himself into the passenger seat and pushed the seat back. It still left his knees against the dashboard.

St. George stepped around the Hyundai and watched the cars whip past him. He could smell exhaust and feel the wind as they passed. He picked little details off each one—chipped paint, flyers trapped under windshield wipers, one driver talking on his cell, another plucking at her hair.

If it was an illusion, it was an amazing one.

There was a lull in the traffic. He stepped over and pulled the door open. The moment he closed it, the Hyundai leaped back into traffic. The steering wheel moved on its own.

"Missed you guys!" said the radio. "The past few weeks have been really weird, y'know?"

"Kind of, yeah," said St. George.

"Where we headed? Want me to take us back to the Mount?"

"First to the Four Seasons on Doheny," said Stealth. "Has it been weeks? We are unsure how long it has been since we fell under Smith's influence."

"Think so," said Cesar. "I mean, it's tough to tell in here, y'know?"

The wheel spun, the tires squealed, and cars around them dropped away. The Hyundai rushed through a yellow light. Horns went off and their honks faded away before they'd finished.

"You've been in the car the whole time?" Madelyn leaned forward between the seats to talk to the radio. She had to squeeze around Freedom's shoulders.

"Yeah," Cesar said. "I been following St. George the whole time. I kept trying to talk to you but you kept zoning out on me, man."

Stealth looked at St. George. "Do you recall any of this?"

"I think I remember zoning out the radio, yeah. Sorry, Cesar."

"No problem, man."

The Hyundai swerved into another lane as they headed down a hill and went around an airport shuttle. It straddled lines to slip past a BMW and then the engine growled again. The light just past the bottom of the hill turned red and the car came to a reluctant stop.

"I find it to be unlikely," said Stealth, "that you found a working model of your old car at the same time Smith altered your memories."

"Hyundais weren't rare," said Danielle. "There's probably at least a thousand of them in Los Angeles."

"It's not a Hyundai," said Cesar. "We're in an old Taurus."

"No," said St. George. "It's my old car. It's a blue Hyundai Accent."

"Dude," said the voice on the radio, "it's a piece o' shit Taurus. Mostly red, but the passenger door and side panel are all primer. Feels like it got sideswiped and they never hammered it out all the way."

Freedom looked at the door by his arm.

"Driver," said Stealth, "what are you seeing right now?"

St. George swore the car lifted itself a little higher on the road. "What do you mean, ma'am?" asked the voice on the radio.

"What do you see on the road ahead of us? How many cars are there on this stretch of road with us?"

"Well . . . uhhh," Cesar said, "there aren't any."

Freedom glanced at a glossy black Hummer as they swooped past it.

"Please explain," said Stealth.

"I mean, there's some wrecks and stuff. Abandoned cars. That what you meant?"

A yellow Volkswagen pulled away as the Hyundai dipped into its lane. A woman on a motorcycle shot them an angry finger as Cesar slipped past and forced her close to the curb. The engine revved and they shot through a red light into a corridor of greenery.

"Donner Pass," muttered Freedom.

Madelyn touched his arm. "What?"

"Nothing."

St. George tapped the steering wheel. "So you're telling me there's nothing else on the road?"

"Nothing moving," said the voice on the radio.

They roared out of the green corridor, past a gas station and the Beverly Hilton. The Hyundai cut across two lanes, ran a red light, and made a wide turn past a fountain. More cars honked and a siren wailed to life behind them.

"Cops," said Danielle.

"Where?" Cesar asked.

"Right behind us," said Madelyn. "You are bussssssssted."

"There's no cops," said Cesar. "We're the only ones on the road."

St. George glanced in the rearview mirror. "You don't see or hear anything out there?"

"I've told you, man, it's not like that. When I'm in here, I'm kind of seeing things by . . . like, by comfort. The same way, like, when you've had a car for years you know if the rear end's near the curb or another car."

"It would seem," said Stealth, "that the Driver's unique senses in this state allow him a different perception of the world around us, much as Madelyn's mind allowed her to resist the false memories."

The Hyundai drove past a crowd of people waiting for a crosswalk. All of them had chalk-colored skin. St. George got only a quick look, but it looked like two of them were missing limbs. Their heads swiveled to watch the car go by.

Cesar said something else, but St. George didn't hear it. His head whipped around to look at the people on the sidewalk. He glimpsed a dead woman dragging a small, shriveled shape on a child leash, and Stealth bracing herself against the back of the passenger seat.

The steering wheel hit him hard in the chest and snapped off as he folded around it. He heard a crash of glass and saw Freedom catching Madelyn and Danielle. Momentum threw them between the front seats and into his arms. All of them were ringed with sparkles, and St. George realized the small lights were little cubes of glass reflecting in the sun just as he bounced off the hood of the car and was thrown into the street.

He hit the pavement head-first, rolled onto his shoulder, and then his knees cracked down against the road. The car appeared for an instant before momentum flipped him over again. The ground slapped him in the temple, the back, the ankle, the forehead, and then he was stopped by a concrete barrier. He sprawled with his face against it for a few seconds before he slid down. It was very gritty on his cheeks and nose. Some of the barrier crumbled away and fell with him.

St. George stayed on the ground for a moment. The sky was very blue above him. The city was silent. He wondered if he'd broken anything, and then he remembered he was bulletproof and nigh invulnerable.

He sat up. His jeans and the fleece jacket were ripped. His shirt had survived unscathed. He flexed his fingers and brushed some gravel and glass out of his hair, then looked down the road.

Thirty feet away, a dust-covered red Taurus sat on four flat tires. Most of the windshield was scattered over the hood and in front of the car. The passenger side was primer gray and looked lumpy.

He saw Freedom shift in the passenger seat. The officer had a gash where his forehead had hit the dashboard. Madelyn shook her head next to him. St. George didn't see any injuries on her.

"Everyone okay?" he called out. He rolled up onto his feet and brushed some more glass off his clothes as he walked back to the car. There were some fragments of windshield in the back of his jeans, but a few hops sent them tumbling down the inside of his pant leg.

"We appear to be uninjured for the most part," said Stealth. She stretched past Danielle and folded down the driver's seat. Danielle pushed the door open and the two of them slid out of the car. Freedom's door opened with a squeal of forced metal. The huge officer climbed out. He kept Madelyn cradled in one arm.

There were a few other abandoned cars on the road. One was nothing but a blackened frame. Two of the others had bodies in them. In one of the cars, the body behind the steering wheel pawed at the windshield. The sound of teeth echoed in the air all around them.

St. George tapped the hood of the Taurus. "Cesar," he said. "You okay?"

The car was silent.

He walked around and leaned in the door. "Cesar?"

The radio was long gone. A rectangular hole gaped in the middle of the dashboard.

"He is not here," said Stealth.

"How can you be sure?"

"Cesar's abilities allow him to possess mechanical devices with a certain amount of functioning electronic circuitry. Based on the dust layer and the degree of fading in the various materials, I would estimate this vehicle has not functioned in at least four years."

St. George looked at the car. "What's that mean?"

"Is he dead?" asked Madelyn. "If he switched over into a car that didn't work, would that . . . I mean, could it kill him?"

"I do not know," said Stealth.

"But it's the car he said he was in," said Danielle. "The red Taurus."

A few yards behind the car, a crowd of undead staggered out into the street. One of them fell off the curb and hit the pavement face-first. The others wobbled but kept their balance.

"We can't stay here," said Freedom. "We've got to get moving again."

"Are we just going to leave him here?" said Danielle. She stood with her arms wrapped tight around herself and watched the mob of exes. There were at least fifty of them now, and more in the distance. The closest were a dozen yards away.

"There is no evidence he is here," said Stealth. She glared at the car as if it offended her. "If we are shifting between realities, perhaps he has been left behind in the other one."

"Except he could see this one," said Madelyn. "He saw the car and the dead people."

"There is too much conflicting data to make a solid hypothesis."

There were scrape marks around the trunk lock, and a dent that could've been from a crowbar. St. George yanked and it swung open with a squeak. "Damn it," he muttered.

Danielle looked at him. "What?"

"Maddy's wheelchair is gone," he said.

Maddy tried to sit up in Freedom's arms. "What?"

St. George looked down at the empty trunk. It had been stripped down to the frame. "Gone," he said.

An ex fell on him from behind and bit his shoulder. Its teeth sank into the fleece and grated on his skin. St. George shrugged the dead man off, grabbed it by the shoulders, and shoved it back at the approaching crowd. It knocked a few of them down. A few more stumbled over the fallen ones.

"We should be on our way," said Stealth.

"I agree," said Freedom. "We might move quicker without the wheelchair."

"Yeah," said Madelyn. "Piggyback?" The huge officer lifted her up and she swung around to hang on his broad shoulders.

Freedom settled Madelyn on his back. "We'll need to cut back and forth through side streets," he said. "We need to start throwing them off our trail before their numbers get any larger."

St. George took a last look at the car. He wondered if Cesar was somewhere else right now, wondering how everyone had vanished out of the car. Or maybe he was in some limbo, not even aware he'd ceased to exist.

Stealth started walking. They all fell in behind her.

* * *

They headed up Santa Monica Boulevard. Exes trailed behind them. St. George and Stealth beat aside the undead and crushed skulls. Freedom grabbed one that got too close and hurled it back across the wide road. After half a mile Stealth guided them onto a road heading east. Half a mile and seven more dead exes after that, St. George saw the hotel stretching up above the skyline.

"It's getting into the afternoon," he said.

"I am aware. From the shadows, I would put the time at twelve-thirty."

He glanced at the shadows. "Is this going to be a long stop?"

"I hope not."

The air rippled and the white noise of chattering teeth vanished. Stealth stepped back and pushed Danielle out of the way as an SUV roared by at twice the posted speed limit. It missed George by inches.

"Jerk," shouted Madelyn.

"Not much of a choice, is it?" said Danielle. "We stay on the sidewalks, we get attacked by random exes. Walk in the streets and we get hit by cars."

"They seem to be happening faster," said Freedom. "The shifts. It feels like we can't go more than an hour without one happening."

"They are," said St. George.

When they were across the street from the hotel, Stealth stopped. "St. George and I shall go on from here," she said. "The rest of you should remain at this location and attempt to locate Barry."

"I'm sorry, what?" Danielle's brows made twin arches over her eyes.

"Which part of my statement was unclear? Depending on traffic and his possible experiences during the shifts, he may have been here for as much as ninety minutes."

"Are you actually saying we should split up?" asked Madelyn. "Have you ever seen a horror movie?"

Stealth's nostrils flared. "On an average day the hotel has over nine hundred occupants. The hallways are less than six feet wide, leaving us very little maneuvering room. If we experience another shift and even half of those individuals were revealed as exes, there is no way a group of this size would escape without suffering losses. Infection at least, although there is a strong chance at least one of us would be killed."

She let the words sink in.

"I guess we're staying out here to look for Barry, then," Danielle said.

"This places a great deal of responsibility on you, Captain," said Stealth. "Do you feel recovered enough to accept it?"

Freedom's enormous chest swelled, and he lifted his head higher. "Yes, ma'am," he said. He managed to keep most of the annoyance out of his voice.

Stealth turned and stepped out into the broad street. Each step was paced to avoid the cars that went back and forth.

St. George followed a few feet behind her. He dodged cars until he caught up. They reached the far side of the street and headed for the hotel entrance.

"I shall go in," she said. "I need you to keep watch outside."

"So we're splitting up even more?"

"I shall be fine, George."

"What about your . . . ummm, your dad?"

"I shall be fine."

"Are you sure? The guy who's supposed to be your father is . . . pretty intense."

She looked at him. Her face seemed especially calm and stoic. "He is my father, George. Almost exactly as I remember him."

"Minus the whole international terrorist thing?"

She said nothing.

"Jesus," muttered St. George. "Why didn't you ever say anything?"

"He had very little to do with my life or upbringing, or our life within the Big Wall. It never seemed relevant."

"Relevant? Your dad's a borderline supervillain who's on a few dozen top-ten wanted lists around the world and you didn't think it was relevant?"

"Would you have trusted me less? Would it have changed how you felt about my abilities?"

"No," he said. "No, of course not. It wouldn't change anything."

He held out his hand. She took it and squeezed.

"In our world," she told him, "my father is dead. If I had any reason to believe you would have encountered him, I would have told you everything. I still will once we have resolved this current situation, if you wish."

St. George managed half a smile. "Are you sure?"

"Of course. It is important to me that we are open and trust one another."

"I meant, are you sure he's dead? It seems like the Quilt family is known for their toughness."

Her eyes dropped and her fingers loosened. "I am certain he is dead in our world."

There was a moment of silence between them.

"Ahhhh," said St. George.

"Again, I will tell you everything, if you wish."

The hotel entrance was a block away. A man with a camera leaned against a car. He perked up when he saw Stealth.

St. George looked at the man, then up at the hotel. "Maybe I should come with you."

She shook her head. "It will attract far too much attention for me to enter the hotel with an unknown man. Also, the Quilt of this world is still enough like my father that he will react poorly to surprises."

"Do I want to know how he's not like your father?"

"I would think not," said Stealth, "but I will tell you if you feel it is important to know."

"I'll probably sleep better if I don't," said St. George with another half smile.

"You will," she said. "Wait here. This should take fifteen minutes at the most."

*　*　*

Stealth marched onto the hotel grounds with long strides, moving past the handful of paparazzi before they could register the chance slipping away from them. A few quick cameras clicked and snapped, but she did not pause for them. She heard one man mutter about the fact she was wearing the same clothes she'd left in the night before.

She had not been here before with her own mind and memories. It was, she could admit, disconcerting to be exposed in front of so many people. To not be wearing her mask.

The doorman pulled open the door for her before recognition sparked in his eyes. Heads turned as she slipped out of her coat and hung it over her arm. She scanned the lobby for any sign of Barry but saw nothing. A few whispers reached her ears while she waited for the elevator. One girl, a Welsh tourist judging from her T-shirt, raised a Canon PowerShot S30 camera and took a picture.

The S30, Stealth noted, had been new in 2003.

The elevator pinged and the doors sealed her off from the lobby. There were thirty seconds of solitude before the doors slid open on her floor. She found the plastic keycard in her pocket and opened the suite.

Two of the couch pillows had been moved, and so had the oversized television remote. The vertical blinds had been rotated to the left. She could smell furniture polish. From the lines in the carpet and the faint scent of an electric motor she knew someone had vacuumed the suite. A subtle odor of tobacco lingered beneath the electric scent. The vacuumer was also a smoker.

The door clicked shut behind her. Her heart beat nine times. The only sounds were the almost subsonic rumble of the refrigerator in the kitchen area and the low whistle of central air conditioning.

She stepped across the suite, the coat-draped arm held out ahead of her. Her feet landed toes first, and the soft carpet muffled her steps. The knob on the closet door scraped as she turned it. The hinges rustled when the door opened.

Two flat cases hung on either side of the closet. They were bright blue, a color chosen to attract attention and thus deflect it at the same time. On casual examination, each one looked like an oversized garment bag. Against the back wall sat an oversized Versace suitcase, a pink monstrosity one would expect to find in a traveling supermodel's closet.

From her memories of this world, she knew each of the blue cases contained an array of frames and straps designed to keep their contents secure. One held an array of hand-to-hand weapons—knives, *sais,* collapsible batons, brass knuckles. The second case contained a quartet of Glocks, a pair of Colt pistols, a trio of Mk23 USSOCOM pistols, two micro-Uzis, and a Heckler & Koch G36 rifle her father had converted into a breakdown model. The pink suitcase held the gun leather, belts, and ammunition.

Stealth reached out and unzipped both of the garment bags at the same time.

Both were empty.

There was no need to double-check. Even before she had finished opening them, the weight of the hanging cases told her everything had been removed. She prodded the suitcase. It felt full, but the contents would be useless without the weapons.

"What are you doing?"

She spun, her arms flying to a defensive position as her weight shifted to her back leg.

Quilt stood six feet away. Just out of reach for a kick. His hands were behind his back. His stance appeared open and relaxed.

They stared at each other for a moment.

His hands came out from behind his back. They were empty. His left forefinger had a small patch of oil, half the size of a dime, alongside the nail. He reached up and adjusted his glasses. He did not blink. His eyes were on hers.

If he'd meant to fight, his gaze would've been at the top of her sternum. It gave a clear view of the body without the distraction of the opponent's eyes. Stealth was not sure why she thought the Quilt of this world would now consider her an opponent.

She lowered her hands. Not to her sides, but low enough to show a degree of concession. "I require the weapons," she told him. "Where are they?"

Her father's head shifted and he allowed himself a single blink. "The pistols are in the safe, as always," he said. "The blades are in my room. They were due to be cleaned and oiled. Why do you need them?"

"It would be difficult to explain."

He dipped his chin, a concession of his own. He turned and took a few steps across the suite toward his room. "Do you require a blade or pistol? Or a combination?"

"I will need all of them."

TWENTY-EIGHT

FREEDOM HAD IDENTIFIED a side door to one apartment complex at the top of some steps. The door swung outward so nothing could surprise them from behind. Exes didn't do well with stairs, so being eight steps up gave them some safety in the front. There were three cars parked on the street in front of the staircase, forming a bit more of a barrier.

The top of the staircase gave him a clear view of the street and half the intersection. He panned his head back and forth across, watching each pedestrian and each car that drove by. Studying the drivers reminded him of the checkpoints in Iraq.

He glanced back at Dr. Morris. "I could use your help," he said. "I'm not entirely sure what Mr. Burke looks like."

Dr. Morris—Danielle—stood with her back to the door behind him. It seemed to calm her to be surrounded. She was still vague in his memory. He seemed to remember her being much larger and brasher. He guessed part of that had to be the Cerberus battlesuit. She hadn't said much since George and Karen Quilt left.

No, he corrected himself. St. George and Stealth. He knew those were the right names, but his mind kept defaulting to the other ones.

"He's bald and black," said Madelyn.

"You just described me."

"And he's in a wheelchair."

"Probably not if he's in a cab," said Danielle. She leaned forward and looked either way down the street. "He's got light brown eyes. He smiles a lot. He's really thin because his power . . ." She closed her eyes and brought up her fingers, but the memories came before she snapped. "His power eats him up."

The description brought an image to Freedom's mind, but it was still too vague.

Madelyn still hung on Freedom's neck. He barely noticed her weight. Every now and then she'd shift her hips against his back. It disturbed him at first, and then he realized she was trying to make her legs work.

Her skin was cold. He could feel it on his neck, even through her sleeves. She gave off no warmth at all. He'd felt bodies like that before. Another reminder of Iraq and Afghanistan.

He remembered the name Stealth had used. The Corpse Girl. He still wasn't sure what it meant. He just knew seeing Madelyn had filled him with a great sense of relief.

A man walked by pushing a three-wheeled baby stroller. He chattered away on his phone and gave only a glance to the people up on the steps. A few more strides carried him past a decorative planter and out of sight. His voice continued for a few moments and then it faded, too.

"This sucks," said Madelyn.

He turned his head enough to see her in the corner of his eye. Her skin looked pale in the bright sunlight. "How so?"

"I figured once we all got back together everything would start making sense again. That everything would be fine."

"Fine how?"

"Just, you know . . . fine. Back to the way things are supposed to be. We'd all get together and something would pop and we'd all be good again."

"In my experience," said Freedom, "most problems aren't solved that easily."

Danielle snorted.

The world rippled around them. One moment the hotel was tall and pristine. The next, the bottom half was wrapped in overgrown ivy. Two balconies near the top were marked with black halos of soot.

A car in the middle of the street came to an abrupt halt and gained three years' worth of dust. Two of the figures across the street vanished, and the other two went from walking to staggering. The planter in front of them exploded with wild growth.

"Be careful what you wish for," muttered Danielle.

"Whoa," said Madelyn.

"You saw it this time?" asked Freedom.

"Yeah," she said. "I'm still seeing it. Home again, home again, like Mom used to say."

"Should we stay here?" asked Danielle.

"We should be good," said Freedom. "The plants hide us a bit more now, and the stairs still give us restricted access."

"Also means we'll have a harder time spotting Barry," she said.

Madelyn looked at the hotel. "You think they're okay inside?"

"They're fine," said Freedom. "The exes can't hurt St. George."

"Stealth's just human, though, right?"

Danielle snorted again. "She's not 'just' anything. If I had to bet, I'd say she has better odds of coming out of there than Geor— shit!"

Freedom turned in time to see Danielle slam herself back against the door. Her breath was fast and her arms pulled in tight against her ribs. Her eyes were locked up above Freedom's shoulder, on Madelyn.

He turned his head and a dead girl looked back at him from a few inches away. Her skin was white, even more so against her dark hair, and her eyes looked like dusty chalk. He could see the retinas, but there was no color or shine to them.

The Corpse Girl blinked twice. "What?" She looked at Freedom, then Danielle, and back. Her hand came up and patted at her head. "Is there a bug in my hair?"

"I think you might . . . you're getting better," Freedom said.

"Yeah?" She shifted on his back and glanced over at Danielle. Then she noticed her own hand. "Oh, that's right," she said.

A scream echoed down the street. It was far away, but it

sounded like a man's voice. A moment later it rang out again. It was words this time, but it was too distant to be understood.

Freedom straightened up and felt Madelyn shift on his back. He listened to the echoes for a moment. It was coming from the north, he was almost certain.

"Was that him?" asked Madelyn. "I'm not sure."

Danielle had her head cocked, listening, with her eyes closed. "I think it might've been," she said.

Freedom went down the stairs in long strides, taking two at a time. "Whoever it is," he said, "they need some help."

The three of them headed north. A few exes spotted them and stumbled their way, but they were easy to outpace. Danielle stayed so close to Freedom she was almost pressed against him. They covered two long blocks.

"Maybe we should yell for him," said Madelyn. "We could try to triangulate or something."

"No," said Freedom, shaking his head. "We don't want to attract any more exes."

"Definitely not," agreed Danielle.

Another shout echoed across the street and she winced. This time Freedom pinpointed the source. A battered yellow cab sat in the southbound lane of Doheny alongside a dark and dusty sedan. A figure in the backseat of the cab slammed against the rear door again and again. The shape in the front moved much slower.

They got closer and Freedom saw the cab had suffered some kind of collision. Most of the driver's side was dented and caved in. The other side was blocked by the sedan. The cab's tires were flat on the pavement and crumbling.

In the backseat of the cab was a thin black man. He had bristle-short hair, as if he'd been shaved bald and let it grow back. His chin had a few days' worth of stubble, too. The man saw them and waved. "Thank God," he called out. "Get me out of here." He'd rolled down the window, but it went only halfway. Probably to discourage dashers.

Captain Freedom checked the other figure in the cab. The ex in the driver's seat was trapped by its seat belt. It had turned halfway around to paw at the divider between it and the man in the back-seat. He felt Madelyn raise herself on his back. "Zzzap," she said.

"Barry," said Danielle. It was almost a sigh of relief. Her shoulders slumped and her hands unclenched.

It was, Freedom realized, probably just what he had looked like when he'd seen Madelyn for the first time.

Barry stared back at her. "You're the redhead," he said. He blinked twice and smiled. "Danielle. The Gundam pilot."

"I have no idea what that means," she said, "but it's good to see you."

"You, too." He looked up at Freedom. "The door's jammed. D'you think you can give it a pull from your side?"

"I think so, sir."

"And you do realize there's a zombie teenager on your back, right?"

"It's come up," said Freedom. He glanced over his shoulder. "You have a good grip?"

Madelyn nodded. "Yep."

Freedom grabbed the latch and pulled. It snapped off, but it jerked the door open enough for him to get his fingers around the edge. He braced his feet, heaved, and tore the door out of the frame. "Do you need a hand, sir?"

"Yeah, that'd be great," Barry said. He leaned forward and Freedom scooped him up like a child. "Oh, and can any of you explain what the *frak* just happened to the whole city!"

"Is this your first shift, Mr. Burke?"

"I have no idea what you're talking about, so I'm guessing yes."

"It's good to see you," said Madelyn.

"I know you, too," Barry said after a moment. "You're the dead girl in my dreams."

"The Corpse Girl," she said.

"Yeah!" He looked up at the huge officer, then at his uniform. "At least someone had the decency to wear nametags during the trippy amnesia fest."

"Just for you, sir." Freedom looked around. The noise of ripping off the door combined with Barry's shouts had attracted some exes. There were five or six in the immediate area closing on them. Maybe another dozen farther out. They had two minutes, tops, before they needed to start moving.

Barry shook his head. "Captain Freedom," he said. "Man, I hate cheap knockoff names. Can't the government put any thought into this stuff?"

Madelyn bit back a laugh.

"My wheelchair's in the trunk. You guys are with George and Karen Quilt, right?"

"Yeah," said Danielle. "They're back at the hotel."

Freedom walked around to the back of the cab. "How'd you end up here, sir?"

"I was taking a cab to the hotel," Barry said, "like she told me. And then a few minutes ago everything just . . . changed."

"The shift," said Madelyn.

Freedom hooked the fingers of his free hand under the lip of the cab's trunk and pulled. It wasn't locked, but the hinges were rusted. They squealed as he pried the lid up, and then Barry swore.

"No wheelchair," said Maddy. "Déjà vu."

"Long gone, if it was ever there," said Danielle.

"Not a problem for now," said Freedom.

"My bag's gone, too," said Barry. "My Weyland-Yutani shirt was in there, damn it."

"We should head back," said Freedom. "This area's getting hot, and it'll be harder to fight while holding both of you."

Barry looked up at Madelyn. "Wait, you can't walk either?"

She shook her head. "Not at the moment."

"Fantastic," he said with a grin. He looked over at Danielle. "Three more people in wheelchairs and we've got a basketball team."

* * *

Stealth watched Quilt pack the weapons into a duffel bag he'd set on the couch. His movements were quick and precise. It was an admirable efficiency of motion.

And it was wrong. She knew that. Terribly wrong.

He used the last pieces of a shredded towel to separate the weapons so the bag would make no noise. He checked the chamber on the last of the Glocks and held it out to her without looking. It was done automatically, the way other fathers would hand over keys or credit cards.

She took the Glock. It felt good in her hand. Not perfect, but good.

He set a clip-on holster on the arm of the couch and followed it with a collapsible baton. The holstered pistol went on her right hip. She slid the baton into her side pocket.

"I have packed the spare magazines," he told her, "and enough ammunition for three reloads on each."

She looked at him. "What have you kept for yourself?"

He zipped the bag shut. "I have the G36 and one of the Mark 23s."

"Will that be enough?"

The edges of his mouth twitched, the barest hint of a smile. She remembered seeing it twice as a child. "Have you ever known it not to be enough?"

It was an echo of what she had told St. George the night before.

Too much of an echo.

He held the bag out and waited for her to take it. She looked at it for a moment. Then she looked at him. He stared back.

"You are not my father."

The words hung in the air for a moment. He blinked once. "And what makes you say that, child?"

"Because my father swore to kill me if I could not stop him," she said. "It is the kind of man he was. No one can change that much. If you were my father, even a version of him ... one of us would not be alive right now."

He set the bag down and blinked again. His fingers flexed once, like ten scorpion tails coiling and uncoiling. Then he reached up with his left hand and made a minute adjustment to his spectacles. "Perhaps I took pity on you."

"I often wished he had. But that was not his way. You are a vestigial childhood dream dredged up by Smith's manipulations. A desire buried deep in my subconscious. I wanted you to be real so . . ."

He waited for her. After a few moments, he raised one brow. "So . . . ?"

"So I could introduce George to my family."

"I see," said Quilt. "And why would that matter?"

"Because I think, in his own way, my father would have approved of such an honorable man, despite their many differences."

"I think he would have."

Stealth set her hand on the pistol.

Quilt nodded. His mouth opened, as if to say something else, and then snapped shut. It opened and shut again. And again. The sound of clicking teeth filled the suite.

In her peripheral vision, the room fell apart. Wallpaper sagged and darkened. The couches were reduced to shreds of fabric and broken wood. The curtains vanished and let in the harsh sunlight.

The duffel bag vanished as well. The weight on her hips changed as the pistol vanished beneath her hand and the baton dissolved into the air. Even the holster was gone.

The dead thing was not her father. Its shoulders were too wide. The hair was too thin, even taking age into account. It was, by her estimate, an inch and a half too tall. The jawline was wrong.

It reached for her and she batted its hands out and away. A strike to either side of its neck cracked two vertebrae. Her heel lashed out and shattered one of its knees. It hit the floor and a second kick cracked the side of its skull.

There was a sound from behind her. Another ex-human stumbled in from the hall, drawn in by the sound. The door had been kicked open at some point, four years ago judging from the shade of the exposed wood, and splinters of the frame were strewn in the entryway.

The ex had been a woman, and was still dressed in the dark uniform coat of the hotel. Two more followed in behind her, then a third and fourth. The third was wearing a staff polo shirt splattered with dried blood. The fourth had been a boy of eleven at most. It was dressed in red swim trunks with dragons on them. Another child tottered in behind them. This one was naked, but mangled enough she could not be certain of its gender.

The sound of teeth grew louder and Stealth turned again. Another pair of exes had wandered out from the master bedroom. She guessed they'd been the original occupants of the suite. The dead woman wore a wedding band and engagement ring. The dead man did not.

Eight exes, six of them in the narrow entryway.

She leaped over the remains of the couch toward the bedroom door. The heel of her palm slammed into the dead man's nose. The ex's face flattened out with a crack as the bones were driven back into its skull. The dead thing staggered back and tipped over. She spun and struck the other ex just below the neck, crushing its throat back to the spine. Her follow-through shattered its jaw. She dropped, spun, and swept its legs out from under it.

Another ex staggered from the suite's office. A high kick snapped its neck. It wobbled and then fell over. Its jaws still snapped open and shut.

Something moved behind her. The ex in the uniform coat had crossed the room and was a few feet away. The others were a yard behind it, still working their way around the couch. Three more had entered the room, and she could hear more in the hallway.

Nine exes between her and the exit. At least six more in the hallway, judging from the echo of teeth and footsteps. Uneven floor. No weapons. While the exes took another step forward, she ran through five different methods of taking on multiple undead opponents. She considered a dozen possible scenarios and outcomes.

Then she did the most logical thing to guarantee her safety.

Stealth drove a kick into the uniformed ex's chest, knocking it back into one behind it, and turned away. On her first step, she reached up and crossed her arms in front of her face. On the second, she grabbed the collar of her shirt behind her head. On the third step, now a full run, she kicked off and dove through the glass doors of the balcony.

* * *

St. George stood at the corner of the hedge that separated the hotel grounds from the public sidewalk. He had a clear view of the main entrance to the hotel, the doorman, and the valet. A Middle Eastern–looking man, his wife, and three small children waited for their car. Two of the children were twins. A few paparazzi stood nearby, but none of them seemed to recognize him as the mystery man seen with Karen Quilt.

It all looked real. He tried to spot an inconsistency in the way people moved or the smells of flowers and fountain water that hung in the air. He studied the front of the hotel for a break in the architectural details. Anything that would hint it was just a hallucination.

A bee wove back and forth along the hedge and then launched itself toward the hotel flowerbeds. One of the paparazzi scratched the side of his mouth. The twins traded colorful cards back and forth between their hands.

Then he heard a crash from above him. The thin sound of breaking glass. His head whipped up. So did everyone else's. He saw the shards sparkling in the sun, the body in the air, and then—

By the time he realized what he was seeing, she was already on the ground.

Stealth ripped her shirt over her head and lashed out with it as she began to plunge. The sleeve wrapped around a balcony railing two floors below hers. It slipped loose of the rail just as quickly, but it was enough to shift her angle of descent, pulling her back toward the building.

She let go of the shirt and slammed into the railing of the third balcony down. She held on for an instant, then dropped to the next one. Then the one below that, and the one below that. Her fingertips grabbed at the balconies like a mountain climber and the holds bled off her momentum. She dropped from railing to edge to railing, and less than ten seconds after going through the penthouse window she was standing on the ground.

People rushed forward. Some of them looked shocked. A few of them had phones out to record the incident. The paparazzi were snapping photos of the scuffed-up supermodel walking around outside in her skimpy bra. She pushed past all of them and marched up to St. George.

"Give me your jacket," she said.

He was still in awe. Still processing what he'd just seen. "What?"

"I will attract too much attention like this."

"You just jumped out of a sixteen-story window, of course you're attracting attention." He pulled the fleece off and held it out. She tugged it over her head and sank her arms into the sleeves. It was big on her.

They headed out onto the street and down the block. The photographers followed at a semi-respectable distance. "The others are gone," she said.

St. George looked up and down the street. "They're probably just out of sight," he said. "Calm down, we'll find them."

"I am always calm."

"Is that why you jumped out the window?"

"When the shift happened, the hotel suite was filled with ex-humans. The balcony was the most efficient and safest way of exiting the building."

He looked at her. "What shift?"

She glanced at him. "You did not experience a shift two minutes ago?"

St. George shook his head. "It's been pretty calm down here. No problems at all."

Her face didn't change, but he recognized the annoyance. "You are certain?"

"Yeah, of course I am. Do you think the world shifted over to post-apocalypse mode and I didn't notice?"

She glared at him, but he recognized the uncertainty in it.

Movement on the sidewalk caught his eye. Freedom and Danielle, a block north. The huge officer still had Madelyn on his back, and now someone cradled in his right arm as well. "There they are," he said. He squinted at the figure Freedom was carrying. "And they've got Barry."

Stealth opened her mouth, then pressed her lips shut again.

They met up on the sidewalk. Barry smiled. "George, I presume."

"Good to see you."

"You, too." He looked over at Stealth. "Both of you."

"Did you just jump out the window?" asked Madelyn. "Was that you?"

"It was."

"That was so cool!"

"Are you well?" Stealth asked Barry.

"A little humiliated that I'm being carried around like a kitten, but fine other than that." He glanced at Danielle. "Just being around most of you is unlocking a lot of stuff in my head."

"Can you change?" asked St. George. "Having Zzzap with us would be a huge advantage right now."

Barry's face dropped. "No," he said. "I can't find the switch. I've been looking for it for a couple of minutes now."

"Crap."

Barry looked at George, then up at Freedom and Madelyn. "It's not just me?" he asked. "None of you have your powers?"

"Nothing past the basics," Freedom said.

"Only those which function on an unconscious level," corrected Stealth. "Neither you nor St. George needs to consciously use your enhanced strength or endurance. St. George does not need to will himself to be invulnerable. Only those abilities which require conscious activation have been repressed. Barry's transformation into Zzzap. St. George's flight and fire breath."

"Makes sense, kind of," said Danielle.

St. George cleared his throat. "I think we can still make it to the Mount before dark if we don't get slowed down."

"You mean, if the world doesn't go all kablooey on us again?" Barry said.

"Yeah."

"I still think we should just hop on a bus," said Danielle. "Having Cesar drive us cut an hour off our walking time."

"And got me thrown through a windshield," said St. George. "What if it'd been you?"

Stealth turned and headed back up the street.

"Great," muttered Danielle.

TWENTY-NINE

THE STREETLIGHT CHANGED, the walk signal appeared, and they crossed Fairfax. A half-dozen other people shared the crosswalk with them. A few of them glanced at the giant Army officer carrying two people, one of them a pale-skinned girl, but he didn't hold their attention for long.

"This is just weird," said Barry. He looked up at a sign for CBS studios. "I mean, walking around LA with people everywhere."

"You're not doing the walking," said Danielle.

"Don't nitpick," he said. "You know what I mean."

"Yeah," she said, "I do." The light changed and traffic surged into life around them. "You think Cesar's back?"

"Maybe," said St. George. He looked at the cars. "Don't know how he'll find us if he is."

"We're heading for the Mount," said Madelyn. "He's smart. He'll find us."

St. George glanced at Barry cradled in Freedom's arm, then up at the officer. "Want me to carry him for a while?"

"Hey," said Barry. "Him is right here in front of you."

"Sorry."

"And you've got skinny arms. It'd be uncomfortable as hell."

Madelyn and Danielle both chuckled.

Freedom shook his head. "It's better to just have one of us dealing with the wounded, sir."

"We're not wounded," said Madelyn.

The huge officer glanced up at her. "The principle's the same," he said. "Wounding one man takes out two, because someone else has to help the wounded man. If we're each helping one of you, we're both hampered as fighters." He looked at St. George. "It's better for me to help both and leave you free to fight if we need to."

"Okay."

"Besides, you're looking pretty beat, sir."

"I've been up for about thirty hours," said St. George. "I'm not even sure when I ate last."

Danielle glanced at a bagel shop and Subway sitting next to each other across the street. "We could grab some food. Eat on the go."

"There is still a chance this is the real world which we are viewing through altered perceptions," said Stealth. She didn't look back when she spoke.

"So?"

"There is no way to know what we might be eating."

Madelyn's face wrinkled up. "Oh, gross."

"There is also the chance we will be eating nothing at all. In which case we would gain no benefit from stopping."

"Okay, I get it," said Danielle. She shoved her hands in her pockets. "No food."

"Please explain again how you found Barry."

The redhead looked up from the sidewalk. "Sorry, what?"

Stealth turned around, but continued to walk backward in firm, even strides. It struck St. George that she somehow made walking backward in an oversized fleece jacket look very no-nonsense. "Explain again how you found him. In detail."

"A shift happened while you were in the hotel," said Freedom. "We heard a yell, investigated, and found Mr. Burke in a cab with an ex."

"He didn't yell," smirked Danielle. "He screamed like a little girl."

"Hey," snapped Madelyn.

"No offense," Danielle said.

"You're not that little," said Freedom.

Stealth raised a finger. "What condition was the cab in?"

"What do you mean?" asked the huge officer.

"Was it damaged in any way? Exterior or interior?"

Freedom looked at Danielle. She shrugged. "It looked like it might've been sideswiped," he said. "The driver's side was pretty banged up. The tires were flat, but I think that was just from dry rot."

"Nothing else?"

He shook his head.

Stealth closed her eyes for a moment, as if she'd been struck with sudden pain. She looked at Barry. "Explain from your point of view," she told him. "Use as much detail as you can."

He looked at St. George. The hero shrugged.

"I got a cab from the airport, like you said," Barry explained. "I asked the driver how far out of the way Universal Studios was. He said not far—which turned out to be a big lie—and I asked if we could drive past it. We came down the freeway and he was pointing all sorts of stuff out to me. Then he got off in Hollywood and we were going along the streets and all of a sudden there was this . . . I don't know. It was like the world switched channels."

Stealth glanced at St. George. "For how long?"

"Half an hour," he said. "Maybe forty-five minutes. I wasn't checking my watch for any of it."

"That's not right," said Freedom. "It was ten minutes at the most."

Barry shook his head. "Half an hour at least."

"In high-stress situations, it's not unusual for time to seem to slow down," the captain explained. "It may have felt like half an hour, but—"

"Half an hour at least," repeated Barry. "I don't know what you guys saw, but I know what I saw."

Stealth focused on St. George. "You still insist there was no shift at all?"

He shook his head. "Nothing."

"Inside the hotel," she said, "the shift was at least ninety seconds. I am not sure it continued after I left the room."

"After you dove out the window, you mean," said St. George.

"Yes."

"That was so cool," Madelyn said.

Stealth came to a stop as the light changed to red. A row of cars turned in and drove through the crosswalk behind her toward a towering parking structure. Madelyn looked back and forth from Stealth, still facing backward, and the stoplight. "How did you—"

"On the opposite corner the crosswalk signal has a beeper for sightless pedestrians. The sound is distinct, even beneath the traffic noises."

"But you couldn't know which way the light was changing off the sound."

"She can't," said St. George, "but she can see the flow of traffic on this—"

The road flickered and the cars slammed to a halt as a wave of dust and decay washed across the street. Cars lost tires and windshields. Buildings lost windows and signs and one even lost a wall. Half the pedestrians vanished and the city went silent.

St. George opened his mouth to yell and took two steps forward, but Stealth was already whirling. The ex behind her caught a strike in the throat and one in each knee. She ducked, grabbed its calves, and flipped the dead man over backward. It struck the pavement head-first and went still. She lashed up with the heel of her hand and caught the second ex under the jaw, spraying its teeth into the air. They clicked and pattered on the pavement while she drove three more hammer blows into the sides of the creature's skull, each one cracking bone. The ex wobbled and then slumped to the ground.

A dead woman with stringy hair grabbed Danielle by the arm. Its fingers had been worn down to bony tips. She shrieked and yanked her arm away, but its claws caught at her sleeve.

Freedom shifted Barry in his arms and slammed his boot into the ex's side. The kick crushed the dead woman's pelvis and rib cage. It flew away from Danielle to crash against a rust-spotted truck. The ex slumped to the pavement and flailed, trying to move limbs that had nothing left to support them.

St. George took two steps and shoved a muscle-bound ex in workout clothes. The dead man flew across six lanes of street and slammed through the side of a bus stop. It tried to get up, but its legs were hooked up and over the steel framework. Too much thought was needed for it to free itself.

"Well," said Barry, "that all looked pretty easy."

"We've had a lot of practice," said St. George.

"It was very cool," said Madelyn. She smiled at him from Freedom's shoulders.

"Thanks."

"Oh frak," said Barry.

St. George turned. Danielle shook as if she was cold. There was a gash in her sleeve. The bony fingers had torn through the camouflaged material as it was hurled away.

"Oh no," she muttered. She thrashed her way out of the coat. "Damn it, damn it, damn it."

"There's no blood," said St. George. "I don't see any blood."

The Army jacket hit the ground and Danielle held her arm up. Her shirtsleeve was already rolled up, and they could all see the white scrape on her arm. There were a few small curls of loose skin around it. She poked at it and they all waited.

The scrape turned pink. At a few places it was almost red. But it didn't bleed.

"Oh, Jesus," she said. Her eyes were wet. "I think I'm going to be sick."

Barry grabbed her hand. "You're okay," he said. "That's all that matters. You're going to be fine."

"I'm so sorry, ma'am," said Freedom. "I didn't mean for it—"

"This is getting ridiculous," said Danielle. She squeezed Barry's hand. "How are we supposed to do this? We're not even halfway to the Mount."

"We've got to," he said. "They're all counting on us back there."

"You don't know that."

"The armor's back there," said St. George. "The Cerberus suit's waiting for you."

She bit her lip. Then she swiped the jacket off the ground and fought her way back into it.

Behind them, Stealth spun on her heel and snapped an ex's neck with a high kick. "Let us be on our way, then," she said.

Danielle muttered something under her breath and started walking. St. George fell in next to her. Freedom helped Madelyn adjust herself on his back, switched Barry to his other arm, and brought up the rear.

* * *

The heroes walked for another hour and put down twenty-three exes. They'd passed Highland and were heading into a more residential area when the world glitched, giving them a quick glimpse of a bustling Los Angeles at rush hour. Then it reverted back to the devastated city they knew. Two-thirds of the cars on the road vanished as quickly as they'd appeared. The rest became wrecks with cracked windows and flat tires. The one closest to them, a BMW, had a dead woman with tangled brown hair in the passenger seat. The ex pawed at the glass between them. It was wearing a faded yellow sundress that had popped too many buttons. Bright red sunglasses were perched above the ex's forehead.

Danielle stared at the creature. "This is going to sound weird," she said, "but I think I remember her."

The zombie smacked its head against the side window. Danielle hopped back and her arms pulled in close. She forced them back out.

Madelyn pulled herself a little higher on Freedom's back. "Was she a friend of yours?"

Danielle shook her head. "I mean, I remember this ex. Trapped in the car with the sundress. She's wearing combat boots too, right?"

St. George stepped up and peered through the window. "Yeah."

"It was a run, a month or two before we met you guys," she said to Freedom. "It might've been one of the times we were gathering cars for the Big Wall. I remember a couple of the scavengers making guesses about the sundress and boots combo. Ilya, Al, maybe . . . Billy? Did we have a Billy? I can kind of picture some-one with short blond hair . . ."

"Billie Carter," said Freedom. "Not a he, she."

"Ahhh."

Stealth looked up at the sky. "We are within half a mile of the Mount and we have seventy-five minutes of daylight left." She gestured them down the road.

"Doesn't sound bad," said Barry. "I mean, as long as we don't think about the few thousand exes outside the Big Wall any given day."

Danielle's back went stiff so fast she staggered. She shot an angry look at Barry.

"Sorry," he said, "just thought I'd voice it because I haven't heard anyone else bring it up."

Stealth lashed out with her foot and sent an ex staggering back. It was a dead man with silver hair in a deep red UMass sweatshirt. As it wobbled, she stepped forward, brought her palm up, and caught it under its jaw. The dead man's head tilted back and it tipped over. The back of its skull hit the curb with the sound of an egg cracking.

She glanced back at them. "We shall get as close as possible and signal the Wall guards. There are several apartment build-ings and other structures near that corner of the Big Wall. We shall take shelter there until a vehicle can be sent out to re-trieve us."

"That still doesn't really answer the question about the thou-sands of exes," Danielle said.

"An actual question was not asked," said Stealth.

They walked on for a few more feet. "Okay, fine," Danielle said. "How are we going to deal with all the exes outside the Wall? They'll tear us apart before we can get into a building."

An ex stumbled out from between two cars and reached for her. St. George lunged forward, grabbed it by the neck, and heaved it up and over his head. The dead thing sailed through the air and crashed down on the street behind them, a few feet from the BMW imprisoning the sundress ex.

"Please note," said Stealth, "the ex went after you, Danielle."

"Yeah," she snapped, "I noticed." She clenched her fists again and again.

"It went after you," Stealth said, "even though Barry and Captain Freedom were closer targets."

Their eyes all drifted between Freedom, Barry in his arms, Danielle, and the gap between the two cars where the ex had been lurking. They looked back at the broken ex in the street. They looked at each other again.

And then they all looked up at Madelyn, still hanging on the huge officer's shoulders.

"The ex in the car also did not react to Freedom when he moved past it. It remained focused on Danielle and St. George. The sensory filter that renders Madelyn near invisible to ex-humans has been active for some time now, most likely since her true appearance began to register in our conscious minds again."

"Yay, me," said the Corpse Girl, smiling.

Stealth turned and continued east. "Her abilities extend to those she has contact with, and it would seem Barry's proximity keeps him included as well. If she can include Danielle as well, that makes the four of you free to reach a safe position near the Wall while St. George and I hold off the exes."

"And if her powers can't cover us all?"

"Then you will have to move quickly."

Danielle sighed and muttered something. Stealth ignored it.

Another two intersections went by. They passed Las Palmas. A handful of exes came after them. Stealth broke several necks. Freedom backhanded one through a wooden fence with his free hand. St. George threw a few of the zombies at the trios and quartets following behind them. They sprawled in the street and cut down on pursuers. He knew it wouldn't be good to have a few dozen exes stumbling up behind them when they reached the dense numbers around the Big Wall.

Freedom paused for a moment. "Pardon me, sir," he said to Barry. He shifted the smaller man into his other hand. "I just need to shake that arm out for a bit."

"Just tell me you wiped your knuckles off. You've been smacking zombies with that hand."

"It's okay, I'm wearing gloves."

Madelyn snickered.

"And I'd just gotten comfortable on the other side."

"Sorry, sir."

"I'll let it slide since you're doing all the— What the hell is that?" Barry tried to raise himself up in Freedom's arms. "Was someone playing Jumanji or something?"

Ahead of them the sides of Beverly were wrapped in green. Branches and leaves reached out to surround some of the nearby houses.

Tendrils and vines had grown out along the long-dead power lines. The vast expanse of green looked like the entrance to an oversized hedge maze. Or a cave.

"The Wilshire Country Club," said Stealth.

"Looks like management gave the groundskeepers the last four years off," said Barry.

She ignored him and pointed down the road. "Beverly continues straight through for five blocks. There are no intersections or exits."

"So it's a killing floor," Freedom said.

"That would depend on how many exes are along this stretch of road. The lack of intersections limits their access as well. However, you and George both retain enough strength to tear though the fences on either side if we require an emergency exit."

"Assuming there's nothing on the other side of the fence," said Danielle.

St. George looked at the green tunnel. "Are we sure we want to go this way?"

"It is the most direct route. The exit is by the southwest corner of the Big Wall. Anything else would require that we detour around the country club, at least eleven blocks in either direction."

Stealth paused to spin and shatter an ex's jaw with her boot. The boot came back around to strike the dead woman in the chest and knock it back over the hood of a low-slung sports car. The ex tumbled out of sight and hit the ground with a loud crack.

"It is not a favorable choice," she continued, "but at the moment it is the best choice. We have less than an hour of daylight left. We must move."

She headed toward the tunnel of green.

They followed her.

* * *

On either side of the street plants grew thick and wild. Branches curled through the fence and over the sidewalk. A few had found street signs and wrapped around them like vines. Some had even reached around broken cars, wrapping them in green and making them part of the walls. It made the street feel enclosed. Constricted.

St. George could see movement ahead of them, but it was hard to break it down into individual figures. There was just enough distance to make the stretch of road blur at the end. He seemed to remember an odd jog in the road, one of the many places where the old neighborhoods of Los Angeles hadn't lined up when they joined together. They wouldn't be able to see the Big Wall until they were right on top of it.

The *click-click-click* of teeth rolled down the tunnel of greenery. The leaves muffled the sound, but not much. Just enough to make it hard to guess how far away it was.

St. George moved to the front to walk alongside Stealth. Danielle stayed behind them. Captain Freedom brought up the rear with Madelyn and Barry.

They'd gone a hundred feet in when the first pair of exes staggered out at them. Two dead men. One wore a blue shirt with a plumber's logo on it. The other was bare chested and missing an arm. Its shoulder was a ragged, half-burned mess.

St. George grabbed the plumber's outstretched arm and yanked the ex close. Its teeth snapped at his face. He grabbed the dead man by the seat of the pants, tried to ignore the soft mass beneath the denim, and hurled the zombie up and over the wall of green.

Stealth dodged the one-armed ex, tripped it, and pushed down hard on its head as it fell. The dead thing's forehead took the full impact of the fall. She kicked it in the back of the skull, just to be sure it stayed down.

Danielle shook her head. "This has been right outside the Mount all this time?" he asked. "How?"

"Nature runs wild," said Madelyn. "I saw a really cool special about it once on the History Channel."

"Well, what I meant was why didn't we do something about it?"

"We didn't have any lawn mowers?" said Barry.

"I don't even remember seeing all this," said St. George.

"It is unlikely you would," said Stealth. "For the most part, neither you nor Barry leaves the Mount on foot. You are more used to an aerial view."

"That's true," said Barry.

Another ex, a woman, stumbled toward them from down the street. St. George could see two more past her heading their way, and another four past that. "They're picking up," he said. "At least half a dozen."

"Half a dozen's not many," said Freedom.

"We haven't even gone one block yet," said Danielle.

"Let none of them past us," Stealth warned St. George. "If a significant number get behind us, we will not be able to defend ourselves on two fronts."

St. George took a few steps, swung his hand like an axe, and crushed the side of the dead woman's skull. The ex slumped to the ground. The next two banged their teeth together as they closed in on him. He let them get close enough to grab at his outstretched hands. They gnawed at his fingers and he slammed their heads together.

An ex pulled itself free of the vines that had hidden it and staggered at Danielle. She stumbled back and Freedom stepped forward, his free hand curled into a fist the size of a football. Before he could strike, Stealth grabbed the ex by its collar and yanked it back. As it fell over she grabbed its skull and twisted. The body thumped to the ground. Its teeth scraped on the pavement as its jaw continued to work back and forth.

Four of the walking dead blocked the road. George grabbed one by its heavy coat and swung it into the air. He slammed it against the other three, battering them to the ground, and then hurled it as far as he could. Three blocks away the ex bounced off the wall of greenery and crashed onto a truck.

One of the others tried to crawl to its feet as they walked past. Freedom brought his boot down hard between the dead man's shoulder blades. The zombie's spine cracked and it slumped back down on the pavement.

They fought through another three blocks. St. George took the brunt of it while Stealth caught the rest. Freedom dealt with the two or three that stumbled up from behind.

St. George chopped through an ex's neck and watched its skull bounce away. He glanced over in time to see Stealth flip a dead man over her shoulder and spin to kick the corpse in the head while it was still in midair. "Now you're just showing off," he said.

"I am testing my muscle memory," she said. "Their numbers are not increasing as much as I expected."

"They're still going up, though," said St. George. He nodded down the road. "It looks like there's another thirty or forty to make our way through."

She looked grim. "As Barry said, this corner of the Big Wall has an average of fourteen hundred exes, drawn here by either sounds or the sight of guards patrolling along the Wall. Even with their random movements, this section of road should contain at least one hundred of them."

St. George walked forward with his arms spread and gathered up half a dozen exes. He looked back at Stealth. "Maybe things are going our way for once." He shoved the exes forward and they stumbled and fell. Their bodies tripped four others staggering at the heroes. He stepped up to the pile and twisted their heads one after another.

When he glanced back, she was still grim.

He looked past her. Since entering the overgrown length of road, Danielle had pulled her arms tight against herself. She'd backed up so close to Freedom he had to push her along. Barry looked annoyed at being carried, but kept one hand on Danielle's shoulder. Madelyn was trying to watch everything. Her perception filter, as she liked to call it.

Up ahead the road curved off to the left. Another dozen or so exes staggered toward them. Three of them wore military helmets with their civilian clothes, while one dead man had on what looked like a batting helmet. Leftovers from one of Legion's many attempts to storm their home.

"Not much farther," St. George called back to the others. "The Big Wall should be right around that bend."

"Want us to go ahead?" asked Madelyn. "We could scout around and make sure they're ready to open the gates or pull us over the Wall."

"The exes may not see you," said Stealth, "but if we have all been gone for any amount of time, the guards may not react well to your appearance."

"We'll all go together," said Freedom with a quick glance up at Madelyn. "All of us or none of us."

"I'd prefer all of us," Barry said.

"Me, too," said Danielle.

St. George tore the hood off a car, held it in both hands, and sent it spinning into the approaching exes. It decapitated two, tore five in half through the torso, and shattered the legs of half a dozen more.

Stealth was a blur. Kicks, strikes, punches, flips. She broke bones, snapped necks, and cracked skulls. Exes reached for her and then slumped to the ground.

Then they came around a corner, and the Big Wall loomed in front of them. The tops of buildings peeked over the barrier of triple-stacked cars. St. George could see the wooden platforms and rails that ran along the top of the Wall, and as they got a few steps closer he could see up Rossmore to . . .

"Oh my God," he said.

THIRTY

THE HOLE IN the Big Wall was twenty feet across. Two stacks of the cars that made up its bulk had collapsed and crashed to the ground inside. The wooden walkways along the top had splintered apart and gone with it. What was left of the Wall on either side sagged inward. One car hung in midair, still half wedged into the layered structure.

Exes were slumped on the pavement around the base of the Big Wall. St. George guessed there were a few hundred of them. Most of them had head wounds, in a variety of calibers. A few had suffered more violent trauma—crushed skulls or decapitation. The ground around them was covered with dark, dried puddles and a few dots of dull brass.

A few dozen exes still staggered in the street. Another dozen were visible through the hole, inside the Mount. Men, women, and children. A few of them noticed the heroes and staggered toward them.

Danielle shook her head and bit her lip.

St. George couldn't see anyone along the Big Wall in either direction. Rossmore curved heading north, but he was pretty sure he saw another hole farther along. If he had it right in his head, it was across from the church.

"What happened?" asked Barry.

Madelyn's head swung back and forth. "Is everyone . . . are they all dead?"

Freedom reached up and put his huge hand on top of hers. His face was a blank, but somehow still grim. St. George had come to know it as Freedom's bad-news face.

"We should move inside," said Stealth. "There is nothing to learn out here, and the number of exes appears lower inside the Wall."

No one argued. St. George battered a few dead people out of the way and cleared a path to the gap in the Wall. Dried blood covered the hood of a car in the Big Wall's bottom row. Lots of dried blood. Someone had lost an artery and sprayed out.

Stealth looked at the dark brown fan with a clinical eye.

St. George heaved against the side of the car and it slid out of the way with a scrape of tire rims on pavement. The sound attracted a few more exes, but let them get through faster. Once Freedom stepped through, St. George heaved against the other side of the car and pushed it back into place. It wasn't much of a barrier, but it was better than nothing. A few exes bumped against the far side and stretched their arms across the hood. They clawed at the air separating them from the living people.

Stealth tapped something with her boot, then kicked it up and grabbed it with one hand. A police baton. St. George remembered several of the guards carrying them as emergency hand-to-hand weapons. Stealth settled it against her arm, then turned and dispatched three of the closest exes with swift swings and thrusts. They hit the ground with a rhythmic *thump, thump, thump*.

Freedom took a few steps along the Wall, then turned and walked the other way. "What was that?" Madelyn asked. "Was that another body?"

Barry closed his eyes and muttered something.

"Sir," said Freedom. He gestured with his free hand.

St. George stepped over. He took a quick look around for exes, then kneeled to inspect the body. He was pretty sure it had been a man. One arm was gone. The other one was missing below the elbow. Both legs ended at the knee. The torso was opened below the ribs and had been hollowed out. There was enough skin left to see the man had been black, and a lone dreadlock of dark hair curled down from the side of the well-gnawed skull.

The flesh was dry and wrinkled. A thin layer of dust covered it all. The body had been there for a while.

"Makana," said Stealth.

St. George glanced up. He hadn't realized she was standing there. "Are you sure?"

"There is enough left for a basic forensic reconstruction," she said. "Approximate height, weight, and age are correct. Skin tone, hair, and gender are as well. There is a scar on his left shoulder which matches one Makana had, although the one on his right forearm was more distinctive and would be more conclusive. He is also wearing a similar belt buckle and holster, although some of the scavengers have been known to trade gear on occas—"

"Okay," said St. George. "I believe you. It's him."

"I do not mean to seem callous. I just wish to be clear there is very little chance this is not Makana. We should be on our way. Moving the car has doubtlessly attracted whatever exes are within the Big Wall."

"Where are we going?" asked Barry.

"To the Mount itself," said Stealth. She pointed northeast with the baton. "It is the logical place for survivors to fall back to if the walls were breached. If nothing else, we should find supplies and weapons there." She glanced at Danielle. "And the Cerberus suit."

"God, I hope so," said Danielle.

* * *

They walked east along Beverly to get as much of the setting sun as possible. Along the way they put down a baker's dozen of exes. St. George recognized two of them. One had been a scavenger named Danny Foe. He tried not to think about it as he twisted the dead man's head around.

The sun vanished behind the corner of the Big Wall just as

they reached Larchmont. Stealth announced the wide street was their best route north to the Mount. They saw more bodies on the sidewalk and lawns. No one complained too much when the light faded.

St. George crushed a few more exes. He tried not to look at their faces, but more of them looked familiar. People from the Mount. People from the Seventeens' camp who'd joined them. Even a few from Project Krypton. He tried to hurl those away before Freedom could see them.

"No chance of lighting a torch?" Danielle asked. "We could tie up my socks in a tree branch or something."

St. George shook his head. "Sorry. Still don't have any fire." He coughed for emphasis.

"Are you out of gas," asked Barry, "or just forgot how to throw up?"

"I'm not sure. Both, maybe?"

"We are less than four blocks from the Melrose gate," said Stealth. "We will be fine." She swung her baton and cracked an ex's skull for emphasis.

St. George heard Freedom say something, but the words were lost as he cracked an ex's skull with his knuckles. He kicked the body away. "What was that?"

"I said there still aren't many, sir," the captain repeated. "If the Mount's the fallback position, the exes should be denser here." He shook his head. "This still isn't much heavier than the standard numbers we've seen everywhere else. Fifteen or twenty per block."

They reached the intersection. There was just enough light for St. George to make out the huge globe of the Earth perched on the walls of the Mount, two blocks away. He could also see a few dozen exes between them and the gate. The sound of clicking teeth filled the air. "Cheer up," he said. "There's a lot more here."

In the dim light he saw Danielle shudder. Freedom reached out, wrapped an arm around her shoulders, and pulled her in close. "I've got her, sir," he said.

"And I've got all of us," said Madelyn. "Keep an eye on Stealth. We're good."

St. George turned in time to see Stealth's baton strike a dead woman's skull three times in a blur of motion. It might've been four times. The last one made the whole head jiggle. The ex wobbled for a moment, its arms went limp, and it fell over.

He marched into the horde and they bit at his arms and face. His shirt was covered with rips and snags. He swept his arms together and slammed four of the dead things against each other. Before they could untangle their limbs, he shoved the mass off to the side. They knocked over two more exes before sprawling over a curb.

Stealth spun through the crowd. Her baton whirled and sliced through the air. At times it lunged out for a precision strike. Once it thrust back to shatter a forehead. Exes slumped and dropped around her. She stepped over their bodies and brought her heels down on the necks of ones that still moved.

They reached the corner of the Mount. The pale walls were bright in the moonlight. George slammed his fists out and felt undead skulls and jaws collapse under his knuckles.

Another hundred yards and they'd be back inside.

"There's no one on the Wall," Barry called out.

St. George glanced back. The exes still seemed to be ignoring Freedom and his passengers. They brushed past or bumped into him, but their chattering teeth never came close. Danielle was curled up almost in a ball. Madelyn looked like she was concentrating. Barry and Freedom were both looking up.

"He's right, sir," said the captain. "No sentries."

St. George looked up. There was no one up near the oversized globe of the Earth that sat on the corner of the Wall. His eyes ran along toward the gate. He didn't see a single guard.

He caught an ex by the arm as it tried to grab him. "We're almost there," he said. "Just a few more minutes."

They pushed ahead. St. George and Stealth cleared the path. Freedom followed before the exes could fill it back up.

They pushed past the last corner and saw the Melrose gate at the end of its short driveway, half-hidden in shadows. On the other side of an overgrown shrub, the guards held the wide gateway open. One gestured them in with slow waves while others held off the exes.

St. George made the last push through the exes. More of them were going after him and Stealth than the guards at the gate. He smashed the dead things aside. She battered them down. He made a last lunge with his arms wide, pushed half a dozen of them into the small garden with a squat palm tree, and left a clear path. Stealth rammed her baton into the side of an ex's head and ran for the opening with Freedom and the others right behind her. The guard waved them in. The wave was an unsteady, somehow mechanical gesture, as if the man wasn't quite aware he was doing it.

Stealth brought her baton up, shattering the guard's jaw, then smashed it down on the top of his skull. The man swayed. She slipped through the gate, smacked aside another guard's hands, and continued the swing into the back of the waving guard's head. His face slammed into the bars and the impact rang through the gate.

Four long strides carried St. George to the gate. Up close he could see the waving man had been Derek, one of the Melrose guards almost from the day the Mount had been founded. He was dead. His skull was cracked and sagging.

From the color of his skin, he'd been dead for a while. One of his ears was gone, and most of the flesh around it. The arm that had been stuck in the bars, waving, was missing two fingers.

Another ex fell on St. George from behind. He let it gnaw on his neck for a moment. A few of its teeth broke loose and slipped down the back of his shirt. They were cool and dry against his skin.

He turned and shoved the ex back. He pulled the gate shut and stood there for another moment while the dead things outside clawed at his fingers. Then he looked around, found the steel pipe they used for a bar, and dropped it in the brackets across the gate.

Behind him, he heard Stealth put down the other exes by the guardhouse.

＊＊＊

No one said anything.

Except for the click of teeth echoing between the buildings, there was no sound. All the windows in the buildings were dark.

A pickup truck was parked near the gate. The driver's seat was smeared with blood. The passenger seat held the withered remains of a woman with an empty pistol in her lap. The back of Billie Carter's skull was gone, and the rear window behind her was cracked and covered with dried gore. It was all through her spiky blond hair as well.

Stealth took the pistol, released the slide, and checked the magazine. She glanced up at St. George and shook her head. She slid the pistol in her waistband.

He checked beneath the truck for any crawlers, then pulled the tailgate down. The truck had two boxes of food in the back, and a third box of random supplies. St. George gave them a quick search and handed out some crumpled granola bars with long-since-expired dates.

There was a large water bottle, maybe five gallons, sealed with some plastic wrap and a doubled-up rubber band. The band crumbled when he tugged on it. The plastic wrap was sticky. He found a clean spot on his shirt and used it to wipe the mouth of the bottle as clean as he could.

Danielle sat down on the end of the tailgate. Her legs dangled above the ground. Freedom set Barry down next to her, then Madelyn.

They ate and sipped water in silence. The Corpse Girl glanced over her shoulder at the cracked rear window. Even in the dark, the splatter of gore on the inside was visible.

There was enough light from the moon and stars to see the garden had turned into a thick mess of yellowed plants. More bodies were sprawled in the rows. Most of them had been stripped of enough meat to make them little more than skeletons.

Some of them were very small skeletons.

"How long?" Freedom asked. "How long have we been gone?"

No one said anything.

"Ma'am?"

Stealth looked across the lot, picking out shapes. "It is difficult to be accurate in such poor light," she said. "I could make a rough estimate from the amount of dust on the truck and the level of plant growth in the garden. I saw similar levels at the Big Wall. The state of decay in the bodies we have seen also allows a general guideline."

St. George looked at her. "And?"

Stealth continued to study the lot around them. "I would say it has been at least four months since this area was used. That estimate may be off by several weeks."

"Four *months*?!" gasped Danielle.

Barry shook his head. "No way," he said. "That's not possible."

"We should get inside," said Stealth, as if none of the others had spoken. "We will attract attention here, and we cannot defend an open area such as this."

"We need to look for survivors," said St. George.

"Agreed," said Freedom. "We can—"

"At the moment, the odds of there being survivors would seem to be very low," snapped Stealth. "St. George and I have both been awake for over thirty-six hours at this point. Barry and Madelyn cannot walk. Danielle is useless from fear."

Danielle looked up and glared at Stealth, but said nothing.

"Our first concern is to secure a base of operations and rest. If there are survivors, we are of no use to them like this. Is that clear?"

They all stared at her. "Yes, ma'am."

"The Roddenberry Building is the logical choice. It is central, it has three ground-level entrances, and the stairwells have isolated any exes inside. I have weapons and supplies secured there."

"Okay, then," said St. George. He stacked the three boxes of supplies, then balanced them in one hand. "Let's go."

They started across the parking lot. An ex with a military helmet staggered out from behind the old studio store and headed for them. Stealth knocked its helmet off with one swing of her baton, broke its jaw with a second, and with the third she rammed the baton through its empty eye socket. It dropped to the ground.

Danielle looked up and her eyes widened. She pushed her way out of Freedom's arms and ran ahead. He tried to grab for her, but the move swung Madelyn across his back.

"I've got her," said St. George. He set the boxes down and took off after her. He knew where she was going. They should've planned on it.

Right behind Roddenberry, one street over, was the scenery shop they'd cleaned out years ago and turned into Danielle's workshop. She'd reconfigured the whole place for the Cerberus armor. She even made a small apartment for herself in the back so she never had to be far from the battlesuit.

The wide doors were open, and she ran in without hesitating. St. George was a few yards behind her. Her scream echoed inside the dark workshop.

He raced in. The moon didn't put much illumination through the skylights, but it was enough. His eyes were already used to the dark.

Danielle stood still. Her arms were tight across her chest, pulling so hard he thought she might hurt herself. She looked unharmed. St. George followed her eye line over to Lieutenant Gibbs.

Gibbs was one of the Project Krypton survivors. He'd been an Air Force officer—not one of Freedom's super-soldiers—who found himself at Krypton when the Zombocalypse set in and the chain of command fell apart. He'd been the intended pilot for the Cerberus suit, and had spent hundreds of hours in a simulator for it. Danielle had even let him wear it half a dozen times.

What was left of him was spread across the workshop floor. He'd been pulled in half, by the look of it. His legs and hips were missing, along with his hands, left forearm, and face. If it wasn't for the nametag on his Air Force coat, he would've been a piece of meat.

The Cerberus Battle Armor System was in pieces. The first thought in St. George's mind was old Universal horror movies, when the villagers inevitably stormed the lab and destroyed whatever they found there. At least a third of the battlesuit was missing. The sections scattered across the floor had been battered and gouged. Wiring had been pulled out in clumps. The gauntlets looked like they'd been attacked with a pair of crowbars.

The helmet sat on the table like a decapitated head. The lenses of both eyes had been smashed. The speakers had been ripped out. There was a dent in the forehead that might've come from a sledgehammer. Broken glass from the interior screens surrounded the metal skull. Half a dozen connectors hung limp, their ends cracked or smashed or missing altogether.

Danielle gritted her teeth. She raised her fist away from her body and then slammed it into her arm again and again.

* * *

They put down seven more exes on the way to Roddenberry. St. George knew almost all of their faces. One was too mauled to be sure. The two in the lobby weren't familiar, although Stealth took down a third behind the reception desk before he could get a good look at it. The main stairwell was clear, but there was one more outside Stealth's fourth-floor office. It had been Rocky, the man who made chain-mail armor for the scavengers. St. George turned the dead man's head all the way around. The teeth kept chattering, so he carried the body to a window and let it drop four stories to the ground.

When he got back to the office, Stealth had pulled open the blinds to let in what light she could. Her office had been the floor's main conference room once, back when the Mount was in the movie business. She'd turned it into a war room of video screens and covered the marble table with maps.

Most of the screens had been smashed. Her many maps of the city, state, and the rest of the country had been torn apart. From the ashes on the table and the soot on the ceiling, it looked like some of them had been burned.

St. George saw a piece of black fabric on the edge of the ashes and realized they'd burned more than her maps.

Danielle's shoulders dropped at least an inch in the enclosed office. Freedom found an office chair with arms and set Barry down in it. Madelyn slipped off his broad shoulders and sat on the edge of the table.

Barry looked at the broken screens and ashes. He traded a look with St. George. "Man," he said. "They must've really hated us."

"They were scared," said St. George. "They needed a target to take it out on. One they could beat. We weren't here, so we were the easy ones."

"Keep telling yourself that," said Danielle. "Nick always had these people pegged. They were glad for us when we were here, but they never liked us."

"We should secure the perimeter," said Freedom. "Make sure this floor's clear and sealed off."

"The elevators are inoperative without power, but there is one other stairwell to secure." Stealth looked at St. George. "Check the other offices and supply closets on this floor. Dispose of any other exes which may have ended up here."

"Don't suppose you've got a flashlight?"

Stealth paused for a moment and glanced at the others. "In my quarters," she said. "In the second closet."

St. George nodded and headed for the door at the far end of the conference room. It was camouflaged to blend in with the wall. He pulled it open and walked through to her spartan apartment. He did a quick check in the small bathroom and both closets. He was pretty sure they'd been cleaned out. Stealth had so few personal things, it was hard to be sure.

He found a trio of big Maglites, and also two smaller ones and an electric lantern. He clicked the button on each Mag to make sure the batteries still worked. The lantern lit up the room.

He went back to the office and handed out the lights. Stealth hung the lantern from a piece of heavy wire she pulled from above the ceiling tiles. Freedom was out blocking the stairwell door with a desk.

St. George headed down the hall. Most of the doors were unlocked, and the rooms bare. Stealth had cleaned the offices out herself back when she'd claimed the floor as her personal lair.

Four rooms away he heard a muffled *click-click-click* through the door. He opened the small office and saw an ex stumbling against the window. The door swung open and tapped the far wall. The corpse turned at the noise. It had been a little girl. He recognized the face, but couldn't think of a name to go with it. The dead thing's left shoulder was a mess of gore and blood.

The ex staggered across the empty room. Its arms reached up for him and pale fingers clawed at the air. Its little teeth tapped against each other again and again.

He let it grab his hand and it gnawed on his fingers. Some of the little teeth broke on his skin, and their shards sprinkled on the carpet like snow. He sighed, then reached down to grab it by the back of the neck. He squeezed and felt the bones splinter and crumble under the skin.

The jaws kept working on his fingers like an eager kitten. Then the weight of the limp body pulled the teeth off him and it slumped to the floor. The head bounced on the carpet and kept gnashing its teeth. He scooped up the dead girl and carried it to the window. It hit Avenue E right in front of Danielle's workshop.

He still couldn't remember her name. He tried to blame Smith's brainwashing and push it from his mind. He closed the door behind him.

St. George checked two more empty offices, then found one filled with desks, chairs, and other pieces of office furniture. It had never crossed his mind that Stealth had to put everything somewhere. He wasn't sure why she'd cleaned out all the offices to start with. It had never come up.

In the hallway on the far side of the building, the knob on the first door stuck. He tried to jiggle it twice, but it was solid. The door was locked.

He thought about leaving it. An ex wouldn't've locked doors. Even if it somehow had, it couldn't unlock them.

He sighed. A twist of his wrist snapped the tumblers inside the lock. The knob turned with a metallic rustle and a scrape.

The room was dark, but it smelled different. His flashlight beam hit the pile of blankets and the bag of empty cans and he realized what it was. The room smelled like the stages in the Mount when they'd first been converted into apartments. It was the smell of living in a small area.

Something moved across the room. He saw the figure, a shadow against the slightly brighter window. It was holding its arms out.

He brought up the flashlight and a gunshot thundered in the room. The round struck his front teeth, right on the left incisor, and made his gums throb. The flashlight and the bullet dropped to the carpet. He brought his hand up to press it against his lips. "Son of a bitch," he said, "that stings."

"Goddammit," muttered the figure. It was a female voice. "I save my last bullet all this time, and then I waste it on you. Makes sense."

St. George heard footsteps running in the hall. He reached down and grabbed the flashlight just as Stealth appeared in the doorway. The woman in the room winced away from the bright light and threw her arm across her face, but his mind had pieced enough elements together to identify her. "Are you okay?" he asked. "We've got food and water, and I think some basic medical supplies."

He lowered the beam, and Christian Nguyen glared at them.

THIRTY-ONE

WHEN THEY GOT back to Stealth's office with Christian, Madelyn was fast asleep in Freedom's arms. Her eyes were half-open, and her jaw hung slack. Her body sprawled like a limp rag doll.

Christian shuddered at the sight and muttered something so low St. George couldn't hear it.

Freedom looked at Christian. "Miss Nguyen," he said. "Good to see you, ma'am."

She said nothing. St. George gestured her to a chair. He nodded at Madelyn. "Is she okay?"

"Just sleeping," said the big officer. "Or whatever it is she does. Recharging?"

"As good a term as any," said Stealth.

"She yawned and almost fell over just before we heard the gunshot," said the captain.

St. George heard a rattling noise. Danielle pushed Barry out of Stealth's office, using the office chair for a wheelchair. Barry looked slightly more comfortable with it than he did being carried. He had a pillow and a blanket on his lap.

Freedom set Madelyn down on the table and arranged her body so it looked natural, careful that her feet avoided the pile of ashes and burned material. Barry handed him the pillow and the huge officer tucked it under her head. He draped the blanket over her and slid her eyelids closed.

"So," Danielle asked Christian, "how did you end up here?"

The Asian woman glowered at them. "It was what I could reach when the exes came," she said. "I thought that psychotic bitch might've set some traps or defenses or something that would make it safer."

"Watch your mouth," said St. George.

"Make me," snapped Christian. "I'm sorry you don't want to be reminded that she finally ran out on all of us, but—"

"More likely," said Stealth, "I would guess he is hoping to make you restrain yourself before I come up with a more direct way of silencing you."

Christian gave the unmasked woman a nasty look, took in a breath to respond, and then she recognized the voice. Her face softened and she shrank back.

"What happened here?" demanded Stealth. "Was it Legion? Did Agent Smith cause this somehow?"

Christian's eyebrows went up at Smith's name. Then her usual surliness surged over her brief surprise. She settled back in a corner of the room and glared at the heroes. St. George wasn't sure if it was mild shock or plain old stubbornness.

Stealth took a step toward the former councilwoman, but he held her back.

"You should get some sleep," said Barry. "You look fried."

"It's been a rough two days," St. George said. "I think I am kind of fried."

"Both of you sleep," said Freedom. He nodded to St. George and Stealth. "You need it more than any of us. We can do shifts until we all get caught up."

"We'll . . . we should . . ." St. George tried to come up with a protest, but part of him realized in the few moments of downtime his brain had started shutting down all on its own.

"I'll wake you up in four hours," said the captain.

Stealth took St. George by the arm and guided him back to her quarters. The small cot still had a sheet on it. It looked glorious.

He pulled the shirt off over his head and popped two buttons off in the process. It smelled like death. There were dark stains and splatters all over it, but not enough to hide the fact it had been white once. A few stitches had split on one shoulder. He let it drop on the floor. He didn't look forward to putting it on again when he woke up.

Stealth peeled off the ragged fleece jacket. There were two or three dark patches on the arms that had dried into little spikes. Blood and gore had soaked through the fleece to make a few spots on her bra. She placed her baton and the pistol she'd taken from Billie's body and placed them on top of the jacket.

They stretched out on her thin mattress. There was no blanket or pillows, but it felt luxurious to not be standing. She pulled his arm around her shoulders and pressed herself against him. Her skin was warm. She was always warm.

He kissed her forehead, and he was pretty sure she kissed him back, but he was already asleep.

* * *

It's the early days of the outbreak. I don't even know it's an outbreak yet. In four days, I will meet the woman who will change my life forever. She will tell me the monsters are the result of an infection. A year and a half from now, we will learn where the infection came from. Two days after that she will tell me her name.

There are almost a dozen monsters—exes—in the parking lot with us. They are hunting homeless people. They won't be exes for another two weeks, when the President refers to them as ex-humans for the first time in a televised statement. The name will stick.

A dead thing grabs my cape and tugs me off balance. I spin around and hit it in the head with a backhand. Its skull cracks under my knuckles.

With me is Gorgon. His vampiric gaze is useless against the monsters—the exes—but earlier we stopped a minor gang skirmish, and for another hour or so he is superhuman. He grabs an ex by the wrists and swings, throwing it across the pavement. His leather duster whirls open as he does. I know he looks much cooler than I do, but I am still proud of my red and green costume.

I'm aware this is a dream. Far more aware than I've been in a long time. This is the past replayed as present.

I slam my hand out and an ex flies across the parking lot to slam into a brick wall head-first. It slumps to the ground. Gorgon—his name is Nikolai, but I don't know that yet—punches the last one in the jaw. Its head spins from the blow, and he grabs it and twists even more. Its neck breaks with a sound like driftwood and it drops.

A year and a half from now Gorgon's body will be twisted by a giant monster—a bastard of the ex-virus and a failed supersoldier project—and his own spine will break in four places. His death will be quick. My friends and I will tell ourselves it was instantaneous.

He turns and looks at me. The dark irises of his goggles gleam in the streetlights. He shrugs and settles the long jacket around his body. The jacket looks wrong without the silver sheriff's star on it, but that is still almost nine months away, and I realize I'm looking at him through my eyes, the eyes that have seen all this before.

This is the point where most dreams collapse. The point where you become too conscious of the dream and start thinking about it rather than experiencing it.

"Okay," says Gorgon, "you're clear this is all in your head, right?"

I stare at him. This is not how the past went. I'm not sure what to say.

"Oh, for Christ's sake, George," the other man growls. "It's a dream. Just a bunch of stuff you dredged up from your memories to help you figure stuff out. You've beat him on this level before, when you saved Karen out at Project Krypton."

Gorgon was dead months before I traveled to Krypton. He never learned Karen's name. No one else did, not until the night—

"It's not me, you idiot," he snarls. "This is all just you. All of it. Smith made you provide all the details, made you build your own prison, but you stuck me in here to help you remember the truth. You're just talking to yourself."

"Like *Fight Club*?"

"Yes, just like *Fight Club*, except I'm way better looking than Brad Pitt."

I snort back a laugh and realize I'm not wearing my mask. My old costume, the Mighty Dragon, is gone. I'm back in my leather flight jacket, the one that was charred to bits fighting the demon, Cairax Murrain. I've got a pair of goggles of my own, but they're pushed up on my forehead, holding my hair in place. "You were just a clue," I say. "Because I knew you weren't supposed to be here."

He nods back and looks down. His body is twisted under the coat. His clothes are wrapped tight around his waist. His toes point behind him. One of his knees bends at a strange angle. "Looks like everyone dredged up some dead people to gnaw at them. Plus you had that stupid parrot sketch and all the clicking sounds. Little things your subconscious was trying to get your attention with so you'd know none of this was real."

The parking lot has vanished into a dark gray blur. The dream is starting to fade away. Or maybe I just can't focus on it because I don't need it anymore. Even as I think this, another ex lumbers out of the darkness behind Gorgon. It's a man in a suit. It has a very colorful tie. Even in death, its smile is broad and insincere.

I step forward to knock it away, but Gorgon stops me. He glares at me through his goggles. "Don't you get it?"

I look back at him, then at the ex. It's only a few feet from us. "Get what?"

"Jesus, you're dense sometimes." He turns and points at the ex. It has a United States flag pin on its collar, and also a small pin showing a bear. The seal of California. "How often do you have to have something set out right in front of you?"

"What are you talking about?"

Gorgon turns and the ex grabs his shoulder. It bites into his bicep, but the leather duster protects him. It gnaws away at the material. He shakes it loose and drives the heel of his palm into its forehead. It stumbles back and tips over. It makes no attempt to slow its fall and its skull hits the ground with a crack. The noise is loud enough that I realize—on that higher dream-level—that it's going to wake me up. The last shreds of memory fall away, but Gorgon says one last thing before they do.

"Why are you still dreaming about me, George?"

THIRTY-TWO

"AS OF RIGHT now, our first priority is to check for survivors," said St. George. "I'm guessing that's going to come down to me. I'll start as soon as the sun's up. I can try to grab some more clothes for everyone and maybe find a wheelchair for Barry."

"I need my wheels, man," said Barry with a nod.

St. George had shaken out his shirt and knocked some of the dried matter off, but it still smelled like death. Stealth, on the other hand, had found a tight black turtleneck that looked like a cross between spandex and body armor. She looked a lot more comfortable in it.

They stood around the far end of the conference table. Madelyn was still sleeping, but there was enough space for all of them to gather around the rough sketch of the Mount Danielle had made.

St. George glanced at Christian. She hovered on the edge of the little group. She still hadn't said much, but she'd been fine with eating their food. "Christian?" he asked. "Any information you've got would be great."

She shook her head, then looked at the map. "There were two families over on Stage 29," she said. "The Dvorskis and the Randolphs. We all talked with walkies for a while, but the batteries ran out. I haven't heard from them in a month, I think. Someone said Father Andy took people into his church when the walls fell, but I don't know if that's true or not."

"I'll check them all out."

Her lip twisted into a sneer. "Some of the scavengers struck out on their own about a month ago. No idea what happened to them."

St. George thought of Billie Carter in the truck with the pistol in her lap. "Second goal is setting up a safe zone," he said, pushing the image from his mind.

Stealth tapped the different gates into the studio on the map. "The Mount is still defendable for the same reasons it was originally chosen. St. George can check the gates with relative safety. Once the perimeter is secure, we can terminate all exes within the studio grounds and better assess our resources."

St. George looked at Barry. "This would be a lot easier if you could power up."

"Don't I know it." Barry shook his head. "I've got nothing. I'm pretty sure the switch is still there in my head somewhere, but it's like I'm feeling around in the dark and can't find it."

"I know what you mean." St. George looked at the map and tapped Danielle's workshop. "Third goal. Cerberus."

Danielle set her jaw.

"If we get everything cleaned out, how long do you think it'll take to get up and running again?"

She tapped her fingers on the tabletop. "Hard to say. From what I saw, I know I'll have to rebuild the lenses and screens from scratch, most of the inter-component connections, too." She glanced at Barry. "Assuming we can get power back up, that's a solid three weeks of work right there."

He coughed into his hand. "A real three weeks," he said, "or are you trying to sound like a miracle worker?"

Danielle snorted, but her lips almost twitched into a smile. "It's a month of work," she said. "If I get really lucky with a couple of things and there's some decent replacement parts kicking around, maybe three weeks. It'll all depend on what I find when I do a full diagnostic. As long as most of the computer systems are still intact and I can find all the missing components, I should be able to get the rest of it running again. Eventually."

"That brings us back to the big, overall question," said St. George. "What happened here?"

They all glanced at Christian, but she stared past them and out the dark window.

St. George took in a breath to speak, but she cut him off.

"You're all so full of shit."

Stealth raised an eyebrow. "I beg your pardon?"

"All this acting so concerned," said Christian. "Acting innocent. It won't work. Are you trying to get me to buy into it so I'll be on your side? Everyone knows what you did." She stared back out the window. "Everyone who's left, anyway."

"I know you're not our biggest fan," St. George began with a sigh. Then something in her tone, her inflection, gnawed at him. "Wait, are you saying," he started again. "Do you actually think we had something to do with this? With whatever attacked the Mount?"

"There wasn't any attack," she spat at him. "It was just you."

Freedom stood up straight and looked at St. George. So did Barry and Danielle.

St. George blinked twice. "What?"

She pointed an accusing finger at him. The nail was chipped. "You were out with the scavengers a few months ago. They said you just abandoned them and walked away, talking about dumpsters or something. No one knew what to do, so they just let you go."

He exchanged a glance with Stealth and shifted on his feet.

She glared at him. "A week later you came back and started pounding on the Big Wall. Just punching the cars. You stopped before it fell over, and then wandered off again. A few days later you came back and knocked a hole in the West Wall. We had guards there for three days straight while we tried to figure out how to make it safe."

"No." He shook his head. "There's no way I would've done that. I was—"

"Then you did it again," she yelled. "Just lording it over us that they couldn't hurt you. Showing off that you were safe."

"Where was I during all of this?" asked Stealth.

"I don't know," snapped Christian. "Hiding somewhere, as always."

"And Danielle?" She nodded at the redhead. "Barry? The gate guards would not have let an unarmed woman and a man in a wheelchair out into the city."

"I don't know all the details," Christian said. "I just know you all left us high and dry, like I always said you would." She pounded her chest. "I stayed. People can depend on me when things get tough. That's why I—"

"Enough," said Stealth. "Be silent."

Christian took in a breath to shout and Stealth's hand slid down to the baton tucked through her belt. The former councilwoman turned and stalked out of the room. Her swears echoed back to them.

"Should someone go after her?" asked Freedom.

"She will be safe as long as she remains on this floor," said Stealth. "We have more important matters to discuss."

St. George looked at his knuckles. "I can't believe this," he said. "I just can't."

Barry shrugged. "If Smith could make us all think the world was normal again, why couldn't he make you smash through the Big Wall and think you're . . . I don't know, in the shower or something?"

St. George shook his head.

"I also do not believe you caused this damage," Stealth said.

"Thanks."

"At the moment, I cannot believe any element from her version of events."

Danielle frowned. "Why not?"

Madelyn yawned at the end of the table. She sat up, blinked her chalk eyes, and took a quick look around the room. "Still just us, huh?"

Freedom shook his head. "Christian Nguyen's survived," he said, "and possibly some others."

"But everyone else is dead?"

Freedom and St. George exchanged awkward glances. The giant officer took in a breath to speak, but Stealth interrupted him. "You remember where you are?" she asked Madelyn.

The Corpse Girl studied the room. "It's your office at the Mount, right?"

Stealth's eyebrow went up. Her jaw shifted as she studied the girl.

Madelyn looked around again. "It is, isn't it?"

"Yes," said Stealth after a moment, "it is."

"And," said Danielle, "you were about to tell us all why Christian's a liar."

"Perhaps not a liar," Stealth said, her gaze swinging away from Madelyn, "but her version of events clashes with many observations I have made over the past forty-eight hours and additional facts I have culled from your own individual accounts."

St. George set his hands on the table. "That's a good thing, right?"

"Perhaps." Stealth crossed her arms. "Christian claims St. George has been present here at the Mount and is responsible for much of the damage to the Big Wall. This would be consistent with the patterns of damage the Wall has suffered. The overall evidence I have seen here confirms that at least four months have passed. During this time, all of us were most likely wandering Los Angeles in a trance or fugue state.

"The most straightforward possibility," continued Stealth, "is that Smith has affected our perceptions. This is within the scope of his powers as we have experienced them."

"Okay," said Barry. "Got it. Smith's playing mind games."

"Which means he's here in Los Angeles," Danielle said. "He needs to talk to someone to control them."

"That makes sense," St. George said, "but how could he have made it into Los Angeles, into the Mount, without any of us knowing?"

"Maybe we did know," said Freedom. "It's possible he just forced us to forget."

Madelyn snorted and flexed her arms over her head.

"However," said Stealth as if they hadn't spoken, "there is the matter of our clothes."

"What?" Madelyn looked at herself. So did Freedom.

"Most of our clothes show little sign of wear. The stains are recent, from the past forty-eight hours, and many have not had time to dry. The damage is fresh and still shows clean edges which have not frayed."

"What's your point?" asked Freedom.

"Where did they come from?" responded Danielle. "If we've been walking around hypnotized for the past four months, where've we been getting clean clothes?"

"Not just clothing," said Stealth. She gestured at St. George. "Your hair smells of shampoo, as does Madelyn's. My hands smell of skin cream. Captain Freedom has freshly cut fingernails. Barry's clothes contain hints of the antiseptic spray used by cleaning crews between domestic flights."

Madelyn pulled a lock of hair under her nose and sniffed.

"But I thought we decided this is all an illusion," said Barry. "I wasn't on a plane."

"You could not have been," agreed Stealth. "Yet these scents cling to all of us. We also have this." She pulled three small cubes of glass from her pocket and they bounced on the table. "These are from the windshield St. George went through when the Driver stopped moving. They were trapped in his fleece coat. If this was all an illusion, where did that momentum come from?"

"If our view of the world has been altered," said Freedom, "it's possible we thought we were in a car when we were just walking along the road. Then we climbed into a wreck and found ourselves back in the real world."

St. George picked up one of the glass cubes. "And me going through the windshield?"

"You can fly, sir," said the captain. "Maybe you threw yourself."

"A solid hypothesis," said Stealth. "Very similar to the one I had formed myself before you found Barry."

Barry blinked. "Me?"

"If this was an illusion," she said, "we could have crossed the city on foot. Barry could not have."

"Unless I was in my energy form," he said. "Then it's like George and the windshield. I could've been flying along, flitted into the cab, and turned human again."

"Except you were found clothed," said Stealth. She looked at Freedom and Danielle. "And the car had suffered no heat damage from proximity to Zzzap."

"No," agreed Danielle, "it didn't."

"Maybe he changed a few yards away," Freedom suggested. His lips twitched as he said it.

"Which still does not explain the matter of his clothing," Stealth said. "There is also the matter of food and water. Even if we had all avoided contact with ex-humans, which is unlikely, four months is sufficient time to starve to death. Yet none of us are hungry or show signs of malnourishment. What have we been eating for the past four months?"

Danielle shuddered. "I don't want to think about it."

Madelyn's lips twisted. "Couldn't Smith just make us believe we've been eating and drinking?"

"He could," agreed Stealth, "but that would not stop our bodies from suffering the effects of malnourishment and dehydration."

"Unless he's keeping us from seeing those, too," said St. George.

"If we are going to accept that Smith has altered our perceptions in . . ."

Stealth paused. A moment later Barry sat up in his office chair. "Son of a bitch," he said. "We're in the ship in a bottle."

Madelyn looked at him. "What?"

"It's a classic *Next Generation* episode," explained Barry. "'Ship in a Bottle.' It's one of the best ones they did. They filmed it here at the Mount. Picard and Data go into the holodeck and encounter the holographic Moriarty, but when they leave Moriarty walks out with them, even though he shouldn't be able to survive outside."

"Barry," sighed St. George, "not now."

"No, listen," insisted Barry. "They spend most of the episode trying to figure out how he did it, because it should be impossible—it defies every bit of science they know—but it turns out the whole thing's a trick. They never even left the holodeck. Moriarty created a holodeck program that made them think they'd left and were out walking around the ship."

They all stared at him for a moment. "Yes," Stealth said. "I believe your analogy is accurate."

"What are you two talking about?" asked Danielle.

"A lot of people thought the Wachowskis were doing the same thing with the second *Matrix* movie," continued Barry. His eyes were wide and he tapped the desk with his fingertips. "See, after *The Matrix Reloaded* there were all these theories about why Neo could use his powers outside the Matrix because people were still thinking the Wachowskis knew what they were doing. And one of the ideas was that the Matrix we all knew was actually nestled inside a *second* Matrix. That way people would think they'd escaped but really they were still hooked into the pods."

"How is it that no matter what's happening you can relate it to *The Matrix*?" asked St. George.

"Because it's the greatest movie ever made," said Barry.

"I'm lost," said Freedom. "Are you saying . . . we were in pods?"

Stealth shook her head. "We have based all of our assertions off that reality's interactions with this one, but we have been doing so under the assumption this is the real world."

St. George got it. So did Madelyn. Danielle saw the look on their faces. "What?" she said. "I still have no idea what you're talking about."

"None of this is real, either," said St. George, waving his arm at the office. "Smith's still got us."

THIRTY-THREE

"IT EXPLAINS EVERYTHING," said Stealth. "There is no conflict of facts if this is another illusion. This is why none of us have been bitten, and also why elements of the other world are carrying over."

"Sounds like this world is kind of sloppy, then," said Madelyn.

"It's not a world," said Barry. "It's a safety net. If we break through the main illusion, this one catches us and bounces us back."

St. George looked at him. "How do you figure?"

"Think about it. You're convinced the world's normal and you start having these 'hallucinations,' right? I don't know about you, but my first reaction was 'Well, *that* can't be real.'"

"So everyone's okay?" Danielle asked. "Gibbs, Makana, all the rest of them?"

"It is best to assume everything we have encountered in this world is another perceptual illusion created by Agent Smith," Stealth said.

"And Cerberus is okay," said Danielle. She almost smiled.

"A question, if I may," said Freedom.

Stealth dipped her chin.

"Are *we* all real?"

They glanced at each other. "How do you mean?" asked Danielle.

"How do we know that some of us aren't just part of the illusion, too? I mean, for all we know one of us could be Smith telling us to see him as someone else."

"Like the Shadow," Barry said. "Clouding our minds so we cannot see him."

St. George looked at the others. "Valid point. How do we prove we're real?"

Madelyn shook her head. "I'm real."

"I think I am, too," said Freedom.

"Maybe I'm the one who's real and I'm just thinking you're both thinking you're real," Barry said.

"That's just silly," said Madelyn.

Barry shook his head. "I have a really vivid imagination."

"Cogito ergo sum," said Freedom.

"Aptly put," said Stealth, "but how can any of us prove to another that we are actually thinking beings and not just hallucinations?"

"And," Barry said, "another 'Ship in a Bottle' reference. You're getting better at this, Captain."

Freedom managed a half smile. "Thank you, sir."

"I've got one for you," said Danielle. She cocked her head toward the office door and the hallway. "Is she real? Christian?"

They all glanced after the councilwoman. "Why?" asked Madelyn.

"If she is part of the illusion," said Stealth, "why is she the only living person in the Mount? If she is in the illusion, as we are, why has Smith isolated her?"

"Because she has power," said Freedom. "He attaches himself to people with power and influence and uses them as puppets. That's how he stays out of the crosshairs."

"But then wouldn't he need her ... I don't know, awake?" Barry asked. "Not trapped in the Matrix with us?"

"Assuming she is real," said Stealth, "and not an element of the illusion."

"If this is another level of the illusion," said St. George, tapping on the table, "how do we get out of it?"

"*Can* we get out of it?" asked Danielle. "When he plants these ideas, they're pretty hard to shake."

"But not impossible," Stealth said. "Several people have been able to create pathways around the blocks Smith creates."

"Like out at Krypton," said St. George, "when I rescued you from the helicopter even though Smith told me I couldn't beat him."

"Correct," she said. "You were able to rationalize a situation which allowed you to act without violating the conditions he had imposed upon you."

"We were never able to do that before, though," said Freedom. "He had most of us believing his lies for two years."

"Until we arrived at Project Krypton," said Stealth, "none of you had reason to doubt the beliefs he created. Once we did, most of the Unbreakables resisted his imposed perceptions within a few days. The same may be happening here. Our minds are working around the imposed images and attempting to show us the real world."

"So, wait," said Barry. "If we've already shaken off most of his voodoo, does that mean we've only been under for a few days?"

"There is no way to be sure," Stealth said.

"So how do we get out of this?" asked Madelyn.

"I'm still not entirely clear how we got out of the last one," said Freedom. "Do we just have to . . . not believe in the world?"

"How do you do that, though?" muttered Danielle. "It's like the old 'don't think about pink elephants' thing."

"I believe I have a possible solution," said Stealth. She walked over to Freedom and gestured him down to her level. She cupped her hand by his ear and whispered for a few moments.

Freedom glanced at her, stared across the room, and then nodded. "Yes, ma'am."

"What?" said Danielle. "Are you going to share with all of us?"

"Smith's suggestions work in a manner similar to dream states," said Stealth. "A simple idea is planted in either the conscious or subconscious, and the brain reworks memories to accommodate this idea."

"Okay," said Barry. "That kind of makes sense."

"I believe there is a simple solution," Stealth said. "There is a common sleep disorder known as a hypnagogic jerk. It is an involuntary muscle twitch. Some biologists believe it may be a holdover from our primate ancestors, similar to the Moro reflex in infants." She looked at St. George. "I suggested it to you yesterday."

"You did?"

She took a quick step back. St. George heard someone move behind him. He turned and Freedom slammed a football-sized fist into his head.

It didn't hurt, but he wasn't ready for it and the force of the blow sent him reeling for a moment. Before he could shake his head clear Freedom had spun him around, grabbed his belt and one shoulder, and was forcing him across the room. The larger man took one step past St. George and lifted him up, the perfect position to—

He flailed, tried to stop himself, but it was too late.

Freedom hurled him at the window. St. George crashed through the blinds and felt part of the aluminum frame snap under his shoulder. All he could hear was the chime of broken glass and the rustle of the blinds tangled around him and the rush of wind in his ears.

Four stories gave him just enough time to turn and see the pavement rush at him like a speeding truck. He clenched his shoulders, his back, everything he could think of. Something would make him fly, but he couldn't think of it in the second before he—

* * *

—woke up.

St. George opened his eyes and took a few deep breaths. He stared up at the distant ceiling. He could see exposed beams and catwalks, all painted black, and a few different lighting fixtures. Most of them were banks of fluorescent tubes, but some big china-hat lights hung up there, too.

His neck flared as he tried to sit up. There was a blanket between him and the concrete floor, but nothing else. His butt and elbows ached. His back and legs were sore.

A spot on his back tingled, right between his shoulder blades. He focused on it and fanned the tingle like a weak flame. It grew across his body and out, pushing down on the floor. On the world.

He rose into the air.

He relaxed his concentration and his boots tapped the concrete. He looked down at himself. Boots, jeans, and a black motorcycle jacket to replace the one Cairax destroyed. He felt his head and found a thick mass of hair that needed a shower and was a month past needing a cut.

His stomach grumbled. He was hungry. He rolled his abs and his stomach growled again. Hungry, but not starved. Maybe a little over a day without food? Two days, tops. He ran his tongue around the inside of his mouth, touched it to his lips, and guessed the same without water.

He looked behind him and forgot food.

Stealth, Barry, and the others were all unconscious. Each of them was sprawled on a blanket. Freedom stretched off the ends of his.

St. George ran to Stealth. She was in full uniform, with her hood pushed back off her head. He grabbed her shoulders and she leaped off the floor into his arms. He was strong again. Very strong. He took a breath, remembered how to treat the fragile world, and lowered Stealth down to the blanket.

She had a pulse, and he could feel her breath through her mask, but she wouldn't wake up. He tapped her cheek, kissed her forehead and lips, and tugged at her mask. He knew from experience that unbuttoning his shirt in the same room could wake her up. Pulling at her mask should've provoked a much more extreme response. Most people would lose teeth.

"Hey," he said. His voice echoed in the empty space. He raised it to a shout. "Stealth! Karen! Wake up!"

Nothing.

He looked at the others. None of them stirred, either. Barry was wearing sweats, the kind of thing he wore just before or after a shift in the electric chair. Danielle was in street clothes, but he could see the collar of her Cerberus contact suit under her shirt. Freedom had his leather duster on over his Army uniform. Cesar and Madelyn were both in regular clothes. Her eyes were open and staring at the ceiling. It looked like they were dusty. St. George put two fingers on her pale neck and confirmed she didn't have a pulse. She also wasn't breathing.

In her case, he took it as a good sign.

They'd been set out in a wide circle, feet pointing outward, their heads toward the center. The placement seemed too deliberate to be an accident. There wasn't anything connecting them, but all of their heads were within twenty or thirty inches of each other.

Not our heads, St. George realized. Our brains. He's got our minds close together.

He looked around. He was pretty sure he was in one of the old studio stages on the Mount. They'd all been converted into living space when the Mount had first been set up, but most of them had been abandoned since the Big Wall went up and people had better housing options. They'd been stripped down and left empty shells, with most of the lumber going to the Big Wall.

Empty shells no one ever went to.

He gave his friends a last look and then lumbered to the door. His limbs were stiff. He forced his legs to take longer steps, made his arms swing higher.

He pushed on the door. It was stuck. He hit the bar again, hard, and dented it. He heard something scrape, a bang, and a jingle of metal. The door swung open.

The sunlight was blinding. He saw a few stick figures heading toward him, and a few blinks put blurry flesh on them. They stopped a few yards away.

"Sir," said one of them. It was a woman's voice. "What were you doing in there?"

One last blink turned the blur into First Sergeant Kennedy. One of Freedom's soldiers from Project Krypton. She was still wearing her uniform, but she'd rolled the sleeves up in tight, military fashion. Makana stood next to her. Alive. A few steps behind them were some other guards St. George recognized.

He looked over his shoulder. A huge, blue 32 was painted on the wall behind him. At his feet were a few broken links of chain and a twisted padlock. "What day is it?" he asked.

Makana raised an eyebrow. "What?"

"What day? How long have we been gone?"

"We?" asked Kennedy. "Is the captain with you?"

"We thought you were all off on a mission," said Makana. "Have you just been sitting in there all this time?"

"How long?" snapped St. George.

Makana and Kennedy glanced at each other. "Maybe two days, sir," the sergeant said. "You all left night before last."

"You said you didn't want to influence the election," said Makana. "So you all went out on some scouting mission for a couple days, to check up on Legion or something."

"What election?"

"The election for mayor," Kennedy told him. After watching St. George's expression, she added, "It was yesterday."

"Yesterday?" St. George shook his head. Dates and times were a jumble. He tried to put everything in order, to make sense of it, and had a sudden understanding of what life had to be like for Madelyn on a regular basis. He took a deep breath while his memories sorted themselves out. "Who said we went away?"

Kennedy and Makana glanced at each other. "Well ... you did," said the dreadlocked man.

"When? How?"

Kennedy nodded in agreement. "You held a big meeting at the Melrose gate with four or five hundred of us. The captain, you, Stealth, Dr. Morris. You all said you were going to step away for three or four days."

St. George looked at Kennedy. "When did he get here?"

"Sorry, sir?"

"Agent Smith," he said. "John Smith. When did he get here?"

The first sergeant's brow furrowed. "Agent Smith?"

"Yes."

"Sir, we haven't seen him since we left Project Krypton," she said. "Last reports had him heading for Groom Lake."

St. George stared at her. "He's not here?"

"No, sir."

"You're *sure* he's not here?"

Kennedy's brows knotted for a minute, and then she scowled. She knew what he had done to her soldiers. And how he'd done it. "To the best of my knowledge," she said, "Agent Smith has not been seen anywhere here at the Mount, sir."

He looked at her for a moment, and then at Makana. "Okay," he said. "Wait here."

He staggered back into the stage. His legs were warming up, and his blood was flowing. He looked at the ring of his friends and made a decision.

He gathered Stealth in his arms, cradled her head, and looked up. The ceiling was about forty feet up. He glanced at her masked face, back up at one of the high girders, and threw her into the air.

Her cloak whipped around her as she soared upward. She rolled once, twice, and reached the top of her climb. Her knuckles rapped on one of the china-hat lights.

Then she plunged back down.

He flew up and caught her in midair. Her cape had wrapped around her like a shroud. She was limp in his arms. He put his ear close to her mouth and felt the same slow breaths.

"Damn it."

He landed near the others and set her back down on her blanket.

"Boss?"

St. George looked over his shoulder. Makana had followed him in. The dreadlocked man gazed at the heroes sprawled on the floor of the huge space.

"Are they all . . . ?"

St. George shook his head. "They're alive," he said. "I just can't wake them up."

Makana looked at him, then at the empty blanket he'd been on. "How'd you wake up?"

"Stealth had Freedom throw me out a fourth-floor window."

"What?"

"Not important. I think Smith knew she'd be the hardest to keep under his control. She probably got a double dose or whatever it is he does."

The dreadlocked man looked at the others. "So you can't wake 'em up?"

"I don't know." St. George shifted, kneeled, and patted Madelyn's cheeks. Up close he could see her eyes were dry. He shook her shoulders and poked her in the side.

"Pinch her earlobes," said Makana. "I heard once that's a good way to wake people up."

St. George tried it. Nothing. He picked her up in his arms. "Stand back," he said. "I'm going to try this again."

Madelyn's body tumbled toward the ceiling. Her arms swayed and her back arched. She reached her high point, her head tipped back, and she started to plummet back toward the stage floor.

Then she blinked twice and screamed.

St. George leaped into the air and caught her ten feet above the floor. She grabbed at him like a drowning person, pulling herself tight against him. "What the hell?!" she shrieked.

Kennedy ran in with her pistol drawn.

"It's okay," St. George said. "I've got you."

Madelyn blinked again. "Where am I? What's going on?"

"I needed to wake you up," St. George said, "and nothing else was working. So I tried the same thing Stealth did." He settled on the ground and let her down.

She shook her head and looked at Kennedy and Makana.

He gave her a tight smile. "Wakey-wakey, Corpse Girl," he said.

"Jerk." She stuck her tongue out at him and stretched. Then she looked down at her legs and grinned. "Oh, thank God," said Madelyn. "I can walk again."

Kennedy crossed to Freedom and checked his pulse. "Is he drugged?" she asked St. George.

He shook his head. "It's Smith. He messed with all of our minds. They're in some kind of trance. A dream." He looked at Madelyn. "Do you remember any of it?"

"Most of it, I think." Her chalk eyes turned up to the ceiling. "Where are we?"

"The Mount."

She blinked and glanced over her shoulder. "Really?"

"You just said you remembered most of it."

"Most of the dream," she said. Her lips twisted as she looked around the stage. "I can't remember the last time I was awake."

St. George took a few steps toward the door. "Try to wake up everyone else," he said. "Use bright light or buckets of water or something. Try to get them oriented when they wake up."

"Where are you going?" asked Kennedy.

"To find Agent Smith."

"But we don't know where he is," said Madelyn.

"He'll be where he always is," said St. George. "Behind the scenes. I'm going to go talk to the mayor."

* * *

St. George stepped out of Stage 32 and hurled himself up into the air. His shoulders buzzed with the sensation of flight. He shot up above the buildings, into the sky, and hovered there for a moment.

The Mount was stretched out below him. Straight ahead was the water tower, off to his left were the facades of New York Street. Los Angeles spread out past the studio walls on all sides. He could see hundreds, maybe thousands, of people—living people—walking in the streets and between buildings. Off in the distance he could see the Big Wall, with dozens of tiny guards walking along the top.

And past that were the exes. Close to the Big Wall they swarmed like ants. They were pinpricks from here, just big enough that he could see them lurch and stagger.

He soared down and swooped over the garden. A few people looked up. Some of them waved. He swung around and landed outside the Roddenberry Building.

Like a lot of the buildings at the Mount, Roddenberry was named after a famous filmmaker. They'd all thought of it as the town hall for years, even when it was nothing but Stealth's offices and a few conference rooms that got used once a month or so. Now it really was the town hall. Almost half the offices were being used. The mayor was on the fourth floor. He remembered Stealth had agreed it was a good symbolic move to put the mayor's office where hers had been, to make it clear to everyone the heroes were turning the governing of Los Angeles back over to the people.

St George marched through the lobby, past the half-dozen or so folks there. Once he reached the stairwell his feet left the ground and he flew up the stairs. His body jackknifed at each landing like a high-diver.

The door on the fourth-floor landing was open.

It was very bright. Stealth had always kept it dark, with plenty of shadows. Now light streamed in through the windows. There was a desk just by the stairs and elevators. A young man sat at the desk and looked up as St. George's feet touched the carpeted floor. Behind him, two large potted plants flanked the doors into the big conference room. They looked plastic. The inner office doors were open, too.

"Oh," said the man. "You. Do you have an appointment?"

They stared at each other for a moment. Then the man's face cracked and he chuckled. "Sorry," he said. "I couldn't resist. We don't even have a schedule set up yet. There's no appointments."

"Oh."

"Would you like some water or anything?" He pointed at the large bubbler across the reception area. "It's cold."

St. George almost said no, but then realized how dry his mouth was. He filled a plastic cup and drained it. It made him feel a bit sharper and more awake. His stomach grumbled again as the water hit.

"The mayor thought you might be stopping by once you and the other heroes got back," said the young man. He waved his hand over his shoulder. "Go on in," he said.

St. George set the cup down and walked past him.

The blinds were up, and Stealth's old office was flooded with sunlight. All the screens were gone. She'd taken them with her when she moved to . . . wherever her base was now. It struck him that he didn't know, and he wasn't sure if it was because his memory was still spotty or she just hadn't told him.

The big marble conference table had been moved down to the other end of the room and turned. It was a massive desk now, covered with inboxes, a phone, two computer screens, and a small collection of photos. It all still looked very arranged. There hadn't been time for any of it to settle and find its natural place yet.

There were three big chairs in front of the desk, and one huge one behind it where the mayor was sitting. With its high back, St. George thought it looked a lot like a throne. He was pretty sure it was a deliberate choice.

He looked around. There was no one in the office but him and the mayor. No sign of Smith that he could see. The mayor was wearing a pant suit and a dark tie. She finished reading the document in her hand, scribbled a quick note on it, and looked up at him.

"Well," said Christian Nguyen. "I can't say I'm surprised you came back early."

* * *

St. George stepped up to the desk. "Where is he?"

"He who?"

"Smith. Agent John Smith, from Project Krypton."

Christian pursed her lips, then shook her head. Each movement looked rehearsed, like she'd practiced to get the maximum effect from each one. "Last I heard, your lot accused him of being some kind of traitor and he escaped to another military base."

"He's here now," said St. George, "and I'm betting he's working with you, even if you don't realize it."

She shook her head. "I can already see where this is all going," she said. "First you'll convince everyone that the government representative you claimed was some kind of supervillain is here at the Mount."

"Everyone from Krypton knows he—"

"Then you'll seize power again," she interrupted. She stood up behind the desk and gazed at him with cold eyes. "'Just for a little while,' you'll say, 'until we've got everything under control again.' And then you'll 'discover' some flimsy evidence that says Smith and I were part of some conspiracy and the election's invalid." She shook her head. "You'll say anything to get me out of this office and one of your little spineless sock puppets in here."

He closed his eyes and counted to five. Then he opened them and glanced around the office again. They were still alone. "Christian," he said, "this isn't about you. Agent Smith is here somewhere and—"

"No, he isn't."

"He's here somewhere and he's dangerous. He kills people for kicks, Christian. No one's challenging the election, but if he's not with you we need to figure out where he is. Who he's using."

She shook her head again. "You're so desperate to start trouble. You just can't stand the fact that people can depend on me when things get tough."

"Christian, please . . . if you aren't going to help, I'm going to have to do this without you." He paused for a moment and decided to risk pushing one of her buttons. "That's not going to look good your first week in office."

She stared at him for a moment. Then the faintest hint of a smile crossed her face. "You still don't get it," she said. "You honestly don't understand what's going on here."

"I think I've got a better idea than you."

She shook her head. "No, I don't think you do." She gestured at one of the big chairs on his side of the desk. "Sit down. I'd like to explain something to you."

"We don't have time for—"

"This won't take long. Humor me, please?"

He sighed and dropped into the closest chair.

She sat down in her own chair and waved her hands at the desk. "This gives me power," she said. "This office puts me on par with you. All the people who listened to me before have been validated. All the people who listened to you, like it or not, are listening to me a little closer. Because they know I've got power now."

She reached out, set her hands on the desk, and laced them together. Then she pushed her two index fingers forward. It was like she had a gun pointed at St. George. "Not power like yours," she said. "Nothing physical. The secret about power—real power—is that it's all up here."

One hand came away from the other and she tapped the center of her forehead.

"People think power is a thing. Something they can seize or gain or take away from others. Knowledge is power, money is power, strength is power." She waved her hand, brushing the words and phrases out of the air. "They're the ones who never get real power, because they're always chasing the wrong thing."

St. George nodded once and tried to make it seem polite. "I think we've got more important things to be doing right now."

"You said you'd let me explain, didn't you?"

"Yes, I did," he admitted, although he wasn't sure why he'd agreed.

"Real power is a concept," she said. "It's an idea. You go out, and you spread your idea with whatever means you can. Posters, newspapers, commercials."

"We haven't had a newspaper in Los Angeles for over four years," he said.

Christian shook her head. "I'm just giving examples. What it really comes down to is talking to people. That's how you get your idea out there. Through communication."

St. George's brow wrinkled. "I'm not sure I follow."

She put her hands out, gesturing like a politician giving a speech. "If someone asks the right question," she explained, "they can suggest a certain answer. Plant an idea in your mind. Maybe it's not much at first—most ideas aren't—but it's there, tickling the back of your mind. And over time that idea grows and gets stronger. And eventually it becomes more than just an idea. It becomes something bigger. It overwhelms rational thought. It becomes power."

St. George stood up. "We don't have time for this," he said. "If you're not going to help, that's fine. I'm going to get the scavengers and the guards to start a search." He headed for the door.

"I'm not done talking yet, George," said Christian. "Could you stay seated?"

He stopped halfway across the room. The hero looked at the doorway, then back at her. He shuffled back and sat down in his chair.

She smiled and adjusted her tie. "Thank you."

It was a broad, fake smile. She beamed it at him for a moment until his eyes widened with recognition.

"Yeah, I know," she said. "It freaked me out at first, too."

People Can Depend On Me
When Things Get Tough.

THEN

I STOOD OUTSIDE Stage 32 and waited for St. George to appear in the sky. Any minute now. This was going to be fun.

Being out on the streets of the Mount reminded me of another day out in the sun with St. George, almost a year ago. I look back on it a lot, even though it's still confusing as hell. The moment that I can remember from two different points of view.

I remember being Christian Nguyen and seeing John Smith nod.

I remember being John Smith and seeing Christian in front of me. "I'm glad to know there are people like you here in the Mount. People we'll be able to depend on even when things are tough." I remember feeling the words slide off his tongue, and echoing in her ears. "I can depend on you when things get tough, can't I, Christian?"

I remember being Smith and feeling the ever-so-faint tingle that told me the question was burrowing its way into her mind, planting ideas.

I remember being Christian and smiling. "Of course you can," I'd said. "I'm always honored to serve the people."

I said, "Excellent." I used my confidential smile, the one that made people think we were sharing a small secret, and I remember seeing the smile as Christian and feeling proud.

It's a weird sensation, I've got to admit. Remembering it all through two sets of eyes, two sets of ears. I'm stuck with it, though. It's the one part of her that's held on, the single most important moment of her life. The moment she met me.

Of course, I wasn't expecting this. I just planted a few deep thoughts and ideas and figured I'd have a happy sock puppet at the Mount. Someone in my hip pocket if I ever needed them.

It turns out Christian had a little secret of her own, though. Nothing big on its own, nothing huge. Every time you hear about someone who could've been the greatest physicist in the world if they put their mind to it, it stands to reason there's a few dozen people who would've been tied for the fiftieth- or hundredth-greatest physicist in the world. If they'd put their minds to it. Hell, I'd bet there's a good chance she never even realized she had it. She was in deep denial, half the reason it never worked on anything past a subconscious level. And even then, it was a timid thing.

Christian had her own superpower. She taps into the gestalt, if I remember those old Psych 101 terms. She brings people together, connects them on a subconscious level. I mean, how else could someone with zero charisma and interpersonal skills be a successful, honest politician?

Of course, if I'd known that ahead of time, things might've gone differently. Instead, we had two sets of mental abilities overlapping and amplifying each other to crazy levels. A harmonics thing, I think. Maybe her gestalt thing, too. The whole being greater than the sum of the parts or something.

I ended up planting a very big idea. Much bigger than I'd planned. And she brought us together.

Of course, being in this body took a lot of adjusting. There were all those mornings Christian woke up and couldn't figure out why her face didn't look right. Plus all the old things she couldn't remember, and the new things she could. Most people would start panicking about Alzheimer's or something, but she was so focused on rallying the After Death movement and her steamroller-style mayoral campaign that she just kept brushing it aside. And she kept saying the phrase I'd given her again and again, like an error-loop glitch that keeps popping up.

People can depend on me when things get tough.

She started forgetting her life and started remembering mine.

St. George appeared in the sky and dragged me back to the present. He spun around in a circle like a kite whipping through the air. Then he dropped down and landed on the pavement a few yards away.

"What's up, Christian?" he said. He always sounded so sincere. It's incredible how fast that can get grating.

"I need to show you something," I told him.

He glanced back across the Mount. "I'm kind of busy," he said. "We're trying to juggle a couple of things before—"

"It'll just take a moment," I said. "You can spare a minute, can't you?"

"Yeah, of course."

I turned away and fumbled with the lock. It was a show. I'd done it three times already at this point. "I'm glad you made that announcement," I told him without looking back. "I'm sure a lot of other people are, too. It will make the vote go much smoother, don't you think?"

"Yeah," he said.

The lock popped open and I pulled the handle. I glanced back at St. George. "Are you coming?"

He reached over and held the door open, then followed me in. One thing I've got to say, men treat women differently. It's a bunch of little stuff, but it's there. It threw me at first, but I've gotten adjusted to it.

St. George walked behind me toward the center of the stage. I'd set up some blankets, just to make things a bit homey. People are always a bit confused when things look homey, and confusion usually works in my favor. Three of the blankets already had people stretched out on them.

"Danielle?" he called out. "What are you doing here? I was trying to reach you for half an hour."

My favorite redhead didn't move, of course. She'd been the

second one I'd grabbed. I couldn't risk her recognizing some speech pattern or habit of mine. It was tempting to use her once or thrice for old time's sake, too, but I don't have that equipment anymore. Still getting used to that part of this, I've got to admit.

"Sorry about that," I told St. George. "She was helping me with something. You don't mind, do you?"

He was going to say no, of course, but by then he'd noticed Danielle wasn't moving. And he'd seen Freedom's bulk spread out on the farthest blanket. And, just past Danielle, a third person. In the dim light of the stage, she blended in and was hard to spot.

To give him credit, he didn't shout her name or anything melodramatic like that. He just charged across the room. Leaped, really. A noble man of action.

I took my time and walked up behind him. He had the cloaked bitch in his arms. He tried to wake her up, pressed his fingers against her throat, and listened to her breathing. I was maybe five feet behind him when he glanced back. "Did you know about this?"

I nodded and smiled. "Do you want to lie down next to her?"

He set her back down on the blanket, placed a fold of it under her head, and returned my nod. "Yeah," he said. "I think I'd like that."

His brow wrinkled, and I saw a spark of fear deep in his eye. He recognized what was happening. What he was doing. It's always more fun when people realize what's going on.

"Just stretch out and relax," I said. "Wouldn't that be a good way to spend the afternoon?"

St. George looked down at one of the open blankets, flipped the edge over to double it up, and sat down on it.

It's a little risky, doing this. Getting them alone one by one and then dropping them. One quick response, one of them puts it together before I can speak, and this fun little experiment is over.

But it's still better than the alternative. I'd heard stories about what happened to me out at Project Krypton. Well, to other-me, I guess. I pushed for details where I could, eavesdropped when I couldn't. I heard about other-me getting dragged out from behind the curtain. Colonel Shelly dying. Professor Sorensen dying.

Stealth planting a knife in other-me's throat before I could escape to Groom Lake.

I couldn't risk that happening here. First rule of building your new empire—get rid of the people who brought down your last one. The people who know how to beat you.

I'm still amazed I got Stealth. Granted, I took her out first so she wouldn't have a chance of being suspicious. Well, any more suspicious. She's so damned fast. But she never saw it coming and four minutes after walking into the stage to check out "safety concerns" she was unconscious on the floor.

Danielle was next. And Freedom's still the same clueless idiot, deferring to anyone he considers above him. God bless the military mind-set.

St. George stretched out on his blanket and shifted a few times to get comfortable. He glanced over at Stealth, then up at me. "You're right," he said. "This is kind of nice."

I plastered a smile on my face. "Why don't you take a nap?" I suggested. "A good long one."

He yawned and blinked twice.

"Wouldn't it be nice to dream about a world where there aren't any zombies?" I asked him. "No exes, no ex-virus, nothing ever happened. You could forget all of it. Just the plain old world where you're a normal guy, doing whatever the hell you did before you became a superhero. Wouldn't that be nice?"

"God, yes," he said, and yawned again.

One great thing about this new, overpowered skill set is the dreams. The old me, the other-me who's out at Groom Lake or somewhere, could force someone to sleep, but eventually they'd wake up. I couldn't control their subconscious. But with Christian's powers in the mix, I can make people combine their dreams and build on each other's memories. Two or three people together can make a great, rich world, each of them filling in the gaps for the others. A world they never need to wake up from.

St. George managed to turn his head toward Stealth before his eyelids got too heavy. Then he just rolled back to center. His breathing leveled out.

I whispered a few more suggestions. I wanted them out of the way, lost in the dreamworld. But any good jailer knows you want a wall around the prison, too, just in case people get out of their cells. Just in case they start to wake up. Nothing too elaborate, just a believable tweak on reality, enough to keep them busy for a few—

"What are you doing?"

I turned around and saw Sorensen's brat halfway between me and the door. The Corpse Girl, she likes to call herself. I should've guessed she'd be here. She follows St. George around like a dog. I wonder if he's doing her. Necrophilia's really not my thing, but I can see the appeal of a body that's almost-eighteen forever.

She marched across the room. In the dim light, her skin looked pure white. Even walking, she had a stillness to her that had taken me days to pin down. Sometimes she stops breathing. It's one of those subtle things, a person's chest moving up and down. You don't realize you register it until you meet someone who doesn't do it. She doesn't blink sometimes, either. It's kind of eerie, and I say this as someone who's been mentally cloned into another body.

I've got to admit, it creeped me out when I became conscious enough to realize who the Corpse Girl was. Little Madelyn, the daughter Sorensen would not shut up about, even after I'd arranged to have her killed in front of him. It was like some bad horror movie. The dead come back to life, you turn around, and there's the girl you killed in act two, back for zombie revenge.

Of course, she had no idea who I was. Then or now.

Granted, I didn't know enough about her, either. She's dead, but she's not your standard ex-human. Twice I've given her simple commands, as a test. They last about a day with her and then she just seems to shrug them off. I've heard she's got some sort of memory problem, which makes sense in a way.

It meant I was going to have to be harsh with her.

She was twenty feet closer when she saw the heroes stretched out on the floor. Her sneakers *chuffed* on the concrete floor as she stopped. There was just enough contrast to her iris that I could see her eyes flitting back and forth over all the figures. Mostly St. George, of course.

I gestured with my hand. "Could you come here?"

The Corpse Girl started moving again. She took a few more steps, then stopped again. She looked at me. "Did you do this?"

"Of course not," I said. "Could you come over and help me, please?"

That was enough. She walked over next to me and I pointed at one of the blankets. "Don't you want to take a nap? You can sleep on St. George's other side, if you like."

She blinked and trembled for a moment.

"Don't you want to go to sleep?" I asked her again.

Her eyelids drooped down, sagged lower and lower, and then snapped open. She glared at me. It was kind of eerie with the dead eyes.

I smiled and laced my fingers together. "Now, don't you look at me that way," I said to her. "Are you a little overtired, maybe?"

And then I hit her across the jaw with both hands.

She staggered back, and almost fell. Then she straightened up and her thin fingers rolled into fists.

I let my own fingers come apart and shook them out. I suck at fighting. I think I may have broken a finger. "Hurts, doesn't it?"

She winced and reached up to touch one of her cheekbones.

"Are you too dizzy to stand up?"

The Corpse Girl swayed and dropped to one knee.

I watched her try to keep her balance and tapped my fingers against my leg. One of Christian's odd muscle memories that shows up now and then. "You were sick when you were little, right? Muscular dystrophy or something? Your dad would mutter about it now and then after I killed you the first time." She teetered back and forth, trying to fight the questions. "He did something to fix you, didn't he?"

She fell over on her side. I took her by the arm and half led, half dragged her toward the circle of heroes. She struggled for a minute and I clucked my tongue at her. "You don't want to act that way, do you?"

She stopped fighting.

"Wouldn't it be easier to just relax?"

She rolled down onto the blanket. She ended up on her side, then tipped over onto her back. She stopped breathing again.

I whispered to her as she settled down. She struggled a bit, but the questions sank into her brain and the ideas took hold. She blinked a few times and then went limp. Her blank eyes stared up at the ceiling.

She was going to be the wild card in all this. I wasn't sure how long I could hold her, and I wasn't sure if holding her would have any effect. I don't think she can starve to death. I was tempted to just stomp her head in, but if the bodies were found that would lead to questions.

And I didn't want to deal with questions. Not yet, anyway.

For now, it's just a nice, peaceful sleep.

THIRTY-FIVE

ST. GEORGE TRIED to get out of the chair. He strained his legs, tensed his back, forced his arms to push up. He focused on the spot between his shoulder blades and tried to hurl himself at the ceiling.

Nothing happened.

Christian grinned at him, then leaned forward in her seat. "Keep quiet for a minute, would you? And were you thinking of trying something?" she added. "I can see the smoke coming out of your nose."

His mouth went dry and his lips pressed together. He glared at her.

"Todd," she called out.

The young man appeared in the doorway. "Could you get on the radio and call the special channel for me? Tell them the word is 'prodigal,' and I'll be coming to them. I'll be there in . . ." She glanced at St. George. "Let's say half an hour or so."

Todd's head bobbed up and down. "I'm sure they can make that happen, Ms. Nguyen." He vanished back to his desk.

She settled back into the throne-like seat. "I'm sure you're dying to ask some questions," she said to St. George. "And your minute's just about up, sooo . . . go ahead. But stay in the chair, okay? And I can trust you not to hurt me, can't I?"

"It's just us," he said. "You can drop the act. Or the illusion. Whatever you want to call it."

Christian blinked.

"Making me see Christian. Is she dead? Or is she just asleep somewhere, too?"

She laughed. "You weren't paying attention at all."

"What did you do to her?"

"Ahhh," said Christian. "Now that's a smart question. I don't think you know it, but it's a good one." She tapped the side of her head. "Really, all that matters is that a few weeks ago the annoying Ms. Ngyuen went to sleep with a headache, and I woke up the next morning."

St. George stared at the woman. The faint accent had dropped out of her voice, and some of her words had a mild twang to them. She sounded younger. The muscles of her face flexed in odd ways. It just wasn't the way Christian held her lips or eyes. He remembered Smith's fake smile. "So you killed her," he said.

"Maybe." She shrugged. "It's not like the ex-virus got her or something. Heart's still beating, lungs are breathing, brain's active. It's my brain now, granted."

"She's going to be the last one."

"I doubt that very much. So do you. And let's be honest—there's no love lost between you guys. There was a lot of serious hatred for you and Stealth and the others floating around in here." Christian tapped her head again. "Don't try to convince me she was your best friend and you need to avenge her or something."

"She was a person. We didn't always agree on everything, but she still mattered."

The woman sighed and shook her head.

St. George tried to stand up again, but his limbs were frozen. "So you're . . . what, controlling her body from Groom Lake?"

"Nope." Christian looked at her reflection in the mirror and adjusted her collar over the tie. "I'm a mental clone, if that makes any sense. Me and the other-me, our lives split right there when the idea of me got yanked into Christian's brain. So I don't know what's going on with him, he doesn't know what's going on with me. I'm Christian Smith, if that works for you."

"If you're not him," said St. George, "then why do all this? Why not work with us?"

Air blurted out between her lips. "Honestly," said the woman, "I don't know what other-me's been up to—not much, I'm guessing, considering how Stealth left him—but I've got a great chance to start over here. Twenty-odd thousand citizens, a few super-soldiers, an armored battlesuit . . . that's the beginning of a new empire. As long as I worked around you, Stealth, the captain, and the rest. So, a few choice words and you all left while everyone in Los Angeles voted me in for mayor."

"Of course they did," growled St. George.

"Give me a little credit," Christian said. She leaned against the huge desk. "It wasn't a landslide. I got a healthy forty-two percent of the vote. Richard got twenty-three. You and Stealth got about sixteen percent between you, although I think she actually beat you by a couple of votes. Mickey Mouse got eight votes and Superman got four. All very nice and believable."

"And what about us? You couldn't've hidden from us forever."

"I'll be honest, George. I'd kind of hoped you'd all just pleasantly live in your little dreamworld until you starved to death, but . . ." She stopped and looked at him. "It was Sorensen's kid, wasn't it? I knew she was going to be a problem."

"She remembered you," said St. George. "She knew you were up to something."

Christian Smith smiled and shook her head. "It's the little details that always get you in the end. She almost got you out of it yesterday. You probably would've woken up if I hadn't been there to give you a few fresh commands." She straightened up and brushed her suit down. "Anyway, we should get going. Could you follow me, George?"

He stood up without thinking.

Christian crossed the room. "And you haven't tried to hurt me so far. That's good. Can you keep that up for a bit longer?"

He knew he wouldn't hurt her, but he didn't want to nod. His head went up and down against his will.

She paused just before the door. "By the way," she added in a lower voice, "you might be having some clever thoughts about trying to hurt me in some indirect way or maybe warning some people. That'd be bad. Don't forget who I am and what I can do. Todd out there will crush his own windpipe if I give him the word. I've got similar suggestions planted in about fifty folks all over the city."

They stepped out to the elevator links. Todd smiled at them. "They said they'd be ready for you, ma'am," he told her.

"Excellent," said Christian. "Those letters on my desk are signed. Could you make sure they get copied and go out to everyone?"

"Yes, ma'am."

She led St. George past the elevators and they went down the stairs. He noticed Christian was wearing flats. He wondered if Smith had trouble walking in heels.

"I had high hopes for you," she said. Her voice echoed up to him in the stairwell. "A couple years ago, when I found out the Mighty Dragon was still alive and kicking ... I really thought this was going to be the big chance I'd been waiting for. And then, goddamnit, even after all you've gone through you still turn out to have this damned moral code."

"Sorry to disappoint you."

She shook her head. "It would've been so much easier if you'd just stayed in your happy place and starved to death, but you're such a goddamned Boy Scout you make Freedom look bad." She hit the crash bar and they stepped out into the lobby. "And he actually was a Boy Scout. He got his Eagle badge from a senator and everything."

Christian smiled at a few folks as they walked out of Roddenberry and into the sunlight. She slipped a pair of sunglasses from her pocket as they stepped out from under the canopy and pushed them over her face with one hand. They walked a few more yards and she stopped near the edge of the garden. St. George could see a few people moving between the plants, pulling weeds and gathering soybeans.

The ground shook. Like any Los Angeles resident, he'd lived

through dozens of minor earthquakes. The tremors barely registered until he noticed they came in slow, steady pulses.

Christian Smith smiled. "You should get ready, don't you think?"

He turned around.

Cerberus loomed over him. The battlesuit had been polished and cleaned. The massive M2 rifles were mounted on its forearms, and the ammo belts looped around to the hopper on its back. Whoever was wearing the armor moved with a heavy stride, slamming each foot against the ground. An eager bruiser. Someone who wanted to fight.

"Lieutenant Gibbs," said Christian. "You remember when I warned you St. George and the others might come back and try to seize power?"

"Yes, ma'am." His voice was an electronic growl through the suit's speakers.

"Lieutenant," said St. George, "listen to me. This isn't—"

"Well, I'm afraid it's happened, just like we feared." She grinned up at the battlesuit. "You know what to do, right?"

"This isn't Christian Nguyen!" shouted St. George. "It's Agent Sm—"

The punch hit him in the face, but the fist was so big the bottom knuckle banged against the top of his chest.

He flew past the old paint building, bounced into the parking lot, and tumbled across the south end of the garden. He came to rest facedown in some dirt with a few blades of grass poking up through it. Dust and dry soil pattered around him.

St. George pushed himself up onto his knees and caught a burst of .50-caliber rounds across the chest. It knocked him back another half-dozen feet. He could hear people screaming. He saw a few figures running through the garden and hoped they were running away.

The hits hurt like all hell. He wasn't sure, but he thought the rounds might have cracked a rib or two. He rolled to the side and back up onto his knees to avoid a second burst of gunfire. A third point on his rib cage flared with pain.

The earth was trembling again. He counted to three, focused, and then shot forward. He crossed his arms and rammed the titan just below the chestplate.

Cerberus bent over and staggered. He took a few steps after it and slammed the palm of his hand up into the armored helmet. The battlesuit tipped back and stumbled a few more feet before it fell over with the sound of a car crash.

St. George turned and leaped at Christian. If he could get one punch—a careful punch—he could knock her out. He didn't know if Smith's powers worked when he—she—was unconscious, but it couldn't hurt.

She smiled as he lunged through the air. One hand came up and waggled a finger at him. "I'm not the one you're fighting, am I?"

St. George froze in the air with his arm back. He dropped to the ground and landed on the balls of his feet. "Bastard," he spat out.

"I think, technically, it's bitch now."

Behind him, he heard the scrape of metal on concrete as Cerberus climbed back to its feet.

"I helped get that suit built, George. I know how powerful it is. If there's anything in this city that can kill you, that's it." She sighed. "Damn. It really should've been Danielle doing this. I guess I didn't think of everything."

"Ma'am," shouted Gibbs from inside the battlesuit, "are you all right?"

"Just fine, Lieutenant," called Christian. She winked at St. George. "At least he hasn't stooped to hurting unarmed civilians. I don't think he'd sink that low, do you?"

He scowled and smoke curled out of his nostrils.

The ground shook and he saw the huge shadow of the arm coming down. He turned and caught it with both hands. The servos whined and Gibbs tried to force the arm down. St. George pushed it back up a few inches and glared up at the huge eyes.

The other arm swung around and caught him in the side. The world blurred and one of the square pillars in front of the Roddenberry doors hit him in the back. The corner caught him right on the shoulder blade. A few cinder blocks crumbled and spun him off into the base of a large palm tree. Dust and grit sifted down from the canopy above.

"St. George," called someone. "You all right?"

A figure blotted out the sun. He shook his head clear and saw three people from the lobby standing over him. More dust drifted down onto their shoulders, but they didn't look up until the first golf ball–sized chunks hit their shoulders.

St. George shook his head clear, leaped up, and shoved them back. He caught the desk-sized slab of canopy on his fingertips, twisted, and pushed it away from the people. It crashed into the pavement and turned into so much rubble. A fist-sized piece of concrete bounced off his shoulder. He glanced at the trio. "Everyone okay?"

He heard the heavy footsteps approaching before they could answer. He grabbed a chunk of cinder block and plaster the size of a basketball and hurled it at the battlesuit. Cerberus tried to block it but the piece of rubble struck the side of the armored skull. St. George leaped into the air and headed back across the parking lot, into the open and away from the buildings.

Cerberus stomped after him. "Surrender now, sir," shouted Gibbs. The cannons came up and traced lines through the sky.

St. George looped around fast, swung down, and slammed his shoulder into the back of the battlesuit's knee. It tipped back and waved its arms, fighting for balance. St. George planted his feet, grabbed it by the arm, and twisted. The armored titan slammed down to the ground again.

His hands slid down the massive arm until he reached the ammo feed for the M2. He tore the belt apart and the rounds and links jingled on the pavement. He leaped over the fallen battlesuit and found the other ammo belt.

Cerberus lunged up and grabbed him. The stunners came on. Electricity arced around the huge fingers as 200,000 volts raced through St. George. His muscles stiffened up and his skin tingled.

It froze him long enough for another punch to slam into his chest. He sailed across the open space and slammed into the short wall that wrapped around the garden. Momentum flipped him over it and he tumbled into the parking area for the scavenger trucks. He bounced against *Big Blue*'s reinforced grille and fell to the pavement.

If his ribs hadn't been cracked before, they were now.

"Holy shit," muttered someone.

"Is he alive?" asked another voice. Hands wrapped around his arms and pulled him up. He heard other murmurs in the background.

St. George opened his eyes, blinked, and looked into a familiar face. Luke Reid, the head driver. He needed a shave. "You okay, boss?"

"Get out of here," St. George told them. "Everyone. Now."

He heard Cerberus stomping across the pavement. The battlesuit still had one M2 left, plus the stunners. And it was stronger than him. A lot stronger.

"Go!" shouted St. George. They saw the battlesuit approaching and scattered. He knew they could see the menace in its movements, too.

He looked around for anything that might give him an edge. There were some tools scattered around, but nothing too useful. He wasn't strong enough to throw one of the trucks, and even if he could it would cause too much damage. There was a case of motor oil, a half-dozen block-like batteries, and two stacks of tires for the big trucks.

He grabbed one of the tires and rolled it alongside him. It bounced against the wall and tipped back. He caught it with his thigh.

"Gibbs," he called out. He raised his hands. "This isn't right," he said. "You know me. I'm not a threat. I'm not your enemy."

"You're a traitor leading a coup against the mayor," growled the titan. "You're trying to overthrow the government."

"No I'm not. What have I said that would make you think that? What have I done that would make you think I'm doing that?"

"Liar!" The gun arm came up.

St. George kicked the tire into the air and smacked it toward Cerberus. The M2 thundered and scraps of black rubber rained down on the parking lot. *Big Blue*'s windshield shattered.

It had given St. George time to step back to the stack. He flung two more tires like thick Frisbees, then pulled another one out of the pile and hurled it, too. He remembered reading years ago about people being killed at racetracks when tires came off at high speed and flew into the stands. He was pretty sure he was throwing them at least that hard.

Cerberus targeted the first two tires and annihilated them with bursts from the big gun. The third one slammed the battlesuit in the side of the chest hard enough to make it twist at the waist. The next one hit it in the shoulder. Then one struck the barrel of the M2 and knocked it down.

St. George threw tire after tire. They slammed into the armored titan and bounced off into the garden or toward the Melrose gate. One or two shot straight back and hit the short wall in front of St. George. It was like a brutal game of dodgeball. They weren't forcing the armored titan back, but they were stopping it from doing anything else.

He was pulling his punches. He knew it wasn't Danielle in the battlesuit, but he still knew it was hers. Part of her, almost. He didn't want to damage it.

He threw his last tire. "Agent Smith," he shouted.

Across the parking lot he saw Christian perk up. The battlesuit did, too. He'd caught Gibbs's attention.

"You remember Agent John Smith," St. George called out to Cerberus. "The one who tricked all of you. The one who killed Colonel Shelly."

The titan straightened up and lowered its arms. All the men and women from Project Krypton remembered Smith. He'd used them all, killed their commanding officer, and then bragged about it.

"Smith is here, Gibbs," said St. George. "He's trying to take control here just like he did out at the base."

The gun arm came back up. "I'm sorry if you're being influenced, sir," said Cerberus, "but it's my duty to protect the citizens and government, and right now you're an immediate threat."

St. George shook his head. "I'm not the one being influenced, Lieutenant."

"What?"

"I'm not the one he's trying to control."

The titan's M2 drifted down from St. George's face to his chest. The loose ammo belt waved back and forth on the battle-suit's other arm like a banner.

"Just tell me how Smith works," said St. George. "Just think for a minute. You were out there. You remember how he did it."

"Lieutenant Gibbs," shouted Christian. "You're not listening to him, are you?"

The armored skull turned to look at her, and St. George saw the titan's stance shift. "No, ma'am," said Cerberus. The battle-suit turned back and the M2 came back up.

St. George flew into the air as the rounds chewed up the wall and smashed into *Big Blue's* engine block. The front of the truck sagged. He was pretty sure it would never move again.

He tried to swoop around the titan and the gun arm tracked him. Another burst fired off with the deafening sound of a bass drum. The rounds almost missed him. Two of them hit him in the thigh, one cracked into his kneecap. He wobbled in the sky just long enough for a second burst to knock him back. He hit a palm tree and dropped out of the air. A yellow parking pylon, one of a dozen or so that still studded the area, caught him in the hip as he fell and flipped him onto his back.

He saw the steel fist plunging down at him and rolled out of the way. It cracked the pavement behind him. Cerberus shifted and tried to stomp, but St. George managed to focus enough to throw himself up to his feet.

The gun arm came up and blasted away. He leaped out of the way and it traced a path after him. He heard the rounds hit concrete, glass, and wood. Screams echoed across the lot. St. George stopped dodging and blocked the last two bursts with his aching ribs. The rounds tore his shirt and leather jacket to shreds.

"Jesus, Gibbs," he coughed when the barrage stopped. "There's people everywhere! Civilians!"

The lieutenant growled and ignored him. Another punch came swinging around. St. George set his leg back to brace himself and managed to catch the fist with both hands. The impact made him slide back a foot.

Sorry, Danielle, he thought.

The gauntlet had three fingers and a thumb. Each one was as thick as a soda can. He grabbed the thumb and the farthest finger and twisted.

There was a squeal of metal and a few sparks as the steel hand tore apart. Cerberus yanked away, but it was too late. St. George let the two digits hit the ground. One of the remaining fingers hung at a strange angle and twitched. The other one kept flexing as Gibbs held it up to check damage. "Son of a bitch," muttered the lieutenant.

The broken hand slammed into St. George's face. The two remaining fingers grabbed his head in an awkward pinch. He reached up to grab them and the stunners fired up again.

His muscles tensed. This time he felt it in his tongue and teeth and eyes. His eyelids twitched. The finger-claw tightened on his skull and lifted him off the ground. He reached up, tried to shake himself loose, but couldn't grab hard enough.

He felt the muzzle of the M2 settle against his stomach and a moment later he was punched in the gut a dozen times. At point-blank range the sound itself was a weapon. The barrel rose and the furious rounds battered their way up his chest. Then the impacts tore him free from the damaged fingers and he tumbled away.

St. George staggered back but managed not to fall over. He took in a deep breath to blind the titan with a burst of fire and his chest screamed with pain. A hundred spikes stabbed between his ribs. He coughed out some smoke, a few flickers of flame, and then slumped to his knees.

The battlesuit stepped forward and leveled the M2 against his head.

THIRTY-SIX

"STOP IT!"

Danielle ran along the garden. Her hair and shoulders were soaking wet, and her shirt was plastered to the dark contact suit beneath it. She pushed past some terrified onlookers, took a few panting breaths as she swung her legs over the wall, and ran toward the battlesuit. "Gibbs, stand down now."

The armored skull turned to her. "Ma'am?"

"That's St. George," said Danielle. "What the hell do you think you're doing?"

"He's gone rogue, ma'am. He's threatened civilians and tried to overthrow—"

"He's been asleep," Danielle said. "We've all been asleep for two days. He hasn't done anything. Now stand down."

"Lieutenant," yelled Christian.

The huge lenses turned her way.

"They're in this together," shouted the mayor. "Don't you realize that?"

Danielle heard the voice. She knew the tones and inflections from back when John Smith was the guy she worked with almost every day and woke up with on more than a few mornings. She recognized the sly smile. Seeing it all come from Christian threw her, but not by much. She'd come to accept pretty much anything where Smith was concerned.

The titan swung back around and glared at Danielle. She'd never realized just how aggressive the armor's face could look. The battlesuit took two stomping steps toward her.

"You, too, ma'am?" the titan said. "I respected you."

"This isn't going to work, Gibbs," she said. "Just stop now. You can't win this."

The M2 swung around. The barrel settled in front of her. "Not really sure how you see it that way, ma'am."

The cannon's muzzle was huge. She looked up at the helmet's round lenses. "Because you're inside my armor," she told the titan, "and you can hear my voice."

Gibbs's snort echoed over the battlesuit's speakers. "Are those your last words?"

"Not quite," she said. She wiped a wet strand of hair off her face and took a deep breath. "Patriotic! Crustacean! Houdini!"

The bright lenses flickered. Just for a moment. Loud *clacks* came from the ammo hopper. Across the armor, two dozen small panels opened at the shoulders and hips and around the waist, each one the size of a matchbook. Four of them popped up around the thick collar the helmet sat on. A gleaming bolt sat under each one.

The cannon pointed at her trembled but didn't fire. She stepped back and Gibbs growled inside the armor. "What the hell have you done?" he yelled.

"A subroutine I wrote a while ago to save time," Danielle said. "Back when I had to do most of this myself."

The steel fingers flexed, and he snarled. It was a rasping sound through the speaker. She imagined him trying to activate the stunners again and again with the optical mouse.

She took another step back. "Cerberus is preparing for disassembly. The weapons systems are offline," she told him. "You can't turn any of them back on without a hard reboot."

The battlesuit took a step forward. She took two more back. The eyes flickered again.

"You might want to stand up straight," said Danielle. "Once I shut it down, the gyros won't keep the armor stabilized anymore."

Cerberus growled and lunged at her. The huge fingers spread, ready to snap shut on her skull. She flinched away and heard a clang of steel on stone.

St. George grimaced as the fingers tried to crush his arm. "Thanks for the breather," he said.

"No problem."

* * *

"Well, that really sucks."

Christian Smith shook her head and pushed her sunglasses up. She'd recognized Danielle, even twenty yards away and soaking wet. And despite some quick improvisation, the unarmed, unarmored redhead had already disabled the battlesuit to some degree.

She was always the clever one.

Smith hadn't expected this combo. She'd expected one or two heroes to fight the battlesuit—hopefully St. George and Captain Freedom. Best case, they'd be killed, worst case they'd all be beaten senseless and easy to control. It had never crossed her mind that Danielle could just shut the suit off from the outside.

She adjusted her glasses and took a few steps along the garden. At least Gibbs would keep the heroes busy long enough to get Plan B up and run—

Something sharp yanked Christian's skull to the left, like she'd slammed the side of her head into a beam or pipe. Her sunglasses tumbled away and the side of her face sagged. Just as the sound of the gunshot reached her, the dark line along her temple burned into her skin and became a stream of hot blood. It soaked her ear and her jaw and rained down on her shoulder.

In the corner of her eye, a shadow slid closer across the parking lot. Stealth had one of her Glock 19s aimed at Christian's head. A faint wisp of smoke came from the barrel. "That was a warning," she said. "Do not move and do not speak." She walked forward and her cloak swirled around her.

"Oh, God!" Christian screamed. She grabbed at her head and her fingers came back wet and red.

"Turn around. Get on your knees."

"Please don't kill me," Smith begged with Christian's voice. "Please. I never meant all those things I said about you and the others. I was just angry. I didn't—"

"Silence."

"I don't want to die!" she wailed. "I don't! I don't think you can hold that gun, do you?"

Stealth's arm dropped and the pistol clattered on the pavement.

"Gotcha," grinned Smith.

The cloaked woman lunged forward, her fingers curling for a strike.

"Punching again?"

She stumbled in mid step and came to a halt. Her fists trembled.

Smith raised a hand. "Let's calm down, okay?"

Stealth froze for a moment. Then she spun and her boot caught Smith in the gut. Air whoofed out of the other woman and she stumbled back. The cloaked woman followed through with a second spinning kick that cracked across Christian's jaw.

"I am always calm," said Stealth.

Smith coughed some blood and sputtered out two teeth. "Let's stop all the violence, then, okay?" Her voice was slurred, but it was clear enough. "Could you help me up?"

She could feel Stealth glaring at her through the black mask. The cloaked woman reached down and pulled Smith up to her feet.

Christian pulled a handkerchief from her pocket and dabbed at her mouth. She spit out a few more fragments of teeth and then tried pressing the cloth on the side of her head. It was soaked with blood in seconds. She grumbled to herself and then waved at Stealth. "Would you take the lead?"

"Where are we going?"

"Back to Stage 32," said the other woman. "It's a lot more visible than I wanted, but it looks like I'm going to have to have you all beat each other to death. And then, if you're still in one piece, we're going to find someplace quiet for a day or two." Smith looked at the handkerchief again and shook her head. "Word is, you caused a lot of problems when I tried to take you hostage out at Yuma, but I'm sure you won't cause any trouble at all this time, will you?"

* * *

Cerberus squeezed and pushed down, but St. George pushed back. The battlesuit couldn't crush his arm, and it didn't have the leverage to force him down.

Then the gunshot and scream echoed across the garden and St. George's head whipped around. He caught a quick glimpse of Stealth with a pistol drawn advancing on Christian, a flash of blood, and then the titan shifted tactics and yanked St. George up in the air.

He forced his way even higher and the battlesuit stumbled. It took a moment for Gibbs to catch up and let go. The steel arm dropped and some of the small panels across the body scraped and sparked.

St. George looked across the lot. Stealth was helping Christian up. The pistol was gone. Christian was smiling.

Cerberus glared up at the hero hanging in the air. Then it ran at Danielle. The steel feet clanged.

St. George tackled the battlesuit and sent it staggering.

The punch whipped past Danielle, missing her by a few inches. St. George put his fists together and slammed them into the armor's side, right under the arm. The battlesuit stumbled another few steps and he wrapped his arms around the leg and pulled.

Cerberus crashed to the ground again.

He looked back toward the garden. Stealth and Christian had vanished. He could guess what happened if Smith managed to get a few words out.

Danielle came running over. He opened his mouth to talk but

she waved him silent. "Echo sierra alpha victor forty-two," she called out.

The battlesuit slammed its mangled hand against the ground and pushed up. The servos whined. The damaged hand sparked on the pavestone walkway.

She frowned. "Echo! Sierra! Alpha! Victor! Forty-Two!"

The armored titan got to its hands and knees, then brought one foot up.

Danielle called out the words one more time and punctuated the phrase with a swear. "Goddammit," she added. "He killed the external mikes. I can't shut it down."

St. George watched Cerberus climb to its feet. "I can," he told her.

"What do you mean?"

He guided her back as the battlesuit straightened up. "Gibbs isn't going to stop until he kills us. Or until we stop him."

Her eyes went wide. "No."

The battlesuit turned around and the lenses locked onto them. St. George grabbed Danielle around the waist and leaped into the air. He flew away from the titan, and realized a moment later it meant he was flying away from Stealth and Smith, too.

Cerberus stomped after them.

Danielle stiffened up as the buildings fell away. Her arms pulled in tight, and even her legs pressed together. She gritted her teeth and managed another "No."

Below them Cerberus smashed through the low wall around the garden and sent chunks of mortar and cinder blocks flying. An angry backhand crumpled the front of *Mean Green*.

They flew over Five and Four. "He'll run out of power using it like that," Danielle gasped. "Without Barry recharging it, the suit won't last long at all."

"How long?"

She was taking quick breaths through her nose. "Put us down."

He dropped down between Stage 4 and the Edith Head Building. A few people watched them land, drawn out by the sounds.

Danielle relaxed as the walls rose up around them and he set her on the ground. "Maybe forty-five minutes," she said. "An hour tops. If you can just keep him—"

He shook his head. "That's too long. If we keep this up, he's going to kill someone. And Smith has Stealth."

"Are you sure?"

"Yes." He turned to the gawkers. "Run," he told them. "Get as far from here as you can."

One man looked around. "What's going—"

"Run!" St. George looked at Danielle. "I have to—"

"I know!" she snapped.

The ground shook. They heard the hiss and stomp of the battlesuit coming toward them. There was a crash of metal on concrete.

"I'm sorry," he said.

Danielle squeezed her hands into fists. "Do it."

Cerberus appeared between two buildings. Gibbs yelled something over the speakers but he'd switched to public address mode and his amplified words were lost in their own echo and the stomp of armored feet.

The battlesuit charged them.

St. George leaped to meet it.

He ducked a punch and then a follow-up swing from the damaged hand. When the next fist came at him he braced his legs and caught it. A few steps to the side kept the arm out straight and St. George far enough away that the other arm couldn't reach him. The titan tried to pull free but he yanked back and kept it off balance. The feet hissed as pistons and servos adjusted.

He pulled again. When Gibbs tugged back, St. George let go with one hand and grabbed the steel thumb with the other. The metal fist clenched around his hand. If he'd been a normal man, his fingers and forearm would've been crushed to powder.

St. George drove his free hand up into the battlesuit's elbow as hard as he could. Metal squealed under his knuckles. At least one servo sparked and blew out.

The steel fingers released him. Cerberus tried to shake him

off but he drove two more punches up into the joint of the arm. The second one got even more sparks. The third one made it go limp and sag at a wrong angle.

The hero grabbed the forearm with one hand, the dead M2 with the other, and wrenched the whole thing away. The elbow joint cracked and some ball bearings sprayed out onto the street like steel raindrops. A half-dozen cables yanked free. An armor plate broke off and clattered on the ground. The M2's ammo belt twisted until some of the links bent and it snapped apart.

The battlesuit took a few heavy steps back. Gibbs raised the remains of the arm. St. George thought he could see the man's own fingertips exposed in the twisted remains of the elbow.

The titan roared and the mangled hand—the pincer—swung around and caught the hero in the side of the head. It slammed him across the road and into the corner of Four hard enough to break cinder blocks. He tumbled across the building and spun out onto Avenue R. He hit the ground face-first, and a spray of rubble pattered around him.

He raised his head and saw people running toward him. Billie Carter was in the lead—alive and well, her face grim under her spiky hair—with Ilya just a few steps behind her and two more past that. He could hear Cerberus stomping after him, getting close.

St. George rolled onto his back just as Cerberus brought a foot up to crush him. The hero drove his heel into the battlesuit's other ankle. He felt it dent under the blow, but it didn't break. It was enough that the foot came down to regain balance rather than do damage. The titan wobbled for a moment as it compensated for the damage.

"We never trusted you," roared Gibbs over the speakers. "Any of you!"

A fireworks display of small-arms fire sparked and pinged off the armor. The scavengers emptied their weapons at the battlesuit. Some of the rounds ricocheted down to slap St. George in the thighs and chest. After the M2s, they felt like bug bites.

It didn't hurt the titan, either, but it distracted Gibbs for a moment. "Traitors," he bellowed at them. The battlesuit pulled its foot back and kicked St. George in the ribs, hurling him at the scavengers.

His ribs tore at his insides, but he managed to twist in the air and miss Billie and one of the others. His hand smacked against Ilya's arm and he was pretty sure he felt one of the other man's bones crack. He hit another building—he wasn't sure which one— shoulder first and left a crater in the wall.

St. George took a breath and his ribs howled. He forced another breath and pushed himself out of the wall. Grit and rubble dropped off him.

Billie and the others were reloading on the move. Cerberus stalked after them. She was shouting something at the battlesuit, but it sounded muffled and echo-y in his ears. He shook his head and the world became a little clearer.

The hero launched himself at Cerberus again. Gibbs saw him coming, the pincer hand came around again, and St. George landed inside the blow. He blocked it with his own forearm and slammed three punches into the titan's stomach—an array of overlapping armored plates. He heard the impacts echo inside the battlesuit. One of the plates cracked under his knuckles.

Gibbs roared again. The titan's arm pulled in tight and crushed St. George against its chest. One of the small open hatches scraped on his cheek. Cerberus looked up at the sky, then brought its steel head down onto the hero's skull with a crack. St. George reeled for a moment, spots swirling in his vision, and Gibbs battered him with the stump of the damaged arm.

St. George stretched his arms out and hammered his fists into the titan's sides. He did it again and again, at least half a dozen times before the arm pinning him against the battlesuit released him. They stumbled apart, he shook his head clear, and then Cerberus lunged forward again, the pincer fingers stretched out.

He threw himself into the air and soared above the titan. It reached after him and he grabbed it by the wrist. He dropped back to the ground, pulled, and threw Cerberus over his shoulder. He didn't let go of the broken hand, and the battlesuit's own momentum tore it loose at the wrist with a crack of metal and electricity.

The titan smashed into the corner of a warehouse. Cracks raced up the wall. Large swaths of plaster and concrete broke free and tipped out over the street. A landslide of rubble raced down the side of the building.

St. George hurled the hand aside and threw himself forward, snatching Billie and a bald man out of the way just before the remains of the warehouse wall smashed into the ground. "Get lost," he said. "You guys can't stop it."

Billie glared at him. "Can you?"

He set them down. "Just stay clear and keep everyone else out of the way." He looked around for Danielle. She'd vanished. He was sure she hadn't been near the wall when it collapsed. She'd either run for cover or couldn't stand to watch the suit get ripped apart.

The rubble shifted around Cerberus. The titan pushed itself to its feet again. It stood with its back to St. George, as if it was gathering strength.

"Gibbs," he said, "There's enough holes in the armor. I know you can hear me. We can still work this out. I know this isn't your fault. Stop now and shut the suit down."

The handless arm swung around and hit him like a wrecking ball.

St. George hit a wall, scraped across it, and slammed into Four again. Momentum bounced him off the corner and threw him back out into the street. He hit the pavement and tumbled another two yards.

The street shook under him. He tried to focus, to throw himself into the air, but his head was spinning and the titan's foot caught him in the side before he was even a few inches off the ground. He crashed into another wall and fell. He heard people shouting, but wasn't sure if it was inside the building or somewhere in the distance.

Cerberus stomped over and glared down at him. A Y-shaped crack ran through one of the eye lenses. Servos hummed as the battlesuit raised its foot over St. George's face and blotted out the sun.

Then the sun leaned to the left and dropped down to light up the street. The foot started to fall and the brilliant wraith struck like lightning, shooting through the raised leg just below the knee. There was a deafening hiss, Gibbs howled in pain, and the two sounds mixed and echoed across the lot.

The half-fused foot clanged on the ground next to St. George's head. Molten metal splashed over it. A few drops hit his arm and burned what was left of his shirt. He swiped them away.

One of the thick toes twitched a few times and then grew still.

Cerberus tried to keep its balance on one leg. St. George reached up, grabbed the still-glowing stump in both hands, and shoved. The titan tipped over and hit the pavement.

Zzzap hung in the air a few yards away, shaking. *Gahhhhh,* he said. He waved his arms. *I hate doing that. I think I'm going to puke.*

"Thanks," said St. George.

You're welcome. Didn't want to risk hitting you with a blast, and I figured we didn't want to incinerate whoever's in there. Gibbs?

"Yeah."

What's up with him?

"Smith."

Figures. Does Danielle know you had to—

"Yeah."

Zzzap made a static-y noise that might have been a sigh.

St. George limped over to the fallen titan. It was like a wounded turtle, stuck on its back with no limbs left to push itself over. The stump pounded on the ground. The handless arm swung at him again but couldn't reach him. Billie, Ilya, and the others approached from the north, reloading as they closed in.

St. George hooked his fingers under the helmet's chin. He braced his foot against the armored shoulders and pulled.

The battlesuit groaned, metal squealed, and Cerberus's armored skull ripped free of the body. Shrapnel sprayed like blood. A tangle of cables dragged loose from the armored collar. Each one snapped, sparked, and popped apart. The thrashing limbs went limp.

The large eyes flared for a moment, one after the other, and then died.

Lieutenant Gibbs's head looked small on top of the huge

torso. He had a bruise over one eye. "God damn you," he snarled at them. "You're traitors. No one will ever trust you again. No one!"

So where's Danielle and Stealth?

"Smith's got Stealth," said St. George. "I'm not sure where Danielle slipped off to."

Zzzap floated a few feet higher in the air. *Did Smith get her, too?*

"Not sure. I'm going to head toward Gower. Can you do a perimeter check?"

On it. The gleaming wraith shot into the air and vanished.

St. George dropped the armored skull on the ground and hurled himself up over the buildings.

* * *

Christian Smith guided Stealth along Avenue C. They'd run into two or three people, but a few words from the mayor had sent them on their way. They could see the cross street up ahead.

"Not long now," said Smith. "I was happy to let you all starve to death peacefully, you know. I really wanted to avoid anything big and showy like this. I'm not big on direct confrontation. Still, I think you'll protect me from any potential threats, won't you?"

Stealth said nothing, but her head jerked up and down once.

Smith smiled. "And you'd warn me if you knew of any trouble up ahead, right?"

"Yes." The cloaked woman stumbled, just for a moment, as if her foot had caught on something. "There is no trouble up ahead."

"Wait, what?" Smith stopped walking. "Why did you . . . What are you hiding?"

"Many things," said Stealth. "Perhaps most important is that someone has been following us for half a block now."

Smith spun around and the gunshot echoed on the street. The bullet whizzed past her, close enough that she flinched away.

Danielle lined up the Glock with both hands and fired

again. Her aim wasn't great, but the round hit Christian Smith in the calf, just under the kneecap. The Asian woman howled and dropped to the ground.

The redhead walked forward. The pistol stayed on Smith the whole time. "You fucking son of a bitch," she snarled. "George had to destroy Cerberus because of you."

Smith tried to speak, but all she could manage was a few angry whimpers as her hands flailed at her ruined leg.

Voices were shouting down the street. Danielle recognized Madelyn's pale figure running toward them. A few guards were behind her, their own weapons up and ready. Captain Freedom loomed behind them, looking groggy but keeping pace.

Danielle aimed the Glock and fired one more time. This time the round took two fingers off a flailing hand and smashed into the other kneecap. Smith screamed and fell backward. Her hand twitched and splashed blood over her shirt.

"Hold the barrel of the pistol in your hand," said Stealth.

"What?" Danielle glanced at her.

"Hold the barrel of the pistol in your right hand. It will be warm to the touch from firing, but will not harm you. Raise the pistol to shoulder height and swing so the tip of the magazine connects with the side of the skull. Your target should be the temple just above the cheekbone."

Danielle looked down at the thrashing woman. Smith was trying to gasp out words, but couldn't focus.

She turned the Glock around in her hand. She swung and cracked it into Smith's head. The woman went limp and slumped to the ground.

Danielle let out a long breath.

"Thank you," said Stealth.

"You couldn't've done that yourself?"

"Semantics."

EPILOGUE

ST. GEORGE FLOATED in the sky above the water tower. It was a windy night, but not horribly so. Enough to make the world feel alive. Los Angeles was lit up below him. Houses, a few small shops, floodlights on the Big Wall and the corners of the Mount.

It was good to be home.

Things were chaotic, granted. In thirty-six hours, dozens of rumors had already sprung up about why the new mayor was shot twice and put into a medical coma. A few of them were somewhat close to the truth. For the moment, as runner-up in the election, Richard Lihart was acting as mayor. He made it very clear he'd step down if anyone had serious objections, but for the moment no one had.

The destruction of Cerberus had caused ripples, too. It had been three years since a hero had fallen. Even if no one had actually died, it was a harsh reminder the world still wasn't safe. If anything, it was a little less safe with the armored titan gone.

Gibbs was under observation. He responded well to Freedom and was coming to grips with the suggestions Smith had planted in his brain. He'd lost most of his right foot when Zzzap burned off the battlesuit's legs. The lieutenant seemed to be taking it as some sort of penance.

St. George heard a ripple of fabric. He looked down and saw Stealth standing on the tower below him. Her cloak whipped around in the wind. The corners of it snapped and popped like small whips.

He floated down to her. They hadn't had any real time together since waking up from Smith's dreamworld. She reached up and checked the bruise on the side of his face, running a gloved finger along his jawline. "Your injuries are healing rapidly."

He nodded. "I should be fine by the end of the week."

"I am glad to hear it."

"Is it just me," he said, "or do I get the crap beat out of me a lot for a guy who's supposed to be indestructible?"

Her face shifted under the mask. He recognized the faint smile. "Considering the battles you become involved in, it is not that surprising."

She wrapped her arms around his neck. He held her by the waist. They drifted back into the air. "I have missed you," she said.

"You threw me out a window."

"To be exact," said Stealth, "I had Captain Freedom throw you out of a window."

"Ahhh, well."

"You were the best choice, George. You have a flexible mind and had already begun to doubt." She shifted against him. "You were also the most likely to survive the fall if it did not cause you to wake up."

He chuckled and shook his head. The wind shifted and her cloak wrapped around both of them. It twisted and flexed like a living thing.

"So how much of it was real?"

"How much of what?"

"Y'know," he said, "you're the worst person on Earth when it comes to playing dumb. For a number of reasons."

"I concur."

"So all that stuff about your parents. Was that all true?"

Stealth shifted her body again. One of her legs wrapped around one of his. "The majority of it," she said. "A few minor details were changed to better fit Smith's illusion."

"Like what?"

Her body tensed and then relaxed. Then it tensed again and he felt a deep breath whisper against his chest. "You once asked me how long it had been since anyone had used my name. You were impressed that I knew it had been twenty-eight months, at the time."

"I remember," said St. George. "When we were going down to spy on the Seventeens, just before that first big battle with Legion."

"Before I told it to you," said Stealth, "the last person to use my name had been my father."

"Ahhh."

"Nine minutes later I killed him."

They hung in the air for a few more moments. George pulled her closer. She was still tense.

"I'm guessing there's a little more to the story than that?"

"There is. Do you wish to hear it?"

"Yeah, of course."

She relaxed. Just enough that he could feel it. "As you have observed," she said, "my father was not a good man. Killing him was an act of self-defense, although he had committed numerous crimes which would warrant execution."

"Did you want to do it?"

She looked up at him. "I beg your pardon?"

"Did you want to kill him?"

Her head went side to side. Just once. St. George remembered the thin man in the hotel suite with the round spectacles and the efficient motions.

"He was a monster in several senses," said Stealth, "and a wanted criminal in twenty-three countries. However, he was my father. I wish he had not put me in such a position. I took no pleasure from it."

"Why did he try to kill you?"

She pressed her head against his chest. "So he would know if I was ready to succeed him or not. It is an inheritance I have attempted to avoid for most of my life."

St. George took her in both arms and hugged her. "I would've stopped him for you, if I could've."

"You could not have."

"Hey," he said, "I'll have you know I'm an actual superhero. I used to be known as the Mighty Dragon? Maybe you've heard of me?"

"You are being foolish in an attempt to distract me from these thoughts."

"Mostly, yeah."

"Thank you."

They drifted away from the water tower and over Rodden-berry. The wind shifted again. Her cloak whipped away from them and spread out behind her.

"Speaking of supervillains," he said, "have you thought about what we're going to do with . . . Smith, I guess."

"I have," she said. "Dr. Connolly believes she can maintain the medical coma indefinitely, provided we can supply certain drugs she requires."

"And if we can't?"

"We have spoken about the possibility of performing an extended cordectomy encompassing the contralateral vocal fold, ventricular fold, and the subglottis. She has never performed such a procedure, but she feels it is within her ability."

St. George furrowed his brow. "What's that mean?"

"If we must, we will surgically remove Christian Nguyen's vocal cords. This should eliminate Smith's powers."

He shook his head.

"This bothers you?"

"Of course it does. Christian was a pain in the ass, but she didn't deserve this."

"I agree," Stealth said. "Unfortunately, Smith's abilities do not leave us many options."

"I know. I get it, doesn't mean I have to like it." He looked at the buildings below them. Light shone up through one of the skylights. "Danielle's up late."

"Yes."

"Honestly," said St. George, "I'm kind of surprised Smith didn't have you preprogrammed to kill her or me. Anyone who tried to stop him."

"He tried," Stealth said. "Using your own experience with him as a guide, I formed a semantic argument in my mind to keep myself from acting on his commands."

"How so?"

"Agent Smith ordered me to deal with any potential threats. I knew we were being followed, and had several reasons to believe it was Danielle, but there was no possible scenario where she would pose a potential threat."

"How could you know that?"

Stealth bowed her head against his chest. The breeze pushed her hood back. "If I was protecting Smith, Danielle would pose no threat at all."

St. George stared at her for a moment and then laughed.

"Once she had fired the pistol," Stealth continued, "she was no longer a potential threat, but an actual one. Smith had not ordered me to deal with actual threats."

He kissed her through the mask. "You're amazing, you know that?"

"This said by a man who is hovering eighty feet above the ground."

She took one arm away from his neck and slid off her mask. He kissed her again. The wind shifted and wrapped her cloak around them.

EPILOGUE II

IT TOOK CESAR most of the day to find her a drafting board, a tall chair, and a full set of tools. Paper had been harder, but just before sundown he'd appeared with a dozen large sheets rolled into a cylinder. They'd been used on one side, but not much. Just a few simple line drawings and diagrams. He promised to get her more tomorrow.

Danielle hadn't done any drafting with pencil and paper since her undergrad years. Everything had been CAD and 3-D modeling since then. But her laptop didn't have any of the right software, and the screen was too small anyway.

She taped down the first sheet and set her straight edge over it. A few quick passes with the pencil gave her a border. A few more passes using the edge and a triangle gave her a title box in the bottom right corner. She filled out her name, the date, and then the project title. It had been a while since she'd had to do the Gothic letters by hand.

CERBERUS MK. 2

Danielle looked at the words for a moment. Then she set her pencil to the paper and began to work.

ACKNOWLEDGMENTS

IT WAS IN the second draft of *Ex-Patriots* that I came up with a bare-bones idea of how I could bring back Agent John Smith. I almost didn't use it, to be honest. At the time, *Ex-Communication* was a sure thing, but it was already pretty full of story with the return of Max and Cairax, not to mention introducing Madelyn as the Corpse Girl. I didn't want to waste Smith's reappearance, so I knew there was no way I'd be able to tell that story until at least the fourth book. And I'm enough of a realist to know that nobody should be planning on any books past the ones they're contracted for.

By the end of the second draft, though, there it was. A set-in-plain-sight clue that Agent Smith and Christian Smith were somehow going to be up to no good together. By the time I sat down to write *Ex-Communication*, it looked like there was a good chance I might get a fourth book . . . so I peppered in a few more clues. I have to admit that—as I write this—it's been two months since that book came out and I'm two-thirds thrilled/one-third disappointed that no one's noticed them. But I take solace in the fact that you're probably all going back looking for them now.

Now here we are at book four, with the possibility of a fifth *Ex-Heroes* story dancing in the road up ahead. And maybe a few clues and hints for that one planted here and there. Maybe some of them set in plain sight . . .

Needless to say, I couldn't've made it here without help from a few people. So, I offer some very heartfelt thanks to the following folks.

David, my agent, made this book a reality, and made sure I was in a place where I could work on it without pressure or panic. Well, not any more than the usual amount, anyway, when you're re-launching an entire series with a new publisher.

Julian, my editor at Crown, offered many tips, suggested a few things, caught mistakes, and overall made sure I didn't fall back on the whole logic-cheat of "it's all just imaginary." Or that I had really good reasons when I did. If this book impresses you at all, it's because he didn't let me get lazy.

Ilya answered some firearm questions for me. Marcus talked at length one afternoon about military hearings, courts martial, and punishments. Mary helped me with emergency-room proce-dures and terminology. Any straying from the facts in these areas is my own and not theirs.

John and CD read early drafts in record time when my sched-ule got tight—they're both amazing.

And of course, many thanks to my lovely lady, Colleen, who continues to offer advice, to listen when I need to think out loud, and to put up with me while I worry and stress out (again) about how I'm definitely going to screw everything up this time.

—P.C.

Los Angeles, September 7, 2013